FALLING INTO THE MOB

FALLING
INTO
THE
MOB

STEVE ZOUSMER

The Permanent Press
Sag Harbor, NY 11963

For information, address:
The Permanent Press
4170 Noyac Road
Sag Harbor, NY 11963
www.thepermanentpress.com

Library of Congress Cataloging-in-Publication Data

Zousmer, Steve, author.
Falling into the mob / Steve Zousmer.
Sag Harbor, NY : The Permanent Press, [2017]
ISBN: 978-1-57962-436-1
1. Life change events—Fiction. 2. Organized crime—Fiction.
3. Mafia—Fiction. 4. Black humor (Literature).

PS3576.O8 F35 2017
813'.54—dc23   2016025190

Printed in the United States of America

DEDICATION

Almost ten years ago I met a woman on a train and had the conversation I've reproduced in Chapter 1. I never saw her again but she stayed in my thoughts and those thoughts led to this book. I didn't get her name but I created one for her: Sylvia Sforza.

I regret that she'll probably never know that she inspired not only a fictional character but a whole novel, but she did both and that merits a dedication. Sylvia, wherever you are, this one's for you.

While Sylvia inspired the book, my agent, Julia Lord, was its tireless supporter through thick and thin, mostly thin. She and her associate Ginger Curwen were invaluable friends along the rocky path to publication. I am very grateful to them.

CHAPTER 1

There must be an age when we stop running for trains. A voice within us whispers, "No more of this. It's undignified, it's risky (collisions, falls, heart attacks) and you're too slow anyway. Add running for trains to the growing list of things that are over."

I'm fifty-nine and nearing this point. But I'm not there yet. I have at least one more mad dash through a train station in me, and I'm making it now. I'm charging across the great concourse of Grand Central Terminal huffing and snorting like a rhinoceros, darting between clusters of waiting passengers who jump back in alarm as they sense my approach.

The cleared path is helpful, but I have (I'm guessing here) only forty-five seconds to make the train. It won't be easy because I've had a big meal with a fair amount of alcohol. And I'm wearing a business suit. My necktie is choking me. My briefcase is confusing my balance. My stiff-soled shoes have no bounce or bend and absorb no shock. My steps slap the marble floor in a jangled rhythm that says: this is so reckless, so foolish, so sure to end in painful and deserved embarrassment.

But I persist. I don't know why. There is no reason for rushing. Nothing awaits me but an empty house. I could easily nurse a drink at the bar, killing a half hour before the next train to the suburbs, but some desperate imperative lashes me forward. I exit the elegant concourse and enter the shadowy lower level where trains await. I am running downslope on a ramp, knees pumping, gaining speed.

My brain flashes warning imagery of the fall that awaits me. I can imagine the sound and feel the impact of my forehead hitting the hard terminal floor, scraping on its rough surface before I come to a stop bruised and stunned, my suit smeared with grime. What makes it even worse are the solicitous young commuters who stop to help me up, brushing me off, calling me sir.

But I keep going. The train is still there, only a few strides away. So many times I've had trains pull away with sadistic railroad humor at just this moment. Not this time. I'm going to catch the son of a bitch.

And I do. But it's close: I squeeze through the automatic door just as it slides shut. The door-closing whistle sounds but I'm in. My entrance is a whooshing arrival, a hyperventilating explosion contrasting with the settled calmness of the seated passengers who glance up at me over their digital devices.

I lurch toward an empty aisle seat, whirl, aim, and land. The woman in the window seat next to me actually bounces from the impact. She has every right to scorch me with a glance or snicker but she has the decency to keep her eyes on the book in her lap.

The conductor, a chunky Hispanic woman, covers her mouth to hide her amusement and pats my shoulder. Congratulations, champ, you made it.

I sit there gasping. I have made a spectacle of myself and it feels like everyone is looking at me, which is not a good feeling at an age when you don't want to be looked at closely because you are trying to pass for something you're not—a person who is obviously not young but not obviously old.

Is fifty-nine old? Not drastically, but it's old enough to see what's coming and develop a Gloomy Gus attitude about aging and its consequences. I know this attitude is socially and politically incorrect and rather sternly frowned upon. I frown upon it myself. I recoil from the thought that I am a baby boomer bitching because the privilege of youth has expired after only 5.9 decades.

I know I'm supposed to enter the twilight whistling a happy tune. I should be a happy camper who never mentions getting old. ("Oh, don't even *say* that," people scold you when you complain about infirmities or forgetfulness.) I should distract myself from the depressing reality of aging by keeping busy, filling my plate from the approved menu of senior activities.

No disrespect to the golfers and gardeners and so on but *activities* don't work for me. I don't want to go gently into a future of *activities*. I want a whole new life to replace the one that's wearing out. I know this is unrealistic. I'm not asking to be young again; I'm not asking to be exempt from time and its punishments. But I don't want to spend the rest of my life playing games or doing exercises or taking bus tours overseas. I want to find something that will kick my discontent in its fat ass and carry me to the finish line feeling that I'd finished strong, finally grasping some sort of intensity or richness or bold embrace of life that eluded or intimidated me when I was young.

But how is this done? I have no idea. No idea whatsoever. A large part of the problem is that I am too free, too unencumbered. My one child, a son, is grown up, a busy twenty-six-year-old graduate student living 1,200 miles away (U. of Minnesota). My former wife is even more distant: Los Angeles. Her solution to aging was to trade up for a more exciting husband, what we used to call a "happening" kind of guy, a doctor with big bucks flowing in, entrepreneurial ventures, a splendid wardrobe, and a glamorous global travel agenda. Who could blame her?

As for work, I'm hanging on but my once-admired career as a freelance speechwriter for some of America's foremost CEOs has come down to one last client. And *he* is retired and getting old too.

As for money, I probably have enough unless I do something stupid.

As for health, I am better than average. I row and run at the gym, and I've been lucky. After my annual physical this year my doctor told me, "You've got the test numbers of a forty-year-old. Too bad you don't *look* like a forty-year-old."

So nothing is holding me back from any good opportunity. I'm grateful for this. I know that many people would kill to be in my shoes but there is still the matter of having no plan to avoid a lonely, empty, purposeless future.

Finding a new woman seemed like an obvious solution. I tried it but the process went nowhere. There are plenty of nice available women my age but I had no energy for the chase. There was no spark, no magic, not even any cheap thrills. I had to drink like a fish just to get through an evening. I was glad to give up.

For a while I thought the solution should *make sense*. I thought self-examination would reveal the way. I scoured my memory for signals about where I've been headed all these years. I slouched down in the video screening room of my mind, reviewing long-past scenes in a quest for illumination.

Believe me, this was no sentimental journey down memory lane. I assessed myself unsparingly, but the effort got me nowhere and I gave it up, concluding that you don't find the big answers in life—they find you.

Or they don't.

ON THAT fateful night there were two rounds of laments about aging, one on the train and the other before it over dinner with my old classmate and friend Charlie Benedict. He and I meet regularly and our conversations tend to center on the transition to geezerdom.

On this night, after recounting recent senior moments, we focused on feeling superfluous, marginalized, pushed to the sidelines. We discussed the latest reminders of the reduced power or presence a senior citizen could exert in any of the more invigorating human activities. We talked about being out of it and living in the past tense, no longer looking forward or believing that tomorrow will be better than today. This last point was relatively new to us and had unexpected bite, causing an unwelcome silence, which we resolved by ordering more drinks.

With bourbon in him, my old friend seems to turn into the wise and courtly Southern senator he might have become if not for his contempt for Southern politics. He is a good fellow and apparently a fine lawyer. His hair is snow white and he has just the right amount of Tennessee in his sonorous voice. He is an international grand master in the art of the reflective pause. Over the years his pauses have stretched to such length that I've speculated on things I could do without missing a word, such as taking a bus to Brooklyn and back.

Dinners with Charlie have always been occasions for excellent wry humor but in recent years the subtext has become less amusing: he has a serious heart condition but is determined to keep working for a few more years to build a nest egg for his wife, daughters, and a profusion of granddaughters. This aspiration is regarded with a cold eye by his youth-minded law firm which, he believes, is attempting to ease him out. Being thrown into the job market as a sixty-year-old in bad health is a depressing prospect. His line is: "I don't know whether to write my résumé (long pause) or my obituary."

I lingered too long with him but finally said good night and was shocked to look at my watch. It was late but if I rushed I might catch the 11:13 P.M. train to my suburb, Hartsdale, in Westchester County twenty-some miles north of New York City. Somehow this seemed like a train I had to catch.

As WE chugged out of Grand Central I opened my briefcase in which I carried a printout of a speech I was writing and a magazine to provide reading material for the forty-one-minute ride. But instead of reading I dozed off. I woke up more than halfway home and found myself listening to a voice from a few rows back, the intrusive voice of a young man of notable callowness, instantly dislikable.

He was engaged in a remarkably uninhibited cell phone conversation with a young woman named Jenna, tenaciously trying to charm her into picking him up at his train stop. They would go for drinks and then (this was close to explicit) they would have acrobatic sex in her car. The sex would be Jenna's reward for getting dressed and bundled up at this rather late hour and taking advantage of an offer that might never come again.

I was inclined to cringe at the shamelessness of the young man's pitch. Is this how young people do these things now? Yet I kind of admired it: he marketed himself with a brashness I had seldom mustered. He understood at least one of the great lessons of life: those who don't grab don't get. I never mastered that lesson. I was a gentlemanly faller-into, not a grabber.

I next realized that while I was waking up into this mini-drama, everyone else in the car was already tuned in to it. The car's population had thinned out but the normal isolation between passengers had been breached by the shared pleasure of eavesdropping. Glances, smiles, and whispers were exchanged as if we were the audience to a titillating soap opera. I imagined a deep-voiced announcer reading a tease saying, "Will Jenna take the bait?—or find the pride to say 'No'? We'll find out after these messages."

Jenna did not say yes or no. She wavered. Perhaps she was tempted; perhaps she was too polite to hang up. The young man's crassness and urgency mounted as his stop approached. It became increasingly clear that the drinks and sex were only sweeteners to his primary motive of getting a ride home on a cold night. Of course if he could get the ride *and* the sex he would have a boastworthy tale for weeks to come.

He tried until the last minute but Jenna dithered and when the train stopped, he gave up abruptly, pocketed his phone, and joined other passengers filing out of the train. I got a glance at him as he passed. He was tall and mildly handsome but he had the look of a spoiled and sullen preppy, and his lightweight blue blazer was not going to keep him warm walking home.

His departure left a silence. That's when the woman sitting next to me leaned sideways and whispered, "What an asshole."

I laughed. And nodded in agreement.

She looked at me directly, her big dark eyes making confident eye contact. "This Jenna is hating herself right now. *Hating* herself. I bet she still lives with her parents and she's sitting alone in her little pink bedroom and she's so bored she wants to scream. Because she has no balls. I figure she's someone he knew in high school but she was below him on the social ladder and he never called her but tonight she got her chance. She could have taken it or rejected it and either would have been fine but she did nothing. It's the story of her life and she knows it."

Probably. But I felt for Jenna. Her offer came from an asshole with shoddy motives but what happens when you get a sudden offer from life? It demands a boldness you don't ordinarily possess but you want to say yes despite the risk because this is your chance and it might never come again. What do you do?

That's what I was thinking, but it's not what I said.

"When I was his age if a girl I had no chance with called up and promised to buy me drinks and have sex in return for a ride from the train station, I would have broken the speed limit to get there before she changed her mind."

"Of course," she said, eyes twinkling. "For the man it's a no-brainer. But it was a decision for her and she blew it. She didn't have enough self-respect to make a decision."

At this point I was thinking that this conversation was pure high school and I was forty years past high school but I was enjoying it. I was also thinking that the last time a young woman started a conversation with me was either in the Pleistocene or Jurassic period but so long ago that scholars no longer give a shit. I'd forgotten how welcome it was. This woman—Italian-looking, strong but plain features, shoulder-length black hair—had a vitality and nerviness that instantly delighted me. I was pleased that she intended to move on from Jenna's dilemma to other topics.

"So, did we have a lot to drink tonight?"

"Jeez, where did that come from?" I said. "Do you have a great sense of smell or are we married?"

"It wasn't the smell I'm talking about. It was your crash landing into your seat."

"You're right, I did have some drinks. I had dinner with an old friend. In fact we talked a lot about self-respect. Not quite as light-heartedly as you and I are talking about it, but the same thing."

"What is it about self-respect that you were so unlight-heartedly talking about?"

"We talked about the erosion of self-esteem as you get older."

"Why is that? My dad's older than you and he has no problem with self-esteem."

"Well, I'm glad to hear it. But a lot of people my age start to lose the things that create self-respect. Everything starts to diminish: your work, your place in the world. Your memory. You're only a step away from sitting around a pool in Florida talking about your doctor's appointment and the early bird special at the new Thai restaurant. You walk down Fifth Avenue and people look right through you. I bet most people my age know the feeling. You're so irrelevant you're invisible."

"My dad is seventy-five and he sure isn't invisible."

"I should get your dad's advice. What would he say to me?"

"He'd say, 'Grow the fuck up.'"

I started to be offended but she cut it off with a smile and pat of my elbow.

I said, "I turn sixty next May."

"Condolences. I turn forty in February. But I never would have guessed you're almost sixty. You've got hair, you're not fat, you don't have an old-fart voice. You're not bad looking. I think you're just playing games with yourself."

I laughed again, enjoying the flattery.

"So you go out with your friend and talk about getting old?" she said. "Isn't this kind of a downer?"

"We enjoy commiserating. It's a good way of dealing with major negative changes in life. You talk about them until they bore you and then you're okay. What does your dad do?"

"He still runs his business."

"What kind of business?"

"It's a family business."

"Doing what?"

"He's not doing much right now. He's been sick."

"So what do you do?"

"I tend my flock."

"Kids? How many?"

"No, no kids."

"Sheep?"

"No. No sheep."

She smiled gently but turned away. I wondered if I'd said something wrong. She was looking out the window (where she could see nothing but her reflection in the glass). I sneaked a good look at her and gathered these details: she wore no makeup, no wedding ring, and no jewelry, and under her black parka she wore something you don't see much anymore, I think they call it a dress. Maroon or some other drab reddish/brownish color. She had a large leather handbag into which she put her book. I caught a glance at its title, something about cancer, which I connected with her sick father.

"I get off at Hartsdale," I said. "How far are you going?"

"One stop past yours. White Plains."

"Well, I'm going to get up now. I've learned to stand up and wait near the door when it opens or I might have a senior moment and forget to get off. I've actually done that." Actually

I hadn't—this was a fib to cover my awkwardness about breaking off.

"You make fun of yourself a lot, don't you? The men I know never make fun of themselves. They'd never admit to missing their stop. They'd go find the conductor and give him a load of crap, like it was *his* fault."

"Really? Kind of a tough guy approach? Do you like that?"

"No. I'm done with tough guys. I'm thinking you're the opposite: not a tough guy on top but solid underneath."

"Thank you, Mrs. Freud. Can I ask how you reached that conclusion?"

"No, but I'm right."

I stared at her.

"I know men," she said.

She certainly knew how to cheer men up. She'd made me feel better in a few minutes than I'd felt in years. I would have to preserve the memory of this encounter and bring it out on days of melancholy and malaise.

"I've enjoyed talking to you," I said. I was halfway through standing up when I looked at her one more time and there it was: *the greatest smile I've ever seen.*

CHAPTER 2

Basking in the radiance of her smile I stepped backward into the aisle and collided with an oncoming force which turned out to be a mountainous and furious young black man. Before I had the vaguest notion of what was happening he spun me around and pounded me just above the heart with a short hard jab that stole my breath and almost dropped me to my knees.

Then came an explosion of profanity. *Mothafucka-mothafucka-mothafucka*. I could barely understand his words but the gist was that I had stepped on his foot, thus disrespecting the entire African American race. Therefore he would beat the shit out of me.

At first I was more dumbstruck than scared. My only clear feeling was embarrassment to be trapped in an appalling racial cliché. In a crazy way I wanted to *edit* it, to make him something other than a young black American bulging with rage and muscles as he terrorized an older white guy.

If my thinking self was slow to react to danger, my more reliable inner sensors fully grasped the situation. I have lived a safe life and could not remember the last time I felt fear but my memory was quickly refreshed: the feeling of alarms going off riotously in every cell, flames leaping up somewhere inside me, the rush of adrenaline, sweat, and some queasy poison that created turmoil in my lower intestines.

It got worse as I realized that I had not just one enemy but three: the screaming guy and his two equally broad and towering buddies who pushed in to surround me, tensing their shoulders and glowering at me.

Then one clear but useless fact came to me: I had not stepped on his foot. This guy *chose* to collide with me and did it with linebacker zeal. This was an attack, not an accident. I wasn't guilty but I tried to apologize anyway. This made him even more furious.

He leaned down and in on me, almost nose to nose. His eyes were blazing. His spittle landed wet on my cheek, his breath was repulsive and his rage was over-the-top, preposterously excessive. I remembered something told to me long ago by an intimidating navy captain: the dominant figure in any encounter is the one who gets angriest fastest. That person sucks up all the energy and aggression in the room. The other person is left with nothing and either surrenders or plays catch-up, surrender being more likely.

I struggled to get some strength in my voice and urged him to back off, raising my hands in a calming-down gesture that he chose to interpret as my preparing to throw punches. His hands went up too, giant fists clenched and cocked.

"Clock his ass, Avon," urged the second guy. "Put the mothafucka down."

I said, "Look, I'm sorry I bumped you but my stop is coming. I have to go."

"You going to the emergency room, that's where you going."

Avon's buddies roared at this.

"Come on, please, get out of the way."

"Why you talking, dog? Did I give you permission to talk?"

So I didn't talk, not just because of fear but because I didn't know what to say. I was blank. How *not* street-smart could I possibly be? I didn't know how to play my part in this drama, though I realized that Peace-seeking White Guy was sure to backfire, inflaming him even more.

"He gonna be in intensive care with tubes and shit coming out his head," said Second Guy.

I looked around the train car for help, hoping the woman conductor or an off-duty police officer would appear and intervene. But the car had emptied. All other passengers had fled via the far exit the moment this fire-breathing monster entered the car.

I had forgotten about the woman though I thought I heard her voice as the three men tightened the ring around me, each growling threats about the violence to come. Perhaps Second Guy heard her too because he now addressed her, asking if I were her "daddy."

She said, "You're lucky he's not my daddy."

Second Guy said, "Avon, you think Grandpa been hustling this bitch?"

Avon looked at her with a predatory leer. "I don't think he been hustling her, Roy. I think he been tapping her."

"With his five-incher?" said Roy.

"More like a one-incher 'bout now," said Third Guy, laughing.

"So you doing him or not?" Avon asked her.

She said, "You just crossed the line, dipshit."

I was amazed by how unruffled she was. So was Avon. Her mix of composure and contempt was so remarkable that his focus shifted from me to her. And I think he and I had the same thought simultaneously but he expressed it: "Lady, you a cop?"

"You'll wish I was," she said.

"What the fuck you mean by that?"

She glared at him with those black eyes and the unanswered question hung in the air but the second guy, Roy, was oblivious and gleefully rattled on with his trash talk, jabbering about my "little white weenie." I wasn't thinking too well but this choice of language struck a false note. Do tough guys talk about *weenies*?

Having been briefly ignored I managed to recover some detachment. I could see that Roy was Avon's suck-up admirer. I figured he was not bold enough to start anything himself but would pile on nastily if Avon went to war. The cheap shots—the kicks in the balls and ribs—would come from him. Third Guy was far less worked up than the other two and my sense was that he wasn't interested but would join in a beating if he had to.

Avon was the one to worry about, but he'd forgotten me. The woman's icy dignity intrigued him. No, *aroused* him.

"I'm gonna call her 'Tiger,'" he said, imitating the velvet voice of a late-night radio host. "I like tigers because tigers like to growl and scratch, you know what I'm saying? But it ends with sweet surrender." This seemed to remind him of a song about sweet surrender because he did a little silent dance thing, singing into an imaginary microphone.

The woman made a puking gesture, fingers down the throat.

"Hey, don't Tiger remind you of Mrs. Katz?" Avon said. His friends nodded back eagerly but he kept his eyes on the woman. "Our principal in high school, Mrs. K. She was one mean bitch, man. You look a little like her. You could get a little foxier, baby. Number one, you gotta stop wearing your mama's old dresses. Number two, put some meat on them skinny-ass bones."

This drew giggles from Roy. The woman turned away in disgust and looked out the window. The train was slowing down.

"Here's where Grandpa gets off," said Avon. Showing me a sly smile, he winked and said to me, "You can split, man. Go home and work on your stamp collection."

"We gonna have us a party with the skinny lady," said Roy, grinning. "We gonna run us a train on the train, mothafucka."

Somehow I knew that "running a train" meant gang rape.

They stood back, clearing the way for me, smiling.

I looked at the woman. She pointed toward the door, making a shooing gesture, urging me to go.

I would have sold my soul to be an action-movie hero capable of ending this scene with swift whirling bone-crunching martial arts panache. In truth I'd never been in a fight as an adult and only a few as a kid.

The train's public address system sang out in a ding-dong chime followed by an automated male voice announcing the Hartsdale stop.

What scared me more than a cascade of blows and even the humiliation of being overpowered and defenseless—I saw myself balled up on the dirty floor, trying to get my head under a seat to dodge their kicks and punches—was the thought of craven behavior in front of this woman.

Abandoning her, dashing off the train and leaving her at their mercy, would be the disgrace of a lifetime. Loss of self-esteem would no longer be a topic for indulgent philosophizing in restaurants; it would be a life sentence of self-loathing.

The train stopped. The sliding door opened and waited.

"Better get gone, dude," said Avon.

"Door gonna close, man," said Roy.

I didn't move. Couldn't and wouldn't. I wished I could have spat out some defiant statement but words wouldn't come. I shook my head—no.

"Roy, you got them brass knuckles?" said Avon.

He seized my elbow and yanked me toward the door. I was off-balance but caught hold of a hand grip on the corner of a seat and hung on to it with all my strength, making it clear I was not getting off, determined resistance offsetting fear, a sense of resistant pride rising to meet a sense of impending doom.

"What you doing, man? You gonna *defend* her? Against *us?* With your little shit-ass briefcase?"

The door slid shut and I was still on the train, which jerked forward and started moving. Except for the five of us, the car was empty.

First, Roy had no brass knuckles.

Second, Avon's rage had crested and begun to ebb. I realized what I should have known from my first whiff of his breath: he was not a monster, he was just drunk. When he banged into me he was at the peak of his high, feeling his oats and lusting for combat, but he'd burned himself out with his ferocious theatrics, the woman had distracted him from his simple plan of punching me out, and in a small but unmistakable way I'd called his bluff.

He'd gotten us into this cliché but didn't know how to get us out. As the violent momentum leaked out of him he seemed to shrink into a frowning, frustrated child, as did his friends. Instead of fearsome brutes I now beheld husky ex-high school football players who'd been drinking and now wanted a little kick-ass before bedtime. I thought about the giggling, the joke about my weenie, the posturing—these guys were not the real thing. I'm not saying they were pussycats. They had been dangerous for a moment and could be dangerous again but the peak danger had passed.

Avon's consistently oblivious friend Roy did not grasp this change and continued agitating for violence but Third Guy saw an opportunity to steer Avon away from it. "Screw this, A-B," he said. "We got work early tomorrow."

Go faster, train, I thought, holding my breath. I knew it was less than four minutes to White Plains. Only a little longer and we'd be okay.

The key was to avoid anything that would reignite their rage. We were still face-to-face and that was bad because sooner or later it would mean exchanging words and the words would not be good-natured. So I slid through the gap between Avon and Roy and resumed my place sitting next to the woman.

We made no eye contact, either between us or with them. We didn't listen to their grumbling; we just sat still and gazed forward. What a relief it was to be sitting; I was exhausted.

And then, blessedly, the train rolled into White Plains station.

"We'll finish this in the parking lot," said Roy, one last threat as the woman and I arose to leave the train.

Avon, perhaps feeling he'd lost face by letting me off the hook, stepped forward and grabbed my briefcase. We wrestled over it for a moment but he yanked it out of my hands and flung it like a Frisbee toward the back of the car. I started to retrieve it but the three of them blocked the aisle. So this fearsome confrontation had come down to plain old school-yard bullying. The solution was simple—I wrote off the brief-case. It was an old and inexpensive Land's End briefcase with replaceable contents.

The woman and I left the train together and joined the flow of debarking passengers on the elevated arrivals platform. A few split off to the left, crossing a connecting bridge to the large parking garage. The rest of us herded to the right and started down the concrete stairway to the street.

The woman and I were near the back of the pack. The three black men followed behind us. We could not make out what they were saying but apparently they decided to break off from tormenting us and hurry ahead. As they skipped down the stairs to pass us, Avon stepped directly behind me and threw an elbow that hit me like a sharp spike in my shoulder blade. I staggered forward but stayed upright.

Roy was next, snarling and giving me an evil eye as he passed. Then came Third Guy, who slowed down and whispered to me, "Hey man, we was just messing with you. Don't mean no harm or nothing."

This was apparently an attempt at graciousness. It seemed to call for a reply in kind: I was supposed to flash a grin signifying that I was cool with the rough manly humor and sign off with a wink or brotherly handshake.

But with pain shooting through my shoulder I not only failed to appreciate his offer but was enraged by it. They had threatened me with a beating and threatened the woman with sexual attack. They'd been hostile, vulgar, sexist, and racist. They'd gone way beyond excusable conduct and frankly they'd created a few minutes of the worst fear and humiliation I'd ever known and which I knew would recur in my dreams for the rest of my life.

So I was not going to offer anything resembling forgiveness. But I'll never know what I *was* going to do because the woman read my emotions perfectly. She put an arm around my shoulder in what seemed like an embrace but it was only to pull me toward her so she could whisper: "Slow down and don't do anything. This will be over in a minute."

I thought she meant that in a minute we'd be out of the station, going our separate ways. But that's not what she meant.

AT THE bottom of the stairway three men appeared suddenly and charged up the stairs like marines storming a beach. It was a sight to remember because in addition to black ski masks and work boots, they were wearing pajamas.

"Yo, where's the slumber party?" Roy howled, seeking a laugh.

The pajama men seemed to make eye contact with the woman, who nodded toward the three black men. The black men did not realize they'd been singled out for attack until the pajama men hit them in a breathtaking collision, driving them up the stairs and backwards until they were on their backs defenseless against an onslaught of sickeningly hard blows, crying out in shock and pain. The black men were bigger but unable to resist the swirl of violence. The beating was systematic and merciless. No passengers stayed to watch, dispersing in a noisy panic.

The woman clutched my arm and pulled at me and we ran back up the stairs. At the top of the stairs she stopped and leaned on me as she removed her high heels. I glanced back at the melee and saw Avon being dragged down the steps face-first, his face bouncing horribly against each step.

The woman and I took off running toward the parking garage. She was a fast, athletic runner. She found a door and threw it open and we were in a dim stairwell, rushing down two flights to street level where we burst out into cold night air. She glanced around the parking lot, then seized my arm again and we ran across the garage entrance and up a sloping sidewalk. I recall worrying that she would cut her bare feet.

We were away from the station now, running across the broad Ferris Avenue and then stopping, gasping for breath, hearing approaching police sirens.

"We'll wait here," she said.

"Wait? For what?"

"They'll be coming."

"Who? Who'll be coming?"

"There they are," she said, pointing. A dark SUV pulled out of the station parking lot and turned left, toward our location. I noticed that it was driven at moderate speed with no screeching of tires.

She waved her arms and the SUV came right at us. It stopped just in front of us and a rear door flew open.

"Get in," she cried, reaching back for me as she jumped into the vehicle. I followed, squeezing in next to her. Two pajama guys were in the front seats and the third was in the rear.

The driver jumped out of the SUV. I thought he was coming to close the rear door behind me but instead he reached in and grabbed me fiercely by the collar, yelling, "Get the fuck out of there."

His arm strength was extraordinary but before he could hurl me to the pavement the woman shouted, "Stop it, George, he's with me."

"With you?"

"Let go of him. Close the door."

He obeyed, slamming the rear door and then jumping back in behind the steering wheel. The police sirens were louder and closer. We drove to the corner, turned right, and smoothly entered light traffic.

My heart was thundering. The woman seemed to be pumping too but the pajama guys were at ease. There was no wild high-fiving, no reveling in victory. Not a word was said as we left downtown and drove through increasingly dark streets until we were in a working class residential neighborhood. I realized that the ski masks had disappeared.

"So you saw Poppa tonight?" said the young guy on the other side of the woman.

"Yeah. He's the same," she said.

We were making a lot of turns. The blocks were short and it was pitch dark. I had no idea where we were.

"Can I ask where we're going?" I said.

"Our house," she said. "I couldn't leave you at the train station. Somebody would have pointed you out to the cops. Then you would have been tangled up in this."

It was a first for me: fleeing a crime scene. I thought of everything I'd said to Charlie Benedict about wishing for a breakout from the dull plod to old age. So here I was riding around with a woman I didn't know and three pro-quality thugs in pajamas.

"You know what's funny?" said the pajama in the front passenger seat. "We were watching *The Godfather* when you called—"

"One, two, or three?" the woman asked.

"One."

"You've only seen it fifty million times."

"Yeah, but what I'm trying to tell you is that we were watching the part where Sonny kicks the shit out of the dickhead who beat up his sister. Feeks was saying, anybody comes near *our* sister, they get a lot worse than that. And at that exact moment the phone rings and it's you with your 10-13 and off we go in our peejays because we didn't want to waste time getting dressed. Is that amazing or what?"

I knew that 10-13 was the "officer needs assistance" radio code that police use to summon help in emergencies. But these guys were not police.

"You made a phone call?" I whispered to the woman.

"In the beginning. When the big one was spitting in your face."

"He won't be spitting in nobody's face for a while," said the kid next to us in the backseat. "His own face just got pretty fucked up."

"This is my brother Jimmy," the woman said, introducing me. "That's my brother George driving and the other idiot is my brother Tommy."

Jimmy shook my hand and said, "Call me Feeks."

Feeks was clearly the baby of the family, the smallest of the brothers. He was my height but unfilled out, wiry, even skinny. But he had taken on the fearsome Avon and easily kicked ass.

"So what's the story on those guys?" said Tommy.

"They were shitfaced and acting up," she said. "They looked serious at first but I saw they were just punks and almost called you off but they kept pushing it. They deserved it. Richly."

"They were threatening sexual attack," I said.

"They weren't going to do anything," she said.

"Sister, who is this guy?" said Tommy.

"I'll introduce you as soon as he reveals his name," she said.

"Oh, my apologies," I said. "Phillip Vail. Phil."

"Pleased to meet you, Phil," she said, shaking my hand and giving me that dazzling smile. "My name is Sylvia Sforza."

CHAPTER 3

George pulled the SUV over and stopped at what seemed to be a random location near a dark intersection. No one spoke. Finally Feeks came to life with an angry snort, muttered something, and got out, slamming the door.

George laughed. "He's pissed because he always has to be the scout. Because he's the little brother."

Feeks started to move away but George rolled down the window and called him back. "Get the T-shirts off the plates," he said.

I asked Sylvia why there were T-shirts on the license plates.

"I'll let you guess."

"To cover the plates?"

"Brilliant," she said.

Feeks retrieved the old T-shirts. When George opened the window again to receive them Feeks threw the shirts in his face. They laughed at this. Then Feeks disappeared into the darkness.

Moments ticked by. Finally I asked what this was about.

"This is to see if the cops are parked outside our house," Sylvia explained. "I doubt if they're here this fast but getting caught in bloodstained pajamas would be pretty incriminating."

"Why would cops be outside your house?" I said. "How would they connect you to the station?"

She looked at me and said, "That's a long story."

The door opened and Feeks got in. "They're there. One car."

"Shit," said Tommy. "Is it Pelikan?"

"How would I know? Was I supposed to press my face against the car window and look in? 'Hey Pelikan, is that you in there?'"

"I bet it's him," said Tommy. "Pelikan never sleeps."

"I was hoping to get back to *The Godfather*," said Feeks. "So do we have to drive around all night or what?"

Tommy said, "If George would drive a little faster we would have got home before Pelikan got here. I bet he was just driving around looking for somebody to hassle and heard it on the radio and beelined his ass right over here."

"Poppa makes me drive like that," said George. "He says it's professional and he's right. So where to now?"

"We could go to a bar or something," said Feeks.

"Feeks, what are we wearing?" said Tommy. "Can we walk into a bar in pajamas?"

"There's a law against pajamas in a bar?"

Sylvia said, "Okay, look. We could go to the barber shop, we could go to storage or one of the car washes—"

"The car washes got no heat," said Tommy. "We'd freeze our butts off."

"I know that," she continued. "I'm just trying to put together the very short list of places we could go, given the pajama problem. We could drive to Uncle Tiz's."

Everyone groaned. "I know," she said. "He was at the hospital tonight. With Aunt Angela. I had to go to dinner with them after."

George said, "We could drive to Greenwich and back, just to kill time."

"I don't see sitting here all night," said Feeks. "What if someone has to take a dump?"

Everyone was annoyed.

Feeks looked at me, as if discovering my presence for the first time. "What would you do?" he asked.

"Me? I have no idea. This is not my normal lifestyle."

"What is your normal lifestyle? Who the fuck are you and what are you doing here?"

I had to laugh—I'd been asking myself the same questions.

"The black guys started on him before they started on me," explained Sylvia. "We were sitting together."

"You were, like, on a date?"

"No, Jimmy. Remember I was at the hospital tonight visiting Poppa and then eating with Tiz and Angela. I was not on a date."

She called him Jimmy. The others called him Feeks.

I tried to understand how Sylvia fit in with these wackjobs. She'd mentioned caring for her "flock." Were they her flock?

"We could go to my house," I said.

No, I didn't say that.

But I did.

It was a lifelong hospitality reflex kicking in involuntarily. I had been taught early on to open my home to friends and neighbors and my son's little schoolmates but this open invitation never extended to fugitives from the law. And yet the words were out of my mouth before my jaws could slam down and break their necks.

George turned the ignition key and the truck came to life. A street light lit Sylvia's face as she gazed at me with wonderment.

Hey, come on over, thugs, and we'll have some fun. I'll whip up a midnight snack and demonstrate the acquired hosting behaviors of my life as a noncriminal. Maybe we can play Clue.

YEARS AGO I purchased a modestly priced co-op apartment in New York City. In the next decade its value skyrocketed insanely and I traded it almost even up for the house in the way-too-affluent suburb of Scarsdale (Hartsdale is the closest railroad station). We in the Vail household were among the town's population of relative paupers, meaning both spouses were hard-working wage-earners without deep pockets or rich parents.

We left the city so our son, Willy, could grow up in a cocoon of peace and prosperity. Manhattan was a somewhat hairy existence in our years there and even as a four-year-old Willy sensed the danger and was frightened by it. It was not uncommon for gangs of marauding teenagers to rampage through Central Park play areas, terrorizing the kids, moms, and nannies. A few months after we moved I asked Willy what he liked most about his new house, hoping he'd say it was his room or new puppy, but he said he liked it "because there are no bad guys."

So now I'd invited the bad guys to drop by for a visit on their way home from a violent assault. I did this under no coercion and in fact I was an obliging host. When they expressed reluctance about parking on the street (because police of every municipality recognize their vehicle), I dug myself even deeper into criminal conspiracy by moving *my* car to the street while they parked the SUV in my garage and pulled down the door.

If I had any concerns about my house being looted and pillaged they vanished immediately. It was a relief that the three brothers were not overly impressed with the house. The reason, it turned out, is that they were in the moving and storage business and were frequently in houses nicer than mine.

What did surprise them was that I lived in a relatively big house by myself. The Sforza family was evidently large and it seemed to touch them that I had no family around me and existed in such solitude. Sylvia asked, "What do you do on Thanksgiving? Are you all alone?" I explained that I'd adjusted to it and I enjoyed the excessive square footage, which gave me breathing room and allowed me to delay the prospect of getting older in the suffocating confines of a sensible bachelor condo.

But I could not hold on much longer. The local taxes were staggering and always rising, my income was falling precipitously, and the divorce settlement that gave me the house gave most of the cash to my wife. It was probably an unwise deal but keeping my home was what I wanted. I thought speechwriting income would replenish my cash but I had not foreseen a bad economy or age discrimination. I looked around one day and I was older than most of the CEOs I wrote for. This was bad because most of them want subordinates to be unchallenging and subservient, which tends to mean younger. I had noticed that prospective clients were interviewing me with surprising deference—as if I were their father or a retired senior citizen—but always hiring someone else.

I led the Sforzas into my house through the side door in case any neighbors were staying up late to watch for criminal infiltration. The normal routine for first-time guests was a room-by-room tour but when I offered to show them around the brothers were as interested as twelve-year-olds so I aborted the tour and sat them down on the couch in the TV room.

My mind snapped a photo of them scrunched together in their pajamas: three men with long, lean swimmers' bodies, three good-looking Italian faces, none of them even slightly thuggish-looking. There was a notable difference in their ages: George was early forties, Tommy about ten years younger, Jimmy (Feeks) in his early twenties. George was the biggest and, it seemed, the dullest. Tommy was sharp and sarcastic. Feeks was speedy verging on hyperactive. If I hadn't seen what he'd done to Avon I would have described him as a playful puppy; he did not seem to have grown into his dramatic face, which strongly resembled his sister's. But the resemblance stopped at the physical: she radiated stability; he could have been a poster boy for attention deficit disorder.

I delighted them by pulling out my *Godfather* CD collection. I left them with Don Corleone while I headed to the kitchen. Sylvia followed me. Sensing my awkwardness, she took command of snack preparation, searching the refrigerator and cupboards. I braced myself for teasing about my supplies—pathetic bachelor food—but she said nothing. She'd said she knew men and maybe that included knowing when to lay off.

"Sorry I'm not prepared for company."

"No problem," she said. "These animals will eat anything. In their world I'm Martha Stewart."

She'd taken off her parka and heels and now, like her brothers, looked slender but fit. She prepared a serving plate of Wheat Thins, cashews, and a bag of baby carrots. I laughed. She said, "Actually this is fine. You're a good guy to let us in. We really appreciate it."

"How long will Officer Pelikan wait at your house."

"*Detective* Pelikan. He'll probably give up as soon as nature calls. Do you have some sodas or something? Don't bother with glasses, just bring the cans."

The snacks were quickly devoured as the five of us sat and watched the movie. The brothers were boisterous but discerning viewers. It ended sometime after two thirty. I hadn't seen this hour in years but it was also years since I'd been in such lively, youthful company. I went to the dining room liquor cabinet and returned with a good bottle of single-malt scotch. This was an unfamiliar taste for them. They debated its merits compared to high-quality grappa.

Sylvia was sitting next to the telephone and asked to use it (instead of her cell) to call her Uncle Tiz to set up their alibi. The story would be that Sylvia had spent the night at Tiz and Angela's house in Peekskill, having driven up with them after their dinner in New York. The brothers, according to the lie, also stayed over in Peekskill, driving up in their moving van from the family residence in White Plains (leaving before Detective Pelikan arrived outside). Starting the next morning in Peekskill instead of White Plains made sense because it subtracted twenty-five miles of morning traffic from their drive to a moving job upstate.

This had to be explained repeatedly to the uncle and aunt. I could hear their loud voices questioning Sylvia. It was evident that they were elderly and hard of hearing but excited to be involved. There seemed to be no integrity issue about lying to police but Sylvia was not confident they would remember the right answers if questioned.

"In his day Tiz had a great mind," she said to me, "but now he's eighty years old with Alzheimer's. And his wife's a ditz. This is not a solid alibi. Poppa will kill me when he hears about this."

My assumption at this point was that my adventure in the world of crime was about to end without consequence. The brothers were clearly guilty of beating up the black guys but Sylvia was creating an alibi for them and their ski masks would make them impossible to identify. I figured the incident would be investigated and left unsolved. My own moral position was ambivalent: I didn't like the idea of people getting beaten up but neither did I like the idea of people being terrorized on a train.

"So Phil, let me ask you something," said Tommy. "When these guys were threatening our sister, what were you doing?"

The question was posed in a genial tone but it was clearly loaded with an implication that my performance under pressure had been unmanly. I knew this was something I would reflect on for the rest of my life, but the reflection process had not begun and I was at a loss to know how I felt about my own behavior, let alone how to frame an answer that would satisfy the brothers.

I knew they would see through any evasion. They were not going to punch me out for being inadequate but no man wants to be regarded as cowardly or unable to defend a woman.

Sylvia said, "I'm going to step in here. I'm going to say this just once and then this line of questioning will end. This guy stood up for me. Against three big fuckheads who were trying to intimidate him. They gave him a chance to get off the train and leave me alone with them but he didn't budge an inch. Fighting with assholes is part of *our* world but it isn't part of *his* world, you know. He was going to take a beating but he didn't back down. Is that understood now?"

Tommy was chastened. The other two were impressed. Feeks lifted his glass and made a toast, "Here's to you, Phil. Thanks for standing up for our sister."

She looked at me and said, "What you did was really brave."

BRAVE?

Am I brave? I've never known. I've never been challenged to be heroic or self-sacrificing. I couldn't think of a single incident in my life in which anyone would have called me brave. Or the opposite. On the scale of courage, I have made no mark.

Until now. It was especially nice to be called brave by a woman, and especially a woman who seemed to know what she was talking about.

I wasn't deluded: I didn't confuse bravery with fearlessness. I was anything but fearless in the confrontation on the train. I wasn't heroic either but I had stood my ground and managed some resistance, thank God.

I refilled the brothers' glasses and we drank another toast. Part of me was ready to drink until dawn celebrating this proud moment. Another part of me was dead tired.

I offered blankets but all declined. I said good night and went upstairs. As I fell asleep I heard the brothers hooting and cheering downstairs as they got into *The Godfather Part II*.

WHEN I came down in the morning they were gone. The house never felt so empty. The TV room and kitchen were immaculate. My car was back in its garage. I half-expected a thank-you note, but tough guys don't leave thank-you notes.

My sense of unreality about the night's experience lasted until I walked to the Hartsdale station for the morning commute and got a look at the front-page headline of the local newspaper. I should have realized that the story of the train station fight had all three of the great news media hot buttons: violence, race, and sex (sex in the form of the mysteriously kinky twist of "pajama-clad assailants").

I bought a newspaper but couldn't bear to read it until I was alone in the little rented cell I called an office, located on a high floor of the Empire State Building. Sylvia and I were not mentioned. Avon (his last name was Boudreau, age twenty-six) and his two buddies identified themselves as construction workers returning from a party in the Bronx. They were treated at White Plains Hospital where Avon was held overnight and the other two, Elroy M. Hastings (Roy) and Vennard Banks Jr. (Third Guy), were sent home after treatment. The injuries were mainly facial and testicular.

I didn't think I was guilty of anything, but it would not enhance my reputation to be linked to a lurid front-page crime story. Thinking of my lost briefcase gave me a scare for a minute but leaving my briefcase on the train could be explained away as accidental. I considered calling Charlie Benedict for legal advice but I wasn't ready to tell this story, even to a good friend with attorney/client privilege. And if I did need a lawyer, Charlie was the wrong one. His specialty was leasing airplanes.

CHAPTER 4

I'd been working on a speechwriting job for my last remaining client but after reading that newspaper article my concentration was worthless so I gave up around two P.M. and went home, buying a bottle of wine on the way. I don't keep a wine supply in the house for fear that wine and I might fall into a meaningful relationship. But this night I would be watching TV coverage of the pajama-clad maniacs story and might require liquid support.

I barely had my shoes off before the phone rang and someone was telling me that my briefcase had been found and would be kept overnight at White Plains police headquarters before being sent in the morning to the railroad's Lost & Found Department in Manhattan, where it might not emerge from the system for seven to ten days and retrieving it would be a bureaucratic hassle involving waiting in a long line and presenting proof of ownership. In friendly tones the caller emphasized that I was better off picking it up immediately.

So I got in the car and drove over to White Plains. The desk sergeant was suspiciously helpful, as if the whole department had been waiting to serve me. A woman officer led me to the elevator and upstairs where she asked me to take a seat in a small room and wait for someone to bring the briefcase. The sign on the door said Interview Room but I recognized it from a million TV shows: this was a room where police grilled suspects or witnesses. You could almost feel its bad vibrations and smell the sweat that had been sweated here.

I sat down. Then the door opened and Sylvia walked in.

IT WAS a jaw-dropping moment for both of us. It turned out to have been stage-managed by the notorious Detective Carl Pelikan who entered a moment later, laughing and carrying my briefcase.

"That double-take was effing hilarious," he said. "Not strictly kosher but hilarious. I watched it through the one-way. Please sit down, Sylvia." He extended his hand to me and said, "I'm Detective Pelikan."

Sylvia lowered herself warily into a chair glaring at Pelikan, who fit the picture of a middle-aged detective: big cop belly and a pocked sallow complexion. He was in jovial spirits, enjoying his stunt of bringing Sylvia and me face-to-face in his interrogation room.

"You gotta forgive my little trickery. My little ruse. I just had to see the reaction."

My internal alarms started ringing again. Last night I faced three drunks on a train; now I was facing a cop in an interrogation situation—both times I'd felt fogbound, slow-witted, unable to rise to the challenge. And I knew why: I was soft from too much time alone with reveries and not enough time being kept on my toes by the real world. But Sylvia was on her toes. She was alert and straight-backed in her chair. The blackness of her business suit, hair, and eyes gave her a formal and impressive presence.

"Want to hear about my day?" asked Pelikan, flipping open his notebook. "It sure didn't start out good. My bosses beat me up all morning over this pajama bullshit. But then I went over to the hospital, had a tête-à-tête with a young African American acquaintance of yours, Avon Boudreau."

Pelikan looked up from his notes and gave Sylvia some fierce accusatory eye contact, then took a quick glance at me.

"At first he came on like a wiseass but I'd run his sheet and he's not much of a criminal, just a few drunk-and-disorderlies. By the way he had high blood alcohol last night, at the hospital. I bet he's bad news when he drinks, eh? Big, scary guy, looking for trouble?"

It was tempting to nod but nodding would confirm that we'd been on the train with Avon Boudreau. I knew the rule for talking with cops: don't volunteer anything, don't be sucked into conversation.

"Okay, here we go," said Pelikan, finding something in his notes. "Mr. Boudreau dropped out of high school and lasted a couple weeks in the marines before they kicked him out for being a shithead. He tells people he's a construction worker— I'm guessing that's a lie because it sounds more macho than his real job, working for a pet foods distributor. He unloads trucks and stacks heavy bags of animal food. That's how he got those big arms and shoulders, not from prison iron.

"We danced around a little but then he was eager to tell me all about his run-in with a Caucasian man and woman on the 11:13 train. Not that he talks so well because he's got a concussion headache and he's missing a bunch of teeth and his jaw don't work right. He says this white man on the train bumped him disrespectfully and then addressed him in a racist manner. And he says the woman sitting with the man got into it too and was abusive and repeatedly used the N-word. And he also says, Mr. Vail, that the man threw his briefcase at him. Which might be considered assault."

"Are you buying this nonsense?" I asked.

"Of course not," said Pelikan. "I've checked you out, Mr. Vail. You're a solid citizen. You are not going to use racist language or throw briefcases or make threats, especially to a drunk young black man who is six foot three and 220 pounds and has two friends with him about the same size. Avon's story is 98 percent bullshit, I know that."

He gave me a big reassuring smile.

"But the 2 percent that *isn't* bullshit is that you were all in that train car together. Avon has given descriptions of you both and while I've never met you, Mr. Vail, he said the woman—his word was 'bitch'—was tall and skinny with dark hair and eyes, big sharp nose, and a sassy mouth. I heard that and two words formed on my lips, *Sylvia* and *Sforza.*

"So then I had to find the man sitting with Sylvia. Avon told me this gentleman tried to get off the train at Hartsdale and it just happened that a briefcase found on the train had a name tag on it from a Scarsdale resident named Phillip Vail who might use the Hartsdale stop. So I took a wild guess that you're the Caucasian male in this story. And then you two walk into this room and it's obvious recognition when you see each other. So I'm thinking you were on the train together last night and had an ugly encounter with Mr. Boudreau and his friends just prior to their getting a royal ass-kicking. Am I Sherlock F. Holmes or what?"

He slid the briefcase across the table at me. "I read the speech you had in there, Mr. Vail. I'm guessing you're the speechwriter for Peter Draybin."

I nodded.

"Draybin's a hot shit," Pelikan said. "I saw him speak at a big cop and firemen event after 9/11. He was great. Did you write that speech?"

"I provided some assistance," I said. The speechwriter code says you never admit authorship of a client's speech.

"I'm curious about how the speechwriter for a superstar like Peter Draybin gets to know someone from the other end of society, like Sylvia Sforza."

Sylvia ignored the insult and said, "We didn't know each other. He sat down next to me on the train. The conductor will confirm that because he came running in at the last minute and fell into his seat so hard she thought it was funny. She'll remember. Ask her."

"I'll do that. By the way, Mr. Vail, I've been acquainted with Sylvia and her lovely family for many years. Sylvia, I understand your father is under the weather."

"If you call terminal cancer 'under the weather.' "

"Terminal cancer? Tough luck for you but maybe good luck for the law-abiding citizens of the State of New York."

Her face flushed with anger but Pelikan made a conciliatory gesture and quickly backed off, apologizing for an "insensitive" comment and smiling to emphasize his lack of sincerity.

"So let me take it to the next step. You and Mr. Vail have your interaction with these three young men. Then the train gets to White Plains, and a few minutes later these young men are waiting for an ambulance due to a beating by three other young men who come out of the night in pajamas and commit assault in a very professional manner.

"So who in this city comes to mind in this category? None other but the Sforzas, even with the baddest of the four brothers temporarily *hors de combat*, thanks to the justice system with a little help from myself."

I was curious about this fourth brother.

"So I'm thinking, Sylvia has an issue on a train, phones home, the three brothers jump out of bed in their pajamas and rush out to save their sister. I'm betting your cell record would show that you called out the cavalry somewhere around 11:40 last night. Have I put it together correctly?"

I was stunned by how well he'd put it together, but Sylvia reacted with dismissive body language and a shake of the head.

"No, but I did make a call around that time," Sylvia said, surprising me. "These punks on the train were just drunks. I'm not surprised they provoked someone at the station and got a beating. The reason I called home was to make sure the boys were on their way to Peekskill to sleep over at my uncle's so they'd be closer to a seven A.M. moving job in Rhinebeck. When I called they told me they were just going out the door. And we don't usually do moving jobs in peejays."

"That's weak, Sylvia," Pelikan said. "You can do better than that."

"I don't have to. Call Tiziano. He'll vouch for the boys arriving about twelve thirty A.M. and staying over with him and his wife."

"Tiziano would vouch for anything. His vouch has no weight."

Pelikan was winning and loving it. "How about the home-owners they were moving? How about if I talk to them?"

"Fine. I'll give you their name and number. They'll confirm that our van was outside their door at seven A.M. There's an embarrassing catch to this—we were supposed to move them at seven A.M. *next* Friday. My bad. I sent the boys a week early. But we did show up and you can check it. All the neighbors saw us. We're noisy."

"That's ridiculous."

"But true. Check it out."

So Sylvia sent the brothers to Rhinebeck this morning to appear at a house where no one was moving. It was hardly a world-class alibi but maybe it was better than nothing.

"Why did Mr. Vail not get off at Hartsdale?"

"I didn't want to leave her alone with those drunks," I said.

"That's very gallant, Mr. Vail," said Pelikan.

"The whole scene was just stupid," Sylvia said. "These guys were looking for trouble. But Mr. Vail and I had nothing to do with it. We got to White Plains, we got off and left, end of story."

"Except that when you walked down the stairs World War Six was going on."

"We didn't walk down the stairs. We walked over the bridge to the parking garage, where my car was. If there was a fight going on we missed it."

"But then your brothers came running out and got in their vehicle."

"Not *my* brothers," Sylvia said.

I felt like I was watching a sports event, rooting for Sylvia who seemed to be rallying after a weak start.

"So you're saying you didn't call your brothers in, you didn't witness the attack, and your brothers were in a moving van driving to Peekskill at the time of the incident?"

"That's it. Are we finished here?"

"One more question. I was in my car when I heard the radio dispatcher sending police to the train station—"

"You've got to get a life, Carl. Don't be driving around by yourself at midnight."

That irked him but he went on. "I called in and found out what'd happened so I pressed the button on my GPS labeled 'Sforza Residence.' But nobody was home. I heard the dogs barking but no one came to the door. I had a patrol car relieve me at three thirty and stay till sunrise. No one showed up. Where was everybody?"

"My dad was in the hospital, my brothers were in Peekskill."

"How about you? Where were *you?*"

I was alarmed but she had an answer.

"I gave Mr. Vail a ride home. He'd been a good guy staying on the train with me and he missed his stop so giving him a ride was the least I could do."

"So you would know Mr. Vail's address?"

"Yes, I do." She passed the test, telling him my address and the color of my house.

"Okay, but I was outside your house till three thirty. You dropped him off but didn't get home till when?"

"About seven or seven thirty A.M."

That surprised him. "At that hour of the night it's a twenty-minute drive from his house to your house but it took you, what, *seven hours?*"

Pelikan lit up, smug over punching a hole in her story.

Sylvia looked away and seemed lost in thought. With a sigh she pulled herself together, turning back to Pelikan.

"I drove him to his house. He invited me in. We had drinks. One thing led to another."

I saw where this was going but Pelikan was so focused on reality that he missed the leap into fiction.

"Meaning what?" said Pelikan.

"Meaning I spent the night at his house."

"Because you figured I'd be waiting outside your house?"

"No, Carl," she smiled sweetly. "Because we made love."

He stared at her, speechless.

"Please don't tell my father," she added, with a perfect straight face.

I fought off a laugh.

"You *made love*? No way."

Nothing knocks a conversation more off course than an unexpected admission of sexual intercourse. Pelikan lost his cool entirely, and he didn't like it. He was chagrined at being slow on the uptake. He was angry at the possibility that Sylvia was putting him on, but he wasn't sure and then he was angry that he wasn't sure. His jocular showing off was gone now—there'd be no more talk of little ruses or tête-à-têtes or *hors de combat*.

He called Sylvia's story bogus and vowed to rip it to shreds. He promised to put her brothers in jail. They could become cellmates with the fourth brother at Ricton Correctional Facility and share the stainless steel shitter.

In his rant against the Sforzas he seemed to have forgotten me but now he turned and caught me struggling not to laugh.

"Vail, do you think this is some kind of *amusing* lark to tell your sophisticated friends about—"

"Not at all, Detective."

"I hope you realize the only reason she slept with you was so she could control you."

"At my age you take it any way you can get it."

Sylvia laughed and Pelikan reddened.

"Can we leave now, Carl?" she said.

"Don't call me Carl, *Sylvia*. Do you hear me?" She nodded contritely.

Pelikan turned to me. "Mr. Vail, I want to hear you tell me whether she's telling the truth or not. I want you to be on the record with this because if she's lying and you support it, you're in the same shit she's in."

Without hesitation I said, "She's telling the truth."

He gave me a long and sorry stare. "That's very disappointing, Vail. You've just thrown away a lifetime clean record of being an honest citizen. What for? To live dangerously? To get a little more gangster snatch? You ought to be ashamed of yourself."

He turned away and said, "Get the fuck out of here."

WE WERE on the street outside police headquarters about to go our separate ways when she kissed me.

"They might be watching," she said, explaining the kiss by nodding up to the windows of the police building. "Remember, we're lovebirds."

"It's amazing that I'd totally forgotten we had sex."

"Typical man," she said, giving me a light punch to the forehead.

She started to turn away but then turned back. "Hey, Phil, you stood up for me last night with thugs on the train and you just stood up for me again with the police. You know how many men would do that?"

Before I could say anything she was on her way to her car.

BY SUNDAY night I was struggling with boredom. I finished and e-mailed the first draft of the speech I'd been writing for Pete Draybin and then sat around, feeling adrift, sensing that life would seem very dull without Sylvia Sforza and the events that seemed to crystallize around her.

I could not remember a time in my recent life that had been as *heightened* as the hours that started with sitting down next to Sylvia Sforza. But now I was coming down from those heights. I was surprised to realize I missed Sylvia but couldn't say exactly why. I liked her humor and the spine she showed on the train and against Pelikan. I liked her old-fashioned, earthy, bright-eyed looks. I was fascinated by all the things I didn't know about her. And then another thought, which startled me: she seemed to have an inexplicable inclination to see good things in me. She thought I was a good guy, a brave guy who stood up for her twice. I liked that; I realized I wanted to look good in her eyes.

Was I attracted to her? Yes, I had to acknowledge attraction and I was delighted to remember what attraction felt like, but mature judgment rushed in to warn me that developing a boyish crush on Sylvia Sforza was supremely inadvisable, if not pathetic. She was too young. She was from a different and apparently unsavory world. The distance between us was uncrossable and not meant to be crossed. It would do me no good to be getting ideas.

I turned on the news. The story of the train station mayhem had not developed. There'd been no arrests or new twists. The only new element was a snippet of Avon Boudreau hobbling out of White Plains Hospital on crutches. The monster who would haunt my dreams forever now looked like a cartoon character covered with casts and bandages. A woman reporter approached him for an interview but he ducked away, covering his mouth to hide the dental damage inflicted by Feeks.

The phone rang. My son, Willy, calling from Minneapolis.

I heard the tension in his voice and I knew it was about Thanksgiving. Last year he'd spent the holiday with me in New York and it had been a forlorn experience. This year his mother wanted to host him in Los Angeles, but he had a different plan. He had been invited to Thanksgiving with the family of a new girlfriend in Minneapolis. His mother had given her reluctant approval and now he wanted mine too. What young man wouldn't prefer to be with a new girlfriend?

Of course I said yes. But I would miss him. Perhaps he heard this in my voice because he quickly promised a New York visit for Christmas.

Ten seconds later the phone rang again. Was it Willy having second thoughts about abandoning his dad for Thanksgiving?

"This is Jacopo Sforza."

"Who?" I said.

"The father of Sylvia Sforza."

"Of course. Good evening, Mr. Sforza," I said, struggling to overcome surprise. "How are you feeling?"

"Pretty good, and thanks for asking," he said. He had a slight accent but there was no weakness in his voice. "My daughter has good words about you."

"Oh," I said, tongue-tied but pleased.

"Mr. Vail, they're going to let me out of the hospital for one day to enjoy Thanksgiving at home with my family. I would be honored if you would be our guest. Unless you have family obligations of your own. Sylvia thinks you do not."

"No, no obligations, no problem. I'd love to come."

"Someone will pick you up Thursday afternoon. Three o'clock."

The phone clicked. A tingle of pleasure swept over me. My adventure with the Sforzas would continue. I would see Sylvia again and I was intrigued by Jacopo Sforza. Far from sounding like a blue-collar Italian papa with a small local moving company and four hooligan sons, he sounded like a polished gentleman—formal, careful, commanding, like many CEOs I'd written for.

For the first time in a while I had something to look forward to.

CHAPTER 5

Peter Draybin, the last of my speechwriting clients, read my first draft at five A.M. His assistant, Jane Dooley, waited until seven A.M. to let me know that Mr. Draybin expected me for lunch. But not in his downtown office. Today he was on his yacht, docked at a marina in Connecticut. There was nothing surprising about this but Jane's voice lacked its usual cheer.

"Is he okay with the draft?"

"Talk to him," she said.

"That doesn't sound good, Jane."

"Call me tomorrow."

I'd been writing freelance speeches for Peter Draybin for fifteen years. He was intelligent and thoughtful to work with, delivered speeches better than any corporate speaker, and paid better than anyone. Without him I could not have sustained my speechwriting business. We always worked well together, producing speeches, videos, and other projects we were both proud of. We'd spent many hours in each other's company and while we hardly traveled in the same social circles (I traveled in no circle at all), we talked freely about almost everything, often in superior restaurants which he preferred to meeting in his office.

The problem with Pete—everyone called him Pete—was similar to the problem with me: a mood change linked to his recently diminished status. He had reached retirement age and been forced to step down as CEO, but because he was a superstar, adored by the news media as well as tens of thousands of employees over several generations, the company made a show of retaining him in the role of corporate wise man, bearer of the institutional memory and keeper of the flame.

That is, he made cheerleading speeches at company meetings and lingered in his office hoping to be asked for advice. He was treated with fawning respect and important visitors stopped in to greet him. But he was out of the mix and powerless.

He understood this and had the good taste to refrain from meddling, gossiping, or second-guessing his successor. We drank large amounts of fabulous wine discussing the challenge of his new position and trying to work out a speech style appropriate to his new role. It distressed him that he now had to give speeches he correctly felt to be deficient in substance and overloaded with morale-boosting "soft" topics including values, leadership, and business wisdom.

After a make-the-best-of-it start, his resentment at being extraneous had begun to take its toll on his sunny personality. And because shit inevitably rolls downhill, his fall from power bumped down into a fall from grace for me. He had never been abusive but now he seemed to want to vent his frustrations by finding fault with my drafts, which came back with cranky comments scrawled in red ink. He sulked and withdrew, leaving it all to me but later accusing me of ignoring instructions he didn't give and ideas he didn't offer. Tension was gnawing at our relationship.

I knew he had spent the weekend on what he called his "boat," though to most people it would pass for a small ocean liner. He held frequent business meetings on board—I presumed there was a sizable tax advantage to this. I had met with him on the boat several times, enjoying informal lunches prepared by his onboard chef. There was a luxurious sitting area in the large cabin topside and a dinner table for six on the deck below. Usually we chatted for a while before eating but this time club sandwiches were waiting in the sitting area and we got right down to business.

Even when you know your client well, reactions to a first draft are unpredictable and you approach these sessions with apprehension. Draybin was more secure and less temperamental than most clients but he could be trouble if his first reading of a new draft caught him in the wrong mood.

And he was not in a good mood today. I boarded the yacht to a greeting that was polite but far from his usual blast of enthusiasm. He held the printed-out draft in his hands and as he riffed through it uncomfortably, I saw no red ink. This told me that he either hadn't read it or had quit after the first page or had some larger problem. He poured me a glass of white wine but took none for himself.

"Phil, this draft just doesn't give me energy. I'm not eager to read it to an audience. I can't point to specific faults— it's not what's there but what's *not* there. I read it and I say, 'Who cares?' Frankly I've had the same feeling with the last few speeches you've written."

That last sentence was a body blow.

"We've had a great relationship. You've done so much great work for me over the years, but you don't seem to have your old pizzazz, that special Phil Vail sparkle. I don't think your heart's in it anymore."

Shit: *I was being fired.* This was a jolt I had not foreseen; I had figured we would just work through the learning pains of his new speechmaking persona, but now it hit me that my working life was about to end, leaving me with nothing. How would I fill the days? What would be the foundation of my identity and what would I do without income? I reached for the wine and downed a big gulp, almost choking.

I looked at his face and saw mounting discomfort. I figured the guillotine blade was about to drop. In a moment my skull would be bouncing on his highly polished deck. Asking for a reprieve or stay of execution would only embarrass both of us. Making excuses or quibbling would be patiently dealt with but would leave a bad taste.

I had lost my pizzazz, he said. So I had to regain it, immediately.

Then my cell phone rang.

Its ring broke the rhythm of my firing. Pete sat back, perhaps relieved, and said, "Go ahead, take it."

I fumbled around with the phone but got it to my ear and said hello.

"It's Pelikan."

Pelikan. It's so nice when the cops call as you're being fired.

"I made a note of your cell number when I had your briefcase."

Pete was staring at me. Of course he was hearing only my side of the conversation.

I made my move. What the hell.

I said, "Mr. Gates, it's so nice of you to call."

"Gates? This is Pelikan."

"Yes, I've had some great chats with Melinda."

"Who the hell is Melinda?"

I paused a moment, not quite sure how to do this, improvising madly. "Of course I've read about it. You're doing inspiring work with that foundation." Then I tacked on, "Bill," as if he'd asked me to call him by his first name.

Pelikan said, "Vail, I'm calling to make you an offer. Your new friends would call it an offer you can't refuse."

"Oh my, that's a *great* offer," I said. "I'm honored, really."

"I haven't even told you the offer."

"Tell me your timeline, Bill. Because I have to tell you up front that I'm just about to dive into the second draft of a speech I'm very excited about it. It'll need maybe two more weeks but it's for my premier client, Pete Draybin, and my loyalty to him takes priority over everything (I didn't have the

nerve to look at Pete as I said this), even the fantastic opportunity of working for you, Bill."

"Are you insane?" demanded Pelikan.

While Pelikan steamed about my insanity I stood up, took
the speech printout out of Pete's hands, flicked off the paper
clip, and threw it overboard. The pages fluttered slowly toward
the water.

Pete grinned broadly.

"I want to see you *today*," thundered Pelikan.

"In fact I'm sitting here with Pete right now. Can I put
him on for a quick hello?"

Pete brightened, reaching out to take the phone.

"Tell him to go fuck himself," shouted Pelikan.

I hoped Pete didn't hear that.

"Oh, sure, Bill. Of course you're in a rush but I'll pass
along your regards."

Pete dropped his hand, disappointed.

Pelikan growled, "Call me when you sober up. *Today*."

"Thanks, Bill," I said.

PETE CLAPPED his hands. "That was beautiful, Phil. What a
great stunt. World-class."

I lifted my hands in a palms-up gesture, modest thanks
for the compliment.

"You did that so well I almost believed you."

I laughed, pleasantly noncommittal.

"Did you think it up on the spur of the moment or was
it planned?"

"Bill sends his best," I said. I was not going to concede
that I'd faked it. Let him always be a little uncertain.

"*That* was the old Phil," Pete said, beaming. "That's the
Phil I want to work with again."

He topped off my wine and filled his own glass.

"Look, here's what we'll do. You write that second draft—
and I hope the first draft is on your computer so you don't

have to scuba dive for it. Let it rip, be the old Phil, and we'll make it work, okay?"

We lifted our glasses. We were both happy—I still had employment and he didn't have to fire me. Pete was built for the good guy role and hates being the bad guy so he was almost as pleased as I was.

I wasn't really confident this era of good feeling would last. He would read the next draft and, no matter how much I pumped it up, it would not make him king again.

As soon as I left the marina I pulled over and called Pelikan. He was away from his desk. I left a message that I was on the way.

I got on I-95 where, as always, traffic came to an instant halt. This was fortunate because it gave me time to make the psychological transition between Pete and Pelikan. I had to shake off pizzazz and shift into paranoia.

"Sit," he said when I entered his messy little office. "I won't even mention that phone call." He put his feet on his desk and stared at me.

"Do you know I'm still getting calls about that train station thing? From all over the world, especially Japan. All they care about is the fucking pajamas. I don't get it. Are they perverts, or what?"

I offered a small, we're-two-unperverted-guys smile.

"So what do you make of it all?"

I shrugged. *Don't say one word more than necessary.*

"So, Phil, I'm thinking that by now, with a couple days to think about it, you'd be willing to level with me. Hey, we've all lied to get laid, right?"

"No comment on that."

"What I mean is, you put the wood to her a few times and it was exciting to be getting criminal tail but now you're coming back to earth. You lied to a cop for the first time in your life and you're wondering how to get off the hook. I mean, what if your name got in the papers? What would Bill Gates think of you then?"

"You're losing me, Detective."

"You're a smart guy but you're way over your head. I read that speech you wrote. I said, this guy knows business but he don't know squat about what he's getting into."

"So you're offering to rescue me? And what's in it for you?"

"Just the truth. I want you to confirm my scenario of what happened. Maybe tell the story again in court, but it probably won't come to that. You can walk out of this building and never see my classically good-looking face again. No more stress for you and you won't have to spend your 401(k) on a criminal lawyer. And you'll have a clean conscience. There's a good deal, right?"

It *was* appealing to get out of this crime story and channel my energies into my revived career with Pete. But I wanted to see Sylvia again. I wanted to meet her father. Something was *opening* to me and I wasn't ready to slam the door on it.

"Appreciate the offer," I said. "But I'll pass on it for now."

"You're going to look back at this opportunity and kick yourself."

"I think we're done," I said, rising.

"Not for long, not for fucking long." These words lit the short fuse of his temper. He got up pushing his chair backward angrily and led me to the elevator, more pissed off with every step.

"Maybe I'm just a slob to you but I'm a police detective and proud of it. I play for the good guys. We defend people like you against the bad guys. And the Sforzas are the bad guys. You're my chance to put three of 'em behind bars but the woman gave you a taste and that's all you can think about."

He glared at me but broke it off when a group of cocky younger detectives walked by and seemed to snicker at Pelikan, who scowled back at them. "These smartass jerkoffs piss me off," he said to me. "They think they're real cops. But I'm the real cop around here. I'm the real fucking thing and don't forget it."

He was burning mad, red-faced, and close to exploding as the elevator arrived. I was surprised by how swiftly his emotions had escalated. Was it frustration with me or resentment at the perceived disrespect from the younger detectives?

"I've been trying to tell you what you're getting into but you still don't get it, do you?"

I entered the elevator, anxious to get away from him. A half-dozen passengers retreated to the far corners of the elevator as Pelikan stepped forward and caught the closing doors.

"The brother John, aka Catcher, the one I put in prison? He's a goddamn weapon of mass destruction. And the father? You never heard of Jacopo Sforza? He's in the *Mafia*, Vail. He's a caporegime in the Vavolizza crime family. *And you're fucking his daughter*."

CHAPTER 6

If the goal was adding spice to my life, I was succeeding beyond my wildest dreams. In a single day I'd almost been fired, I'd improvised a ridiculous stunt to save my career, I'd been told that I was celebrating Thanksgiving with the Mafia, I'd been screamed at and embarrassed by a detective, and I'd found myself daydreaming about a woman twenty years my junior whose father was a mob boss.

When I got home there was a voice message from Sylvia: "My dad suggested that I call and give you a warning—"

A *warning?*

"—Dad has always felt that Thanksgiving is an important American holiday and we should dress to show respect. But he's aware the rest of the world feels otherwise and he didn't want you to feel uncomfortable by showing up in casual clothes that any normal person would wear. This doesn't mean you can't play basketball with the boys, it just means the boys will be wearing suits. See you."

I Googled Jacopo Sforza. There was a Wikipedia item about a Jacopo Sforza who'd led a mercenary army in Italy in the 1400s and a few other obviously innocent Jacopo Sforzas were mentioned but then I started finding *my* Jacopo Sforza, though there wasn't much about him.

He was an upper echelon mobster who didn't get his hands dirty, was rarely mentioned in the press, and had a reputation as "untraditional," although that wasn't explained.

I didn't find anything violent other than references to a short but furious mob war years ago in which his brother's two sons were killed.

The prospect of Thanksgiving with the Sforzas created some trepidation but also some playing-with-fire giddiness. I imagined arriving in my standard L.L. Bean Thanksgiving outfit of chinos and a sport shirt and being glowered at by guests decked out in gangster swag—gaudy stolen jewelry, designer dresses that had fallen off trucks, elite-label men's suits that were freebies from terrified extortion victims. So instead, I would wear my best dark business suit. This would be appreciated by the undertaker who would not have to re-dress me if I got whacked. The big question was whether I should run out and buy a pinky ring.

Mafia jokes skipped merrily through my brain. I was amused until I realized this was a wrong way to prepare myself. I could not go into this seeing myself as Billy Crystal or Woody Allen spending a holiday with the Corleones or Sopranos, giggling when frisked and doing jokes about mob-ster nicknames. This was reality, not comedy. The answer to how to comport myself was simple: I would take it seriously. Because it *was* serious and because I *wanted* it to be serious.

The clarity of this resolution put me in an upbeat mood that transferred smoothly into my effort to pump pizzazz into Draybin's speech. It was one of those infrequent times in the writer business when everything flows, effortless and right.

I would e-mail it to Pete on Thanksgiving afternoon when he'd be on his yacht en route to Cape Cod. Maybe he wouldn't read it until Friday or even Monday. Maybe I'd also send a copy to Pelikan with a cover note saying, "Yo, Carl, this is what I do when I'm not banging Jake Sforza's little girl."

PROMPTLY AT three P.M. on Thanksgiving Day a vintage Cadillac Fleetwood sedan pulled up in front of my house. I'm not a car person but this car was sensational: fire engine red, twenty feet long, with great lines and fins and an attitude of unabashed world-beating bravado.

A dashing young man jumped out and hurried around to open the passenger door for me.

"Good to see you again, Mr. Vail."

"Feeks? Is that you? You look like a movie star."

"Nah, just the same old piece of shit."

But there was no resemblance to the Feeks of the other night, the hyperactive loon in pajamas. He *did* look like a movie star, trim and athletic, black hair brushed back. He wore stylish black sunglasses and a pinstriped charcoal suit that may have been the best-looking men's suit I'd ever seen.

"Brioni," he said. "We buy American for everything else but for suits, hey, you gotta go Italiano. Want to hear some music?" He turned on the radio to a golden oldies station.

"Did you program that station for me?" I asked.

"Yeah, the stuff I listen to would blow up your head, Mr. Vail."

"Call me Phil."

"Not today, Phil. Today you're *Mr. Vail*. You're the guest of honor. And we've never had a guest of honor. Maybe we never even had a guest."

"Is this a big event? How many people show up?"

"Enough to fill the house. Good people, for the most part. A few nutjobs. Uncle Tiz is getting demented. My brother Catcher's wife, Vera, is a piece of work. And her two sons are little psychos but I can't complain because I was like that at their age."

"You were a wild kid?" This was no surprise.

"Oh, the worst. I really feel bad about the trouble I caused, especially for my father because my mom died having me. I know it wasn't my fault but, you know, Dad went to the hospital with just mom and came home with just me. She had a heart attack."

"That's horrible, Feeks. I'm sorry."

"It really fucked up my dad. Not to mention what it did to Sylvia's whole life because she was about to go to college but had to stay home to be my mother. I owe her everything. That black dude on the train who fucked around with her?— he's lucky I didn't kill him. My brother Catcher might kill *me* for not killing *him*. But it wasn't Sylvia's fault I was a screwed-up kid. I had to take pills. I saw shrinks. All the doctors I saw got me interested in medicine. I've taken some nursing courses, which may be a surprise considering how bad I did in school, but that was mainly because of maturity issues. I used to be a fucking maniac, believe me."

We were in White Plains now. At a traffic light a car carrying four young Hispanic guys pulled up next to us. The Hispanic guys ogled the Cadillac. They were not hostile but Feeks gave them the finger. I was shocked. The light changed and we pulled away.

"Can I ask why you did that?"

"Because they're punks," he said. "You tell them before they tell you."

"I'd never flip the bird to people I don't know," I said. "You never know who you're dealing with. What if they want to fight?"

"So we fight."

I noted the *we*. It apparently went without saying that I would join the fight.

"I haven't been in a fight since third grade," I said.

This seemed to surprise him. Maybe he heard a tremor in my voice. He thought for a moment and said, "Okay, just keep the fourth one busy till I get there."

Oh, good. I only had to fight one of them. Feeks would take the other three, and then finish off my guy who by then would be pounding my head against the pavement. Feeks was untroubled by the prospect of combat. He didn't care that it was pointless. He gave no thought to where it might lead. On the other hand, I was flattered that he considered me worthy of joining him in battle.

"So I was telling you about how screwed up I was? In high school Sylvia got me into boxing. My dream was to fight in the Olympics. I blew that the same way Catcher blew baseball. He was a legend in high school. Drafted by the Dodgers. They invited him to spring training. This was back when they trained in Vero Beach, Florida."

"Wow. Did he get to the major leagues?"

"No, he didn't even make it to the end of the first week."

"Why?"

"Fighting. That's our curse. Some people say the four of us are brothers but really we're just sparring partners."

"But you're good at it. Most people avoid fighting because they know they'll get their ass kicked."

"You never worry about that. We have a family friend, Uncle Kim. You'll meet him today. He's not really an uncle, he's Korean. He trained us when we were kids. Partly martial arts but more like dirty street fighting. We called it *die kwan do*. Kim's an easygoing guy but you wouldn't mess with him. He also trained our dogs. You'll also meet Vico who runs our barbershop. Gave me my first haircut. He's another guy you seriously don't want to piss off."

Okay, I'll scale back my plans to piss these killers off.

IT WAS a three-story white house at the head of a cul-de-sac called Sycamore Court. The neighborhood was nondescript, somewhere between middle- and lower-middle class. The Sforza house was the biggest on the street but far from grand. Its only eye-catching detail was an oversized flagpole flying a huge American flag.

Feeks rolled down the window, stuck his head out, and yelled upwards, "What's shaking, Carmine?" A voice I presumed to be Carmine's yelled something I couldn't make out.

Feeks told me Carmine was the lookout, watching the street from a small third-floor balcony.

The driveway circled around behind the house where there was a basketball court. A few young boys were playing fiercely. Their good clothes were smudged. Big George Sforza, with a beer bottle in one hand and a cigar in the other and wearing an unbuttoned Brioni suit, was apparently the referee.

"Hey, Mr. Vail, how ya doin'?"

"Good, George. This looks like a wild game."

"Calms them down for dinner. I just step in to break up the fights."

Feeks insisted on leading me around to the front of the house. "Front door for you, Mr. Vail," he said.

As I stepped through the door two enormous Doberman pinschers snapped to their feet and eyed me alertly. I love dogs but Dobermans worry me. Feeks waved them away.

A beautiful little girl in a pink dress ran to greet me. She was about seven but had the Sforza looks, the black hair and strong facial bones.

"Happy Thanksgiving," she said boldly, offering her hand in a handshake. "I'm Amanda Sforza. I'm the greeter. Aunt Sylvia's waiting for you. Follow."

She turned and I followed her past a modestly sized living room to my right, filled with people. The noise level of their conversation dipped as I went past. I felt many hard eyes appraising me. I waved in awkward acknowledgment but Amanda took my sleeve and dragged me to my left through a dining room in which the dining table had been moved aside so a second table could be squeezed in. Both tables were handsomely set for dinner.

Passing through a swinging door we entered a fragrant kitchen full of women. One of them cried out, "Holy shit, he's here!" I scanned the smiling faces for Sylvia but did not see her, until she popped up from behind a busy island stacked with trays and bowls and plates. Apparently she'd been kneeling to look into the oven.

Recognizable as she is, I almost didn't recognize her. I think that because of her black hair, pale skin, and subdued wardrobe my image of her was in black and white, but now she was transformed with color. She wore a bright yellow apron over a cherry-colored silk blouse. Her jewelry was bold and gold and she was towering in high heels.

She was not the plain woman on the train or the all-business woman in the police station; she was knockout beautiful. It occurred to me that she could turn beauty on and off like electricity, turning it off for external camouflage and on for family or, maybe, for me.

The other women were giggling with excitement. It was an infectiously tingling moment—I realized this was a traditional scene in which I was the boyfriend or gentleman caller, showing up to meet the family. I was being inspected by the womenfolk. The cliché called for a bashful Sylvia but she was far from bashful, striding around the kitchen island, tossing off the apron.

She wore tailored slacks in the same color as her blouse. Frankly I wanted to step back and gaze at her but she quickly closed the distance between us, giving me a kiss on the cheek, saying, "You're even braver than I thought to walk into this kitchen."

I was waiting for the knockout smile. She said, "I'd like to introduce you to the seventh graders assembled here today." She introduced Rose, the longtime family cook and helper. She introduced two older ladies, Aunt Paola and Aunt Angela, and Angela's adult daughter Beatrice. She introduced George's girlfriend, Maria, and Tommy's ex-wife, Pamela, the mother of Amanda.

Rose said, "This is not an ugly man, and not that old," and gave me a hug.

Aunt Paola handed me a glass of prosecco and they all drank to welcome me. It wasn't their first prosecco of the day.

"Take over, girls," said Sylvia, taking my elbow and leading me out of the kitchen. Chatter exploded behind us as we went through the swinging door to the dining room.

"Are you still breathing?" she asked when we were alone in the dining room.

"That was amazing," I said. "Am I the boyfriend?"

"That's what they think. I haven't had a date for so long they think I'm a lesbian, so a man showing up is news-at-eleven. But you ought to know that you're here because my father wants to meet you. You're *his* date, not mine."

I guess she could spot some disappointment on my face.

She took my arm and steered me toward the living room. "I'm so glad you came," she said. Then came the smile, which made me weak and strong simultaneously.

"You don't look at all like Mrs. Katz," I said, hating myself for making such an obscure and roundabout compliment.

"Yeah, Mrs. Katz. Avon's high school principal. No woman forgets being compared to a high school principal. His words were razors to my wounded heart."

I must have looked surprised at that.

"Poppa's a Shakespeare nut. We've grown up on quotes like that. We don't *understand* Shakespeare but we quote him."

The mob boss was a Shakespeare nut?

"I just meant that you look beautiful."

There, a brave straightforward compliment, breaking the bounds of my inhibitions. She looked at me hesitantly but otherwise did not acknowledge it. Then she asked, "Do you like the prosecco?"

"Yes, it's delicious."

"It's family-made, near Venice. Uncle Viv has a vineyard, among many other things. You just met his wife, Paola, the blonde one. She's Venetian so she's blonde. Finish your glass, you'll need a lot more."

I finished it in a big gulp. Sylvia opened the door to the kitchen and called for Amanda, who came running. "Mr. Vail needs a refill. Catch up with us."

Sylvia took my arm and steered me toward the living room. "Let's finish the introductions. Poppa's napping but he's eager to meet you later."

I had snobbishly expected a gangsterish house of ill taste but it was far from that. The living room was bright and comfortable. A coffee table was crowded with Italian appetizers and a grand piano was covered with framed photographs. Guests stood around with glasses in their hands. Most of them were sneaking glances at me.

The basketball game was over and George and Tommy and several boys had come inside. George introduced me to his young son Vincent. The names and faces were beginning to blur.

I heard a door open and a toilet flush and a short, rough-looking older gentleman with a bewildered expression entered the room.

Sylvia reeled him in. "Uncle Tiz, I want you to meet our guest today, Phil Vail."

"Are you Jewish?" he asked gruffly.

Everyone laughed—apparently this was his standard opening line. I told him I wasn't Jewish.

"How should I know? Maybe you told me already but I forgot. I got CRS disease."

I didn't know what to say to that.

"CRS—Can't Remember Shit."

Tiz winked and everyone laughed again. Sylvia whispered, "Now you've heard all two of Uncle Tiz's jokes."

Tiz wanted to show me the pictures on the piano. He seized my elbow and tugged me away from Sylvia. "Sylvia, let the fuck go of him for a minute."

She said, "Enjoy. I've got to get back to the kitchen."

"So this is the family," Tiz began. "This is my mother and father. They look like they just got off the boat at Ellis Island, right? Like a pair of peasants, because that's what they were. Here's me and my two brothers in the old days. These were my two little boys, Rocco and little Frankie, rest in peace. Here's my wife, Angela. Here's Jake's kids before Jimmy was born. This one is John, who became a catcher but no Yogi Berra, believe me. More like Rocky Marciano. Here's the two Sylvias, mother and daughter. Are they gorgeous or what? They look serious till they smile but then the fucking sun comes out, you know?"

"You're right."

"You bet I'm right. Who's that movie actress, the tall one? Played a hooker. Looks like no other woman you've ever seen and has a crazy laugh. That's Sylvia to me. Are you hot for her? You're a little older than I thought. What are you, fifty, sixty?"

"Fifty-nine."

"Fifty-nine?" he said, slapping me on the back. "I forget how old Sylvia is, but you're a fucking cradle robber."

T iz seemed fatigued as the photo show ended. I was then approached by Vico the barber who introduced me to Kim, the trainer of fighters and dogs. Both were of indeterminate age, maybe midsixties. Kim was bright-eyed and muscular; Vico was craggy, small, and bent. We didn't have a lot in common but we made a good-humored try at conversation.

Kim and Vico stepped away when Uncle Viv approached. A moment earlier I had encountered Viv as a skinny teenager in the photo with his older brothers; now he was close to seventy, although he looked vigorous and healthy. He was very much the European gentleman, tall and dignified and beautifully dressed. He and his wife, Paola, had flown from Italy for today's event. With his eyes and tone of voice he conveyed a fact that could not be spoken aloud: he expected this to be the last holiday the three Sforza brothers of his generation would celebrate together.

Then we talked about Venice, where he owned small hotels and other businesses. He began an interesting story about his decision many years ago to leave the United States. The "cut-throat nature of American business competition" (I took this as a euphemism for crime) suited his two brothers but he lacked the stomach for it. Though he and his wife were born in New York and had never been to Italy, they felt the pull of the old country and relocated to Venice in their twenties. Aunts and uncles took them in and helped Viv get his start as an entrepreneur.

Viv's story was interrupted by the highly perfumed arrival of Catcher's wife, Vera. As she pushed between us, Viv made a discreet withdrawal.

My take on the politics of the room was that Kim and Vico backed off because Viv outranked them but Viv moved away because he was uncomfortable with Vera. In contrast to his cosmopolitan style, she was—there is no other word for it—a bimbo. Until she appeared I hadn't seen a single Cosa Nostra caricature. The men in the room looked like rough working-class guys dressed up conservatively for a visit to the boss's house, and their wives were anything but flashy, but Vera tested my vow about not seeing gangster satire everywhere I looked.

She must have been a sensation in her prime but now, in her early forties, everything about her suggested desperate overspending. Her face was unnaturally chiseled, her dress was skintight and excessively colorful, and her breasts came at me like great twin weapons that might be used to ram enemy ships in naval battles. She was tall in stiletto heels and if you didn't count the big hair, we were the same height. Her two teenage sons, Todd and Jeremy, whirled around us raucously as we talked. Both boys were scuffed and sloppy from basketball, both were rowdy, and neither heeded her orders to shut the fuck up.

"You I've been waiting to cast my eyes on," she said. "You are the talk of the town around here but I don't get what you did. On the train you didn't even throw a punch but everybody thinks you're the hero? And then you go over to your fancy house where you serve carrots? And then you did something else good with Pelikan but I don't get what? Why does Poppa want to meet you?"

"I haven't met him yet. After I do, I'll tell you what he said. Okay?"

"You would?" She seemed disarmed by my cooperativeness. "That would be fucking amazing."

Then, perhaps thinking she'd finally tapped into an information source, she stepped closer, pressing a marble-hard breast into my shoulder and lowering her voice. "So what's going on with you and Sylvia? I'm glad she finally met somebody. Most men find out about this family and run. But her clock is ticking, know what I mean?"

Even Vera could read my discomfort. "Oh, hey, listen to me. But look, like I said, after you see Poppa if you can tell me what went down because I visit my husband and he's always grilling me about what's happening."

"I'm sure it's difficult for him to be away like that. When does he come home?"

"They say March 19th unless he kills somebody else." She laughed to show she was joking. "Those shit-fucks won't even let him come home to see his dying father. They can talk on the phone but it's a party line with J. Edgar Hoover, right? But there's conversations they should be having, given that my husband would be taking over the family if Poppa passes, God forbid."

Tommy came to my rescue, pulling me away from her. "Sister wants me to give Mr. Vail a tour of the house," he explained.

"A tour of the house?" said Vera. "Why does he get a tour?"

"Sister said so."

"*I* never got a tour," she said. "To this day there are places in this house I haven't been." Then she dropped her protest and turned to me. "Talk later, okay, hon?"

Tommy whispered, "Let's go out to the kitchen and get you another drink because you probably need it after that."

Sylvia was hurrying out of the kitchen. "He's ready," she said. "Take him up, Tommy. Send the nurse down and we'll give her a plate."

CHAPTER 7

The Dobermans followed us, their nails clicking on the wooden stairs.

The second floor was nothing but bedrooms but the next level was a landing with two opposite doors, both closed. Tommy said, "Carmine's balcony to the left, Poppa's den to the right."

He knocked once and opened the door, revealing a small room with floor-to-ceiling bookshelves, a chocolate-colored rug, and a couch where a nurse sat reading a magazine. She jumped up and squeezed past us with a polite smile, leaving the room. The dogs rushed in and curled up on the floor. Tommy disappeared.

I've been shown into CEO offices many times and CEOs don't make me nervous but this was a bit different, I was meeting a bona fide mob boss. But what I found was a frail old man, bald from chemo, oxygen tube in his nose, and black-framed reading glasses which he removed as I entered. He was seated in a leather recliner, wearing a dark suit with an American flag pin in the lapel. We shook hands; I could feel him trying to put strength into the handshake.

He motioned to the couch. I sat down and we looked at each other. Later, when I gave myself a hurry-up reading course on Mafia culture, I learned that veteran gangsters have an extraordinary gift for sizing people up quickly and accurately. When this happens it feels like being stripped to your underwear—poses and motives seen through, soft spots pin-pointed, manhood diminished.

There was a knock on the door and Amanda came in carrying a glass, which she handed to me. Mr. Sforza nodded to her and she left.

The drink's aroma told me it was single malt scotch, probably of a higher quality than I'd served at my home on the night of the train incident. I presumed it had been identified as the official Phil Vail drink. Someone had been sent to buy a bottle for me. These people paid attention.

"Drink, please," he said. "I wish I could join you."

I took a sip. "Excellent," I said, testing my voice.

He seemed weary but otherwise he had what I now recognized as the Sforza look: a long and rangy body, a face somewhere between plain and handsome with big dark eyes and a large straight nose. I supposed I'd expected a beefy thick-necked Mafioso.

"I'll call you Phil and you call me Jake."

There was no way in the world I would call him Jake.

"Do you read Shakespeare, Phil?"

"Not much anymore," I said. "Of course I read him in college. I used to try to read at least one Shakespeare play every year but I'm a decade or so behind on that."

"Look around," he said, gesturing toward the bookshelves.

I scanned the shelves of the bookcase to my right. I had never seen so many Shakespeare titles: he had the Shakespearean plays in many editions, leather-bound and paperback, as well as biographies and critical studies, and he had videos of the plays, more than I knew existed. The bookcase to my left, in contrast, was packed with most of the big-name business best sellers of recent years and stacks of business reviews. The business-book side of the room reflected my own professional library and was equally disorderly, with place markers and paper clips plainly visible, telling me these books had been studied.

"Italians love opera but I was a reader. Over the years Shakespeare pushed out all other authors, even Dante. Sometimes

I find Shakespeare difficult, I don't follow what he's saying. English was not my first language and I was not educated and some things he writes I don't understand even with the footnotes and explanations, but I always come back to him."

"You also read business books, I see."

"Yes, there are many useful ideas in these books. But Shakespeare is even more useful. You know, I don't invite people to this room and I don't spread it around that I read Shakespeare because ignorant people would take it as a sign of weakness. You and I know it's a sign of strength."

It was gracious of him to include me among the knowing.

"I tried to interest my children in Shakespeare," he said, "but it never caught their imagination. To my regret."

"Sylvia just quoted Shakespeare to me downstairs, about razors to her heart."

"Her *wounded* heart," he said, smiling as he corrected me. "*Titus Andronicus.* I'm delighted. Maybe she was listening after all."

"I have a favorite Shakespearean quotation scotch-taped to my computer at home," I said, surprising myself by volunteering this, knowing it was unwise to get into a Shakespeare-quoting contest with him. "I don't remember where I found it but it seems to apply to where I am in life, or what I feel about my life. I'm fifty-nine. It's a little depressing."

"Seventy-five is even more depressing. What's the quote."

I blurted it out: "I wasted time and now doth time waste me."

"Oh, that's a good one," he said. "*Richard II*, I think. I'll ask Sylvia to type it up and tape it to something I see every day, such as my oxygen canister. But Phil, tell me why this quote is significant to you."

"I feel like time is getting even with me for wasting so much of it. I spent a vast amount of time writing words that were forgotten two minutes after they were read. It was just a bunch of bullshit, pardon the expression. And now time's starting to run out and I'm wearing down, feeling wasted."

"I think you don't give yourself enough credit for what you've achieved. Do you think it's too late to do something worthwhile?"

"I'm still hopeful. But if the big opportunity hasn't come along by this point, maybe it's not coming."

After a long moment he said, "I also have regrets. Maybe everyone does, or at least people I would respect. The fool doth think he is wise, but the wise man knows himself to be a fool."

I took a sip of the scotch, stalling as I struggled to catch up to the unexpected nature of this conversation. My notion of Mafia bosses was based entirely on wise guy movies and I had the common stereotypical notion of what mob bosses were like—gruff, gross, thuggish, profane—but he was miles from the cliché.

"You say you're unhappy about what you *didn't* do," he said, "but my regret is what I *did* do. Yes, I built something for my family. I fought for it and protected it and that's good, but the nature of it is bad. As a young man I had two models to choose from, my older brother Tiziano's, and my younger brother Vivaldi's. Vivaldi sensed the honorable way and pursued it. Tiziano found a darker path. My mind was smaller then so I followed Tiziano. I committed my life's work to that error."

He seemed sincere but I had to ask myself: is he seducing me? Is he a wolf in sheep's clothing? Or the opposite? And my instinctive answer was: he might be a philosophical man who means every word he's saying but there is *also* a wolf in there. I felt that unmistakably. There was not a single describable hint of menace from him or anything in the room other than the snoring Dobermans, but his presence radiated danger just as some movie stars radiate sexuality. Reading Shakespeare could be a misleading or meaningless clue. It didn't mean he was a softy; perhaps he studied Shakespeare for lessons in treachery.

Most remarkable is that rather than being frightened by him I was exceptionally stimulated. I heard myself eagerly letting down my guard, surrendering innermost thoughts as if we were close friends or father-and-son in a long-awaited heart-to-heart. And—was I wrong?—he was doing the same. Having known each other for only a minute, we were summing up our lives, confessing to the regrets of our lifetimes.

He was gesturing at a handsomely framed photo hanging in a rectangular gap in the bookcase behind him. It was an enlargement of one of the black-and-white snapshots I'd seen downstairs. It showed the three young brothers standing shoulder to shoulder. They wore short-sleeved summer shirts and baggy slacks. They had abundant slicked-back black hair. Sitting Indian-style on the ground in front of them were two small boys.

"This was 1962. That's me on the left, in my early twenties. Vivaldi is the teenager on the right. The one in the middle is Tiziano. Look at that bulldog mug on him. People would cross the street to steer clear of him. Those two boys were his sons.

"Our father had a hard life but his dream was bringing us to America. He wanted us to have opportunity. His greatest pleasure was owning the 1964 Cadillac you've just ridden in— the car is ostentatious but we keep it as a symbol of dreams coming true in America. Did you notice the flagpole? He put it up. My mother said, 'Does it have to be so effing big?' and he said, 'It's not big enough.'"

"You also wear the flag lapel pin."

"You have to know who you are and what you value and demonstrate it to your children in a way they'll remember. My children are named for the American presidents. George after Washington. John after Adams—the truth is that Sylvia was the second child and we should have named her Abigail after Abigail Adams. To be honest I didn't know until the TV series what a wonderful woman Abigail was, and it would have fit Sylvia well but instead she was named after her mother. And then Tommy was named after Jefferson and Jimmy after James Madison."

I wondered how he squared this patriotism with crime. Of course I didn't ask.

"Do you have children, Phil?"

"One son, William."

"Named after William Jefferson Clinton?"

I laughed. "No, my father-in-law."

"That's good. Names should mean something and preserve something. I hate these asinine names people make up. My brothers and I are named in honor of great heroes of Venice, our native city. Vivaldi, of course. Tiziano Vecellio was the real name of the great artist Titian. I am called Jacopo after Tintoretto, whose real name was Jacopo Comin or Robusti."

"What are the dogs' names?" I asked with a smile.

"Scylla and Charybdis," he said, and both dogs opened their eyes at the mention of their names. "It's not original but I liked it. You know that in mythology Scylla was the monster on the Italian side of the Strait of Messina and Charybdis was the whirlpool on the other side. Passing safely between them was a long-shot proposition. These dogs are getting old but they retain the essential attribute of instilling fear."

"I presume you've been to Venice many times," I said.

"Yes, but always on business and always rushed for time. Tell me about your work, Phil. Sylvia says you write speeches for very important businessmen."

"Yes, I'm a freelancer. I've written for several dozen CEOs."

"Give me their names." I tried to squirm out of this but he insisted and I ran through my résumé.

"An impressive list," he said. "I know nothing about writing speeches. It interests me that these great men allow you to put words in their mouths."

"Many of them could write their own speeches perfectly well but it takes a lot of work and they're way too busy. Some of them can't write so it's smart to hire a writer. And a few are not thoughtful so they hire someone to make up thoughts for them."

"You must provide good value or they wouldn't keep hiring you. I'm thinking you must have the skill of putting yourself inside their heads so you could think like them and speak like them and maybe even make business decisions for them."

"I would never say that to them."

"Because bosses don't like the idea of anyone getting into their heads."

"Exactly. Who would?"

He gave me the Sforza smile again and we contemplated each other for a moment.

"We don't want to delay dinner by talking forever up here, Phil, though it's been an opportunity for me to spend time with an honest and intelligent man like yourself. Sylvia described you well. But let me get to what I want to say."

This unrelaxed me and drove me back to the scotch.

"I wish to thank you for supporting my daughter when she was in a threatened position. In fact you supported her twice. The story has certain absurd aspects but the fact is that you did not back down or put your own interests first. We have a debt to you and I will use my power to repay it."

"There's no debt," I said.

"No debt? Those are words I've never heard," he said, smiling. "In my world, women say 'thank you' and men say, 'I owe you.' Among men there is a debt for every favor or good deed. Most of the people I know would be eager to have me indebted to them, but you're not that way, are you?"

A moment went by.

"Will you ask the nurse to come up? Tell Sylvia it's time to serve the meal. Tell George I'm ready."

The dogs scampered downstairs ahead of me.

My mind was spinning with questions.

SYLVIA TOOK a position in the entrance to the dining room, wordlessly summoning the family to the tables. She looked majestic, stunningly different from the woman I'd met on the train. Avon Boudreau should see her now.

The guests took seats at the table but then waited until George came down the stairs carrying Jake, whose long legs dangled like sticks from George's arms. I sensed that being carried humiliated him and being humiliated drained his spirit. At the table he barely spoke and hardly ate. What might have been a boisterous holiday celebration was painfully subdued. Afterwards the family adjourned to the living room for a sing-along with Tiz's quiet daughter, Beatrice, at the piano. The sing-along didn't work because Jake fell asleep, snoring, and the sight of him being carried upstairs was, many knew, the last time they would see him.

My Mafia adventure had taken an unexpected direction with unexpected dimension. It was not the voyeuristic walk on the wild side I'd looked forward to but an intimate experience with a family that was heartsick facing the cancer death of the man who had defined it and guided it through dangerous times. If I felt a small amount of disappointment at the lack of colorful mobster theatrics, I felt a far larger amount of compassion.

Guests gathered near the door saying good-byes. Sylvia told me she was driving Viv and Paola to their hotel and would drop me at my home on the way back. She pulled around in the Cadillac and off we went, the four of us dead silent.

We drove to an inn called Auberge Bignan. It was small and so exclusive I'd never heard of it or the hamlet where it was located, even though I lived only a few miles away. Viv is a connoisseur of hotels and the Auberge Bignan is his choice in New York.

As we pulled into its circular driveway Viv rallied and insisted that Sylvia and I come in for what turned out to be several rounds of nightcaps. The inn's bar was a welcomed haven, lively and sophisticated. It felt like a secret club serving a mix of in-the-know travelers and upscale locals winding down after a long family day. Most were in my age bracket, probably making Sylvia the youngest person in the room. All eyes looked her up and down as we entered. I took some pride in sitting down next to her in a candlelit booth.

Viv and Paola were effusively welcomed by the bartender and staff. A waiter delivered four grappas. The alcohol and the late hour lifted our emotions. It also dissolved some of the usual Sforza guardedness. Paola reported with a giggle that Vera had come into the kitchen going on about how *amazing* I was.

"Be careful with her," said Paola. "She's a good girl but not judicious. She'll tell Catcher about your visit today and what he'll hear is a strange man in the house, a secret session in Poppa's library, possibly a new and threatening element in the family chemistry. And then she'll say exactly the wrong thing, telling him how *amazing* you are, and then you'll have the next eruption of Mount Etna and the lava—"

"We get it, dear," said Sylvia. A moment of paralysis seized the conversation. A new subject was urgently required so I jumped in asking when Viv and Paola would return to Italy.

"We hope tomorrow night but we may need to extend," said Viv. "There's a big sit-down tomorrow. We have to face a decision about family leadership after Jacopo."

That was a stunner: Catcher was *not* a sure thing to succeed Jake. Viv obviously should not have said it in my presence. Both women stirred uncomfortably but it was quickly clear that Viv had lost control, taken off the tracks by emotion. His hands fluttered, his cosmopolitan poise faltered, and he seemed on the verge of sobbing. I knew I shouldn't be seeing this. I had a notion about an unnecessary trip to the men's room to get away from the table. But then Sylvia said, "Uncle Viv, we shouldn't bore Phil with family business."

"Of course not," he said, trying to brighten. "Let's talk about my favorite subject, Venice. Sylvia, you were just a girl when Jake brought you to visit us. When will you return?"

But he couldn't focus on Venice. He couldn't get his conversation off the family. He began a rambling narrative about its history and origins and its legendary leaders dating back to the fifteenth century when the Sforza dynasty ruled Milan. A Sforza had become a cardinal. A Sforza daughter married the Holy Roman emperor.

The story seemed to refresh him. He signaled the waiter for more drinks. He mentioned a crisis which forced the family's relocation from Milan to Venice. Then he jumped ahead to his father who, as a World War II soldier, was shot through both legs by American troops but never wavered in his fascination with America. He had spent his student years studying English and reading American literature. His language skill earned him a job as a translator for the American Army. He was sent to Naples where the family's history reached its turning point: his boss, the chief translator, was Vito Genovese.

Vito Genovese, a Hall of Fame Mafioso, the founder of the Genovese crime family.

Sylvia said it was time to go. But Viv had momentum. "Doesn't Phil want to hear the Genovese story? Don't you, Phil?" I gave no signal either way but knew a line had been crossed. For the first time a Sforza had mentioned the mob in my presence.

"Genovese killed somebody in Brooklyn and had to flee to Italy. At this point the Mafia was working for the US Army because the Americans needed the antifascists of the Mafia to fight the communists. Genovese built a black market empire. Italy was starving for goods Vito could get from the Americans.

"So here comes our injured and innocent father wandering into the clutches of this mastermind. At the end of the war Vito is extradited to New York. My father begs to come along. So Vito brings him and gives him some help getting started. What else is my father going to do? He can't do labor because of his ruined legs. He wants to get away from Vito—that's why we moved to White Plains—but he had to accept help. Which in turn created a lifelong debt. The hook was in."

"We've got to go," said Sylvia, abruptly standing. Paola stood too. So I heard no more about Vito Genovese. On the way to the door Viv put an arm around my shoulder and said in a low voice, "We are a proud family. But history has taught us that survival depends on the right leadership."

Sylvia was clearly disturbed about the last few minutes of conversation. Driving home we were alone together for the first time but I did not break the silence with questions and she volunteered no answers. Pulling up in front of my house she said, without looking at me, "Maybe I shouldn't have gotten you into this."

I asked what she meant but she only shook her head.

I managed a kiss, not a great kiss but at least it was a kiss.

CHAPTER 8

My bedside phone rang at six forty-five A.M. I looked up at the ceiling and yelled, "Fuck Draybin."

I always recognize the ring of the phone when Draybin calls. The ring is penetrating, intrusive, and insistent. It asserts priority and commands instant action. Usually it comes when I'm asleep.

On the other hand, maybe it was Sylvia.

It was Draybin.

"Phil, I've had a spectacular idea. Fly up to the Cape today so we can discuss it. There's a plane that arrives in Province-town at 3:59 P.M. I'll pick you up. You'll be home by lunch tomorrow."

"Okay," I said. "How'd you feel about the speech draft I sent you?"

"The draft? Oh, great. Wait till you hear what I've got in mind."

I hate clients, even the ones I like. They own you, even when they're nice about it, like Draybin. They call on Friday afternoon and demand a new draft by Monday morning and instead of jetting to Rio with a sex-crazed supermodel you spend the weekend writing something you hate.

FROM THE plane I looked down at the glistening Atlantic and tried to guess Draybin's idea but the unfolding drama with the Sforzas eclipsed my interest in Draybin. I scolded myself: don't let your distraction show when he unfurls the big idea. Whatever that idea is, *love it.*

Waiting at the airport, Draybin was clad in perfect island outerwear. He was in grand spirits, giving me a rib-crushing bear hug and a knuckle-crushing handshake. This may have been the first notably physical moment in the years of our relationship and I had forgotten that he was a big strong guy. His résumé as a golden boy included football stardom at Stanford. A photo of him making a game-winning catch had appeared on the cover of a national sports magazine. A wall-sized enlargement of the cover hung prominently in his CEO suite.

He tossed my overnight bag into his Land Rover and we sped off, making shopping stops en route to his house. We went into a fish market where Draybin peppered the counterman with expert questions about the day's catch. We (meaning "he") then bought great-looking pastries in a pastry shop, several bottles of wine, charcoal briquettes, it went on and on. In each store he generously distributed cash and exuberance and was hailed like a king.

I was initially uncomfortable with this excess but got to enjoy the good cheer that followed him around. He told me his wife, Ginger, was bored by shopping but he loved it. He said it had been a valuable asset as a CEO to relate to the true consumer spirit, though I had never seen a consumer with a spirit as gung-ho as his.

I was looking forward to seeing his house, which I expected to be as sensational as his yacht, but to my surprise the house was relatively modest, even funky. An earlier incarnation of the house, described as a shack, had been purchased in the 1950s by Ginger's father, Dr. Leon Hoffman, a psychiatry professor at Harvard. Dr. Hoffman, now retired, was visiting for the weekend—"You'll get a kick out of this old bastard," Pete told me.

The house's original purchase price was four digits long but several rounds of renovation had probably doubled the number of digits, especially because of the spectacular view from the top of a cliff that towered over the beach way below. The rooms were comfortable and toasty and the kitchen was a kitchen-lover's dream but to me the house's main attractions were two decks, one open and one glass-enclosed. When we arrived it was too dark to see anything but in the morning I would stand on the open deck, feeling a bracing wind and gazing out through crystal-clear air at a beautiful bay.

We carried the shopping bags into the kitchen and Pete started unpacking them. He told me that Ginger and Leon were out on their daily hour-long bike ride.

"Leon is eighty-five going on forty-five," Draybin said. "You think he's a kindly little retired doctor but you find out he's sharp as a nail, which he then hammers into your skull."

We went out to the open deck where, coatless but unbothered by the cold, he got the coals burning in a supersized outdoor grill.

"You know what we need now, Phil? *Cocktails.*"

WE ATE on the glassed-in deck. Aside from a few twinkling lights from across the water there was nothing but blackness outside. Dinner conversation was freewheeling, covering what I assumed were the household's standard topics: the New England Patriots, politics, and gossip about encounters with high-powered friends on the island.

I helped Ginger carry out dishes and in the kitchen she whispered, "Phil, do you have any idea what's got him so pumped up? He said he wasn't going to tell anyone until he had us all together."

Ginger, though always cordial, had never before spoken to me with any real interest; to her I was only the speechwriter, just another member of her husband's entourage. I was surprised by my apparent promotion to the inner circle.

I wondered if his retirement was wearing her out. I knew that she and Pete were both sixty-six. They had been college classmates, married soon after graduation. When women employees talked about Pete he was always saluted for not trading her in for a younger wife. When I met her on speechmaking occasions she was formal befitting her role (she also had her own career as a philanthropic fund-raiser), but now, in jeans and an old winter sweater, she was easy and engaging. Her hair was white and short, her face was lined and lively, and she had become handsomely weathered, as if she'd spent her life on the water sailing with Katharine Hepburn.

In conversation she participated actively but was overshadowed by the sharply probing, wisecracking style of her father, Leon. I guessed that Leon had been an asset to Pete-the-CEO, helping him think through business issues. Meanwhile Ginger seemed to have an intuitive ear for flaws and clinkers. My theory was that Pete's gift was to accept scrutiny from these two in a constructive spirit and somehow to blend their realism with his optimism. By the time he got to the office after weekend sessions with them he would be a steamroller, capable of charmingly overriding resistance from doubters or challengers.

We had written about leadership in many of his speeches but now I saw the whole formula: start with a good mind, high energy, and a popular manner, and then back it up with an effective home support team and you have exactly what it takes to be a world-class alpha dog.

"Okay, let's talk some turkey," the alpha dog said as we settled into couches. "I don't want to overdramatize this but I've concluded that my retirement is suboptimal. I'm not made for the sidelines. I thrive only at the center. I had a great run as a CEO but that's over. So now what? I could hang around the office and drive everyone crazy. I could do good works, like

Phil's close personal friend Bill Gates. I could be on boards and travel around playing golf with other has-beens. Have you ever thought about the reservoir of talent and energy this country has in ex-CEOs with nothing to do? What a resource that could be."

"If you like herding cats," said Leon. "Cats with huge egos."

"I could buy my way into just about anything," Pete went on. "Any outfit would be thrilled to see me walk in and they'd make me president or chairman the minute I flashed the checkbook. But I need something I believe in. I want to feel that I'm doing something exciting and beneficial, and not just for myself."

He paused to light up a Cuban cigar. Then he asked, "What do you think so far?"

I was annoyed, annoyed that Pete's discontent was so similar to my discontent, which of course made my discontent less special.

"I wish I had a toasted English muffin with jelly for every time I've heard this story, especially at Harvard," Leon said. "Ambitious people often feel this way about retirement. They insist on doing something momentous to fight off depression about getting old. But getting old is an entirely reasonable thing to be depressed about. You're losing your power, potency, prestige, purpose, and your professional place on the planet. Freud called them the P-words of life."

"Freud the great alliterator?" asked Ginger, playing along.

"No, Marvin Freud the bassoonist."

An old family joke, deftly played.

Leon continued. "Look, Tolstoy—and I don't mean Henry Tolstoy—said, 'The biggest surprise in a man's life is old age.' This is true. It shocks the shit out of you. The mistake is thinking you've got some unique condition no one ever had before. Hey, it's life. You get old and useless and fall apart. You knew this would happen. Live with it."

"You must have been a great comfort to your patients," said Pete.

"It's an entirely predictable emotion. Relax. Have four glasses of wine and call me in the morning."

"But I want to do something about it," said Pete. "I want to be proactive."

That word, *proactive*, makes me heave. Corporate people love it. I figure some corporate speechwriter like me invented it.

"You want to be proactive?" asked Leon. "Then here's what you should do for Christ's sake: *get a life.*"

"Oh, Dad," said Ginger, jumping in to scold her father for being too blunt, but Pete cut her off. "Yes, Leon is right. I've had a great life but now I have to get *another* great life. I have to reinvent myself." He was beaming.

I don't like *reinventing* either. It's indispensable corporate-speak and I've probably used it in every speech for ten years. Like *proactive* it works because it sounds so energetic, sug-gesting positivity and initiative, finding the core of value by slashing years of accumulated dreck and getting back to what made you great in the first place.

Ginger may have shared my doubts, asking with a trace of sarcasm, "Have you figured out how you are going to do this reinventing?"

"I don't have the specifics yet," said Pete, with a big smile. "That's why we have task forces. And you're the task force. Ginger, Leon, and Phil. Known from now on as Team Pete."

I really hate *teams*. People should contribute cooperatively to the organization's goals but this phony bond of *team* is nothing but manipulation.

On the other hand, strip away the corporate jargon and Pete was playing my tune. Watching him now gave me a sneaky sense of opportunity. I would spy on this master problem solver in action, learn from him, and maybe borrow his solution. Except he had no solution at this point. And the punch line was that he wanted *me* (of all people) to join Ginger and Leon in figuring it out for him.

He said he'd been thinking about this for months. The big picture had not come entirely into focus yet but he knew where to start.

"And that's where Phil comes in."

"WE'RE GOING to write a book."

That silenced the room.

"It'll be a giant of a book, a 700- or 800-page mother-fucker. It will give me a new and wider identity. And that will lead to the new life. Every great march begins with a first step and this is it. Phil writes, Ginger edits, Leon spots weak points. I provide overview and sandwiches."

"Have you gotten around to thinking about what the book is about?" asked Ginger.

"In a broad way. It's how to solve everything, told by someone who's solved every problem that ever came at him. A mix of enthusiasm, confidence, and ball-busting realism as seen by someone who ran a major corporation for years with recognized success in every area. A CEO, a captain, a man for all seasons. Pardon me for sounding like an egomaniac but this is how we pitch it.

"We look at every major issue and show how good people can effectively evolve things for the better. The basic American can-do spirit harnessed with nuts-and-bolts American problem solving. Agree on the desired outcome and work back from it to find out how to get there. Americans are great at this. We've been up to our nose in asshole partisanship for a bunch of years now but we want to get back to working out solutions. And nothing's off-limits—social issues, religion, gender, economics, politics, racism, crime, ignorance, everything. A comprehensive, fearless, positive, and proactive agenda. I know this sounds like bullshit now but Team Pete will make it work."

We would solve all the world's problems? I was speechless. So was Ginger and even Leon.

"I'm sacking out," said Pete, rising, and with a straight face he added, "Have it on my desk by morning."

WAKING AT six on a Saturday wasn't my style but I heard Pete's car door slam outside, then footsteps pounding up the stairs to the guest bedrooms, then a sharp wake-up rap on my door.

After a fast shave and shower I hurried down to the kitchen and found Pete, in running shorts and a T-shirt, at the table on the enclosed deck, drinking coffee as he read the *New York Times*. He had purchased four copies of the *Times*, one for each of us. Leon, in an Oriental bathrobe, was deep into his paper. Ginger was cooking breakfast. The room smelled delicious.

"Have you got the book charted out yet, Phil?" asked Pete.

"Not quite," I said.

"I think we start with a great proposal. Doesn't have to be long but it has to capture the excitement, breadth, and relevance to readers. Ask for any resource you need and you'll have it in two seconds. I'm thinking we can get a book deal on this mother in a month or two after we've signed off on the proposal. We sell it to a publisher who can fast-track the publication and back it up with megamarketing. We write it in less than a year."

"Finding a publisher can be very difficult," I said.

Yes, difficult for the likes of me but not for Pete. He said the first thing you need is a hotshit author for global name recognition, and we had that—him.

Then you needed content and substance that would electrify the market and win the respect of critics. I was apparently in charge of that.

"Then you need a little backdoor rhythm, a little juice," he said. He had plenty of that. The key was his personal relationships with the heads of the conglomerates that owned the biggest and best publishers. He knew them all through countless business, social, and philanthropic ventures in the US, Europe, and Asia; he had directed big-money contributions to their causes, been a speaker at their dinners, served on their boards, played golf with them, and gotten their kids into Stanford. They would not hesitate to pass him along with their strongest personal endorsements to the presidents and chief editors of their publishing subsidiaries, who would fall all over themselves offering him a contract and a mountain of money.

"And you're in for 50 percent of the mountain, Phil. You'll earn it. The other fifty goes to Ginger's charities. I don't take a penny from this. I need a new life, not more money."

He got up and pulled on a sweatshirt.

"I'm gonna run on the beach. When I get back I'll grab a shower and take you to the airport."

Then he was up and out and the room fell silent.

"You're not feeling any pressure, are you Phil?" Leon asked with a sly grin.

"I'm exhausted," I admitted. "He's a hurricane."

Ginger carried over her coffee cup and sat down with Leon and me. "He's consumed with this," she said. "He was up all night scribbling notes, which he's already e-mailed to you, Phil. This is the way it'll be until the book is finished. By the way he's also marked up your speech draft but it'll be easy—it'll take you ten minutes to make the changes."

There was some good news. Fixing the speech would take ten minutes and then I could spend every minute of the next year on Pete's book.

"Dad, what's going on with him? He's so excited about this. Is this some sort of guy thing or getting-old thing, because I'm the same age and I just want to take it easy."

"Why not take him at face value?" said Leon. "He says he wants to reinvent his life and serve mankind. That's a good thing, isn't it? Let him try. It's better than channeling his energy into making you insane."

We sat there in silence. A breathtaking dawn was coming up outside and Pete was down there somewhere, churning through the sand, driving forward, speeding toward his new goal. I went out and looked at the beach for a while, then returned.

"I just realized what he wants," I said.

They looked at me.

"He wants to be president."

"President of what?" Ginger asked.

"Of everything. The United States of America."

"Holy shit," she said.

CHAPTER 9

Now priorities had flipped: the Draybin story eclipsed the Sforza story. The idea of Draybin running for president was a bombshell suggesting life changes of a magnitude that Team Pete could not immediately comprehend. I *knew* I was right but the question was whether Draybin himself realized where he was heading. Leon said Pete probably sensed it but hadn't taken the thought to its logical extension—if you're going to solve all the world's problems you might as well be the world's paramount leader—but it wouldn't be long before revelation struck. At that point the challenge would be much greater than writing a ridiculously ambitious book. It would be charting a course to the White House.

Did Draybin have a chance? I could reel off the obvious negatives. He had no elected-office experience, no campaign experience, no voter constituency, and no political agenda. We'd often talked politics but he'd never mentioned a party affiliation. I would guess he tilted Republican on business issues and Democrat on social issues. Which is not a profile that galvanizes single-issue zealots voting in primary elections.

Perhaps more relevant was the question of whether a former CEO, accustomed to a regal lifestyle, fawning subordinates, worshipful audiences, and, most of all, an orderly universe *which he controlled* could stomach the chaotic mud fight of competitive politics.

On the other hand, Pete was an unstoppable competitor and his personal attributes were top-notch. He was a big, handsome, athletic guy, a natural leader who looked like a president. He had a wonderful wife and four attractive grown-up children. His achievements in business and public service were widely respected. The leadership he displayed after 9/11 was heroic and broadly admired. He had a clean record, no vices, no enemies. He was smart and rich with rich, powerful friends. He was not just good but great on television, articulate and good-humored but firm. In a TV debate format he would stand out and might even kick ass. So yes, maybe he could win.

And I could be with him. We could go all the way. And if I managed to write his book I would be set for life. I had not focused on the size of his offer but it dawned on me that my 50 percent of the book's earnings could be a seven-digit number. That would be more than enough for a low-maintenance guy like me.

Given my prospects only two weeks earlier, I had to recognize that a miraculous turnaround had taken place. My sensible mind told me it had taken place just in time to rescue me from the staggering folly of an entanglement with the Mafia.

But then Sylvia called.

WHEN THE phone rang early Monday morning, I shouted "Fuck Draybin" and wondered if I could bear waking up yelling "Fuck Draybin" every morning for years to come as we wrote the book, campaigned, won, ran the world for two terms, and then wrote his memoirs.

My heart warmed at the sound of her voice but Sylvia was all business, asking where I'd be today. I told her my office in the Empire State Building. She asked for the floor and suite number (the "suite" consisted of a small square room with drab gray walls and a narrow window that hadn't been washed since World War II).

She said, "I'm sending a messenger with your ticket for tonight's Rangers game."

"Great. I didn't know you liked hockey."

"I don't know the first thing about hockey and I won't be there. Go to your seat and a man named Ron Taubman will sit down next to you."

"Who is Ron Taubman?"

"You need to talk to him."

THE ENVELOPE containing the ticket arrived an hour later. Long before game time I walked over to Madison Square Garden, remembering great times there watching Knicks basketball when Willy was a kid. I remembered him jumping into the aisle and dancing frantically to catch the attention of a TV camera panning the crowd for shots of excited fans.

My seat was up in the rafters and in the end zone, looking down from behind one of the goals. I was still the only fan seated in my section when I saw two men trudging up the concrete stairs toward me. The older man led the way carrying a cardboard food container. He was very tall, ungainly and slouchy, wearing a black velour warm-up suit. The other man, much younger, was an oversized block of muscle. He wore a business suit that seemed about to explode at the seams because of his pumped-up physique.

When they saw me, the older one, gesturing to the younger one to stay behind, entered my row and sat down in the seat next to me. He put his oversized feet up on the back of the seat in front of him. He wore spotlessly new white running shoes.

No eye contact, no greeting, no introduction, no handshake.

Van Dyke goatee, big beak, bald head, designer glasses.

In his food container were three hot dogs and one beer. The strong smell of the hot dogs tickled my appetite but he had no intention of sharing. He knocked off the first dog in two alligator bites and used a paper napkin to wipe the mustard off his mouth.

"I don't give a rat's anus about hockey," he said. "A bunch of toothless Canadians knocking the shit out of each other."

He inhaled the second hot dog and wiped his fingers on the used napkins.

"I know you're not wired but I gotta check anyway. Lean forward." I leaned forward and he ran his hands under my jacket, up and down my back, around and under my waist, then from my crotch to my socks. He patted my pockets, studied my buttons, looked under my lapels. Then he sat back.

"Talking to you goes against my fucking grain, know what I mean?" he said, still without eye contact. "But the old man says do it, and if you don't do what he says, you get creased. Understand?"

I nodded.

"I'll tell you right out what I am. I'm a gangster. I'm also a certified public accountant. A combination you don't run into every day, right?"

I nodded again.

"See that kid with the muscles? That's my son. His name is Sheldon." He waved to the kid. "Shelly, give a wave." Shelly waved.

"He looks like a leg-breaker. But you know what he is? A lawyer. He's a public defender in the Bronx. Another year or two he'll get out of that and join my office and he'll know the ropes. Being muscled up like that breaks the ice with his jail-bird clients. Did you know 'lifting weights' is slang for being in jail? 'Hey, you seen Anthony around lately? Nah, he's lifting weights.'"

He smiled at that and continued. "I'll tell you who else is lifting weights. The other brother, the baseball player. Thinks he's the next boss. As a matter of fact, the College of Cardinals is meeting right now on this very issue and it's a tense table, believe me."

He turned and looked at me for the first time.

"Okay, you want my last dog?" he asked. I shook my head.

"Good," he said, devouring it. "The old man wants me to fill you in on a few things. Maybe because the girl doesn't want you kept in the dark. Maybe something else. The old man's mind works in ways the average yutz cannot comprehend. But can I ask you something? What's going on between you and her? Are you schtuping her?"

I recognized a trick question. If I said I was *not* schtuping her, the next question would be why not, or did I have some sort of erectile dysfunction problem. If I said I *was* schtuping her, I'd be marked as a fool for admitting it. If I said I was doing her but was lying, I was a boaster and creep. If I gave *any* answer, I was indiscreet.

"I'm not gonna answer that."

"Taking the Fifth, huh?"

My smart answer must have emboldened me because I then did something unaccountably stupid. I lied, pointlessly. "I got a daughter her age."

He gave me a disappointed look. "No, you don't. You got a *son* and he's not her age. He's twenty-six. William Gregory Vail, lives at 235 Malmedy Avenue, Minneapolis, apartment 3F. Want to know how much rent is? Want to know what car he drives? Want to know about his Vietnamese girlfriend, Janice?"

The Mafia knew all this about Willy? They knew his *apartment number*? And his *car*? Even I didn't know Willy's girlfriend was Vietnamese and named Janice. Had my Mafia escapade exposed my son to danger?

"Hey, relax. We had to check you out."

I started to blurt out something but he shushed me. "I've known Sylvia since she was a girl, but she was never girl-ish. She never wore pink. She never screwed in the backseat. She never had forty bottles of cosmetics more expensive than cognac, like my wife.

She's an old-fashioned no-bullshit woman. And she's by a mile the smartest of them all, equal to the old man. The brother who's away in college"—Taubman winked at me:

"away in college" must be another euphemism for being in jail—"is smart too but he's a hothead and doesn't think. The other three brothers are good soldiers but not officer material, you know what I mean? No judgment whatsoever. They know it. They accept it. The girl would be hands down to be the new boss except for guess why."

"She's a woman."

"There you go. You gotta be a man and you gotta be a *made* man. You know, an initiated member. There's no such thing as a made *woman*. But she also don't have the other thing."

"Which is?"

"She don't want it. You gotta *choose* the life. She hates the whole thing. She runs the family's legitimate businesses—moving and storage, car washes, barbershop, some other stuff, good cash businesses. Remember in *The Godfather* where Brando tells Michael, 'I never wanted this for you'? That's how it is with her and her father. He wants her kept out of trouble. That's a strict rule. But she'd be a great boss. I go in the house and see her vacuuming and I laugh because it's like seeing the queen of fucking Spain taking out the palace garbage."

Fans were arriving. Four excited high school boys wearing Rangers jerseys were about to sit down directly in front of us. When the first one sat, Taubman kicked the back of his seat. "What?" said the kid.

Taubman leaned toward them and said, "My friend and I are talking. When we finish talking, you can sit down."

"Blow me," said the biggest of the boys.

"I'm hearing inappropriate language," said Taubman.

He stared at the boys. Then he twisted around in his seat and unzipped the pocket of his warm-up jacket, revealing the black butt of a gun. He held the pose as the boys looked at each other nervously and sheepishly moved away.

Taubman said, "This is how it is with wise guys. Wherever we are, it's our turf. We own it. We make the rules. We dictate what happens. But look, here's something else about Sylvia. Her whole life, she's only made one tactical mistake. And you were there when she did it. The thing on the train."

"On the train? What was the mistake?"

"Calling in the brothers. A tremendous mistake."

"Why?"

"Because the brothers could have been incarcerated just as we're about to have this transition when Jake dies. We've got plenty of muscle but those three are the palace guard. Poppa went bullshit when he heard the train story. He figured the soft spot in all this was you, Phil. You're the only witness who knows who did the beating. If you spilled the details, that could have put the brothers in jail. As a preventive measure you could have got two behind the ear."

"Two what?"

"Two *bullets*, dickhead. Usually .22 caliber. But she stuck up for you. Saved your fucking life, Phil. And then you saved that fat detective's life because if he'd arrested the boys, Poppa would have smoked him. Which he wanted to do once before, by the way, but the commission said No."

"The commission?"

"*Oy, he knows nothing.* The commission is the heads of the five New York families and some of their top guys. They don't have the power they used to have. Too many convictions, too much family politics, RICO, etc. But still, if you got disputes between families or need certain permissions, you go to them. And you definitely need a commission sanction to ice a cop. But with the pajama thing, he would have iced Pelikan without a sanction and fuck the commission, because the security of the family was at stake. Of course we wouldn't have done the work ourself. We would have outsourced it to the zips."

"Zips?"

"Sicilians. Lawless fucks with no rules about hitting cops. They got no records because you just fly them in on

Wednesday and they don't give a shit who they whack out because they're back in Palermo by Friday night. Or sometimes Montreal. You look like you're about to stroke out."

I felt green and must have looked it. Reality was breaking through. Jake Sforza, who told me that going into crime was the regret of his life and invited me to his house for Thanksgiving, had considered having me murdered by Sicilian hit men.

"You want a beer or something?" Taubman asked.

WE STOOD up and, with Shelly following, walked to the wide corridor circling the Garden. Rowdy fans flowed past us toward their seats.

"Let's get to the thing you wanna know, which you probably already know," Taubman said, while Shelly stood on the beer line. He led me into a men's room. We went to the two far urinals. "Make like you're draining the lizard," he said.

We both unzipped and pretended to pee. Taubman said, "The FBI's got listening devices that can pick up what you're saying almost anywhere."

"They bug men's rooms at Madison Square Garden?"

"Probably not but if they do, the air-conditioning and the flushing and the loudmouth fans drown it out. So look, let's get to the part that really goes against my grain because I have to say the magic word. *Mafia*. We don't use this word. But I'll use it while you're learning. And of course your big question is, are we Mafia? Part of the oath when you get made is to never give a straight answer to that question. If you do you get clipped. I'm not made but I don't need to get clipped."

"Clipped means killed?"

"No, it means they put a big paper clip on your schwantz."

He reached over and flushed my urinal repeatedly, apparently so the FBI wouldn't hear what came next.

"The answer is yes and no. The Sforza crew is part of the Mafia organization chart so that's the yes. But the Sforzas *hate* the Mafia and don't consider themselves Mafia, so in daily practice it's a no. Most of the time we work *outside* the Mafia. There's never been a set-up like this before. We have our own independent business entity, our own business model. Outsiders would tell you this could never happen, but it happened. Zip up."

We zipped up and headed for the sinks, turning the water on at full force but not washing our hands.

"Okay. Tiziano and Jacopo were obedient mob guys for years. Tiz was the capo of the Sforza crew which is one of twenty-four crews in the Vavolizza family. When Tiz started getting demented and had to step down, Jake took over.

"But before that, Tiz and Jake realized they were stuck in a shithead organization. They had a lot of good ideas but the bosses blocked everything because they're paranoid fucks, afraid of anything new. They're aggressive and—what's the word—*cunning*, but in the end they have no judgment. Long-term thinking does not exist. They won't let you build an intelligent modern organization. The only thing they care about is you giving them fat envelopes every month. The bite is worse than income tax, even in the top bracket. It can be *double* the top bracket. The bosses set the rate and you can't complain or you know what happens."

"I can guess."

"Tiz and Jake are entrepreneurs and know you can't build a good outfit when you're wasting so much capital and working under buffoons with rocks in their brains. So they decide to get out. Which has never been done before and is absolutely impossible."

He turned off the faucets. You could hear the Garden announcer and blaring music outside as game time approached.

Much as Taubman protested that he hated being forced to talk to me, I could see that he was relishing his performance. He particularly enjoyed the next part.

"Jake's a natural CEO. He and Tiz were talking about innovation and change and process reengineering long before they became the subject of every article in the *Harvard Business Review*, which is Jake's favorite rag. They were already the top earning crew in the Vavolizza family. Also the biggest. Most crews have eight, ten, twelve guys. The Sforzas got many more than that. Many. But the bosses wouldn't let them grow. So the Sforzas finally decide, okay, if we have to have a war over this, we'll have one. So they hired a lot of ex-marines. Have you met Richie Roncade? He's the boss of the troops. Former sergeant, won some medals in the Sandbox."

"What's the Sandbox?"

"The Middle East. You know the Powell Doctrine? Three principles: overwhelming force, clear-cut goals, exit strategy. Bush Junior forgot this with Iraq but it was a great strategy, which Tiziano followed. The Sforzas went in with overwhelming force. Plus the Korean guy was amazing. The cousin with the scissors, Ludovico, turned out to be a fucking artist of mutilation. He struck terror. The things he did—I'd tell you but you'd puke on your shoes."

"Ludovico? Is that Vico the barber? Nice old guy?"

"Not nice, believe me. We kicked ass but, you know, in a war, you take some hits. Both of Tiz's sons got hit, Rocco and Frankie. We found their bodies strapped to the flagpole outside Jake's house, which was then Tiz's house. They were just sitting there, heads drooping, soaked with blood. The whole war only lasted a couple days but the mess got out into the public. The cops came down on us. But the Sforzas had their goals and exit strategy.

"They knew the mob would never let them out so they made a big show of accepting defeat even though they won. They said they wouldn't leave *but* they demanded autonomy *within* the mob, which they knew all along was the best they could hope for.

"Autonomy meant they could operate their own way but still pretend to be part of the larger picture. As long as they kept kicking up great earnings. They'd share some assets. They wouldn't poach on other guys. They wouldn't threaten other family members. Vico would go back to the barber shop.

"That wasn't enough for the greedy prick bosses but the Sforzas had an answer for that, which is the thing that made it work: they promised that the Sforza crew would *always* kick up more than any other crew. They promised if they ever failed to be the top-earning crew for two months in a row, that would nullify the deal. Also, they'd forego revenge for Rocco and Frankie."

We walked out into the corridor, empty now except for concession workers and Shelly, holding three beers. I took my beer and gulped it.

"Walk ahead of us, Shel," said Taubman. He explained to me that Shelly was better off not knowing this story at this point in his career, though I suspected that Shelly knew a lot, if not everything.

"So a lot of shit went on but in the end the bosses said okay, because they have no choice and because they're greedy pricks with no vision. This shows you how soft the American Cosa Nostra is now. Over in Italy a few years ago a leader of the Calabrian Mafia, the 'Ndrangheta, was in a bar saying the 'Ndrangheta should have autonomy. Two seconds later he's a corpse. Famous story. *Omertà?* It used to be sacred, but now people get arrested and rat each other out as fast as they can get in to witness protection."

"So autonomy was granted?" *Autonomy* did not seem like a gangster word.

"Yeah. Not granted but allowed. The exit strategy was to get out while pretending they'd stayed in."

"The Mafia leadership fell for that?"

"Not really but they didn't lose face because there was no formal change. It was done on a handshake and kept quiet. The bosses hated it and still do. They know they were fleeced. I think they said yes because they figured they'd find a way to cheat and get the deal nullified."

"But they didn't?"

"We cheat better than they do. We know what the other crews are making. If necessary we sabotage them or move cash around to make sure we have more."

"How do you know what they're making?"

"We have an excellent intelligence-gathering system. A guy named Paul Bazzanella does a great job running it."

"Do you launder your revenue through Venice?"

Taubman came to a dead stop and looked closely at me. Looked *down* at me—he had to be six foot six, even slouching. "Where'd you get that?"

"I know you've got growing family businesses in Italy. I'm sure that requires massive capital. So I figure cash from this side is moved over and invested on that side. I write speeches for global corporations, you know. This isn't a new idea."

"All the Italy businesses are legitimate, or close to it. Viv is a helluva businessman. And he plays it straight. That's all I'll say about that. If you care about the kid in Minneapolis you'll never even think that thought again. *Capeesh?* Now stand here and think about that for a while. I gotta use the phone."

He walked a few steps away, turned his back, and put the cell phone to his ear.

Then he came back, calling Shelly over.

"Phil's going to the Vatican," he said.

"What does that mean?" I said, fearing that it was a Mafia euphemism for the last rites before getting two behind the ear.

"Go with Shelly. You're gonna have an audience with the pope."

LATE-ARRIVING fans were still streaming into Madison Square Garden as Shelly and I walked out, crossing the street to the parking lot where the attendant looked at us with surprise and said, "Why you leaving so early?"

Shelly replied, "Because you're an asshole."

These guys just say whatever they want, anytime to anybody. They seem to assume impunity. What a wonderful feeling that must be. What freedom. Yes, it's appalling and despicable and so on but part of me envied it. Never in my life have I had a moment of really satisfying I-don't-give-a-shit obnoxiousness.

We pulled out of the parking lot and headed uptown.

"Where are we going, Shel?"

"The hospital. Mr. Sforza sent for you."

"Do you know Mr. Sforza?"

"He came to my law school graduation. Gave me a good envelope. That's the only time he ever said a word to me."

"Do you know if Sylvia's at the hospital?"

"I don't know. Hey, can I ask you a personal question, and if this is over the line, just say so and no problem, okay? Sylvia's like, a legendary babe. So I always wondered about her. You know, what she's like."

"You mean what's she like *in bed?*" I asked, finishing the awkward question.

Apparently everyone in the New York metropolitan area believed I was having sex with Sylvia Sforza. I just shook my head and said nothing.

Shelly shrugged and moved on to a new topic, telling me his father had once given him the same briefing I'd just received. "It's like the birds and bees speech for mob kids," he said.

I said, "This is something that happens on your sixteenth birthday?"

"Nah. But my dad being on the white collar side, I didn't really get the picture. But then I saw something and told him about it and he sat me down."

I kept silent knowing the story about what he'd seen was on the way.

"I was in this restaurant in Little Italy with a couple law school buddies. All of a sudden there's this big uproar and everybody's looking out the window where this big guy's beating up a woman on the sidewalk. Apparently he'd been in the restaurant with her but got mad and dragged her outside.

He's got her down on all fours and he's yanking her hair and cursing her and slapping her really hard. She's a blonde in a low-cut dress and her breasts are falling out and her knees are all scraped up but she's trying to fight back."

"What did you do?"

"We got up to run out and help her. But at the door there were these two huge goons in suits, holding their hands folded over their nuts like security guys, blocking the door. We knew enough to realize these guys were wise guys. The guy outside was their boss. So we backed off.

"Of course everyone in the restaurant calls 9-1-1. The cops are there in two seconds. I'll never forget this: the mob boss steps back and pretends it's over. Mister Cool. He's actually adjusting his cuffs and straightening his necktie like a gangster in an old movie. But at the last second he decides the woman deserves one more shot. So he gives her a tremendous kick in the butt. She goes down, face into the pavement, busted nose, very bloody."

"What did the cops do?"

"I think the cops might have treated the guy differently if he hadn't kicked her but the kick was like telling them he didn't give a shit whether cops were there or not. The first cop gives him a nightstick in the gut and the other three gave him a beat-down until a sergeant runs up and stops it. The guy was a fancy dresser but he was a mess when they got him up and stuffed him into a squad car. So I told the story to my dad and he said, 'Sonny boy, our world is a little different than most people's. Let me explain.'"

Shelly laughed.

"The next day the story was in the papers with a big screaming headline like MAFIA ANIMAL BEATS WOMAN. Lou Turco was the guy's name. He was well-known, a stud on the way up, but the bosses don't put up with headlines like that. It's negative for business. They gave Turco a warning to cease and desist. A warning like this you ignore at extreme peril. But he ignored it."

I waited for more but that seemed to end the story.

"Shelly, are you saying they killed him?"

But Shelly had clammed up, perhaps sensing he'd said too much.

"Shel, was Lou Turco whacked for hitting a woman?"

Shelly punched a button on his cell and said, "We're a minute out."

CHAPTER 10

I emerged from the elevator on the hospital's top floor and walked down a quiet hallway. Feeks was waiting just outside a sitting room with a spectacular picture window view of the Manhattan skyline. Jake Sforza, wearing a bathrobe and slippers, his bald head seeming to glisten, was in a wheelchair facing out the window.

"This is a view I'd like to take with me," he said. "I prefer sitting here than in my box of a room. I'll be in a real box soon enough."

Another patient, closer to my age than Jake's, sat at the far end of the room, surrounded by wife and family. I could feel their wary eyes on us.

Mr. Sforza called to the other patient, "Max, say hello to my wills and estate attorney. Phil, this is Max Waxman and his lovely family."

The Waxman family was ill at ease, obviously aware of Jake's line of work.

"Maybe they'll leave soon," Jake said to me in a stage whisper. He offered his hand for a bony handshake and gestured to me to sit.

"Did Ron put on a good show for you? What was he wearing?"

"A warm-up suit."

"The black velour Sergio Tacchini? That's his gangster outfit. It's called an Italian tuxedo. Did he show you his gun?"

"Yes. He flashed it at some high school kids."

He laughed. "I wish I'd seen that. By the way, that's not a real gun. Ron wouldn't be dumb enough to carry a real gun. But it's a perk of his job that he gets to play the big hoodlum now and then. Usually you'll see him in a gray suit, preoccupied with business, which he's brilliant at by the way. Creative and careful. And loyal. His son is a good boy."

"He said he was a lawyer."

"Yes. Received a full scholarship to Fordham from the Sforza Foundation."

"You have a foundation?"

"No, of course not, but we've made sure the children of our best people get good educations. We want the next generation to be capable people. In the old days there were plenty of talented kids in Italian neighborhoods who wanted to be in our business but now those kids go into investment banking and we get the dregs. The next generation will be no match for the fresh competition coming in: Russians, Colombians, Albanians, the Asian and African syndicates. The Arabs are next. As soon as they see the potential of global crime they'll lose interest in terrorism. It's like the Russians. All that natural talent for chess and math producing only chump change until they channeled it into cybercrime."

I said, with a smile, "The profit motive shows the way."

"Tiziano and I saw this coming years ago. Our goal was to design a cohesive long-term enterprise like the corporations you've worked for."

He paused and gazed out the window at the brightly lit skyscrapers of Manhattan.

"Look at these great buildings. We studied the companies that built them. We took their best ideas and adapted them. What caught my interest about you, in addition to your gallantry with my daughter, is that you understand the world we want to grow into. You understand it at the CEO level. We don't have any people like you who've actually seen how CEOs operate."

"My knowledge rarely goes deeper than the generalities I need to write a speech."

"I doubt that. Sylvia tells me you always self-deprecate. Phil, this is not understood in my world and you should be careful with it. Have respect for yourself. You sit with some of the smartest executives in the world. I would bet that often your words sharpen their ideas."

"Speechwriters like to think that," I said. "Sometimes speechwriting feels like transforming nebulous bullshit into actual policy. Other times it's just stenography."

He smiled. "Meaning the boss just wants you to spit his thoughts back at him, correct? It's the same in my business. People are too afraid to add anything to the boss's thoughts so thinking becomes dull when what you need is *sharp* thinking. That's the reason I love Shakespeare—his sharpness, ideas sharp as knives. Clear insight. Precision. That's what makes me strong."

Jake Sforza read Shakespeare to *weaponize* Shakespeare.

"Phil, don't you wonder, while putting words in the mouths of these CEOs, whether you could be just as good a CEO as they are, because you have such a clear view of their thoughts?"

I recalled that he had asked a similar question on Thanksgiving. I couldn't understand why it interested him.

"Never," I said. "Not for one minute. I would only be a pretender, an amateur. Amateurs should never compete with professionals."

"But they keep trying," he said, smiling. "You know who's a big professional on Wall Street? My friend Max." He had Max on his mind apparently, trying to will him to leave. He turned and waved for Max's attention. "Max, an amateur investor goes up against you. What happens?"

Max, eager to reply to the gangster with a show of big balls, said, "We take his pants off. We give it to him up the poop chute. Right up the Hershey Highway. You know what I mean, Jake. We're both up from the streets."

The Waxman family grimaced at the patriarchal crude-ness. Five seconds later the Waxmans were standing up to go. Jake winked at me but he was simmering and when they were gone he leaned forward and said, "Yeah, we're both up from the streets, but he could wash the streets off. He could start a Wall Street firm and be a CEO. Could I do that? A wop with an accent and a record and a father who worked for Vito Genovese? I couldn't wash it off. I couldn't deliver coffee on Wall Street. But soon Max and I will be equal again, in death."

Then he smiled. "I offered him a $1,000,000 cash bet on which of us would be the first to die. He almost took it. Then he asked me who I would bet on to go first. I said, 'It's a sure thing, Max—*you*.'"

I laughed. "He thought you'd kill him to win the bet?"

"Maybe I would have. But he'll outlive me. He's got months, I've got weeks."

He asked to be wheeled back to his room. This was obvi-ously the VIP floor of the hospital. His room was a luxury suite. The curtains were drawn back on windows that offered another skyline view. He said, "Viv and Paola are flying through this dark night on their way back to Italy."

Did that mean the succession problem had been resolved?

The big hospital bed was the only clue that this suite was a bad place to be. A nurse arrived to get him settled in. He told me to pull up a chair and waved the brothers out of the room. Then he called Feeks back in. "Jimmy, pour Mr. Vail a large sambuca. And a small one for me."

Feeks opened a cabinet to expose a varied stock of alco-hol, presumably not provided by the hospital. He poured and served the two glasses, then departed.

"Why is Jimmy called Feeks?"

"It's juvenile nonsense from high school. He'd encoun-tered the term 'fecal matter' and to the teenage mind this was hilarious. He couldn't stop saying it. 'Fecal this, fecal that.' It turned into a nickname, 'Feeks.' I've never used it. We are not delicate people but I find it unbecoming. He was named after a great president, James Madison, who drafted the Bill of Rights."

I said, "I agree with you. I won't use it either."

"Thank you. I'm glad to hear that. It adds to my confidence that I've made a good decision."

He gazed at the skyline view for a moment and then turned back to me.

"Phil, there's a Shakespeare line, 'I and my bosom must debate awhile, and then I would no other company.' I finally got some time to debate things with myself with no other company. I've reached a decision and it's been vehemently discussed, regarding the leadership of the family after my passing. I know it's extremely unorthodox. I would like to invite you to succeed me as the boss of the Sforza family."

AFTER A moment he asked if I intended to taste the sambuca. I'd forgotten the glass in my hand.

The two pillars of this man's life were the family he raised and the business he built, and he was offering the leadership of both to *me*, someone he barely knew, someone from a different solar system. Someone he'd considered killing.

The offer was serious. It was also preposterous, but it came at me like a bullet whizzing past my ear.

"To your future," he said, raising his glass.

We drank and the rich flavor of the sambuca was an instantaneous balm, a flash of luxurious ease. It filled my mouth with a seductive taste that was both serene and exciting. I tried to fight it off because this was the wrong moment for intoxication.

"I see it as an interim position," he began. "It would begin with my death and continue until John—Catcher—returns in late March. Today is November 30th. So if you took over in a few weeks that would mean three months in the job, *presuming* you step down when John returns. My guess is that having tasted this experience and gotten over your initial trepidation, you'll want to take permanent command. That would be my preference."

"John would kill me."

"No, the family is behind you and he'll accept that. This was my idea but everyone has come around to it, after initial resistance. More than resistance, to be truthful. They were shocked. They were outraged. You're obviously not one of us. They thought I'd become deranged. But everyone knows John doesn't have the temperament and perspective to lead the family over the long-term. Sylvia is ineligible to lead. Tiziano is sick. Vivaldi has the brains but not the balls and we need him in Italy. So I had to look outside for new blood, and to be creative. But I was finding no one and my time was running out.

"And then you came along. And I discovered that your career makes you well informed about sophisticated leadership and the values and practices of a modern organization. That's what gave me the idea."

Someone should have told me years ago that I was building a résumé for a senior management position in the Mafia.

"Your corporate experience would put us in a different league from the other families. The job is not so hard. You would get good advice. You are educated and could learn quickly. You're not a gangster but you've shown courage and character. And frankly we had no better candidate, meaning that Nicky Vavolizza would be able to step in and put his own puppet in the job. Nothing could be more disastrous. So finally the family saw that you are the right choice. And the only choice."

"What did Sylvia think?"

"She opposed it. Fiercely. She said it was ridiculous. And she said it didn't matter because you'd never take the job."

"What about John? I thought he was the successor."

"I've communicated with him. He's in a bad mood. I would not want to be his cellmate. I've assured him his talents are valued and that if you remain as boss you might make him underboss, which I would recommend, to keep him on your side. There is a lot of politics to this, including external politics. The other families would have a big problem with John as boss. He's like Romeo: too rash, too unadvised, too sudden. Of course they will have a big problem with you as well."

"Because I'm an outsider."

"To say the least," he said, smiling. "They would test you for weaknesses. I sent Ron to explain to you the basics of autonomy within the overall structure. This autonomy is precarious because the predators are always sniffing for weaknesses, and my death will create a time of weakness.

"When I die Nicky Vavolizza will see an opportunity to revoke our autonomy. He'll try to intimidate you. Rebuff him. Convince him he's got a good set-up already and should be glad to keep it. The alternative is war, which would be mutually destructive. Meanwhile his political position with the other families is not strong. He is volatile, tactless, careless, he drinks too much, and his judgment is unreliable. Try to find a way for him to save face but don't give an inch on autonomy because that would begin our undoing."

"What if I can't persuade him?"

"Kill him."

It was impossible to believe I was in a conversation like this.

"If you need to go to war we are equipped for it, but it's a last resort. The newspapers and police will jump on us, the other side will want reprisals, revenue will dry up, and people will get crazy and unpredictable. And then the mayors and senators go for their sound bites and prosecutors get off the leash."

"How would I know when to use this force?"

"When it's time, you'll know it, partly because you can't avoid it. The Sforzas are outnumbered but far more professional. The Cosa Nostra talks about its 'soldiers,' who are just street rabble. Even the Sicilians who come over are peasants with no educations. Our family employs *real* soldiers, retired sergeants from the marines and special forces. We keep them on retainer—we pay them good money to do nothing until we call them but when we call them, we have the best. Common street mopes have no chance against them. We would win in the short run but the public wouldn't tolerate it. Have another sambuca."

"I think I'd better keep a clear head."

"Sometimes a small amount of drink can make you more audacious. You should work on your audacity, Phil. But let me discuss Sylvia. I have not asked either of you how you feel about each other or what you might see in the future and I don't want to intrude but I have the sense that there's a spark between you."

"Have you noticed that there's also a Grand Canyon-sized age difference between us, among other differences?"

"Don't let your age be an excuse, Phil. Think of it as a source of wisdom and strength."

"Sylvia might not see it that way."

"No. She's fine with it."

Wow, I thought. But he could be lying. He could be lying *about everything*.

"Sylvia has not had the life she deserves. And I'm thinking, what if you, Phil, are the right man for her? And what if you are her last chance but drift away? This is not what I want to think about on my deathbed. So why not take a chance and keep you closer for a while, to see if things develop. I wouldn't be the first father to tempt a prospective son-in-law with a high place in the family business.

"Now, let me hear your questions."

QUESTIONS?

I had no questions. Questions would have implied temptation or serious interest. But he obviously enjoyed a good exchange and I could give him that.

"Okay, well, one would be why should I accept this position on an interim basis? Three months later I'm either dead or unemployed. Why risk that? Speechwriters don't get whacked. And if I survive, what would I do when my three months are up? I couldn't go back to my old life. I don't have the means to create a new life somewhere else. What's my exit strategy?

"More important, how could I do your job? You say it's not hard but I have no idea how to run a crime family. I've never even stolen a stick of gum. How could I lead an organization when I have no knowledge of the business, no respect or credibility from subordinates, no vision, and no authority? And no desire to do it? Why should I become a criminal? I'm not a criminal. I'm *against* criminals."

"So many good questions," he laughed.

Amazingly, we were having fun. I freshened my drink and gave him the floor.

"Let's start with getting killed," he said. "Tiziano is eighty and hasn't been killed yet. I'm seventy-five and haven't been killed yet. If this were television you'd get killed but this is reality and you're *not* going to get killed. As for the interim situation, you're right that you won't be able to return to your old life. But you were discontented with that life and looking for a way out of it.

"If the problem is how to finance a new and better life, I can solve that the old-fashioned way. If you accept my offer, the brothers will come by your house tomorrow morning and deliver a signing bonus. Let's call it $250,000 in cash. On the first day of the next three months, you'll receive $100,000 and if you want to leave in March, you'll receive another $450,000 to round off at a million dollars. Call it a golden parachute. Tax-free, of course."

My second million-dollar possibility in less than a week.

"Why wouldn't you save the last $450,000 by just killing me?"

"We've hurt people because they owe us money but we have never hurt anyone because *we* owed *them* money. That's very bad business. We would pay you because we would want your goodwill as you walk away."

"But why let me walk away? Especially with the knowledge I'd have by then?"

"Because you would have a professional appreciation of the consequences of revealing that knowledge."

"Meaning you'd kill me and stuff a dead canary in my mouth to show I'd 'sung.' Isn't that how's it's done?"

"That kind of colorful behavior disappeared long ago. Look, Phil, I know you're skeptical talking about mutual trust with a man like me but there is no greater trust than what I'm offering you—my family and its future. What more can be said about trust?"

He paused. I kept quiet.

"But this is a job offer so let me get back to the financial package. At your age you appreciate the value of superlative medical, dental, and life insurance coverage. I see you smiling at this but don't think people in my line of work are unconcerned about health coverage. Most of them find ways to get it through the unions we work with. But your coverage would come to you as president of Sforza Moving & Storage Company and it's a very good plan."

"I'd run the moving company?"

"No, Sylvia would run it but you'd be its titular president. We'll give you a salary for that. You'd pay taxes on it and have the normal deductions. I've paid myself $145,000 a year. How would that be? And you'll get an annuity, paid vacations, and so on. Add this to the million I've already mentioned and whatever you get for selling your house and you'll have more than enough to launch a new life far away, if it comes to that.

"Of course if you decide to keep the job, you'll be the boss and the boss pays himself whatever he wants. You'll never worry about money again. One piece of advice: keep it in cash. Hide it. Never put it in a bank or brokerage account. The feds will seize it under the RICO law.

"As for doing my job, the hard part—building the structure—has already been achieved, over many difficult years. The business runs itself. You'll have several good advisers, some in the family and some we retain. And don't be concerned about getting dirt on your hands. Or blood. Bosses stay far removed from that sort of thing.

"As for respect and credibility, remember that crime families are dictatorships. No one questions your authority. There is no insubordination or disrespect. No one even talks behind your back. They die for that. Most bosses will not even speak to underlings, who shake like a leaf when the boss is in the room. As for being a criminal, what can I say? I don't feel like a criminal. I feel like a businessman."

"You told me you regretted your life in crime, but now you want to get *me* into crime."

"What else can I offer? These are the cards I was dealt. You have a choice. Every choice comes with risk. But let me tell you a bit, only a bit for today, about what we do, because this might factor into your thinking.

"First, I'll tell you what we *don't* do. We don't do street crime and we don't do narcotics. Drugs is where the big money is but it's dirty and full of monsters. You traffic drugs and before long someone's got a gun pointed at you, a cop or a competitor. There's not a single person you can trust in the drug business.

"We've never been into the girl businesses—prostitution or pornography or the strip clubs. In the early days we did gambling and loan sharking, which go hand in hand, of course. These are excellent revenue sources but we got tired of them. No challenge. It might be different now with the Internet. We've got a brilliant young guy, Hiram Tack, leading us into cybercrime.

"Now we get to the main thing, the bulk of our business. We call it full-service contracts with legitimate business partners. Our principle is that rather than sucking these businesses dry until they collapse, which is the traditional modus operandi, we treat them as partners and help them prosper, which of course means they get richer and pay us on a long-term basis, like paying big dividends to shareholders. Capitalism is good for us. Treating victims as partners is our greatest innovation.

"I'll give you a simple example. You're a restaurant. You got a problem with a customer, an employee, a rival restaurant, or some hoodlums trying to shake you down—we can fix these things easily, probably a strong-arm solution. Or you've got a more difficult problem with suppliers, unions, inspectors, garbage haulers, cops, maybe a tax auditor giving you a hard time. You need a permit, you need a friend in the bureaucracy or the courts. We've cultivated connections in all these areas. A restaurant is a small example but the concept scales up nicely. We have many large clients. But most of all, we have our unique strategic advantage—the acronym is USA."

"What's the unique strategic advantage?" I asked.

"We're *criminals*," he laughed. "That's the advantage. We're not restrained by laws or regulations. We cut corners, we use fear and sometimes violence, we pull strings and apply pressure to get things done, faster and usually cheaper. This is the full-service aspect. You got an issue, we resolve it. Then you owe us a fee and a favor and maybe you return the favor by helping our other partners when needed. This enhances our network. Expands our footprint. Almost every provider in the chain is a partner of ours and we move to a new dimension.

"The revenue compounds dramatically because almost everyone is paying us. And usually, after a while, they start *depending* on us to solve their problems. We become indispensable. They fear doing business *without us*. And as long as they're good partners and show respect, we treat them well."

"I can't believe this works," I said. "I wonder if you're not sugarcoating a little."

He smiled. "Difficulties arise. When everything's going smoothly clients might suddenly forget the reason for paying us. This is human nature. Shakespeare said, 'How quickly nature falls into revolt when gold becomes her object.'"

"So what do you do when they don't want to pay?"

"We give them a taste of the old days. But we're not gorillas. A small amount of correction goes a long way."

Just a little knuckle-slapping, a little scolding.

"Phil, I've kept this sketchy but you'd understand it if you saw it up close. Providing value is a fundamental money-making concept but it's never occurred to anyone in organized crime. Mobsters have a petty thief mentality. Grab the money out of the cash register and run out the door with it. But we have a growth mentality. We reinvest and expand, diversify, provide an excellent value proposition, leverage our prime asset of being outside the law and having access to different types of persuasion, and watch the business grow."

The capitalism-loving audiences I've written for would have greeted this finish with a standing ovation.

"What do you think?"

"I'm impressed. I appreciate your candor. But—I can't believe I'm saying this to you—it's still criminal. It's illegal, immoral, and wrong."

"Phil, on Thanksgiving you sat in my library and poured yourself out about a life that was failing you in many ways and showing you no future. You saw no options. Now I'm giving you an option. It's your chance to be the CEO instead of the ghostwriter. Aren't you cheating yourself by always hiding behind someone else and putting your best thoughts in someone else's mouth? I told you when we first met that I was in your debt. Now I'm paying you back with this offer."

We looked at each other for a long moment.

"I'm suddenly very tired, Phil, so what is it: to be or not to be?"

This was easy. "I have to say no. I'm sorry."

"Of course," he said wearily. "The offer's still on the table. I have to sleep now."

He closed his eyes. I sat there for a moment and a sickly, hollow feeling seemed to spread inside me. I stood up and looked down at him and didn't leave until I was sure that he was breathing.

THE BROTHERS were in the hallway chatting up a blonde nurse. I said good night.

"See you later, Mr. V," said Jimmy. "You need a ride or anything?"

"No thanks, Jimmy."

I walked to the elevator and when the elevator doors opened, I beheld Mr. and Mrs. Max Waxman. Max was in a red silk bathrobe and matching slippers.

"Look, Max," said Mrs. Waxman. "There he is, the lawyer for Mr. Gangster."

I tried to edge past them but they seemed to move in tandem to block my way.

"How dare that man intimidate us?" she said. "How dare he?"

His wife's words were Max's cue to erupt in a pugnacious fury, his voice rising to top volume as he hurled foul-mouthed outrage at me and over my shoulder down the hall toward Jake's room.

I looked into his face and thought: Max is someone you could read in an instant, as if the word ASSHOLE were tattooed on his forehead. You thanked your stars you were not under his thumb because you knew he was a man who bullies his wife and screams at his secretary, abuses subordinates, screws customers, lies to clients, and directs deductible company funds to charities which throw banquets at which he is hailed as the humanitarian of the year.

"You ain't so tough," he was shouting. "I fought my way up. I can kick your guinea ass."

"Actually I'm from Ohio," I said. "Episcopalian."

Max's wife was now trying to restrain him. I looked into his ugly inflamed face and without thinking I grabbed his little round nose. I squeezed his nostrils as hard as I could and pulled him toward me as he honked desperately, eyes bulging. Mrs. Waxman jumped back gasping, then screaming.

I released his nose and pushed him roughly to the side as I stormed into the elevator.

This was the kind of thing tough guys did. I thought it would be cathartic. It wasn't.

CHAPTER 11

The moment I said no to Jake's offer I started wishing I'd said yes. I'd searched for an alternative to the bleak and lonely future I'd been heading into and here it was, presented to me on a platter. Of course there was a little catch to it—the part about embracing a life of crime. What a cruel temptation that was, what a mockery of my needs. Satan was fucking with me and probably laughing his big red ass off. But the offer was clearly out of the question. I could not enter a world whose every value I opposed and taught my son to oppose.

So why was rejecting it so painful? Why did it feel like a failure of courage or imagination? Was saying no an affirmation of morality and citizenship or just a spineless fallback to a safe default position? It does not take major strength of character to decide *not* to join the Mafia.

The one easily identified cause for regret was that Sylvia was at the center of the world I'd rejected. The immediate consequence was a heavy sense of loss. All I could think about in the week after turning down Jake's offer, as I tried to focus on Pete's solutions-to-everything book, was the emptiness of life without her.

Of course I could call her but I cringed at the prospect of being refused because the romance I couldn't help envisioning was just an old man's fantasy. We'd liked each other, yes, but our relationship was not even a relationship. Half the world thought we were copulating like jackrabbits but the reality was two little kisses.

I remembered asking Sylvia in our conversation on the train what advice her dad would give me and she said, "Grow the fuck up." Now was the time to do just that. Get serious and move along. Stop acting like a teenager with a crush and a boner. Some day I would look back with incredulity that I'd even been tempted by a mobster's offer and relief that, when the chips were down, I'd chosen sensibly.

JAKE DIED.

Sylvia called.

"I've been dealing with it since this morning," she said. "The only way I could get away from it was to come to the Auberge. I just got here. Please come over."

"I'm on the way."

So much for growing the fuck up, so much for choosing sensibly. The moment I heard her voice I knew I was in love with her.

"Are Viv and Paola there?"

"Flying in tomorrow. If he can get Paola on the plane. She's upset about spending three months in New York while Viv runs the family. And he *dreads* running the family."

At the Auberge a quartet of tuxedoed musicians was playing and a few couples were dancing as I walked in, finding Sylvia alone in the booth we'd occupied with Viv and Paola. She wore a plain black dress and had a bit of a 1,000-yard stare, the battle fatigue look. An untouched glass of red wine waited in front of her.

Instead of sitting across from her I sat next to her and put an arm around her.

She said, "I didn't know if it was okay to call you. Whether you'd washed your hands of us."

"I thought you'd washed your hands of *me*. I said no to your father. I figured I was out of the picture."

"Oh no. He believed you'd change your mind. The offer was never withdrawn."

"The offer—" I laughed. "I've never seen anyone with real responsibility make a more out-of-the-box decision than your father did by offering me that job. But of course he and his brothers apparently used this same imagination to build their business. It could be a case study in business school. I could see it as a cover story for *Fortune* or *Forbes* or a business review."

"It won't be," she said. "Let's dance."

"Dancing's not one of my talents. But I'm good at wine drinking."

"You always underestimate yourself." She stood up.

There is a lot to be said for that notion that great performers make lesser performers better. I'm not hopeless but I'm hardly the guy you want to be dancing with on the day you've lost your father and ask nothing more than a few minutes of escape on the dance floor, yet somehow she raised my game and made me competent. When my ex-wife and I danced it was a model of disharmony, one of the top five things we did poorly together. Dancing with Sylvia was the opposite. She responded fluidly to the lightest signal; in fact she seemed to respond *without* signals, as if we'd practiced each step a thousand times.

Of course the cabaret music was perfect too, lush, upbeat romantic music for adults. I glanced at other couples and they seemed to be cruising along as smoothly as we were. Then an interesting thing happened: the song came to an end and the pianist, speaking softly into his microphone, seemed to be announcing a short break.

Sylvia lifted her head off my shoulder and made eye contact with him. Nothing more than eye contact. The pianist said, "But first, one more song," and the music resumed. And they were playing just for us. The other couples had left the floor. My instinctive reaction was self-consciousness but she put her cool hand on the back of my neck and I relaxed and we finished the dance. We even received a riffle of applause leaving the dance floor.

Back at our booth she picked up her black purse and, without sitting down, said, "Let's go upstairs."

We walked out arm-in-arm. The maitre d' rushed over and held the door open for us, whispering condolences.

"How many rooms in this inn?" I asked.

"Eight."

I took a guess: "Do you own it?"

"We have a piece of it."

We stopped at Room #1. "Look at this," she said, opening her purse and pulling out a brass key. "Remember these? They're called keys. Not a little plastic card."

I presumed the inn was a former farmhouse and this was the bedroom of Farmer and Mrs. Brown, laid out in a time when folks did not go in for oversized rooms. But the room's smallness emphasized its coziness. It was lit by a bedside Tiffany lamp. It had a fireplace, solid furniture, a nice little bar, a desk covered with books and framed photos. There was no TV but she had a high-quality radio which she switched on and tuned to an FM music station.

Then she kicked off her heels and before she'd walked the two steps to the bed she'd pulled her dress over her head and tossed it on a small sofa. She reached behind her back, elbows out, to unsnap her black bra. Then she pulled down her panty hose and turned around to face me, long and lean and naked. And utterly unself-conscious.

We sat down on the edge of the bed.

"This is my room," she said. "It's never rented to guests. My father bought it for me. He said a woman who lived with her father and brothers should have a sanctuary where she could sneak off and have some peace and be a woman instead of a mother superior."

She paused for a second, gazing past me. "I was hoping he'd live until Christmas. Was that so much to ask? Two fucking weeks?"

Her voice cracked on these last words and she started to cry. She didn't cover her eyes but sat straight up, palms on her knees. Modest tears grew quickly into full-fledged weeping and then the dam broke and she bent forward trembling, shuddering, gasping, unrestrained grieving, the old country way. She wrapped her arms around my thigh and rested her face on my knee. I could feel her tears through my trousers. I looked down at her black hair, her neck and spine, her ribs.

"Let me pull back the covers," I said.

She rose for a moment and stood unsteadily, and then dropped back into the bed, sliding under the covers to the far side where she curled up in a fetal ball. I stroked the curve of her back as she wept. I was hungry to lie down with her but—forgive me if I'd reverted to the age of chivalry—I wasn't sure it was honorable to get into bed with a woman in this state of vulnerability. I managed a few stumbling words to that effect but she shook her head and without turning her face, flung a fist at me, to punish my stupidity.

So I undressed and when I got under the covers with her she moaned and stretched out. I pulled her heavy quilt over us and put my arms around her and she pushed back against me. She squeezed my hands to her breasts. Her crying continued for a long time until we were both asleep.

THE BIG crossover in our lives began at 4:04 A.M. I read the time in the large red numbers of her digital alarm clock as I sneaked back into bed after a bathroom trip. She had shed every tear and it was now time for luxurious kissing followed by a drowsy progression to better things. It was perfect, a silky ride with a glorious finish and an intensity of bonding I think we both recognized as permanent.

"Let's do it again," she said.

"*Again?* At my age it takes awhile to bounce back."

"How long?"

"Three years."

She laughed out loud.

"Really, it's been at least three years since my last time."

"You can do it."

"Can we sleep a couple hours and then try it?"

"No."

"It's not going to work."

"Yes it will. Watch me."

I WOKE to the smell of coffee. Sylvia was sitting on the edge of the bed in a blue robe unloading a silver platter, a breakfast she'd carried up from the inn's kitchen. The clock said 6:50 A.M.

"There's something I want to say," she said. "It may sound schoolgirlish but it's true and it'll always be true: I love you."

"That sounds kind of schoolgirlish."

"Want some steaming hot coffee on your dick?"

Instead she poured the coffee into cups.

"I just said I love you," she said, looking right at me. "Is that, like, good news, or not? Would you be happier if I told you the NASDAQ had gone up twenty points or something?"

"No. It's great news. Sorry, I'm just a little stunned. I was unprepared for that. I'm a little groggy. This wasn't an average night for me."

"Now is when you say, 'I love you too, Sylvia, and I want you to be mine forever.' Can you say that?"

"Yes," I said. "I love you too, Sylvia."

"And?"

"I want you to be mine forever."

"We're giggling now but this is serious and it will get more serious, and not just in a fun way. There's always a weight, a pressure, to being in the family or even around it, even if you're not directly involved in the business. And sometimes it's really bad. Can you handle that?"

"Yes," I said, taking a giant step away from the play-it-safe instincts that had always ruled my life.

"I fell in love with you on the train. I told my dad you were the guy for me. I may have told him at just the right time because he had something pretty negative in mind for you."

"I heard about that. You saved my life."

"Yeah, it could have been a short romance."

I wasn't finished trying to screw myself out of the best thing that ever happened to me. "Let me just suggest one thing," I said. "Your father has just died. My life has gone from nothing happening to so many things happening that I'm completely dizzy. Doesn't it make sense that we're both at points in our lives when we're needy and vulnerable to big mistakes? Aren't we rushing into this too emotionally and not thinking about what happens when reality sets in?"

"Go fuck yourself," she said. "Do you remember what Brutus said in *Julius Caesar*? He was in a debate about whether to attack the enemy now or later. He said there is a tide in the affairs of men which, taken at the flood, leads on to fortune. And then he said, 'On such a full sea are we now afloat, and we must take the current when it serves, or lose our ventures.' So Philly, are we going to take the current or lose our ventures?"

"Let's take the current."

She crawled in next to me and we quietly pondered the ceiling.

"So we're going to do it," she said.

Life was good. Then my cell phone rang.

"Fuck Draybin," I said.

I SPRANG out of bed, grabbing my suit jacket, looking for the pocket, finding the cell phone on its tenth ring. It was Jane Dooley, Draybin's assistant.

"I called you on your home phone and you didn't answer. Where are you at seven in the morning?"

"Don't ask, Jane. What's up?"

"Lunch at one. He's running for president, but you saw that coming. We're now full speed ahead. Dick Tindall will be joining you at lunch. Do you know him?"

"No, but I've seen him on TV a million times. Is he Pete's campaign manager?"

"Looks like it."

"Lunch is at the boat or office?"

"The Tower of Fear. Forty-fifth floor. Executive Dining Room #1."

Sylvia was waiting to ask, "Who's Jane? Do I have to kill her?"

"I want to get back in bed."

She let her robe slide off her shoulders. We embraced and fell back to the horizontal.

"Is this the famous Peter Draybin you're lunching with?"

"He's my last remaining client."

"How did you know it was him calling?"

"I know his ring. Actually it was his assistant, Jane. Nice woman, don't kill her."

"Why did you say 'Fuck Draybin'? Is he a bad guy?"

"No, but his priorities take priority over my priorities. I must do what he says at any hour and I have to be enthusiastic about it."

"That's so different from all the other jobs in this world."

"What do you have to do today?"

"I have to finish the arrangements for the funeral and burial. I have to get the house shipshape because everyone will end up there this afternoon. Then I have a thousand other problems including security."

"What's the problem with security?"

"When the word gets out that Poppa's gone we'll be vulnerable. We have a guy, Paul Bazzanella, who'll be trying to find out what's going on with the bad guys. And there's another guy, Richie Roncade, who'll be making sure we're safe and the bad guys are not safe."

"The bad guys are who?"

"Don't ask."

"You can't say 'Don't ask' to me anymore now that we're floating on a high tide with all our ventures."

"Okay. The bad guys are everybody else in organized crime in the world. But mainly the Vavolizza family, the family we're supposedly part of. The boss is Nicky Vavolizza. Who is some spicy meatball."

"He's the boss but you regard him as a threat?"

"Oh yeah, a big threat. Viv will have to deal with him. Viv hates this. He went back to Venice thinking you'd be the acting boss and Nicky would be *your* problem. But you said no."

"Part of me wanted to say yes, Sylvia. But it's not my thing either."

"I'm glad you said no. It's an ugly business. It's also boring. It's either ugly or boring and I don't see you as an ugly or boring kind of guy."

"But Catcher is?"

"Catcher isn't boring but he's good at ugly."

"Will he hate me?"

"Don't expect a big kiss. The job he wanted and expected all his life was offered to you instead of him, by his own father. Now it looks like he'll get the job by default. But you'll end up liking each other. You like Jimmy and Catcher's the older version of Jimmy. Did you know he had a good shot at major league baseball?"

"Jimmy told me he screwed it up by fighting."

"Yeah. He went down to Florida spring training and had a problem with two Hispanic players who were hot prospects. They were pitchers, he was a catcher. They didn't like his signals or something. They thought they were tough dudes from the islands and he was just a pretty boy from New York. They got in his face."

"They attacked him?"

"I think it was more of a taunting thing. It takes very little to get Catcher in demolition mode. When it was over the Dodgers were looking at two kids who could no longer throw a baseball and a catcher from the Cosa Nostra. End of three careers."

"Why is he in prison?"

"Parole violation."

"What did he do?"

"If you must know, he killed a guy in a bar. This was about two years ago. But it was self-defense and he got off, which pissed off the legal establishment which doesn't like to see a mob guy get away with a high-profile killing, even if the victim is also a mob guy. Catcher had done time on another thing and was on parole, so they got him for associating with known armed criminals in a bar after midnight and called it a parole violation and sent him back upstate."

"What was the other thing?"

"It was an assault thing, business related."

"Have the other brothers been in jail?"

"Nothing serious. They're good when they have to do something but they're not really into it. What's going on with your friend Mr. Draybin?"

"He wants to run for president. Of the United States."

"He's running for president of the United States? And *you* write for him?"

"You can't tell anybody about his wanting to be president. That's a huge secret."

"Oh, like I can't keep secrets? I'll tell you what: I won't spread the word about Draybin and you don't reveal the existence of the Mafia."

"I'm sorry."

"Can I explain something? In my world we keep secrets every minute of every day. Can I tell you how shitty that is? If we accidentally let something slip or break any of the many rules, we can be killed for it."

"I just read a federal report saying the New York mobs kill about thirty people a year. Do the Sforzas contribute to that?"

"I doubt it but no one would tell me. What are you doing reading federal reports like that?"

"There's an organized crime chapter in the book proposal I'm writing for Draybin."

"You're writing a book about us?" Her eyes widened. "Are you spying on us?"

"No, no, no. Calm down. It's just one chapter in a book showing Draybin can be a problem-solving president. I'm not spying on you. Your father invited me to your house for Thanksgiving. Do you think I was trying to infiltrate the family?"

"The FBI has infiltrated the families several times."

"Do you think I'm an FBI agent?"

She laughed, genuinely. The idea of me being an FBI agent was so absurd she dropped all of her suspicions.

"Why do they have the rule about never admitting the Mafia exists? Everybody knows it exists. Mafia guys have admitted it in court."

"They admit it because it's part of the deal when they bargain their way out of forty-year jail sentences. Of course they can never go back on the street again or they're dead ducks. Phil, what's going to happen to us when Draybin's running for president? You can't be hanging around with a woman from the notorious Sforza crime family."

To my astonishment, this had not occurred to me. I suppose I'd regarded my writing life and my mob adventure as parallel realities. Now I realized they would inevitably intersect.

"Are you going to drop me?" she asked.

"No. Of course not."

"You will," she said. "You'll have to."

"I won't. We'll get through this somehow. What else can we do?"

"Don't ask me. You're the smart guy who writes for presidents. I'm just a high school graduate."

"Isn't it fun to be lying here naked and having our first fight?"

"It's the best thing ever. But I have to get going. I'll understand if you can't come over today but I hope you can come to the funeral tomorrow."

"I'll come today if I get home on time and definitely to the funeral. Sylvia, will the cops and newspapers be there? Taking pictures and such?"

"Probably. Does that bother you?"

"A newspaper photo of me at a Mafia funeral might not be a good thing for me."

"Okay. I can see that. Wear a hat and sunglasses and stand behind me and probably no one will notice you."

"Okay."

"Can we do it again?"

CHAPTER 12

I was so mellow leaving Sylvia that I missed the train to New York. When I arrived, forty minutes late, Draybin and Dick Tindall and a small young woman in a black suit were in deep conversation around the gleaming table in Executive Dining Room #1, high above the streets of Manhattan.

I had been in this room a few times, always wondering how shareholders would feel about the splendor in which their company's leaders dined. I particularly enjoyed the wall-sized oil paintings of Hudson River Valley scenes and the large window with its postcard-perfect view of the Statue of Liberty.

The woman looked up at me with a scowl and then looked at her watch, reminding me I was late.

I'm not keen on rudeness from people half my age. She turned away and stared out the window as Draybin and Tindall rose to shake my hand.

I recognized Tindall from his countless appearances on political talk shows which love him because he seems so well cast as a political operative. He looked like a retired army colonel, in his sixties but still trim and hard-bodied. His hair was close-cropped; he had a December tan; he wore his standard no-frills uniform: blue blazer, starched blue button-down dress shirt, and never a necktie.

We did some mutual ass-kissing: I was honored to meet a man with his long record of achievement and expertise. He was thrilled to meet me because he'd had his eye on me for years. Or since yesterday.

Tindall said, "Let me introduce Kitty Fromkin from my staff. She's the best campaign speechwriter I've ever known. She's been in the business since she was a teenager and she's written for everybody. Plus she can knot a swizzle stick with her magical tongue."

"Fuck you, Dick," she said in a flat voice.

"No, sincerely, Kitty is number one," Tindall said, patting her shoulder. She flinched at his touch.

I realized that if Kitty was number one, I was now number two. In every sense. I was chagrined that I hadn't seen this coming: Draybin's deal with Tindall obviously included moving Tindall people into key roles while Draybin people would be moved out. Starting with me.

> Kitty Fromkin,
> Dressed in black,
> Is here to stab me
> In the back.

"Great to meet you, Kitty," I said with false cheer. She didn't reply, her eyes shifting between Tindall and Draybin, looking for signals.

I wondered if I was ever like her: so avidly on the make, so primed for combat. I had no chance against her. She was a campaign professional and I was not. She would be tireless and whip-smart. Her young brain would have every detail on instant recall, while I had almost nothing on instant recall. I dreaded the thought of my first senior moment in her presence. There would be no mercy for doddering dad.

Tindall leaned toward me and smiled. "Phil, Kitty and I have studied your speeches for Pete. We're in awe of your talent for catching Pete's optimism and humor and the richness of his spirit. That's pure gold in a campaign. Eh, Kitty?"

"Yeah," she said. "Great touch with the froth."

The froth? Was I about to become the froth writer?

"Pete," said Tindall, "can I get away with a cigarette in here?"

"I don't know. Go for it."

"Don't want to set off alarms but it's in my political genes to think best in smoke-filled rooms," he said, a tension-breaking laugh line he probably used often. He lit up and took a deep puff, then a thoughtful pause. I saw this was part of the staging as he launched his big speech.

"What I've learned in my years in this business is that the key is coming out of the gate with everything internally defined in lucid language so all your troops are aligned on the same page. What is the Pete Draybin brand? What is the unique Draybin imprint? These questions need answering at the most granular level. Because if you don't have this blueprint in your head you look like a stupid shit the first time a reporter asks you a tough question. I go back to Ted Kennedy on this."

I could barely listen as this dreary charade unfolded. My mind turned back to Sylvia, warm and toasty under the covers at the Auberge Bignan.

"Therefore, we've brought together two master articulators. I see Kitty and Phil as our one-two punch, an all-purpose tag team that kicks ass when we roll into battle."

I laughed. "You're rocking with the mixed metaphors today, Dick."

"Yeah, a writer would catch that," he said with a mirthless smile before getting back to his script. "But what I'm saying is that nobody can formulate issues like Kitty and nobody can write Pete-talk better than Phil."

Pete-talk. Froth. My new domain.

The waiter came in and took lunch orders. The three of them opted for girl food but I scorned the salads and displayed the unique Phil Vail imprint by ordering a greasy but fancy and expensive fish I'd always avoided.

Tindall resumed his spiel. "I won't get into all the usual campaign details because today we're focused on the bedrock clarity of our marching orders. As I see it, we start by painting a picture of Pete in the Cincinnatus mold. He has no lust for office but he responds to the call of duty. He's a results-oriented leader, a solution-finder. He's an antipolarizer, an antipartisan. This is where we need to lay out an aisle-crossing policy agenda that sounds good to all but the rabid lunatics. We reinvent the middle of the road. Kitty whips the issues into shape. Phil brings them to life with dynamite wordsmithing."

"What about the book?" I said. "I'm in the early stages of putting together a proposal for a big book—Pete's idea—that would lay out a comprehensive view of major problems and solutions."

"Forget the book, Phil," said Tindall. "Pete's shown us your preliminary outline and you've done a helluva job but it's too risky."

Kitty explained the riskiness. "You rush this book out and if it isn't Nobel Prize brilliant the critics ream your ass and you're a joke before you get to the starting line."

Frankly I'd thought that from the start but when *she* said it I felt like my infant child was being ripped from my arms and tossed in an incinerator, along with my million-dollar payday. I was being systematically stripped of power and position: the book was gone, the money was gone, my integral spot on Team Phil was apparently gone, and my fantasy of an office in the White House was probably gone too. What next?

Tindall took another puff and charged forward. "Now, Phil, we come to the road warrior part. Your résumé is dazzling but shows zero campaign experience so I'll just tell you that you cannot imagine what a grind it is to be on the bus. There's not enough caffeine or uppers in the world to keep you going but you have to keep going. You lose all connection to your personal life—I've lost two wives to this. And the pay doesn't come close to compensating for the crisis atmosphere you have to put up with 24x7x365. What I'm saying, Phil, is that this is a job for the young. Kitty is twenty-eight and aging fast—"

"Thanks, Dick. My boobs are drooping as we speak."

"So let's not kid ourselves, this is *not* the role for you, Phil. You'd hate every minute. So the way I see it is Kitty is the chief road writer while you're the chief headquarters writer. Your job is maintaining the big picture vision and being the stabilizing backstop at headquarters, at the center of the action."

I'm sure Tindall was right about campaigning being a young person's game but the notion of headquarters as the center of action was bullshit. Everyone knows the center of action is where the candidate is. Headquarters is where the candidate rarely sets foot.

I would be hundreds or thousands of miles from Draybin. I would lose access to him and without access I would be an irrelevant disgruntled crank in a distant cubicle. And then I'd be forced to share the cubicle with two teenage volunteer workers. I'd be deadwood. They'd show me the door.

Unable to look anyone in the eye, my gaze wandered to the window and the panoramic view of New York Harbor with the Statue of Liberty out there standing tall and true. Then the waiter returned, wheeling in our lunches. The fish was surprisingly tasty. I thought about Sylvia spending the day struggling with the sad details of her father's funeral as I dined in luxury while being elegantly shitcanned. Why did they bother with all this flattery about my future importance? Why not just fire me? I knew why: Pete felt guilty. He couldn't stomach an ugly scene. He'd signed off on getting rid of me but only in an upbeat, feel-good context.

I looked at him pointedly, seeking some message in his eyes. But he kept his head down, staring fixedly at his salad, engrossed in an especially fascinating tomato slice. This could have been his moment to save me from being Tindallized and Fromkinated, but no. I was condemned. I understood that presidential ambition is a fever that distorts decisions but I could barely believe he'd betrayed me so shabbily, so cravenly.

What clogged my thoughts and seemed so irreconcilably upside down was that the world I'd always been a proud and loyal member of was trying to jettison me while the Mafia *of all things* was embracing me. I'd spent a lifetime aspiring to share a table with big-name players like Draybin, Tindall, and Fromkin and now that I was with them, I felt surrounded by assholes. They didn't love me like Sylvia or see potential in me like Jake Sforza; to them I was disposable. They sat quietly now, drumming their fingers, dying to check their devices, waiting for me to stumble though some awkward last words that made no difference because whatever I said, I was out. Out now or out later.

The moment cried out for a cinematic fuck you scene in which I would overturn the table and send plates and glasses flying into their laps as I walked out giving them the finger. This would have been great messy fun but still fine with them because I'd be gone, mission accomplished. And it would be fine with Sylvia too because I'd be ending my ridiculous parallel existence with Draybin and the Sforzas.

So it was fine with everyone, *but not with me.* Maybe because I simply wasn't ready to abandon the life I'd known and replace it with some unknowable combination of useless retirement and a life with Sylvia in which it would be impossible to steer clear of involvement with the Mafia. I was committed to her but becoming a full-time mob spouse was crazy—I was in love but not insane. Cathartic as it would feel to erupt in a spectacular table-flipping exit scene, it would forever cut the cord to legitimacy and a normal life. There would be no way back if my Mafia adventure backfired.

As for Draybin, for fifteen years I'd defined my professional self by my relationship with him. I'd liked him, had great times with him, admired him, considered him a friend, a star, even a hero. I was reluctant to see that flushed away. Maybe I hoped my feelings about him could be repaired so I would not have to spend the rest of my life tasting the acid of his betrayal.

And one more reason: maybe I had some ambition of my own. Maybe I didn't want to shut down my speechwriting career only a few steps from the summit, writing for a president.

All this added up to an unappetizing conclusion: instead of going, I would stay. I would hang on and see what came next. I wouldn't be the first person to live with a shitty job. The big fuck you would have to wait. It was time to suck up. With enthusiasm and shameless insincerity.

"This has been a true learning experience for me," I said with a slight tremble in my voice as I tried to disguise contempt as earnest wet-eyed sentiment. "I've seen a top pro, Dick Tindall, in action up close. And Dick, I buy into everything you say. Kitty, I look forward to working for you and accepting your leadership. We'll be an awesome team. And Pete, this is an exciting first step. The Draybin Express is leaving the station. Next stop: 1600 Pennsylvania Avenue. *Toot, toot.*"

As they stared at me I added, "Do you think I could get some white wine with this fish?"

I GOT the wine but had to gulp it because the meeting deflated abruptly, with everyone glancing at their messages, avoiding eye contact, then rising to disperse as we congratulated ourselves on a terrific meeting which was, of course, a horrendous meeting. It was flattering that they'd dedicated an entire lunch just to tossing me overboard. I took dirty pleasure in clinging to the boat. But my pleasure faded as the hurt kicked in. We're never too old to be wounded when told we're not wanted. Lucky for me, I was welcome elsewhere.

CHAPTER 13

There he was, rumbling toward Jake's gravesite just as the service ended. I didn't need to be told this was the big from-age himself, Nicky Vavolizza. He had all the standard mob boss markers: the bouncy swagger, the snazzy outfit, above all the wise guy talent for exuding about-to-explode violence. He was about fifty but I pictured him in younger and leaner days, lording it over a city street corner on a hot summer day, muscled-up in a wife-beater T-shirt and crotch-gripping pants. What a classic thug he must have been.

He was still formidable. Big guy, big belly, big blast of badass vibrations. Paul Bazzanella, the Sforza intelligence chief, had predicted that Nicky would come late to show disrespect but also to claim the spotlight. Nicky loved the big boss role. He brought only one henchman with him, a lame-looking sidekick who was no threat to cut into Nicky's charisma.

We were taking our first steps toward the parking lot when Nicky made his appearance, bringing all movement to a stop. I was standing near Richie Roncade, the Sforza's chief tough guy, who stood next to Paul Bazzanella. I heard Roncade ask Bazzanella, "Who's the little creep with Nicky?"

"One of his capos from the Bronx," Bazzanella said. "Jackie Uddone."

"Jackie Uddone the knife guy?" said Roncade, not quite whispering.

"That's him."

"He kind of looks like a rat, don't he?"

"Everybody says that. But not to his face."

Vavolizza and Uddone were a contrasting pair: Vavolizza was a life-of-the-party extrovert; Uddone was sullen and fidgety. Vavolizza's brawn was decked out in a Burberry overcoat over a pinstriped suit with a black fedora pulled down over his forehead; Uddone was a hatless scarecrow in a drab suit and soiled *Columbo* raincoat. Vavolizza's face was round with pasty features that seemed smudged by too much flesh; Uddone had a pinched nose and chin and his complexion had a rough dingy pallor. The rat resemblance was not much of a reach.

"So which one's the brother?" Vavolizza boomed, but he had no trouble spotting Viv, pulling Viv into a bear hug. "We never met in all these years, eh? My condolences on your loss. And this is Tiziano?" Another bear hug for Tiziano, who looked baffled in Vavolizza's embrace.

Then Nicky stepped toward Sylvia with bear hug intentions but she slipped out of his grasp and held him back while she found his hand for a handshake, giving him a polite smile. It was a snub but he let it pass. Then he nodded at the brothers, at Bazzanella and Roncade, and a few others he recognized. Then his eyes swept over the rest of the funeral party and stopped for a moment on me. Perhaps his radar detected me as an outsider or perhaps it was my Blues Brothers outfit (including sunglasses and a 1940s gangster's hat Sylvia found in an upstairs closet). We had a moment of eye contact; I felt his intimidating force but resisted an instinct to turn away.

I was relieved when he took a step back and puffed himself up to deliver his official remarks as our boss. He said he just wanted to come by to extend a farewell to Jake Sforza. Jake, he said, was "a class act who had gone off course in recent years, but it's never too late to make things right if we're gonna do great things, hey?"

Then he dropped his bomb.

"So without further ado, it's my pleasure to introduce you to your new capo: Mr. Jackie Uddone. Of course I'm not going to talk business on this sad occasion. I'll respect your mourning period but right after Christmas I'm sending Jackie over to take command of the Sforza crew. So everybody say a big hello to Jackie Uddone."

Nicky seemed to have applause in mind but no one applauded. Jackie Uddone took a step forward without smiling and flipped a small wave.

In public the Sforzas are expressionless but someone behind me, speaking sotto voce, said, "This piece of shit's replacing Jake? Is he kidding?"

There was muffled laughter. Vavolizza must have heard it but showed no reaction. I think it was something I've seen with many public speakers who think they can wing it but, bumped off track by something unexpected, go blank at the key moment.

Sylvia stepped forward and said, "Nicky, you honor us with your presence today and we gratefully accept your condolences. We appreciate your suggestion of Mr. Uddone to become our new capo."

"Sylvia darling, it ain't a suggestion," Vavolizza said. "It's a done deal."

She ignored him. "Just one thing. If Mr. Uddone is coming by the house, I have to ask whether he is comfortable with Doberman pinschers, because when they sense discomfort they get highly volatile and it's not a good situation."

"What are you saying, Sylvia?" asked Vavolizza.

Uddone, silent until now, stepped forward and said, "I got no fear of your fucking dogs."

Somehow this shocked everyone. Mafia people use the word "fuck" a thousand times a day but not at funerals for venerated leaders. And Mafia people have a code of respect, or at least a pretense of respect, which Uddone had violated. Sylvia picked up on this and, with perfect pitch, tossed it in Vavolizza's face.

"Nicky, for God's sake, this is my father's funeral. I think your man owes everyone an apology."

Vavolizza put a restraining hand on Uddone's chest but Uddone wasn't done. "I ain't apologizing for anything. And I'm not waiting to give my first order. Here it is right now: when I come over I want those dogs gone. I see them, I cut them."

"Nicky!" cried Sylvia, and the family joined in a murmured chorus of indignation.

"Hey, calm the hell down," ordered Vavolizza, this time pushing Uddone back firmly and glaring at him before confronting the crowd.

"I don't like what you're starting here, Sylvia," Vavolizza said, pointing a finger at Sylvia.

Jimmy stepped forward and said, "You don't point fingers at my sister."

An angry cloud came over Vavolizza's face. "Hey, punk, you don't talk to me. I'm the boss and you show respect."

Jimmy wanted to fight but Tommy pulled him back. Vavolizza seemed to realize that things were getting out of hand and chose to retreat. "Okay, that's it for today. I got business elsewhere. Emotions are high so we'll give little brother a slide for today. But Jackie's taking over, and when he comes by, no bullshit with dogs, got it?"

He paused for a warning glare and then pivoted, stalking off with Uddone following behind. The rest of us exhaled and watched them go.

In the parking lot everyone stood around smoking, reluctant to disband. Sylvia and I stood with Viv, who was rattled by Vavolizza and upset by Paola, who'd decided that she could not tolerate New York mob life for three months and was therefore returning to Italy immediately. Her absence would make running the family even more difficult for Viv. Everyone knew he was the wrong man for the job and the contrast with Vavolizza accentuated his wrongness. Vavolizza possessed the menace and malice it took to run a crime family. Viv didn't have it.

Sylvia stepped away as Roncade and Bazzanella joined us. Like Vavolizza and Uddone, they were a contrasting pair: Bazzanella was a cheerful, curly-haired three-hundred-pounder;

Roncade was a hard-looking commando with a buzz cut and deep tan suggesting years in the Middle Eastern sun.

Viv said, "Paul, speak."

Bazzanella gave his analysis. "Nicky came here to make the point that he picks the next boss, not us. He could pick a lot better than Uddone but it's a stunt, a calculated insult. The message is you don't need a guy who reads the *Harvard Business Review* to run the Sforza crew, you can put in a no-class mutt like Jackie Uddone and do just fine."

Roncade said, "Has he forgotten there was a war over who names the boss? And his side lost?"

"He's drooling over getting his hooks into us," said Bazzanella. "He's ambitious and this is his big moment. He wants prestige and power. He wants to move up another rung in the hierarchy. He's embarrassed he could never control us, so this is his chance to get control."

"He couldn't even control Uddone," said Roncade. "Sylvia pushed his buttons and he almost lost it."

"Uddone makes people nervous, even if he's on your side," said Bazzanella.

Viv said, "Look, we've got a succession issue here. What will the other families do?"

"They'll support Nicky, no doubt about it," said Bazzanella. "He'll promise them all a big bite of the pie when the Sforza treasury gets looted. They envy what Jake built and want to see us brought down. And they hate the idea of an autonomous crew naming its own boss. That's got to be done away with once and for all."

Viv broke in, "We don't budge on this. They don't name the boss of our crew. They didn't name Jake. They won't name John. *We* do the naming."

"Nicky will say it was a one-time deal for Jake and now we go back to the old way and Uddone gets the job."

"My brothers didn't build this organization to have some rat-faced psycho stuck in at the top. We can't operate like that. No compromise on that."

This was impressively firm and I was liking it. But at that moment I heard someone shouting my name. It was Carl Pelikan, calling from his car window. "You sure had me fooled, Phil," he yelled, in front of everyone. "I'll give you a buzz on the cell."

"What does that dick want from you?" Roncade asked.

I shook my head. Pelikan drove off with a wave and a honk.

"Okay," said Viv. "When Uddone comes calling we'll give him a coffee, keep the dogs off him, and tell him the status quo is great for everybody and shouldn't be changed. If he insists he's in charge, we insist the Sforza crew will run better if the Sforza crew names its own boss. We never say no, we never say yes. Meanwhile Richie sets up a full-scale battle plan. Show him we'll fight if we have to."

No one spoke until Bazzanella said, "Nicky said he won't do anything until after Christmas. That's to build pressure. And fear. He's hoping we'll give in without a war."

"The repast is waiting at home," Sylvia announced. "We decided against a restaurant because of the notoriety."

Viv said, "Phil, ride with me." We took the red Cadillac with me driving. Sylvia and Paola got into one of the other cars.

VIV SAID, "I understand why you said no to Jake."

"Part of me wishes I'd said yes. It was tempting."

He laughed. "I wish it tempted me." He fell silent again, but then said, "Jake was going to retire and join me in Italy. He might have stepped down a year ago if John hadn't gone to jail."

"Will John be a good boss?"

"Who knows? They say he's too hot-tempered but there's always been a place in the business for hot tempers. You know, when Johnny was a teenager he was getting in trouble so Jake shipped him over to us in Venice. We had him for a year. He was great. He was popular. He picked up Italian and also the Venetian dialect. He was a protective brother to Gina, my daughter. Did well in school. From the time he left Italy until prison, Paola would phone him every Sunday night and they'd gossip like girls."

"I've met his wife."

Viv smiled. "Vera is something, isn't she? John brought her to Venice for their honeymoon. She brought the whole city to a stop with those *meloni*."

"What's your take on Vavolizza?"

"Just another hoodlum. I've known those guys all my life but I'll admit they intimidate me. They didn't intimidate Jake. He was *amused* by them. He enjoyed making fools of them. I don't have that in me. I want you to be my adviser, Phil. I'm going to be very dependent on you."

Apparently the Italian post-funeral meal, which the Sforzas call a repast, traditionally turns festive but not this time. Vavolizza and Jackie Uddone had cast an ominous cloud over the future. Only Jimmy was in lively spirits, perhaps pumped up by his near fight with Nicky. He broke the mood at the table by telling the story about me pinching Max Waxman's nose. Everyone laughed heartily at the image of mild-mannered Phil getting physical with the spluttering Max.

Halfway through the meal Sylvia surprised everyone by wrapping her arms around my neck and giving me a movie-quality kiss that set off a round of applause at the table. I took this as Sylvia's way of declaring that the long-running drama of her love life had reached a happy ending and also that I had been upgraded to a new status in the House of Sforza.

For several years loneliness had been my steady companion but now I parted with loneliness and moved on. Sylvia and I had become a committed couple.

CHAPTER 14

Over coffee the next morning I realized what I would give Sylvia for Christmas. It was just right. There could be nothing else.

Then Carl Pelikan rang my doorbell. Next to Pelikan, towering over him, was a big good-looking black guy.

Pelikan said, "Meet Special Agent Kenneth DeSens out of the FBI's White Plains field office."

I'd never had an FBI agent at my door. I wondered if I was in even more trouble than I thought. My knowledge of FBI agents, derived solely from TV fiction, was that they were invariably pushy, arrogant bastards, despised by everyone including other police. But DeSens seemed amiable.

Pelikan was holding a stack of three Starbucks containers. "I figured you for Peppermint Mocha Twist Frappuccino. Can we come in?"

I led them into the kitchen and gestured at the table. I felt disadvantaged in every way but especially by my clothing (jeans, T-shirt, and bare feet) in contrast to DeSens, who looked like he'd just slipped into an immaculate suit after winning the Olympic decathlon, and even Pelikan, who looked refreshed as if he were coming from an invigorating session beating confessions out of prisoners.

Pelikan said, "Let's start with my compliments for the way you keep fooling me about Sylvia. I bought your tale about being an innocent dupe meeting her on the train for the first time but then you show up in the funeral party. And where the hell did you find that hat you were wearing? Did Jimmy Cagney leave it to you in his will?"

"I did meet her on the train for the first time."

"But three weeks later you're like a member of the family. So I'm thinking you've been involved with her and the family for a long time. I figure you're connected."

"Which means what?"

"'Connected' means you're in the Mafia orbit but not a made man. I'm figuring you provide something in addition to stud services. But I never heard of the mob hiring speechwriters."

I said nothing.

Pelikan said, "You know I could arrest the Sforza brothers anytime."

"Do you have evidence or would this just be your clear bias against the family?"

"Maybe someone saw them without their ski masks. Maybe somebody got the license plate off their vehicle."

Bluffing.

"The media would eat it up. And a bunch of a-hole junior detectives might see that I can still reel in the marlins."

"Phil," said DeSens, "let me jump in here. My agency is hoping you'd like to bank some goodwill with law enforcement by helping us out with your observations on what's happening in the Sforza family post-Jake. This could be informal or we could do it on an ongoing for-profit basis."

Here was a new career option: I could be a snitch, a paid informer. I said, "I know Sylvia Sforza but I have no knowledge of family business."

"I'll remind you that I'm a federal agent. Lying to me is a crime."

"I'll remind you that you're in my house and I'll ask you to get the fuck out if you threaten me again."

"What are Nicky Vavolizza's intentions regarding the Sforza crew?"

"Mob bosses don't share their intentions with me."

Pelikan said, "We hear Vivaldi Sforza is running things until Catcher comes back from upstate but Nicky Vavolizza wants to put his pet scumbag Jackie Uddone in charge. This sounds like a potentially dangerous clash of intentions. How do you see it?"

They knew all this already. They must have had listening equipment picking up the conversation in the cemetery parking lot. Now they were fishing for more while testing whether they could recruit me as a spy.

DeSens asked, "Would the Sforzas go to war to resist Uddone?"

Pelikan said, "Vail, what Ken's saying is that if this means violence in the streets and 'going to the mattresses,' that would be a very bad idea. Carry that message back to the nest, okay? Public warfare will not be tolerated."

"I'm going to ask you to go now," I said.

They weren't surprised. Both stood up. DeSens pulled out a business card and left it on the table. Pelikan tossed his card on top of DeSens's card and said, "You're over your head, Phil. You're gonna need us."

They were halfway to their cars when I called out, "Excuse me, I wonder if I can have a private word with Detective Pelikan."

Pelikan loved this and hustled back inside.

"It's something I overheard before Jake died," I said. "He was very disturbed by the prospect of his sons being arrested at a time when the family was in a sensitive transition. Even if the brothers were in custody for just one day."

Pelikan grinned. "You've just given me another incentive to pull them in."

"No, I'm giving you an incentive *not* to pull them in. If you'd arrested them, or if Jake *thought* you'd arrest them, you would have made a very dangerous man very angry."

"Do I look like I give a shit?"

"You should have given a shit, Carl. A really big shit."

"Are you saying he was going to—what?—have me *killed*? He couldn't do that. The mob commission wouldn't green-light a hit on a detective."

"You think that would have stopped Jake if the family's survival was at stake?"

It sank in slowly but it did sink in. I saw a glimmer of fear in the Pelikan eyes.

"Of course this is moot because Jake is no longer with us," he said.

"You think he didn't discuss it with the powers-that-be?"

His bully-boy expression was gone now.

"What about me?" I said. "What if I'd implicated the brothers during that session at the police station? You and I *both* would have been on the endangered species list."

I knew I was out of my league playing this kind of game with police, but it seemed urgent. Having Jake Sforza dead and all four Sforza sons behind bars would have offered an opportunity Vavolizza couldn't resist.

"I didn't have to tell you this, Carl. It would have been safer for me to keep my mouth shut."

"Okay," he said. "Maybe I'll back off, for today anyway. No arrests. But you don't mention this to anyone. And tell them if warfare breaks out all bets are off, understand?"

He turned and marched toward his car. Without turning around he said, "Thanks."

I said, "Don't say 'Thanks.' Say 'I owe you.'"

He gave me the finger but nodded his head.

I may have saved a cop's life. Did that bank me any good-will with law enforcement?

I HAD many fears about the Mafia—being killed, being jailed—but a deeper fear was about identity: who would I *be* when I belonged to a Mafia family? In some irrational way I thought it would be excusable because I could never be a *real* gangster, I would always be good clean Phil at heart, an upstanding guy with no evil in him.

But really, no one would buy that. On the contrary, I would be harshly judged. My motives and the story of my falling into the mob would never be understood. Valued friends and family would turn away from me, shocked and uncomprehending and perhaps fearful. Most important, I might lose the love and respect of my son, Willy.

It was a call from Willy that got me thinking like this. He wouldn't be able to visit for Christmas because he was too busy in Minneapolis—the girlfriend, teaching demands, and so on. My disappointment was quickly replaced by a wave of relief. If he came home I would not be able to conceal the Mafia story. I would have to tell him all or most of it. Sylvia would want to meet him. Police would be at the door. Danger would be a fact of life.

Willy would not take it well. Our relationship would never recover. Did this mean I had to choose between Sylvia and Willy? No, I would not accept that.

THE NEXT day UPS dropped off a brown carton which I naturally assumed was a bomb from Nicky Vavolizza. Looking closer, I realized it was a case of very primo red wine from Pete Draybin, his annual Christmas gift.

My first thought was that someone forgot to scratch my name off the gift list. But I found an enclosed note from Draybin telling me he was leaving tomorrow for Cape Cod— "Could be our last quiet holiday for a long time"—and adding, "Kitty's turning out stacks of issues stuff, but it's heavy reading. It needs your touch after the holidays, okay? Merry Christmas." Apparently Draybin wasn't ready to get rid of me.

CHRISTMAS EVE was wonderful. We had a big meal, went to church where I pretended to be Catholic, and enjoyed the kids' excitement over the gifts they'd rip open in the morning.

At four A.M. Sylvia and I woke up to exchange presents. By coincidence we gave each other rings. She gave me a gaudy plastic pinky ring, purchased for $6.95 at a Times Square novelty shop because, "If you're gonna hang around with mobsters, you gotta dress for it." I gave her an engagement ring with the biggest diamond I could afford. "If you're gonna be a wife, you gotta dress for it."

CHAPTER 15

Catcher was murdered on Christmas morning. He was on a line filing into the prison chapel for a holiday service when another inmate stepped in behind him and slashed his throat. The killer whirled away and disappeared into the line of prisoners.

The call from the prison chaplain reached Vera as she was preparing her boys to go to the Sforza house. She collapsed in hysterics. The younger son, Todd, phoned the Sforzas. George picked up the phone.

George may have understood the distress in Vera's house before he grasped the reality of his brother's death. He shouted, "I'm coming," and ran for the door, finding Viv and Paola in the living room. They joined him and the three of them ran out the door coatless, finding Richie Roncade who put his men on full alert and organized a security escort as George, Viv, and Paola took off in the Cadillac.

Sylvia and I arrived minutes later, unaware of what had happened. Sylvia was eager to display her engagement ring. As we entered Sycamore Court we could see that Roncade's men were in a hair-trigger defense condition, making no effort to conceal their weapons.

We rushed into the house, encountering Amanda who cried, "They killed Uncle Catcher."

This was a stomach punch for Sylvia. The air went out of her and she started to fall. I caught her and held her around the waist as she gasped for breath. By this point the family had gathered in the living room. Someone jumped up from a couch to make a place for Sylvia.

The shocking news contrasted painfully with the festive decorations in the living room. The big tree was lit up. Brightly wrapped presents lay under it and Johnny Mathis was singing Christmas carols.

"I was about to send him a card for his birthday," said Angela, who was crowded onto a couch holding Tiz. "Thirty-seven years old."

Sylvia asked, "Was he in a fight?"

"No, Sis, he was going to church. It was a hit, for sure," said Jimmy. "Remember Vavolizza talking about how he'd respect our period of mourning for Poppa? This is how he respected it."

A Roncade guy standing at the window said, "They're back."

The room fell silent. Amanda opened the door. From across the room I could feel the blast of cold air.

Vera needed a dramatic entrance. She is built for opera: larger than life in every way. Her grief, I knew, would be titanic. The room braced for it and then felt its shock wave as she burst in, supported on each arm by George and Viv with her boys and Paola following. Her face was ashen and twisted. She gave a terrible cry and then her knees buckled and she went down heavily. The men could not keep her on her feet. On all fours she wailed and beat the floor with her fists. The kids were horrified.

Viv barked, "Get the children downstairs," and the children seemed to vanish.

Sylvia rushed across the room and knelt over Vera, and then all the women were there, huddled around her while the men retreated helplessly. Vico the barber walked in as this was happening. He inched around them, transfixed by Vera's suffering. You could see a transformation on his face, from kindly senior citizen to savage avenger, his small peasant face set in homicidal fury.

Viv had disappeared. I guessed that he had taken refuge in Jake's den. I went up and knocked on the closed door. There was no response. "Viv, it's me, Phil," I called. A moment later the door opened.

He was red-eyed. He stepped back and let me in. An open bottle of vodka was in plain sight on the coffee table. "John was a son to me," he said.

We sat down and looked at each other.

"I can't bear this, Phil. I can't bear the thought of Jake being gone and me thrust into this hoodlum world. I hate this."

I WAS surprised to hear raised voices from outside. There was a window and I peeked down from three floors to see an intensely emotional basketball game getting underway on the backyard court. The brothers were in the game, as were Catcher's sons.

Viv leaned forward and screwed the cap onto the vodka bottle. That was a relief.

"I know this is a tragic time, Viv, but I wanted you to know that I proposed to Sylvia and she said yes."

He looked up and his eyes glistened. "Such good news with the bad," he said. "This makes you a member of the family. Paola will be thrilled. It might help us balance the pain. I can't bear to think about what comes next. Whose lives will be lost? Jimmy? Tommy? Georgie? I'm past the point of believing this makes sense. Let's go downstairs and see how people are feeling."

"Viv, can I put on my consultant's hat?"

"I would value that, Phil."

"The people downstairs need leadership. Listening to people is compassionate but if we're under attack it isn't the right leadership."

"So what am I supposed to do?"

"I'd hate to find out that everything I've written about leadership was bullshit but my main client was Peter Draybin and he's sort of a leadership expert. He did a great job after 9/11—he actually watched the attacks from his office window."

"And?"

"Draybin says a lot of people think leadership's about charging into battle or shouting orders or slogans but in his view the really important thing a leader has to do is provide a convincing version of reality. A crisis is kind of a reality vacuum. People can't think straight and they're about to panic and do the worst possible things, starting with following the hotheads. The leader has to jump in before the bad ideas take over and replace them with a version of reality that creates stability. As people calm down they realize the problem can be faced intelligently. Their confidence returns. Once they get to this point, you can lead them in constructive directions."

"So you're telling me I can't go downstairs until I have a convincing version of reality, right? But I'll let you in on a secret, the only reality I know is that John is dead and I don't know what to do, other than turning Richie Roncade loose to go out and kill a lot of people. Which is very tempting, believe me."

"But it's more of an emotion than a strategy."

"I suppose you're right. Jake would have found something smarter."

"But maybe not in the first ten minutes?"

"True, maybe not that fast."

"So how about this for reality: Vavolizza killed Catcher to intimidate us and show us we'd already lost the succession fight because our leader-to-be was dead. But it's not going to work. We're going to mourn Catcher but at the same time we're going to keep our heads and develop a plan for dealing with Vavolizza. What's important is getting through the next few days without big mistakes."

He nodded but didn't speak.

I said, "How about if I get Roncade and Bazzanella and the brothers. We'll sit down and talk about what comes next."

"Now?"

"Yes. And I'd like to include Sylvia."

"No. Not Sylvia. Jake had a rule that Sylvia could never be brought into anything she could be prosecuted for."

Fine. Instead of getting her advice in a meeting I'd get it in private.

Jimmy opened the door. "The cops are here. Pelikan and the agent."

"Tell them I'll be down in a moment," said Viv. "This will be a warning against striking back at Vavolizza."

"The *victims* get the warning. That doesn't work for me," I said. "Why not make it a little harder for the cops? Turn the tables and ask what they can do for you. How can they help you avoid a war?"

"No, Phil. We do not ask the police and FBI to save us from a war with the people who just killed John."

"Maybe the cops would create problems for the Vavolizzas. Disrupt their momentum or something."

He got to his feet shaking his head. He looked exhausted but I was primed. That foggy, lethargic feeling I'd had on the train and in the first encounter with Pelikan was a thing of the past. I was in the game now, revved up and ready.

IN MY freshman year of college I took a French literature course from which I remember nothing except a quotation from Baudelaire: "We descend into hell by tiny steps." I think it was memorable because it was such a plausible explanation of how people get in deep trouble. One small step down the ladder is followed by another and another until you're up to your chin in a world of shit. I thought of this with each stair as I came down from the den shoulder-to-shoulder with Viv, the reluctant capo.

Pelikan and DeSens were waiting outside, trading hostile glances with Roncade's sentries. When Pelikan saw me coming out with Viv he snickered and said, "Every time I see you you've moved up a notch. What are you now, the *consigliere?*"

The sight of Viv was not encouraging. This encounter was going to be tough for him. I decided I would put aside my reservations about my undefined standing in the family and jump in as helpfully as possible. The backyard basketball game was over so I suggested that we find some privacy by walking around to the back.

DeSens spoke first, which was probably prearranged: he was obviously smoother than Pelikan. Speaking softly he said he knew that members of the Sforza family would suffer from Catcher's murder for the rest of their lives. He knew it would be very stressful, especially since they were still absorbing Jake's death. He said he did not know Catcher well and would not pretend that he liked him—Pelikan harrumphed at this—but no one should die like this, on a prison floor on Christmas morning.

Viv did not reply. So I asked, "What can you tell us about what happened?"

DeSens gave the answer. "Not much. He was slashed with a box cutter blade. Prison contraband."

"There must be witnesses?"

"Plenty of witnesses but no one saw anything. Prisoners are masters at seeing nothing when these things happen. The killer was white or light-skinned Hispanic, that's all we know. The blade was wrapped in cardboard. Not much chance of fingerprints."

"Maybe someone will rat on him?"

"Possibly but of course that's dangerous," Pelikan said. "There'll be scuttlebutt and rumors. Sooner or later a name will bubble up. It's hard to keep secrets in prison. But assume the contract was laundered through several layers so it's hard to trace. I'm betting the guy who did this has no Cosa Nostra connection and didn't even know Catcher, but there'll be a fat envelope waiting for him when he gets out."

"I don't care who did it," said Viv. "What counts is who *ordered* it. We all know who that was."

"You don't know nothing," said Pelikan. "You're assuming."

"Fuck *assuming*," snarled Viv. I think it was the first four-letter word I'd heard out of his mouth. "Nicky Vavolizza made this happen. We all know that."

DeSens made his obligatory statement: "Mr. Sforza, we urge you in the strongest terms to forego any retribution at this time. I don't have to tell you the consequences would be very dire."

"You're telling me to forget about this?" said Viv. "Have a beer and forget my brother's son had his throat slit on his way to church on Christmas morning? Forget a threat of violence to every member of my family?"

Viv was about to boil over. In another moment he would be saying disastrously wrong things, vowing revenge, and perhaps naming victims in advance. I had to interrupt somehow, changing the direction. Some ancient schoolyard impulse had caused me to pick up the basketball and I was tossing it lightly between my hands but now the ball came in handy. I bounced it hard on the asphalt and launched a thirty-foot shot. We all watched the ball's arc toward the basket. It came down hard and shuddered on the front of the iron rim.

DeSens mouthed the word, "Brick."

Pelikan turned to me and said, "Excuse me, are we boring you?"

I said, "You're picking on the victim. This man's nephew has been murdered and you're standing here threatening *him*. Maybe you could be a little more constructive."

Pelikan was about to go belligerent but DeSens stepped in. "What are you suggesting, Mr. Vail?"

"I suggest you do something more useful than covering your ass. Have you seen Vavolizza yet?"

"Not yet."

"Don't you think that's in order, since he's the obvious instigator of this crime? Give *him* some of your goddamned warnings. Tell him if he wants peace he'd better start making offers. Maybe Mr. Sforza will promise to keep things from blowing up pending some quick results from you."

This I never had in mind: I was taking over the discussion, setting terms for a settlement between the Mafia and police and doing so without any thought or authority.

"You want the *cops* to broker a settlement?" said Pelikan. "That idea would get big laughs in Sicily."

"Carl, hold on a second," said DeSens. "Mr. Vail is asking us to serve as intermediaries. Okay, that's unorthodox but if he's offering it how can we say no, in the interest of preventing bloodshed."

Pelikan was disgusted. "Ken, are you going to invite me to Stockholm when you receive the Nobel fucking Peace Prize?"

DeSens said, "Do we just give them warnings and walk away? Will that stop the war these guys are going to start, probably *today*?"

Viv and I were amazed to see them arguing in front of us.

DeSens said to Viv, "Look, we'll try it but you got to give us your word that nothing will happen till we talk to Vavolizza and get back to you."

"Does that work for you, Viv?" I asked.

He nodded, biting his lips.

"This is bullshit," said Pelikan. He picked up the basketball and angrily threw it, baseball-style, at the hoop. It hit the backboard with a clatter and bounced away.

"We'll make a visit right now," said DeSens. "He lives up in Weaver Ridge. It's, what, twenty minutes from here. Just don't do anything till you hear from us."

"We should let 'em kill each other," said Pelikan.

"Good cop, bad cop," I said.

Viv headed up the stairs toward the den.

"Do you want me up there?" I said.

"If you wish."

"I'll get us some coffee." I knew he was heading for the vodka bottle.

In the living room, Sylvia seemed to have restored domestic tranquility. She sat in a straight-backed wooden chair pulled up next to the tree and from this position she supervised the gift-opening proceedings.

Jimmy grabbed my arm. "Phil, how soon are we going to hit these fucks? Viv says the word and it's on."

"Be patient, Jimmy," I said.

Sylvia broke away from the kids and intercepted me.

"What did the cops want?"

"Warning against retaliating."

"I saw you shoot that basket. That was the loudest shot I ever heard."

"I never had a good three-point shot."

"What's your role in this?" she asked, looking upstairs.

"I don't really know, but Viv is faltering."

She put her arms around my neck and sighed.

"Phil, I ditched the diamond the second I realized something bad had happened—"

"*Ditched*?"

"Put it in my pocket, out of sight," she said. "Do you think I'd throw my engagement ring in the bushes?"

She pulled the ring out of her slacks pocket and showed it to me. "I obviously couldn't walk into the house ecstatic about being engaged while everyone else was devastated. But now that the news has sunk in a little, it might raise spirits if we made an announcement. How about now?"

A minute later we had everyone including Viv gathered in the living room. Sylvia raised her voice and the room went silent, thinking this was something about Catcher.

"This is a Christmas we'll never forget. Poppa just died and today we've lost our beloved brother. It's a horrible day for all of us but especially Vera, Todd, and Jeremy. We all have to be sensitive to their needs in the times ahead, and I don't mean just a few days.

"But there's also some very good news today."

She held up her left hand to reveal the diamond. The Sforza smile lit up her face and a whoop of pleasure went up in the living room. A hug line formed. I was squeezed, cheek-kissed, and wept upon.

But I couldn't enjoy it for long.

CHAPTER 16

Staging a meeting wasn't that easy. The house was packed with people and there was no place to gather for serious talk. When I asked Sylvia's advice she said, "Why do you want to hold a meeting?" Jake didn't hold meetings, he gave orders. The meetings concept was a giant leap from dictatorship to democracy. Sylvia shrugged and suggested the basement so the basement became our war room.

I'd attended strategy sessions in high-tech Fortune 500 boardrooms that felt like the operations center of the Strategic Air Command. The Sforza basement was at the other end of the spectrum: a shitty suburban rec room, 1950s style. The bar didn't work, the neon Budweiser sign behind the bar didn't work, the carpet and furniture were stained and torn. It was clearly the domain of the brothers, where they sloshed and spilled beer, hooted at the tube, played video games. Perhaps high school sex had happened here. In one corner was a freezer and the house washer and dryer; in another was a weight-lifting area. The weights were old-fashioned black iron, not the high-end chrome or plastic stuff found in health clubs. Ventilation was minimal. It smelled like a gym in Bulgaria.

The seven of us descended the rickety stairs and found places to sit. Viv exercised his prerogative as boss and took the best seat, a ragged easy chair. He signaled me to sit to his right on one of two colorless couches. Roncade and the broad-beamed Bazzanella filled the opposite couch. The brothers dragged over metal folding chairs from a dark recess under the staircase. They were ready to be led into war, excited by visions of payback. Any other plan would be a hard sell.

Viv started with no preface, describing the conversation with DeSens and Pelikan. Roncade and Bazzanella were aghast.

"Boss, that's not how it's done," said Bazzanella. "With all respect, wise guys don't ask cops to deal with their enemies. This is between us and Nicky."

"It was my idea, Paul," I said. "I wanted to get the cops into the game, maybe disrupt Vavolizza's strategy."

"There's no strategy," replied Bazzanella. "There's only one move. They kill one of yours, you kill one of theirs."

"Bazz is right," Richie said. "The military calls it 'proportional response.' The other side takes out your target, you take out their counterpart target. Catcher would have been our capo. Vavolizza wants Uddone to be the capo. Uddone is the target."

"Yes!" said Jimmy. "I volunteer."

Bazzanella said, "But you know what I'm wondering? I'm wondering whether Nicky brought Jackie to the cemetery to set him up as our target. He's *sacrificing* Jackie. He's saying, 'Hey, you wanna kill somebody? Kill this little psycho. I won't mind being rid of him.'"

"Except Jackie's so stupid he thinks he's getting promoted," said Tommy.

The brothers chuckled over that.

Viv said, "Killing this worthless runt does not make up for losing Catcher. We could just as well step on a cockroach and call that revenge."

Roncade said, "We have to hit back, Boss. Would Catcher want us to *not* hit back?"

"This is such an old story," sighed Viv. "We take revenge, then Nicky takes revenge for our revenge. You begin the never-ending cycle, *vendetta*. The village halfway up the hill goes to war with the village at the top of the hill because somebody's honor has been offended. Cousins kill cousins.

Nephews murder their uncles. A whole generation of women has no husbands. All you see is widows in black. No one even remembers why. What a great solution. It makes me sick."

To me this was an eloquent statement but it fell on deaf ears. Viv's logic—the outcome of revenge-seeking—was exactly what Pete Draybin would call a convincing version of reality, except it wasn't convincing to anyone but me.

Viv seemed to have one last effort in him. "Paul might be right that Nicky is setting up Uddone. But maybe Nicky is shrewder than that. Let's say we kill Uddone. That allows Nicky to go to the commission and say, 'Look at this outrage. The Sforzas whacked one of my capos. I got a rogue crew on my hands. That can't be tolerated. We got to put this down with all our strength or other crews will get ideas.' And then Nicky gets exactly what he wants: the five families are behind him in a war against us."

"Except we win it," said Roncade. "We strike hard and fast, take out everyone who threatens us, and they all back down. That's what happened the last time. This time we're even stronger. We've got a world-class professional outfit, they got a bunch of undisciplined pasta-fazool lardasses."

I summoned my nerve and got into it. "Richie, I'm thinking of something Jake said to me, that we would win the battle but lose the war, meaning that law enforcement would be all over everyone and by the time it was over we'd all be dead or in jail."

"So we sit on our ass and do nothing?" asked Bazzanella.

"No, we use our heads," I said. "We stay away from predictable behavior that plays into their hands. Don't you think the Vavolizzas are expecting us to come at them? Paul just said there's only one move. They know that, don't they?"

"Who gives a shit if they know it?" said George.

"George," I said, "how about you and Tommy and Jimmy jump in the car to go off to kill somebody but get gunned down before you're halfway to the highway? There goes the heart of the Sforzas, wiped out. That's the end of the war, right there. It could happen ten minutes after you're out of the house."

Jimmy said, "Remember in *The Godfather* when Sonny jumps in the car to beat up the brother-in-law again and gets ambushed at the toll booth?"

That clicked with everyone. My argument was rescued by a film reference.

Tommy said, "Well, I don't like letting the cops into our fight."

"We can't keep them *out* of the fight," I said. "The minute shots are fired it's a three-way with the cops in it too. And Richie, you're not going to turn your army on the cops, are you?"

"We could take 'em," said Roncade, smiling.

Viv scoffed.

Bazzanella said, "Phil—hey Viv, all respect but I got to ask something. What is Phil doing in this argument? I mean, Phil, shouldn't you be upstairs with Sylvia?"

A moment of truth, but Viv rose to it. "Phil is one of us, Paul. I want you all to understand this. Phil is marrying Jake's daughter. Perhaps Phil will become the father of Jake's grandchild. Phil was Jake's first choice to run this family because Jake believed Phil was a better choice than any of us, including Catcher and including me. All of you agreed to this. And the offer to him is still on the table. Is that understood?"

Bazzanella backed off quickly. "Okay. Sorry. No offense, Phil. No disrespect." The others mumbled similar sentiments.

I said, "No offense taken. Before we walk out of this basement we're all going to agree on what to do, but we haven't yet figured out what it is. We need a different approach."

"Like what?" said Jimmy.

I had no idea.

THE CHOICE was war or *something else*. I was the sole advocate of *something else*. Viv seemed to lean my way but he was in and out, not fully engaged.

It was hard for me to understand why the brothers, Roncade, and Bazzanella seemed unable to fathom the idea that a Mafia war would destroy all of its major participants *including them*. They were bright people but under pressure they had a single ingrained response: *kick ass*. There was no space in their minds for consequences, such as outraging not only the public but the legislative, judicial, and executive branches of municipal, state, and federal governments and bringing down the full policing and prosecuting powers of all of the above.

Maybe this is the traditional leadership mind-set of mobs and mob-like regimes: if you have a problem, shoot people. If that creates another problem tomorrow, shoot more people. If all this shooting fails and you end up dead, what the hell— you never planned on a long life anyway.

Jake, the wisest mobster, saw farther than that. It dawned on me now that what he'd seen in me—perhaps the solution to the mystery of why he offered me the family leadership— was that Catcher would not hesitate to let slip the dogs of war while I would grasp the wisdom of keeping those foaming hounds on the leash. The family would not survive with Catcher; it had a chance of surviving with me. My shortcomings were insignificant if I could achieve just one thing: preventing war.

In fact, preventing war had become *my* problem. I seemed to have taken charge. Six men were staring at me intently, waiting for a solution *now*. I needed, at the very least, a short-term tactic that might catch their imagination, meaning it had to make doing *nothing* sound like doing *something*. What I needed was time—time for an idea or, more likely, time for events to create an opportunity. That led me to the same tactic I'd used with Draybin, Tindall, and Fromkin: stall, and give no satisfaction.

"Here's what we do," I said. "We stall, we feint, we never do what they expect. They expect a head-on attack so that's what we *don't* do. They expect a traditional fight but instead we invite the cops into it. Everything in the Cosa Nostra play-book, that's what we *don't* do."

This was a bold start but not enough to run the table. I saw unconvinced faces all around, though Roncade seemed intrigued. Military guys love the frontal attack but they also savor the tricky maneuver.

Bazzanella said, "You're saying play games with them. Fuck up their heads?"

"Something like that," I said, because I really didn't know what I was saying. Then I realized he'd set a trap for me.

"Catcher gets killed and you want to play head games," he said. "Instead of going out and disemboweling these cunts you want to play guerrilla warfare with them?"

But Viv came to life and saved my butt.

"What Phil's saying is that instead of starting a disastrous war, we allow some other situation to develop and maybe that gives us a way out. I don't know what it's going to be but what we need is a chance of coming out of this with something like the status quo. John wouldn't want us to blow up our whole enterprise just for revenge. If we go to war we probably lose everything. So any other plan is worth a shot."

Well done, Viv. He defined a new reality. The doubters were momentarily silenced but I had to act fast to close the deal.

I pulled out my wallet and searched it for Ken DeSens's business card.

I REACHED DeSens in his car with Pelikan.

"We're just leaving Weaver Ridge," he said. "We had a fine old time, didn't we, Carl? Carl says yes." I was surprised by his rollicking tone.

"When we got over to his house we saw all the fancy cars outside and realized Nicky was hosting a big holiday shindig. I bet he had all his capos in there plus wives, family, kids, and assorted other garbage.

"We decided if we had to be working Christmas day we could at least have some fun. So we went for an old-fashioned roust. Carl ordered up some reinforcements and we pulled up outside the Vavolizza residence with a bunch of cops and wagons."

"I like where this is going," I said.

"Nicky comes running out on the lawn all dressed up in his host outfit. He's showing off for the family, throwing F-bombs all over the place. So Carl says to him, 'Mr. V., we just thought we'd swing by and arrest you and your family and all your guests because somewhere among you is the person who engineered the murder of John Sforza. So bring 'em out and we'll go downtown for Christmas dinner behind bars.' "

I gestured to the basement group that they were going to like this story.

DeSens continued. "So the whole Vavolizza family and their guests are now pressed to the windows watching this. A few of Nicky's guests are actually trying to run into the woods but we grab 'em back. Carl is saying, 'Okay, everybody into the vans, let's go.' Carl is complimenting Nicky on his WASPy red Christmas vest with brass buttons and his green plaid Christmas slacks. Telling him how nice it'll look in lockup.

"And we keep this up for a while but then Carl says, 'Tell you what, in the holiday spirit we'll back off for today. But Nick, take this as an illustration of what happens if there are any acts of violence against the Sforzas in the next few days.' So we wrapped it up there and that was the end of our fun."

I said, "It sounds good enough for now. Congratulations."

"Good. Needless to say we expect your promise to desist from any provocative acts until we can have a little cooling-off period and then find a way to get this settled peacefully. Do I have your word?"

"Hold on," I said. I muted the phone and turned to Viv. "This is a good story but I have to give him an answer. He wants a guarantee we won't strike back right away at Vavolizza. I think we should give it to him."

Viv nodded. Bazzanella rolled his eyes.

"You got it," I said to DeSens. "Not open-ended but for now. Now why don't you guys go home to your families and enjoy Christmas. Thanks, Ken."

I hung up. Bazzanella said, "You're calling him *Ken?*"

SYLVIA HAD arranged a church memorial service for Catcher. As we were standing up to go, Jimmy said, "I'm okay with this but somebody killed our brother. We have to know somebody's going to drop for that. Just tell me we're not going to forget about getting even."

There it was. I thought of political debates where finally a citizen asks that no-loophole question that forces even the slipperiest politician to give a clear answer.

I thought killing Jackie Uddone was bad strategy but I understood the ancient instinct that cried out for a violent settling of scores. It wasn't smart but it could not be double-talked away. Further, I realized that for any plan to work, the family had to trust that bloody reprisal was in the cards.

It was Viv's call but Viv said nothing. Instead he passed the buck to me. "What do you say to that, Phil?"

I said, "I think everyone wants that, Jimmy, and you'll get it. Not right away, but you'll get it."

Those words sealed the deal, forever changing my standing in the Sforza family. I was now a partner in an agreement to commit murder. Tiny steps are one way to descend into hell but you can get there with big steps too.

CHAPTER 17

Emerging from the basement we came faces-to-face with Vera, who loomed over the kitchen table surrounded by the family's women. She was massive in a red Sforza Moving & Storage sweatshirt. Her hair was a mess and the desolation on her face was so extreme I wanted to turn away. It was the first time I'd seen her without her glitzy makeup and she seemed nakedly revealed, a heavy, haggard, ordinary woman having the worst day of her life.

The supportive women and a pill she'd been given had drained the explosiveness out of her but the sight of us brought it roaring back. She rose to her feet and wailed, "Kill them! Kill them! They killed my husband. Are you going to kill them for this?"

The women tried to pull her back into her chair but she was fighting now, breaking away. The killers were cocksuckers, she cried. The brothers should be sent to kill them now. And take Vico. Find Niccolò Vavolizza and carve him up like a turkey. Carve out his eyes. Cut off his balls.

Viv whispered to George and the brothers stepped forward to ease her forcefully back into her chair where the family's women clustered around her, stroking her arms, rubbing her shoulders. It occurred to me that this scene of women consoling women after men murdered men could be replayed as soon as tonight or tomorrow.

This misery continued all day. I had little confidence that the peace I'd won in the basement could survive the emotion in the kitchen or, later, in the church where Vera's wracking sobs drowned out most of the priest's words. Afterward we brought her back to the house and put her to bed, sedated. The brothers and children went downstairs to watch TV. The neighborhood's Christmas lights glowed in the evening darkness.

When I came in Paola was waiting to tell me Viv wanted to see me in the den. He was sitting on the little couch and gestured for me to sit in Jake's chair.

"Phil," he said, "I want you to reconsider Jake's offer."

THINGS HAD changed in the month since Jake made the offer. What seemed farcical then seemed inevitable and dramatically inescapable now. I'd been sucked into a leadership vacuum. The decision was not whether to take the job but whether to admit that I already had it.

When I went downstairs Sylvia was sitting alone in the living room. She read my face. "You said yes?"

I nodded. I couldn't find my voice. I felt dizzy and over-whelmed, wondering what I had done to myself.

"Let's take the dogs for a run," she said.

The dogs behave perfectly in the house but they go out the door like the running of the bulls. We got them into the SUV and, with a Roncade car following, drove to the high school where we released the dogs on the football field. They dashed off into the darkness.

"Are we going to get in trouble for letting them off the leash?" I said.

"Phil, you're a Mafia boss now. A Mafia boss doesn't worry about leash laws."

I had to laugh at that.

The metal bleachers would have been too cold to sit on but Sylvia brought a blanket.

"Where'd you leave it with Viv?"

"He told me to sleep on it and confirm my decision by eight in the morning."

"So this will be my last night sleeping with a respectable citizen?"

"I guess so. But aren't bad guys sexier? With huge sex organs?"

Now it was her turn to laugh. "I don't think so."

"Do you think this job is going to change me? Will you be sleeping with a different me?"

I meant that half-seriously but she took it full-seriously. "We'll deal with it," she said.

"Do you want me to turn it down? I'd much rather have things be right with you than have this job."

"Well, it scares me, of course. I wish I'd never gotten you into this. But I think you need to do it. And the family definitely needs you. And I don't want to hear you complaining about what-might-have-been for the rest of your life."

"Where are we sleeping tonight?"

"I think it's time for you to move into my house. The head of the family sleeps in the family house."

The night was too cold to linger. Sylvia put two fingers in her mouth and let loose with a whistle that would stop a taxi at fifty feet. It took a moment to realize she was summoning the dogs who came running at breakneck speed and then, trotting on our flanks, escorted us to the SUV.

"We're between Scylla and Charybdis," I said.

"You've been waiting to say that, haven't you?"

AT MIDNIGHT I awoke to voices and footsteps. It was Roncade's men on the stairs, changing shifts in "Carmine's balcony." I had finally met Carmine face-to-face. He was a pleasant-seeming man in his fifties, content to man his lonely post. He had a stool, a radio, a coffee machine, binoculars, an intercom, and a button that triggered a loud alarm. A rifle and a shotgun were mounted on a wall rack.

My cell rang at seven. Sylvia shouted, "Fuck Draybin."
I answered the phone laughing. It was Kitty Fromkin.
"Merry Christmas," I said.

"Yeah, well, change of plans. He's going to declare his candidacy on New Year's Day, on Cape Cod, and do a photo op on the beach. You'll be there to hear him give the remarks you're about to write. So if you had any plans for today, forget 'em."

She was talking in this brusque manner to a Mafia capo? Then she hung up on a Mafia capo.

By this time Sylvia was brushing her teeth, standing naked at the sink in the bathroom adjoining her father's bedroom. I was entranced by the sight of her long, tight body and stood watching her. Then she saw me and, with toothpaste in her mouth, said, "Pervert," and kicked the door shut.

We'd slept in her father's bedroom. Her own room, a cramped little chamber with a single bed and a treacherously slanting ceiling, was not inviting. I'd discovered that the bedrooms of the Sforza house were spare and utilitarian, even monastic. This is apparently common in Mafia homes. When they are out in public—"bouncing" among nightspots—mobsters flash their wads or "knots" of cash and pretend it is unlimited but their domestic lives are thrifty because their earnings are so brutally reduced by sharing with crime partners and outrageous mandatory kick-ups to bosses. Factor in also the costs and staggering debts incurred through reckless activities that come with their lifestyle: drinking, drugs, gambling, and (most expensive of all) mistresses.

Jake Sforza had contempt for this hedonistic behavior but he also had a wife, five children, and a long-term retirement nest egg building in Viv's Italian ventures. The bedroom he shared with his late wife was spartan. The furniture was heavy, dark, and musty. There were two small windows, a small bureau, and one small closet in which I found about ten identical black suits and a few pairs of old but well-polished black shoes. The only personal touch in the room was an enlarged black-and-white photo of his wife, the original Sylvia.

As Sylvia showered I sat down and I studied this photo with interest because of the striking resemblance between mother and daughter. Original Sylvia was wearing a summer dress, walking on a boardwalk with a boy of about five years old. This was either George or Catcher but I guessed Catcher because he looked livelier than stolid George. Original Sylvia was glancing with squinting eyes at the ocean to her left and may not have been aware of the camera. She had shoulder-length black hair and her face was rougher than my Sylvia's but what the two women had in common was that while both seemed unremarkable on first glance their impact seemed to deepen until you saw a vibrant confidence in their womanliness that emerged unexpectedly, making them beautiful and taking your breath away.

I remembered my Thanksgiving Day conversation with Uncle Tiz who compared Sylvia to a film actress (whose name he couldn't remember) who has a crazy laugh and "looks like no other woman you've ever seen." I realized he meant Julia Roberts. Neither original Sylvia or my Sylvia had the faintest *actual* resemblance to Julia Roberts, but what Tiz might have been saying was that they had Julia Roberts's ability to take you by surprise with a sunburst of personality and beauty.

Sylvia came out of the bathroom wrapped in a towel, hair wet and stringy.

"Phil, you're going to have to do something about having both jobs. Do you actually intend to jump back and forth between capo and speechwriter?"

"I have to think about it."

"I asked you about this the first night we slept together and you said you'd think about it."

"I'm a slow thinker."

"Seriously, Phil. What if it comes out that a guy running for president has a crime boss writing speeches for him? That's so crazy. The media will go berserk. It'll be a worldwide news story. It will make a joke out of Draybin. And they'll look into *your* life. And my life. Not to mention Vavolizza finding out who you are. And Vavolizza's *bosses* finding out."

"I know. You're right."

"Do you really want this job? I mean, the job with us. You're not just—what's the word . . ."

"Dabbling? Playing games? Fantasizing?"

"Yes. Are you?"

"No."

"Do you want out of it?"

"No."

"Don't do it for me. If you don't want to do it, just tell Viv."

"What would happen if I did?"

"I don't know. Viv would run back to Italy and Vavolizza would get everything he wants. There'd probably be no need for a war but it'd finish our family. And sooner or later Vavolizza would come after the Italian businesses. None of us would be safe."

"I'm not backing out."

"Then you've got to break off with Draybin."

"I know. I know. I know. I know."

"It's almost eight. Time to meet with Viv. I suggest you put on pants."

"Do I have to?"

"Maybe not right away," she said, dropping the towel.

The meeting with Viv took a minute. With his handshake I became a Mafia caporegime. Then I had breakfast and wrote a draft of Draybin's remarks declaring for president of the United States.

CHAPTER **18**

"**H**ow the hell do you write such great shit?"

Draybin was in flattery mode when he called two days later. I was at the wheel of the red Cadillac, driving home with Sylvia from Catcher's funeral.

"This is so perfect, Phil. Even Fromkin didn't pee on it."

God had given me the talent to write "great shit." I'm not ungrateful but it's not precisely the talent I would have chosen.

Sylvia, in black, was slumped against the door on the passenger side with a hand over her eyes. She had held herself together until we stood by the grave. Then the tears came and when Sylvia's tears came, everyone's tears came. It was a bitterly cold and rainy day and we'd huddled under large umbrellas and clutched each other, and as we trudged out of the cemetery everyone had the same thought: burying two family members in two weeks is much too cruel. We have to stop meeting like this.

"Pete, it's great to hear such elegant praise."

"Is it too short? Can I declare my candidacy in only three pages?"

"The Gettysburg Address was short."

"Yeah, but I'm up to here with everyone's goddamned memos and suggestions. How about coming up to the Cape on Thursday in case I need your help. Tindall and Kitty and some others are coming, plus the kids. We'll polish off the speech, then uncork the good champagne and do New Year's

Eve." As an afterthought he added, as a clever inducement, "These folks will massacre your draft if you're not here to protect it."

"Pete, I've got some personal news for you. I'm getting married."

"What? That's wonderful. You've been divorced, what, about eight, nine years?"

"Three." The events of my life barely registered with him. That's how it is with stars.

"Ginger will be delighted. Who's the lucky girl?"

"She's a dispatcher for a moving company."

Not what he would have guessed. "A moving company?"

"Yeah. Sforza Moving & Storage in White Plains. You should hire them when you move to the White House. I promise they won't break your china."

Sylvia was starting to laugh through her tears.

I knew the image of Sylvia that now filled Draybin's mental screen: a broad-shouldered mama in overalls who could carry a piano up a staircase.

"How about if I bring her up to the Cape?"

Sylvia punched me in the shoulder. There were two, maybe three long beats before Draybin answered. "Sure, we'd love to meet her. Of course this'll be a working weekend, not a whole lot of fun."

He'd just told me we were going to uncork the premium bubbly and party in the New Year. Maybe he was reluctant to let the celebration of my engagement intrude on the celebration of his candidacy. I didn't care; I wasn't letting go. "I think she'd enjoy seeing us in action and she could use the getaway. She had a recent death in the family."

That did it. "Okay, bring her," he said. "Get here before sunset."

We drove along in silence for a moment. At a traffic light I glanced over at her. She was wet-cheeked but smiling broadly, the smile that always sends a wave of warmth circuiting through me.

"You're out of control," she said.

"You'll enjoy this," I said. "I won't but you will."

"What do people wear in Cape Cod?"

"I'd say jeans and heavy sweaters. The idea is to look like an upscale person's version of downscale people."

A surprise was waiting at the Sforza house. The mourners coming from the cemetery had forced off their gloom and gathered around the dining room table for a combined farewell to Viv and Paola and a toast to me as the family's new boss. Later, after Viv and Paola had left for the airport (before departing Viv hugged me and whispered, "I owe you a very great favor"), Ron Taubman took me aside and said, "Mr. Green has arrived."

"Who's Mr. Green?"

"Come on, I'll introduce you." I followed him up the stairs to Jake's den, where a small brown suitcase was sitting on Jake's chair. I opened it and understood about Mr. Green. It was packed with cash.

"It's the signing bonus Jake promised you. A quarter million in small bills laundered better than your shorts. Remember to stash it where the feds can't find it. Good luck, Skipper. *Mazel tov.*"

I stood there looking at the cash. I said to myself, this is not honest money. The moment I touch this money I'm tainted and maybe prosecutable.

Then I touched it and felt the thrill of an ill-gotten windfall, an undeserved and unreported capital gain. I may have thought of myself as above a seduction like this, but I wasn't. My lifelong clean slate was no longer clean. I had switched sides. I was a criminal.

WHAT A kick to speed along the New England highways on a crisp winter's day, driving a Cadillac the size of a nuclear submarine, blasting music, catching the admiring or disdainful eyes of other motorists, basking in the presence of a smiling and happy damsel, having a presidential campaign to think about and my own Mafia crew to lead. No one in history had achieved this combination of pleasures.

When we pulled into Draybin's driveway he heard the gravel crunching under our tires and came striding out to greet us. He was wearing one of his always-perfect country gentleman outfits. He'd gotten some rest, lost a few pounds, and his hair, normally more white than blond, now seemed more blond than white. He did a double-take at the Cadillac, not a vehicle you see in his part of Cape Cod.

"I never would have figured you for this car," he said, laughing. "Didn't we used to call them *boats?*"

He opened the passenger-side door for Sylvia and as she emerged he lit up with enough electricity to provide light and power for all of Massachusetts. It was only one second before he got himself under control but in that second he looked her up and down with unconcealable lust. I'd never seen Pete do this. Sylvia, modestly dressed in dark slacks and a green ski sweater, was as stunned as I was.

"Pete, meet Sylvia Sforza."

Smiling and offering her hand she said, in a shamelessly perfect suck-up line, "You're the first future president I ever met."

Draybin breathed it in like the sweetest air on the planet. But he had recovered his poise. "How about some hot chocolate?" he said. "Ginger's gone to her workout. Leon's grabbing his nap. The others are arriving later."

A half hour later we'd toured the house, stood on the enclosed deck gazing out at the view while sipping hot chocolate, and welcomed Ginger's return. Then the four of us climbed down the steep slope for a walk on the beach. Pete showed us where tomorrow's photo op beach walk would take place, following his brief announcement of his candidacy in a tiny park designed around the town's memorial to its war dead.

We started out walking four abreast but before I knew it our formation became mixed doubles, with Pete and Sylvia paired off and leading the way.

"Look at him, eternally young," Ginger said to me. "He sees a lovely woman and the magnets come on. His and theirs."

"Will I be able to get her back?" I asked.

"Don't worry, he's just playing. He's also testing his vote-getting skills. Denny Rudd's saying his early strength will be with women, especially middle-class women who like him because he seems like the perfect husband—handsome, smart, nice, rich as hell. Later on he'll start looking good to male voters who'll like him because he's a stud athlete and superstar businessman."

I asked her if all those things were true. She said, "Yeah, they're true."

"How do you and Leon feel about campaigning?"

"We'll be fine. We're good soldiers. I was hoping to relax but this is what he wants and you can't argue with ambition. But tell me about Sylvia."

"I met her on a train six weeks ago. We have very little in common and I've got twenty years on her but for some reason it works."

"It's all about timing, isn't it? Look at her: it's the prime of her life, she's beautiful, glowing. I met her ten minutes ago and already she feels like a lifelong friend. I think you came into each other's lives at just the right moment. Age doesn't matter."

Darkness was coming on fast and when we turned around we could see people waving to us from the Draybins' upper deck, the outdoor deck.

"They're here, Pete," called Ginger.

Three people: small, medium, and large. Kitty-the-F was the small, Tindall the medium, and I didn't know the large.

"The third guy is Denny Rudd, the pollster. Smart guy. Knows everything."

Back in the house I reclaimed possession of Sylvia. As Pete greeted the newcomers she said to me, "This guy's a charmer. I bet he can win."

Then her voice dropped: "But he's hollow at the core, Phil."

"What? Where do you get that?"

"First, he didn't stand up for you at that meeting, which I don't forgive. Second, he just acted like a puppy on the beach, flirting with another man's woman in front of his own wife, which can get you a bullet in my world. Third, I know it because I know it."

Deep down I knew she was right, though I resented her being right so fast. It had taken fifteen years for my doubts about Pete to bubble to the surface, or almost the surface, but she'd nailed him in a matter of minutes.

"I can see you're upset, but you shouldn't be," she said. "I'm just telling you that you're a better man than he is."

Add this to the greatest moments in my life list.

We shook hands with Denny, Dick, and Kitty. They all seemed surprised and even fascinated by Sylvia. She was something these hotshots seldom see: the real thing.

Ginger had to do additional grocery shopping and took Sylvia with her. I found our cozy little bedroom, carried in our suitcase, took a shower, and sprawled on the bed. Wasn't it nice to be having New Year's Eve on Cape Cod in an atmosphere of high purpose, even if I was about to abandon this purpose? I wondered how I'd feel watching Pete give an inaugural address written by someone else.

WITH THE start of Draybin's campaign so close I was braced for an intense evening but things were remarkably relaxed. The plan for tomorrow—Pete's six-minute speech in town followed by his beach walk with his family—was simple and all the arrangements were in place.

When I sat down Pete brought up my draft of his remarks. He said he'd gone over to the park early this morning and practiced reading them aloud. Smart speakers do things like this. He said he'd decided to make no changes—the ultimate compliment to the writer.

Rudd said, "I think the remarks are fine. The autobiographical stuff is all-American. I like the enthusiasm/positivism/ and business approach to problem-solving, which appeals to pragmatism over partisanship, because everyone hates partisanship even though everyone is partisan. The speech is aspirational without being celestial. The beach walk B-roll echoes JFK. Patriotism, beautiful family, ex-jock, high-achieving CEO. I think that's a damn good package to open with."

"It leverages all the Draybin brand points," said Tindall.

"Unless you want to know what he actually stands for," said Kitty.

"We'll get to that with the vision speech at the Waldorf," Tindall said. "That's where we roll out the substance."

No one had mentioned anything to me about rolling out the substance. I was alarmed to learn that this Waldorf event was just eight days away, with Pete's speech as the centerpiece for a gala fund-raiser where 1,300 public-spirited rich people would be flown in from all over the nation to hear him speak, interrupt with applause many times, and write big checks to his campaign.

I said, "Can I ask about this Waldorf speech, because this is the first I've heard of it. I'm nervous, to say the least, about getting it written and polished in just a week, especially considering that everyone will want to contribute thoughts and ideas." I meant *meddle*.

"Rest easy, Phil," said Tindall. "We've got a clear line-of-sight on it. Kitty just has to integrate a few more inputs and we're done. When do we see a first draft, Kit?"

"Tomorrow," she said, carefully avoiding eye contact with me.

Almost done? And I'd never even heard about it? Where was I while she was integrating the fucking inputs? The answer was: *not in the loop*. Just as I was appreciating Draybin for blocking any tinkering with the draft for tomorrow, I now had to take another punch, a flagrant violation of the rule that says when you're being pushed out of your job you should at least be told about it.

Apparently this realization of another betrayal registered on my face and everyone saw it, understood it, and felt a natural impulse to move away from me swiftly to avoid catching loser disease. Suddenly people were on their feet and hurrying off to freshen up before Pete started cooking on the outdoor grill.

My FAVORITE moment of the evening came when Ginger and Sylvia returned from shopping with Ginger wearing a red Sforza Moving & Storage sweatshirt. It was a funny and good-natured gift from Sylvia and Ginger wore it in that spirit.

Then it hit me that it would be catastrophic for the wife of a presidential candidate to be photographed wearing what amounted to the colors of a Mafia family. I whispered this to Sylvia; somehow she was not accustomed to assessing the media impact of her smallest acts but caught on quickly and was horrified that her innocent gift could have damaging consequences. Her solution was to take Ginger aside and tell her that, on second thought, the sweatshirt wasn't such a great idea because of a vaguely described local lawsuit. That was enough for Ginger, who vanished briefly and returned in a blue blouse. We later found the sweatshirt folded neatly on our bed.

Aside from that awkward incident it was a good party. The food and wine were abundant. Draybin was at his best as chef and master host. Denny Rudd entertained with political stories. Leon jumped in with wisecracks. Even Tindall was funny. Kitty Fromkin curled up in an easy chair and poked away at her laptop, working on the Waldorf speech. I took her a glass of wine as a friendly gesture. She thanked me but didn't touch it.

Around ten the Draybin children and grandchildren arrived en masse and the evening turned into a noisy family affair. They were a dazzling family, bright and beautiful.

At midnight, with the TV blaring "Auld Lang Syne," champagne corks popped and there was a lot of kissing and wishing each other well in the momentous New Year. From somewhere out in the blackness we could hear the whiz and thud of fireworks rising into the sky, exploding colorfully, and reflecting on the water.

At the same moment, about 250 miles away, four men with submachine guns emerged from two cars that had turned into the Sycamore Court cul-de-sac. Standing side-by-side they opened fire at the Sforza house, where the family and its guests had gathered to celebrate the end of a painful year.

CHAPTER 19

The attackers were wrong if they thought their gunfire would be mistaken for—or masked by—New Year's Eve fireworks. They were also mistaken if they thought Richie Roncade's security force would be inattentive at the stroke of twelve. Roncade's man on Carmine's balcony set off the house alarm and returned fire immediately, as did the rest of Roncade's security force. One of the attackers was hit. His cry was audible above the firefight engulfing Sycamore Court.

Reacting quickly to the deafening alarm, party guests dived to the living room floor. The bullets went over their heads, chewing holes in the wall and splitting the Christmas tree in half. No one was hit, but Roncade's wife, Pauline, and young Amanda were injured by flying glass. Every street-facing window of the Sforza house was shattered. Bullets splintered Carmine's balcony; the Roncade man on duty there retreated when it appeared that one of the shooters had been assigned to fire exclusively at him.

Inside the Sforza house the first to respond was the sixty-seven-year-old Uncle Kim who, shouting orders in Korean, threw open the door to let the dogs out and followed at a run. The dogs responded as if they had spent their lives waiting for this moment, sprinting headlong into the attackers' fire. They blended into the darkness and were nearly invisible, approaching the attackers in low, fast strides.

The attackers ceased firing and turned to flee but one stumbled and the dogs overtook him. They brought him down hard on the pavement and went at him savagely until Kim, who'd been hit in the hand by a ricocheting bullet, arrived and sharply ordered them off. The man was screaming. Kim silenced him with a kick to the temple.

The other attackers, dragging the one who'd been shot, reached their cars in a panic and escaped with squealing rubber. By this time the Sforza brothers had reached the shooter who'd been knocked senseless by Kim. They picked him up and carried him to the house.

With the firing stopped the street went silent, though police sirens filled the night. Terrified neighbors peeked between their curtains and then crept out cautiously to assess the scene of brief but spectacular mayhem outside their homes. Many ambulances arrived; Pauline, Amanda, and Kim, all walking without assistance, were taken off to the hospital.

I collected these details in a series of calls, the first coming from George Sforza about ten minutes after midnight. I'd stepped out onto the open deck to take the call. I could see the concern on Sylvia's face but she kept her cool, chatting with Draybin and Ginger. As soon as I understood what had happened and that there were no life-threatening injuries to our people I motioned to her to come out and join me on the deck.

I told her what had happened while still listening to George's report. "George says everyone is shook up but they'll be okay. The injuries don't look bad."

I asked George if the cops were there yet.

"They're pulling up outside."

"I want everybody to cooperate. We're the innocent victims in this story. Understand that, George?"

"Okay, I'll get the word around. I gotta get off."

"Is Roncade there?"

"He went over to the hospital with Pauline and the others. He'll call as soon as he can. Tommy and Pam are with Amanda."

I handed Sylvia the phone; George's ex-wife Maria came on to talk to her.

"Ask if Vera's there," I said. It was all Vera needed, to be shot at and have her kids shot at.

No—Vera stayed home and took a sleeping pill but her boys were at the Sforza house, unhurt but frightened.

At this moment Draybin came out onto the deck. "What's up, Phil? Is something wrong?" Inside the partying had paused as everyone waited to be told what was happening.

"Sylvia's cousin had a stroke," I blurted. "It's a very close Italian family and everyone goes into a frenzy when something happens. The stroke appears to be minor. She's had several of them."

Draybin and I went back inside and explained. My assurances about Sylvia's cousin seemed to get things moving again. I drifted back out to the deck.

Sylvia handed me the phone. Jimmy came on. "You should see this house, Phil. Looks like a bomb exploded. Sister's gonna freak when she sees this."

"Try to clean it up before we get home," I said. "Tell me about this guy you caught."

"We got him in the basement."

"Do you know who he is?"

"I don't know him."

"Take out his wallet. Get it off his ID or credit cards."

"Skipper, mob guys don't carry wallets. Just cash. And if they have credit cards, they're stolen so you're not going to get a real name. But Bazzanella's down there with him now so he'll find out who he is. Or we could have Vico give him a haircut."

"No. None of that."

"We won't need it anyway. We can scare him enough with the dogs. You should have seen those dogs haul ass down the street."

"As soon as you know who he is, give him to the cops."

"His piece too?"

"His piece? You mean his gun? You got his gun?"

"Sure. It was lying there in the street. An old Uzi. My father would have stuck that gun barrel down the fucker's throat and blown his head off."

"And then he would have been arrested for murder. This is better, Jimmy. We get rid of the guy and we're not guilty of anything."

"I guess so. Here's the fat man."

Bazzanella came on. "Hey, Skip. I know this guy. Stevie Leccisi. He's been around a long time. Too old for this kind of thing. He's from Uddone's crew."

"Uddone's crew? I just told Jimmy to give him to the cops as a gesture of cooperation. Cancel that. He's a bargaining chip. Hide him somewhere, okay?"

"You got it."

"And see what you can get from him."

"I'm not gonna get much from him right now. He's kind of fucked up."

"What do you mean?"

"Well, first the dogs got him, then Kim kicked a field goal with his head, and then he accidentally fell down the basement stairs. In fact—" Bazzanella chuckled, "he accidentally fell down the stairs twice."

"Is he conscious?"

"More or less. He don't like Dobermans."

"Put him in a closet or something. Get the dogs off him. Are the cops in the house yet?"

"They're just coming in."

"Is Pelikan there yet?"

"I don't see him."

"Call me later."

"You got it, Boss."

I disconnected. Sylvia and I stood in the darkness.

"It could have been a lot worse," I said.

"What did you tell these people?" she asked, meaning the Draybin group.

"I said your cousin had a stroke."

"My cousin had a stroke? Where the hell did that come from?"

"It just came out of my mouth. Name a cousin. Female."

"Tessa?"

"Yeah, Tessa. Another stroke for poor Tessa."

"You have unsuspected talent, Phil."

My phone vibrated. Sylvia went inside to spread the lie about Tessa. The call was from Richie.

"How's Pauline?"

"She got a heavy piece of glass on the back of her head but it's not serious. Amanda had superficial cuts on her arms and back. Seven-year-old girl gets hit like that—that's out of bounds, Boss. You know the Italians don't usually hit people's families."

"Bazz says the guy you caught is from the Uddone crew."

"Really? Man, these guys are so stupid. They should have used people from any other crew but they use Uddone's."

"Do you think Uddone himself was there?"

"No. Bosses don't go out on these things."

"Richie, the thing I have to know is, is this a warning or the start of a war? They killed Catcher and shot up the house. That sounds like the war is on but we have to know for sure."

"Want to know how I see it? I'm guessing they killed Catcher so the Sforzas no longer had a designated successor, which would clear the way for Uddone. Step two was shooting up the house and maybe killing a few more people as a terror tactic. They're hoping we cave in and accept Uddone without a full-scale war. It's also Vavolizza showing his balls."

"I want a meeting with Vavolizza. Tell the fat man to set it up. Have him tell Vavolizza I'll give him Stevie Leccisi as a token of goodwill."

"He don't give a shit about Leccisi. Leccisi fucked up by getting shot. He's damaged goods anyway. Worthless to Vavolizza."

"He's not worthless in terms of the damage he can do. Look, he fired on a residential home with a machine gun. A housewife and a seven-year-old girl and a Korean-American senior citizen are hurt. We've got his piece. He's a known Mafioso. It's a slam dunk for the DA. Leccisi's going to jail for a thousand years. And when he's looking at that thousand-year sentence, he's gonna rat on everybody. Am I right about this? So Vavolizza should be thrilled to get him back."

"Yeah, and he'll waste him a minute later."

"Get the meeting."

"They call it a sit-down."

"Whatever they call it."

"Okay, Boss. What are you going to say to him?"

"Do I have to run it by you, Richie?"

"No, no. You're the boss. You don't have to tell me nothing."

"Talk later," I said, disconnecting.

SYLVIA AND I went back into the party but after briefly embellishing the lie about Tessa's medical history I announced that it was time for us to head to bed, since we'd have to rise early for the drive to Tessa's bedside. We would regret missing Draybin's historic announcement but would be watching the TV coverage. We said good-byes and good nights and went to our bedroom where we spent more time on our cells.

We rose at five thirty, hoping everyone would be asleep so we could sneak out without further socializing. But Draybin and Ginger had risen early to see us off. Draybin was making us bacon and eggs. When a man who is hours away from declaring for the presidency is up before dawn standing in his kitchen in a bathrobe making breakfast for me, I'm tempted to remove his name from my shit list.

Just as we were sitting down Leon came in, dropped down on the living room floor, and started doing pushups and sit-ups.

"Pete, let me ask you something," I said, making conversation but also looking for leadership insight I could apply to the Sforzas. "I was thinking about this when I was drafting your remarks. Politicians running for office always talk about change but aren't there times when it's better if things *don't* change, when keeping the status quo is better than gambling on something new? What do you do then?"

"I thought about that every day when I was CEO. For the most part, the company was in great shape. You wanted to spray it with something that would freeze it that way forever. But that's a fatal error because there's no defense against change. Everybody who fights change ends up losing."

"But what if you finally get something perfectly right?"

"You have to change it anyway because it won't be right for long. Shuffle the deck and deal yourself new cards. Try to be the master of change instead of the poor doofus change happens to. You've written this stuff many times, Phil. Isn't it a rule that every CEO speech has to say that 'Change is the only constant' and therefore we have to 'embrace change'?"

"I may have heard that once or twice."

"Yeah, it sounds deep. But it's true. In fact it's why I decided to run for president. My retirement wasn't working. It had to change."

Leon called out, "Feeling in a rut? Run for president."

"You have to find a pain-in-the-butt like Leon who keeps sticking in the needle about what you're doing and where you're going. What's your objective? What's the most dramatic way to refresh your strategy?"

"That'll be $300," Leon shouted, in the midst of sit-ups. "Pay the receptionist on your way out."

I pushed on. "You also have to talk your people into change. Maybe changing from something they like to something they hate or fear."

"That's right. You know what they call it? *Leadership.* See the need to change before everyone else and get them to follow you. Define the new reality. And here's a big point: sooner is much better than later. Sooner means you stay ahead of everybody. Later means you play catch-up and most of your moves are blocked by then."

"If it ain't broke, throw it out anyway," shouted Leon.

Kitty walked in, yawning and waving good morning as she headed for the coffee.

"We should get going, Phil," said Sylvia.

HALFWAY INTO the first hour on the road Sylvia said, "You were actually milking the next president for free advice."

"Yes. And while I'm at it, how about some free advice from you?"

She went quiet and pondered, and while she pondered, so did I. Talking to Draybin made me realize that my corporate experience might be an asset that would compensate for my lack of crime experience. Instead of playing by mob rules, which I didn't know, I needed to bring something over from corporate thinking and use it as a transforming innovation. I also needed to transform *myself.* I could never pass for a traditional godfather but I might be able to pass for a mob executive. What I needed was strategic perspective. I'd spent hours sitting across the desk from Draybin and other top executives, trying to get in step with the thoughts that guided and stimulated them. I'd gotten through all the bewildering PowerPoints and the jargon and acronyms and all the military and football metaphors. I believed that much of it was bullshit *but not all of it*—somewhere amid the chaff was some of the best strategic thinking in the world.

Sylvia said, "I try to think of what my father would do. I wish we'd asked him."

Yes. Somehow I had to emulate Jake Sforza. Ron Taubman said Jake was a natural CEO and he was right. He transformed the primitive and insular unit of a crime crew into a sophisticated, autonomous organization. He deemphasized the risky impulses of traditional crime mentality and substituted his own version of long-term value creation. He prized ideas and intelligence gathering. And he overcame incredible resistance, not just stubborn preference for the old ways but a shooting war against his family.

THE DRIVE from the Cape to White Plains took about five hours. We arrived around noon, shocked by the scene on Sycamore Court.

TV news trucks were parked in front of the house. Reporters had undoubtedly been on the air all morning with breathless accounts of the midnight gunfight. Police barriers blocked the street. Sylvia had to show ID proving she was a Sforza to get us through.

In the living room bullets had stitched patterns across the wall, taking out large chunks of plaster and destroying two paintings of Venetian scenes (which I had barely noticed). The house was cold because the windows were gone; workmen were filling the window space with plywood. Cleaners were using industrial-strength vacuums to pick up debris. I was surprised to learn that the cleaners were employed by a small company George and Maria created during their marriage and still operated together.

Police technicians were in every room. Roncade, suspecting that they were using their access to plant listening devices, had men standing over the shoulders of each police technician. The Sforza IT and cyber specialist, a gangly redhead named Hiram Tack, stood by to do an electronics sweep when they left. Tack, I learned, had been a "contract hacker" for the National Security Agency. Friends in the military led him to Richie Roncade who led him to Jake.

Most of the family was drinking coffee in the kitchen.

I whispered to Tommy, "Is the guy in the basement?"

"Yeah, in the closet, like you said."

"The dogs are down there?"

"Right outside the closet door."

Sylvia and I sat down and listened. Now that the shock of the attack was subsiding, serious anger was kicking in. I had to put something into motion before the pot boiled over.

CHAPTER **20**

Bazzanella pulled me aside and said, "I got you a sit-down. Tomorrow night."

I was full of questions but he shushed me with a finger over his lips. We couldn't talk in a house swarming with people.

"Let's take a ride," he said. "I borrowed the keys to George's van."

He led me out the back door and we got into the van owned by George's cleanup company. The smell of cleaning fluids gave me six different headaches.

Bazzanella squeezed in behind the wheel and we shot out of the driveway, causing people including a cop and some TV reporters to jump aside. Bazzanella hit the pedal and we were off down Sycamore Court, weaving through an obstacle course of barriers, parked cars, and gawkers milling around hoping to see real mobsters.

"Don't say nothing in the truck," he said. "I got a good spot to talk."

It was a pleasure to tune out for a few minutes. I paid no attention to where we were going, though things got less residential. We turned into a vast parking lot and got out of the van walking toward a cluster of brick buildings I recognized as the state university, SUNY Purchase.

"Are we going to take a class?"

"Follow me." The fat man was light-footed and seemed more at ease than usual.

"I grew up around here," he said. "I used to bring girls over and throw 'em a fuck in this parking lot. My current size, I'd need a flat-bed truck for that. We also took off some good wife cars here."

"What do you mean?"

"We boosted cars. Rich wives would come over to go to the museum in their luxury cars. We'd glom the cars and run 'em down to a chop shop in the Bronx."

"You did this when you were in high school?"

"More like junior high school."

We arrived at the art museum but the door was locked. "Fuck," he said, "I forgot it was a holiday."

"Too bad," I said. "I was in the mood for some art."

"They got good stuff," he said, not realizing I was teasing him. "Terrific African shit. Let's take one of these benches."

The afternoon light was fading. We chose the only bench that was still in the sun.

"I was gonna take you into the café. Sometimes I bring my reports here. Museums are good because you're not going to bump into wise guys. Down in the city I use the Guggenheim and the Frick."

"What do you mean by reports?"

"The people who report to me. Direct reports. Isn't that a corporate word?"

"It is," I laughed. "Who are these people and what do they report about?"

"The reports are usually civilians. I got politicians and bureaucrats, I got union guys, I got cops, I got a couple newspaper writers. They need to talk somewhere quiet. Wise guys I don't bring here. The stuff I get from them is from hanging around the bars, pizza joints, luncheonettes, and so on, picking up shoptalk.

"Mostly my wise guys are around middle level but I got a few higher-ups and I got young guys who feed me stuff because they like to show off how much they know. Of course pissed-off guys are the best. Also the ones who are into the shys—shylocks. If they get too jammed up they got a life-threatening problem because no boss trusts a guy who's shaky for cash. So I help them out if they're willing to tell me things. It can get expensive but it's worth it."

"Their bosses would kill them if they knew this was going on, right?"

He made a dismissive gesture and said, "These guys are not loaded with good judgment or integrity."

"So you're basically a spy, right? Why do you do it?"

"Because Jake told me to. He calls me in—this is years ago—and says, 'Paul, we should have our own little CIA and you're it.' He says, 'You're an outgoing guy and you know the goodfellas in all the families. Take your time and see if they'll take a few bucks just to shoot the shit and tell you what they're hearing. Build a network. Don't show too much curiosity but hang in there and pick up a lot of tabs.'

"Picking up tabs is important because wise guys get talkative when they're getting something free. Another thing, mob guys spend most of their time hanging around bullshitting. A lot of them gossip like teenage girls. I could tell you—true story—about a very high-up guy back in the day who would have Sunday meetings with the big boss himself, Castellano. Then he'd go home and sit in his kitchen dinette and spend the day on the phone having chatterbox conversations with half the Cosa Nostra, telling them everything the big guy said, including really major shit. The FBI figured it out and got a bug into the dinette."

"So there's a code of silence but everyone likes to talk?"

"If they trust you. These guys know me since we were kids so they think I'm okay. I'm a made man so I can stick my beak into conversations other people can't get into. And every now and then I slip a guy a beaner."

"A beaner?"

"A C-note. A hundred dollar bill. People love the beaner. It's just the right amount."

"They're not suspicious?"

"They're suspicious of everything, but for only a hundred what the fuck. Maybe they think I got something going on the side, some small thing for myself, but it never comes back at them so they're okay with it. So what happens is over the years they get more comfortable telling me stuff and after a while I have my own data base of who did which jobs and who knocked off who and what the take was and who the inside guy was and so on, like Jake wanted."

"You're into all five families? You've got information on everybody? Going back how far?"

"About thirteen years. And I'll tell you this, whenever Nicky V. had a beef with Jake, Jake was way ahead of him because he knew the lay of the land going in."

"You must have an incredible amount of information."

"Oh yeah, more and better than what the FBI has. They got informants but nobody likes telling the FBI anything and nobody gives them anything extra. They always hold back a little. I talk to made guys every day and these guys *like* to tell me their tales. I even get sex stuff, like who's putting it to who and the rumors and so forth. This all goes into the notebooks. Another great source is women. I got a couple of *gumaras* and ex-*gumaras*—mistresses of mob guys. They call 'em parakeets. Chirp, chirp, chirp. Get 'em talking and you can't shut 'em up. I got some guys' wives who want a little extra cash from what they get from their cheap bastard husbands. They hear stuff, they don't think it hurts nobody to tell me. They don't give a shit about *omertà*. They know I love a good story. It's like, 'Hey Paulie, have I got a good one for you!'"

His eyes glittered. Bazzanella was proud of the work he'd done for Jake and the responsibility that Jake had given him.

"I mean, it's not like we can listen in on what Nicky V. is saying, though Hiram Tack's put in some bugs here and there. We had a bug in Nicky's car for a while but he was careful in the car as most wise guys are so we took it out before it got found. But the best stuff I get is word of mouth. You'll be getting my reports."

"You mean written reports?"

"Oh no, once or twice a month we'll sit down face-to-face. But I've got it all on paper for myself because there's too much to remember without writing it down."

"You've got thirteen years of this stuff *written down*? Did Jake know that?"

"Jake ordered me to do it. Keep a good record. Every now and then he'd make me show it to him to make sure I was still keeping up. He'd give me pointers, telling me just what he wanted in it, what facts to get in and things of that nature."

"Why did he want it written down? That seems dangerous."

"He said it would come in handy sometime. That's all he said."

"You mentioned notebooks. Is that where you write it down?"

"Yeah. Jake's rule was it had to be handwritten, not on the computer like Nicky does it."

"Nicky takes notes *on a computer*? That's insane."

"Worse than insane. He takes notes because he's got twenty-four crews reporting to him and he can't keep it all in his head like the old guys could or like Jake could. Maybe it's all the Chivas Regal flowing around his brain. He holds capo meetings at midnight in his basement and sits there pecking away on his Mac. He likes to show off how tech savvy he is. He shops on the Internet. Sometimes he makes his guys sit around watching Internet porn with him. I don't think he texts but he sends e-mails, which is even stupider than taking notes, although he uses his wife's account."

"How do the other guys feel about this? It's such a security risk."

"Well, it makes everybody nervous and we're nervous to begin with. The old guys like Carlo Gambino didn't even own a telephone. But you say anything about it to Nicky and he explodes on you, which could be life threatening. He says he's got passwords and firewalls and so on. He hired some kid to install an encryption program, which he thinks is safe. I'm sure Hiram Tack could get into it. Hiram hacked into Chinese and

Russian shit with the NSA. Jake said, 'Nobody can hack into old-fashioned notebooks so that's what you keep.'"

"But what if someone finds the notebooks? Where do you keep them?"

Bazzanella looked around nervously. "This is my biggest secret. Nobody knows but me. But you're the boss so I'll tell you if you want to know."

"Just a hint."

"Okay. Let's say they're in a boat and the boat's in a boat-yard somewhere and somebody else's name is on it. The boat's out of the water and lifted up on a thing, a cradle, so you need a ladder to get into it. It's an old shitbucket so nobody's looking to rob stuff out of it. I got a steel safe welded under the deck in the cabin. About once a week I drive up, smoke a cigar, and write a few new pages. It's kind of my hobby."

His labor of love. His posterity. His secret trust from Jake.

"How many pages?"

"I got 1,563 pages. Takes up three fat loose-leafs."

"Who knows about this?"

"Ron Taubman knows, because he needs to know what the other crews are earning so we can top it. Richie knows. Jake knew, of course. Now you."

"The brothers don't know? Sylvia doesn't know? Does Viv know?"

"None of the above. They know I got a network but they don't know how it works. But here's something you should understand, Skip. Guys are fairly careful *before* a score or something, but they'll blab afterwards. So my advance infor-mation is only so-so."

"So tell me about this sit-down with Nicky."

"Okay, but it's not with Nicky."

"It's not? So who's it with?"

"Rat-face."

"Jackie Uddone?"

"Skip, there's rules to this. First, they didn't know you even existed until I told them last night. They thought Viv was still here. And they don't accept that Viv was a righteous capo because they say *they* name the capo, not us. So I told them Viv's gone, this guy Phil's our capo now. They say, 'You're telling us we got a crew being run by a guy named Phil who's not even made? Who's not even Italian? Who's just some civilian Sylvia met at a singles bar or something? Are you fucking kidding me?' And I said, 'Yeah, we got a boss named Phil and we also got the firepower to blow your ass to kingdom-fucking-come so let's have a sit-down.'"

"So then what?"

"They say maybe we can do something but not with Nicky. Nicky's too high up. Maybe Jackie. So we got Jackie. You'd have been better off with Nicky. Nicky's stable compared to Jackie."

"What's the Jackie story?"

"He isn't a guy you like to schmooze with. Partly the rat look but also you'll be talking to him and he'll be saying kind of nonsensical stuff and suddenly he'd show you some Charles Manson thing in the eyes that nobody was too comfortable with. He was never especially good at anything *except* wet jobs, always with the knife. They say he killed more people than lung cancer. But then he got ambition."

"Doesn't sound like he's exactly cut out for a leadership position."

"No, but he's loyal to Nicky and he bugged Nicky night and day until Nicky finally threw him a bone and made him a capo of his worst crew in the Bronx."

"Do I have any chance of a useful conversation with this guy?"

Bazzanella laughed. "The only predictable thing is he wants to be boss of the Sforza crew because that's a very big step up the prestige ladder. Which means you're in his way. But he doesn't have the final say on anything. He'll take whatever you say to Nicky and Nicky will decide. Another possibility is he kills you."

"*Kills me?*"

CHAPTER 21

Jake assured me I'd be safe. Roncade told me bosses didn't put themselves in physical jeopardy. Getting killed by Jackie Uddone had never entered my mind.

"Hey, Boss, don't worry about it. It's not likely. I mean, he knows we'd kill him for it. That'd be automatic and he couldn't avoid it. But if Nicky tells him to do it, that's something else. We gotta worry about it because it makes sense. Catcher's dead, Jake's dead, Viv's gone. If you're gone too we got no more leaders on the bench. They win."

"Can you kill somebody at a sit-down? Isn't that a violation of the sacred rules of the brotherhood?"

"It's not cool but what if he just says you tried to kill him and it was self-defense. So some guy named Phil is dead. Who gives a shit? The big guys might accept that."

"How would he do it?"

"How? He pulls out his switchblade knife and sticks it in your heart."

"No, I mean how would he set up the attack?"

"I don't know. All he has to do is get in stabbing range. The best way is to kill you when your back's turned."

"There's another honor code violation."

"Forget honor. Richie says the camel jockeys in Iraq got more honor than the Mafia."

"Do I have any protection at all?"

"You mean is Richie sitting next to you with an AK-47? No."

"So let me sum up, Paul. I have a sit-down with this guy who's too crazy to talk to but might have orders to kill me, which we have no way to prevent. Is that it?"

"You wanted a sit-down. This is the best I could do."

"What do you recommend?"

"I recommend you and Sylvia go down to the opera tomorrow night and while you're watching the fat lady sing, Richie cleans up the vermin problem. We call it pay-back for Catcher and shooting up the house. I mean, why take a chance with this fuck?"

Because the point of the sit-down is to get something done, not just to kill the other guy. Because I have an ego and think I can win my way, without playing their usual Neanderthal game. Because, even though I don't have much of a strategy, I think I can outwit this little rodent Jackie Uddone and save the day for the good guys.

"Where do we sit down for this sit-down?"

"At eight o'clock tomorrow night we pull up outside the Department of Motor Vehicles office in Yonkers. You get out of our car and into their car."

"And then you follow their car?"

"We'll follow but they'll shake us."

"Where will they take me?"

"I'd guess a restaurant. I got their word it won't be a basement or back room."

"Can't your network find out where they're taking me?"

"We're trying but probably not. Like I said, it's hard to get stuff *before*. I usually get it *after*."

"After my death? That's just wonderful."

"I know what you're thinking, Skip. You're thinking this is like the scene from *The Godfather* where we tape a gun behind the toilet and you walk out and shoot Jackie and then escape to Sicily and marry the *bella signorina*. The catch is, they've seen *The Godfather* too."

Pelikan had come by again while I was out with Bazzanella. I knew he'd be back. I was planning on blaming him for the attack on the house. My strategy was to keep smashing the ball back into his court. Force the cops to take the initiative instead of us.

Sylvia sat down with me to watch the evening news report on Draybin announcing his candidacy. Draybin performed beautifully.

"Is it exciting to see an important person get up and read words you've written?"

"I hate it," I said. "It's like being a parent watching your kid in the school play. You don't really hear what he's saying, you're just praying he doesn't screw up."

"This is the first time in my life that I watched national news with any sense of having any involvement with it," said Sylvia.

"We should call and congratulate him."

My mind was stuck on the meeting with Uddone. I didn't know how to talk to him or whether I'd keep my cool. Then I had an idea: I'd practice on the thug in the basement.

I went down the stairs and found Jimmy was watching television, eating popcorn. The dogs were sleeping outside the closet door. I said, "Let's play *Meet the Prisoner*."

Jimmy got up and opened the closet door. The guy was sitting in a scrunched-up position with his knees under his chin. He squinted against the room's bright light. The dogs sprang to their feet, growling.

"Stand up. Stretch your legs," I said.

"Get those fucking dogs away from me," he said in a rough voice.

Jimmy took the dogs upstairs to the kitchen and returned. The guy struggled to his feet and stood unsteadily. He was close to my age, tired, and overweight. He had a lantern jaw and a face that looked like it had been carved out of stone but with a very dull chisel. I had no doubt he'd killed people. Probably most or all of them were defenseless.

He looked me up and down, sneeringly, and said, "Who the fuck are you?"

Jimmy started forward with fists cocked but I raised a hand and Jimmy put on the brakes. One look at this guy told me nothing useful would be *said* but something useful might be *learned*. Having him in front of me was like having a specimen under glass.

He was the essence of thug and I had never had a good look at a true thug. We instinctively turn away quickly from his kind, fearing eye contact that might flare into trouble. Now I could give him a good look and what I saw was that he was nothing, what they call a "garbage can," unworthy of fearful fascination. I understood how Jake Sforza regarded men like this: they were potentially dangerous but so was an open manhole. You don't *fear* the manhole, you're just careful about not falling into it.

So I did not wither as he glowered at me, deploying the full range of intimidation theatrics he'd practiced since boyhood. True, without Jimmy behind me I would have been less brave, but my dread of these hoodlums was taken down a notch.

Leccisi said, "*What?*"

This was a good moment for me, a bit of helpful insight just when I needed it: there was nothing special or exciting about these guys, they were just brute criminals. I won't say I felt tough-guy power but in a small and secret corner of myself, I felt a tiny surge of gangster cockiness.

Without a word, I turned and headed upstairs. The Dobermans were waiting eagerly when I emerged in the kitchen. I held the stairway door wide open for them and they shot past me as if there were steaming sirloins waiting on the basement floor.

PELIKAN RETURNED and I laced into him. "Thanks for doing such a great peace-keeping job. You saw what they did to the house. Three people injured including a little girl. I thought your big show with the paddy wagons was going to discourage this."

"We don't know who did this."

"Give me a break. Do you think it was Islamic jihadists?"

"You know your security guys killed one of these people."

Killed? That was news to me.

"His buddies took him to the hospital 95 percent dead and he just went the last 5 percent. Name is Jerome Leccisi, fifty-three, Bronx address. You ever heard of him?"

"I never heard of him." But I had his older brother in a closet and it sounded like Stevie might soon be joining Jerome in the dead mobster department.

"Detective, I counted on you to keep these people from attacking us. I want you to acknowledge that we've been cooperative and nonviolent."

"Jerome Leccisi wouldn't see it that way."

"We defended our home with licensed security personnel but took no offensive action pending efforts by you and Special Agent DeSens to calm things down."

"Yeah, yeah, yeah."

"What's your next move, Detective?"

He didn't like being pressured. We went around a few more times and as this game went on I had an idea about my safety in the Uddone meeting.

I said, "In the interest of peaceful negotiation, I'm going to ask you a favor—and you owe me a big one given my advice about avoiding a threat to your longevity."

"What's the favor?"

"I'm having a sit-down tomorrow night and I'd like you to come along as my security. I'm thinking you keep a low profile and just try to blend in. I don't know where it'll be. Probably a restaurant. Somebody's gonna meet me in front of the Yonkers DMV at eight o'clock and take me to the meeting spot. You could just follow along."

"You've got plenty of security of your own."

He was right but if something happened and Richie stepped in, there would be dead bodies. If Pelikan stepped in, there would be arrests. Also, the Sforza tough guys would be kept out of trouble, and the incident would have no strategic value to Vavolizza.

I said, "I don't think this guy would appreciate me bringing my own people."

"Like he'll appreciate me instead? Nicky won't talk to you if he sees me. In fact, I'm surprised he'll talk to you at all."

"He won't. It's not Nicky. It's a capo named Jackie Uddone."

"That batshit asshole? I don't believe it. This would be funny if he wasn't a stone-cold killer."

"I'm told he likes knives."

"He's not going to knife you in a restaurant. Maybe in the john. Have an empty bladder. Do not go to the john."

Was he kidding or was that a valuable tip?

"Have you taken over the Sforza crew, Phil. What happened to Viv?"

"Viv is not in the picture right now."

"Wow, a star is born. I'm one of the little people who knew you on your way up."

"See you tomorrow, Carl. Eight o'clock at the Yonkers DMV."

"I wouldn't miss this."

What a day it had been. The possible next president made me breakfast. I walked through the shot-up destruction of my new home. I went face-to-face with an old hoodlum and wasn't afraid of him. I made Mafia history by asking a detective to provide my personal security at a meeting with a man who might kill me.

It's not what I'd had in mind for my sunset years. I was afraid but also exhilarated. In bed I told Sylvia about the Uddone meeting.

"It starts," she said, and slowly turned away from me.

CHAPTER 22

I was in a shabby little room with bare walls and only two pieces of furniture: a bed with dirty linens thrown back and a cheap wooden chest of drawers. I could not stop myself from snooping in the chest. Pulling open its top drawer I discovered a glittering array of knives. There were several dozen of them, lovingly arranged. They were diverse and elegant, with different lengths, styles, and colors. I picked one up, a big pearl-handled switchblade, and clicked it open. The blade flicked out like a snake's tongue. I could feel the knife's strength and balance. I could feel the power it would give someone who desperately craved power.

And that someone was coming. I heard footsteps in the hallway and they were getting closer. I could not be caught with the knife in my hands. I struggled to make the blade retract but couldn't do it. I dropped the knife into my coat pocket and felt its blade slice through the pocket lining just as Jackie Uddone entered, incensed to find me in his bedroom. Then I woke up, shuddering with fear. Sylvia held me, stroking me as I caught my breath.

She didn't ask what I'd been dreaming. We lay side by side on our backs, looking at the ceiling, silent. If we'd known it would snow heavily during the night we might have slept at the cozy Auberge instead of bedding down in Poppa Sforza's drafty and charmless bedroom. Through partly open curtains I saw the white glow of what looked like a fantasy snowfall, enormous flakes floating down in slow motion.

I got out of bed, braving the chill, and went to the window. The backyard, never anything but ordinary, was a veritable winter wonderland. There was no moon but the view was luminous, and then Sylvia moving with quick steps on the cold floor was behind me, naked, hugging me with her chin on my shoulder as we looked out at the view.

I thought: if today is my final day on earth, this is a worthy awakening. If the end of this day finds me lying in a pool of blood on a men's room floor, I will fight for a moment's recollection of this perfection before letting go.

AT SEVEN P.M., Stevie Leccisi climbed into the Sforza SUV and was driven to a street corner in the Bronx. He climbed out of the SUV and took a long look around before getting into a waiting car.

At seven thirty, with just a casual kiss from Sylvia, I set out for my Saturday night date with Jackie Uddone. The casualness was part of the professional drill, downplaying the tension we were feeling. We'd made a special effort to shield Vera from the sight of another man in the family going into mortal danger.

I insisted on going, unmouselike, in the red Cadillac. Roncade drove with Bazzanella spread out across the backseat. Two other cars followed at a distance—five ex-soldiers "riding heavy," meaning they carried more firepower than the North Atlantic Treaty Organization.

After much deliberation about appropriate attire I had chosen a Jake-like black suit and red tie, a dress-for-success outfit aimed at providing stature at the negotiating table. Richie offered body armor and tracking devices and concealable weapons but I declined them all on grounds that they would be found if I were searched and that would abort the proceedings, possibly with extreme prejudice.

It is strange the way the mind works: halfway to the big showdown in Yonkers I realized I'd forgotten to call Pete

Draybin. I took out my phone and speed-dialed him, hoping this would be a bullfighter-like demonstration of coolness in the face of danger, impressing Roncade, Bazzanella, and most important, me.

I told Draybin he'd done a better job of declaring than any candidate I'd ever seen. (Two tips for speechwriters: shameless superlatives are the *minimum* when complimenting speakers, and the minute a successful speech is over everyone forgets that a ghostwriter wrote it, so there was no issue of praising my own work.)

Draybin accepted this praise graciously. He was in a good mood and still at the Cape. On Monday he would return to New York and plunge into fund-raising. By midweek he would focus on the Friday night Waldorf speech. He wanted me to meet with him and other advisers to go over Kitty's second draft, which he had not yet read.

Then he moved on to Sylvia and new energy came into his voice. She was beautiful and delightful and impressed everyone. He wondered if she would be willing to take on a working role in his campaign. If she could run a moving company, she could run campaign events. Ginger and Leon sent their best.

Then it was back to squalid reality. We had entered downtown Yonkers. The streets had been cleared of snow but were still wet and glistening. Richie had done a thorough reconnaissance but he had no confidence that his fleet could follow successfully once I was in a Uddone car. I had my cell with Richie on the speed dial, meaning that if I was about to be knifed and knew my precise location, Richie could be there in ten minutes and my body might still be warm.

We got to the DMV but there was no car to meet me. After an awkward moment or two I sent the Richie car away and stood on the sidewalk feeling very alone, making myself as visible as possible.

Many minutes passed. It felt like thirty but five was probably accurate. I was thinking about Richie and Bazzanella laughing about me shivering in the cold. I hoped Pelikan was out there too. He would definitely be laughing.

A dark sedan approached, driving slowly. A man was at the wheel and another was in the backseat. The car pulled over and stopped, the window rolled down.

"You Phil?"

"Yeah."

"Hop the fuck in."

IN MOB lingo, shaking off a tail is called "dry cleaning," which involves driving around endlessly, turning at almost every opportunity, circling back, stopping and waiting, making U-turns, and speeding through empty streets in increasingly dangerous-looking neighborhoods. I felt safer in the car with two enemy hoodlums than out on those streets.

"Okay, we're clean," declared the backseat guy.

I hoped Pelikan knew some fancy pursuit tricks and was out there in the darkness. This seemed like a faint hope.

The car stopped. The driver gestured for me to get out. It was a dark and grungy street in a seemingly abandoned neighborhood. I'd expected a convivial Italian restaurant with great pasta, Sinatra music, brassy broads in low-cut dresses, and guys with pinky rings conversing loudly at the bar.

I was standing in front of a two-story building that was probably in decent condition during World War I but was now a firetrap that might collapse any minute. I stepped back and looked up. In a second-floor window a flickering orange neon light said, "KARATE."

Out of nowhere came voices speaking Spanish. A Hispanic man and woman rounded a corner with their teenage daughter, who was wearing a white martial arts uniform under her parka. They opened a door in the firetrap building and over their shoulders I could see a stairway, badly lit. The father held the door open for me so I went in and climbed the stairs.

Now I was in a waiting area crowded with excited parents and children who tossed their coats and hats onto the cushioned benches which ringed the room and hurried toward a larger room where rows of metal chairs had been set up around an expanse of gray floor mats, obviously the location for karate training.

There were two closed doors, marked "Office" and "Locker Room."

All the psyching-up and preparatory visualizing I'd done for this experience was down the drain. I didn't know what to do, whether I should stand around waiting with my hands in my pockets or go into the larger room and take a seat. I was not even 100 percent confident I was in the right place.

For one of the few times in my life I was the tallest and most expensively dressed person in the room. My guess was that most of the families were Mexican, striving immigrants working hard to become successful Americans, proud to provide karate lessons for their children. The parents were dressed up for a Saturday night out. The kids were wild-eyed and hyper. This atmosphere clashed badly with the role I intended to play—the somber man of respect, tough, terse, not a guy who hung around the waiting rooms of grubby karate schools.

How would a true mob boss behave in this situation? I decided he would exert an aggressive take-no-shit presence. So, feigning the imperious annoyance of a CEO whose time is being wasted (I had seen this many times), I threw open the door of the office without knocking and walked in.

And there was Jackie Uddone, standing up and half-dressed. The jacket of his karate uniform was unbelted and hanging open, exposing a thin but muscled abdomen. He wore black jockey shorts and was stepping into his white uniform pants. A stone-faced Japanese man in a black-belt karate uniform sat on the other side of a metal desk, which was piled sloppily with cash in small bills.

"Hey, are you a parent or what?" Uddone asked, incredulous that a parent would barge so disrespectfully into his office.

"I'm Phil," I announced, in a bold tone I'd practiced all day. "Oh right, Phil. Phil the Thrill."

He gave me a long penetrating look as he finished getting into his pants. He swept the cash into a desk drawer and locked it with a key hanging from a chain around his neck.

"This is awards and new belts night," he said. "Mr. Katsu runs it but I'm the boss. And in the middle of all this I have to have a sit-down with you."

Then he glanced at Mr. Katsu and said, "Showtime, Kemosabe." They pushed by me, out the door.

I tagged along after them into the large room, which they entered like rock stars coming on stage. Parents and some grandparents filled the chairs. The kids sat cross-legged on the mats, demonstrating obedience (probably a rare sight to their parents).

There were many faces but my eyes immediately found Carl Pelikan, seated among the parents. He laughed when he saw me with Jackie and Mr. Katsu.

Uddone said to me, "Grab a couple chairs out of that closet and sit in the corner and I'll come over." Then he picked up a microphone and greeted the crowd in confident but obviously bad Spanish.

I dragged two folding chairs out of the closet. I had looked forward to drama but this was more sit-com than sit-down. I'd assumed the Mafia would have a higher standard for an important meeting which, to me, implied a serious negotiation in a dignified atmosphere.

The kids began sparring under Mr. Katsu's direction. Uddone came over and sat down next to me, without making eye contact. "This is one great cash business. Almost no overhead. We charge for lessons and belt promotions. We run a bingo game for parents while the kids are going at it and we run blackjack at night and when you've got gambling, you've got loan-sharking. For a while I had a hooker giving head in the men's locker room but the wives got pissy about that."

He snickered. He had a jittery manner heightened by—what do they call it?—restless leg syndrome. He had a bad case of it. It started when he sat down and he tended to lean his palms on his knees as if trying to subdue it.

"We're gonna take it national. Nicky's totally behind me on this. Low-cost martial arts centers giving high-speed black belts in all of America's most badass neighborhoods. Someday we'll be taking a big chunk out of every karate dojo in America. But here's the best part. The dojos give us a base for operations across the country, especially in the boondocks, like Nebraska and shit, where the families got next to nothing going on. This is how we get the edge on the new gangs from Europe and Asia. I came up with this idea. It's my vision and guys with vision rise to the top. One day I'm running the Sforzas, the next day who knows? What do you think?"

It wasn't what I wanted to talk about.

"I know what you're thinking. You're thinking I can't run the Sforza crew? I'm so sick of hearing about how the Sforzas are so sophisticated and Jake is so smart and the rest of us are ignorant douche bags. But you know who I am? I happen to be a captain in an outfit that's been in business for 150 years and we've never had a year in the red. Never. We know how to run a business. It's in our bones."

His attention switched back to the kids, who were all on their feet, kicking and punching each other. "These parents are gonna sign one-year, maybe two-year contracts with me. And they pay, my friend. They think karate is going to protect their kids. Why don't they just buy the kid a Glock? I never took a single karate lesson, by the way. I just put on the uniform. I don't need karate. I got a knife."

He looked at me straight-on for the first time.

"Want to see it?"

He pulled up the sleeve of his martial arts jacket and there it was, taped to his forearm, an orange switchblade.

My heart skipped.

Jackie knew he'd unnerved me.

He asked, "You know who my inspiration is?"

"Your inspiration? No, who?"

"Somebody very big, very famous. Guess."

I didn't know what he was talking about.

"Putin."

Putin?

"Vladimir Putin. We're a lot alike. Small in height but huge in balls. Worked for the KGB. Fought his way up to become head of Russia. He's got a black belt in martial arts, which he probably faked, like me. They say he's squeezed so much money out of the oil companies and whatnot, he's maybe the richest man in the world. What is he, five foot six? Exactly the same height as me. I'm hoping someday I'll do some deal with Russia and we'll meet and give each other hugs because we recognize each other as soul mates."

He grinned at this. I looked him over, a ratty little guy unblessed in every way, boiling with delusions which might have amused me if he was anything but a psychopathic murderer with an orange knife on his arm and legs that twitched nonstop. My interest in a battle of wits had vanished along with my notion of a cinematic negotiation scene. Frankly I was close to bailing out and getting away from this guy, but I couldn't leave without discussing what I'd come to discuss. I had to accomplish something in this meeting, even if Jackie Uddone was too wacko to deal with in any normal way. I needed to improvise, as I'd done with Draybin and Bill Gates.

If Putin was Uddone's inspiration—which wasn't illogical given that Putin was nothing but a big-time mob boss himself—why not put my argument in a Putin context?

"Okay, Jackie, let's say you're Putin. Your best province, the one that has the most oil and timber and platinum and so on and kicks up excellent earnings to you—let's say the chief of this province dies. Like Jake Sforza dying. Does Putin then say, 'I'm going to let the province continue doing a great job by doing things in its own independent way?' Or does he install his wife's nephew to take over the province and risk fucking everything because the nephew doesn't know what he's doing?"

He didn't seem to be listening but I had to keep trying.

"Because that's what Nicky's doing throwing an outsider into the Sforzas, even if the outsider's a smart guy like yourself. And letting the province function on its own means no risk to you, no work, no pains in the ass. And maybe there's an increased taste of the revenue for you and Nicky. Let's say $300,000 a year into your pocket for doing nothing at all. And you'd be free to develop the karate idea."

I knew this was a slovenly first draft of an analogy. It was weak and confusing and I was embarrassed by it. Yet it seemed to catch his interest and get him thinking. Would Putin retain the successful status quo or dick with the autonomous province?

"You know what I'd say?" he asked. "I'd say fuck you and put the nephew in charge of the province. *Because that's what Nicky wants.* And because you're *patronizing* me, motherfucker. You think I don't know patronizing when I see it?"

He glared at me and I hated myself. I'd tried to be clever and it didn't work. I'd blown it. The whole negotiation died on a bad analogy.

He said, "I don't know why I'm listening to you anyway. You ain't the boss of the Sforzas, pal. Nicky knows it and I know it. You ain't the boss of anything."

CHAPTER 23

I was dumbfounded. He was smiling, the first time I'd seen him smile. We watched the kids sparring for a few moments and he said, "You know what Nicky says to me when we're leaving Jake's funeral? He leans over and says, '*The broad's the new boss.* She's the smart one, she's the tough one.' But a broad can't be a boss. So she needs a—whaddyacallit?"

"Penis?"

"No, don't be a wiseass. She needs a man who can play the part. The right age, good talker with a good vocabulary, halfway bright. Like you. That's what they brought you in for."

"You think *Sylvia* is the boss of the Sforza family and I'm the front man?"

"I don't think it, I know it. But the commission would never accept it. A broad can't run a crew. Maybe in San Francisco, but not here."

"Why in a million years would I *pose* as the head of a Mafia crew?"

"Because it was getting you the hottest piece of tail in the mob, which is exactly what Sylvia was until a few years ago. She was a knockout and she had class. She was on her way to being queen of the whole American Cosa Nostra back when she was fucking Lou Turco."

What? Who?

"Turco was on the fast track. He was about to be upped to underboss. Marrying Sylvia would have put the Sforzas in his pocket and then he would have moved up to boss and in another few years he'd be at the top, which the newspapers call *capo di tutti capi*, boss of all bosses. You don't know any of this, do you?"

I was on the verge of hyperventilating. I looked across the room at Pelikan who frowned as he read the distress on my face. My discomfort spurred Jackie's enthusiasm.

"But then Lou goes to this big family wedding in Brooklyn. He's on the dance floor with Sylvia. She's shaking it and guys are checking her out. Lou's drunk and this gets under his skin. He's burning. Calls her a slut or something. She says something back. So then he hauls off on her."

"Hauls off?"

"Decks her. Knocks her out cold. Broke teeth and everything. Then he straightens his tie—that was his move, that tie-straightening thing he did—and strolls off.

"So his friends are like, Louie, you just coldcocked Jake Sforza's daughter. Plus you've been warned about smacking women. You are a fucking dead man. Lou says, I ain't scared of Jake Sforza. And they say, you *should* be scared of Jake Sforza because he's gonna kill you. And Lou says, fuck him, fuck everybody, let 'em try.

"Jake's ready to kill him that night. But Lou Turco is a made man and somebody slows Jake down long enough to ask the commission for an okay to clip Lou. This is one senior boss with all kinds of respect asking permission to hit an up-and-comer from another family. This is real fucking politics, you know?"

Jackie was loving the story.

"The commission has no balls and says to Jake, we won't sanction a hit but do what a man's gotta do. We'll look the other way."

"You're telling me the Sforzas killed Turco?"

"John Sforza killed Turco."

"*Catcher* killed Turco?"

"Him and Turco never got along. Since childhood. They were the same kind of guy—tall and good-looking, great in a good mood, your worst dream in a bad mood. Two trains on a collision course, you know.

"All four Sforza brothers wanted the work. Jake gave it to Catcher but he makes him wait a couple days to cool down a little so he don't botch it up. But Lou goes out and has a few drinks and drives up to this bar in some little French hotel in Westchester where Catcher hung out—"

The Auberge.

"He walks in late at night and finds Catcher at the bar with some of his guys. They don't see Turco coming but suddenly he's at the bar with his piece out. Waving it around. Now this is a made man. Catcher and his buddies are not made. Catcher was on the books to be made but it hadn't happened yet.

"And Lou is laughing and doing the tie thing and says, 'Catcher, before I smoke you I just want you to know how much I enjoyed cracking your sister in her fucking snoot.' So Catcher killed him."

"But Lou had the gun."

"Catcher goes right over it. Lou gets off one shot that goes into the ceiling. Catcher gets his gun arm and holds it flat on the bar with one hand while he's bashing Lou in the face a dozen times with the other, and finally he twists the gun back on Lou and puts it against his chest, yanks the trigger and Lou does a back flip off the bar stool, deader than shit."

I was speechless.

"I heard the Sforzas later bought a 49 percent piece in the hotel at a very high price and took good care of the owner and employees to ease their pain."

I looked around hazily and noticed that Mr. Katsu was fighting an exhibition match with another Japanese instructor.

"Catcher's buddies tell him to run. But he won't budge. Takes out his phone and calls his father. Then he calls this White Plains cop who'd pinched him a few times—"

Pelikan.

"Catcher says, 'Come get me. I just capped a guy. But he was a piece of shit and it was self-defense.' Then he turns around and finishes his drink.

"All the people at the bar ran for cover when Lou walked in waving the piece, so the only people who saw Catcher off Lou were Catcher's buddies. And they all say the right thing so Catcher gets self-defense and walks, but they get him on a parole violation.

And there's a PS to this. It was a front-page story. The newspapers were *already* on Turco's case for his women beating so they blew it up. It's a fucking catastrophe. The commission don't know what to do. All they can think of is putting a hold on Catcher getting his button. So he goes off to the joint without being made, which isn't so good for him, even with everyone knowing not to screw with the Sforzas. If he'd had his button, there's no way the commission would okay a hit in prison. He'd still be alive. And what does that mean?"

"I don't know. Tell me what it means."

"It means Sylvia got him killed. Not directly but if she hadn't had the thing with Turco, Catcher would be the head of the Sforzas today instead of being dead and Sylvia wouldn't be running the Sforzas. And you would be selling panty hose or whatever you do. You didn't know all this, huh? I can see I shocked the shit out of you."

Yes. The shit had been shocked out of me.

"I gotta give out the awards," he said, jumping up and heading for the middle of the room where he took the mic and broke into painful Spanish.

I GOT a sign language message from Pelikan: "Are you okay?" I nodded but I was miles from okay. I suppose I hadn't thought much about the dark side of Sylvia's life.

There was a standing ovation for Uddone and Mr. Katsu. Smiling Japanese women came in with a rolling bar, coolers packed with beer, and trays of snacks. Loud Mexican music came on. A party broke out.

I watched Uddone working the room, handshaking and complimenting the performance of the youngsters. My mind was spinning from the Turco story and I was slow noticing that Uddone's victory circuit would bring him face-to-face with Pelikan. Pelikan saw this happening. I watched him look around for a way out but he was unable to back into a wall of parents surging forward to press the flesh with Jackie.

And then it happened. Uddone's back was to me. I saw Pelikan smile and offer a handshake, pretending to be a happy parent, but nobody in the world looks more like a cop than Carl Pelikan. Uddone stiffened. Pelikan made a surprising move, putting his arm around a Hispanic woman in a red dress who was standing next to him, introducing her to Uddone. The woman acted the part of the karate mom. Uddone ignored her, whirling around looking for me.

He'd made Pelikan. Turning away from Pelikan he pushed smiling parents out of the way and ran across the room at me. He pulled up his sleeve and ripped the switchblade loose from his forearm.

"YOU BRING a fucking cop to my dojo? No wise guy would come in here with a cop. Are you fucking wired up?"

He was behind me in a quick step. I was still seated on the metal chair. "Listen to this," he whispered. I heard the knife blade snick out of the sheath. He held its point against the back of my neck so I could feel its sharp point scratching the base of my skull. One hard upward thrust and that blade would be coming out inside my throat.

"On your feet," Uddone ordered. He had my elbow, forcing me across the room. In the party atmosphere no one seemed to take note of this.

We barged into the locker room. Some boys were using the urinals. "Get the fuck outta here," he shouted. Their friendly karate master had turned into a madman. They left fast.

He dragged me back into a section of floor-to-ceiling lockers.

"Get that suit off," he said. "Fast. If you're wired I'm cutting you."

I stripped as fast as possible. "Hurry. Shirt off. Pants off."

My hands were shaking so much I could hardly unbutton buttons. He was searching my body and clothes for a recording device. He felt inside my pockets, took out my wallet and went through it.

"They sometimes put these fucking transmitter things in wallets," he said. "How much cash you got here? Yo, two twenty-dollar bills? I said you wasn't no wise guy. No wise guy goes out with forty bucks."

He pocketed the forty bucks and threw the wallet on the floor.

I heard the door open on the other side of the lockers.

"Get the fuck outta here," Uddone yelled at whoever had come in.

"Gotta take a helluva whiz," came the voice. *Pelikan's.*

I thought Pelikan's arrival was a godsend but maybe not: it clearly rattled Uddone. His glance flickered back and forth between me and the direction of the urinals.

"It's that fucking cop, isn't it?" he said, meanwhile gesturing at me to undress faster until I was naked. I learned that the prospect of a knife through bare flesh is much scarier than through clothes.

"Everything okay back there?" called Pelikan.

"Get out of here, cop," he yelled.

"Me? I'm no cop. I'm a dad. My kid got his green belt."

Uddone, loving my fear and humiliation, leaned in grinning and whispered, "I could slice off your johnson but then Sylvia would have no use for you."

"Nothing beats a good piss," shouted Pelikan. "I had to go since we sat down."

"Stay the fuck where you are," Uddone yelled at Pelikan. Then, satisfied that I wore no wire, he gestured at me to put my clothes back on.

The locker room door swung open and what sounded like a dozen jubilant fathers charged in to use the urinals. Uddone yelled to everyone to get the fuck out but he was drowned out by the voices of the fathers, who were already high on free wine and the rush from seeing their kids win new belts.

Pelikan peeked around the corner of a section of lockers. I was up against the wall. Uddone's back was to Pelikan, blocking me so Pelikan couldn't see the knife held at a possible entry spot between my ribs as I tried to button my shirt. I held my breath, tried to keep focus, tried to keep my mind from imagining how it would feel if Uddone jammed that knife just a few inches forward.

Then Uddone decided against killing me in a room crowded with people, including a cop. He leaned forward to whisper in my ear, holding the knife under my eye.

"Tell Sylvia she's working for me, starting Monday. She doesn't go along, I'm gonna cut her heart out with this knife. Carve her heart out and feed it to the fucking Dobermans and watch them gobble it up like strawberries."

Then he stepped back, retracting the knife blade as he retreated around the corner of the lockers, pushing roughly past Pelikan.

Pelikan grabbed my arm and steered me out of the locker room toward the stairway. I was a mess: shirt flaps out, necktie gone, socks lost, shoes untied. We squeezed down the steps around some slow-moving families and emerged into the street. The cold air hit me like a slap. My adrenaline, pumped to a peak in the locker room, now seemed to be reversing, with energy pouring out of me and waves of heavy fatigue rising into my legs and shoulders.

I'd had my first experience with nearly being murdered. It brought me a little closer to understanding the reality of life in the Mafia.

CHAPTER 24

On the street I looked around for the Roncade cars but of course they were not in sight because they didn't know where I was. *I* didn't know where I was.

"You okay?" Pelikan said to me.

"Yeah. Thanks for coming in."

Standing with Pelikan was the woman in the red dress. Pelikan said, "I want to introduce you to Milagros Soto. Milly."

I shook hands with her.

"I figured I needed a date for this," Pelikan said. "I thought I'd be sitting in a nice restaurant for dinner. One person alone at a table gets noticed."

Milly Soto gave me a big smile and said, "We met once but you don't remember me, do you? I'm a conductor on the Metro-North. I saw you fly in the door like a maniac, about a month or so ago. I patted you on the back, remember?"

"That was you?"

"I had to check out your story," said Pelikan.

"I vouched for you," she said.

"One thing led to another," Pelikan said.

I wanted to know how he got to the karate place, even before I got there.

"I tried to follow from the DMV but they lost me after about two turns. So I called up a buddy at Yonkers PD. He knows Uddone very well. He said this karate dump is Jackie's hangout so I figured it was the place. Do you have a ride out of here? I can't leave you on the street. Why don't you jump in with us? We could grab a beer. I'm guessing you need one."

Grabbing a beer was the best idea I ever heard. My new instincts ordered me not to drink with a cop but my old instincts demanded a break from my new instincts. I wanted to decompress, relax, drink beer, and be normal for a while. Meanwhile Milly Soto's presence softened Carl Pelikan and turned him into a potentially likable drinking companion. I said yes. "But no business talk." He agreed.

First I had to call Sylvia, telling her I was safe but couldn't talk because I was with people. Then I called Roncade, telling him I was fine and had a ride home—obviously I didn't tell Roncade that the driver was Detective Pelikan. I told him to go back to the house and provide maximum security for Sylvia. If the Vavolizzas really thought she was the Sforza boss, she would be their number one target.

THE ONLY Yonkers bar Pelikan knew was a cop bar. He asked if I was okay with that. I was taking the rest of the night off from being a Mafioso so I said fine, no problem.

It was a no-frills neighborhood place but at ten thirty on a Saturday night the music was loud and there was a rowdy crowd of off-duty cops, wives, and girlfriends pressed up to the bar. None knew Pelikan but a few nodded to him as they passed our booth. Pelikan was instantly recognized as being "on the job."

I asked him, "Did you become a cop because you look like one or do you look like one because you *are* one?"

"I've wondered about that," he said. "What if I'd wanted to be a priest or a golf pro or something? Would they have let me in with this face?"

"Oh, it's a *beautiful* face," said Milly. She was a bubbly, happy person, full of affection. She showed me photos of her ten-year-old son in his football uniform. I figured Pelikan had been alone for a long time but finally got what he needed.

The beer was good and we ordered deluxe hamburgers. I could feel myself winding down although the sharp scratch of the knife was a disturbingly fresh memory. Pelikan sensed the need for distraction and launched into funny police anecdotes.

Milly went off to the ladies' room. Pelikan watched her go and said, "I've been thinking: Phil Vail gets on a train and gets off involved with a Mafia boss's daughter and because of that, I get involved with a railroad conductor. Amazing, huh? I guess our fates intertwined or whatever."

"It was a fateful night," I said. "And since then I may have saved you from getting killed by the Sforzas and you might have saved me from getting sliced up by Jackie Uddone."

We were sliding into male-bonding territory. This was not wise. And how stupid was it to risk the lip-loosening effect of alcohol?

On the other hand, I wished caution could be shoved aside because Pelikan would be a good conversation partner for the questions flying around my mind about Jackie's threat to Sylvia. The threat—cutting out her heart, feeding it to the dogs like *strawberries*—had gone by so fast I'd barely grasped it but now it hit me full force. Was Uddone *serious* or was it only hoodlum scare talk? Would he need Vavolizza's permission to murder Sylvia?

But why was I asking questions? There was nothing to *contemplate*. Sylvia's life had been threatened by a certified killer. There was only one thing to do.

Milly was back, full of chatter. I was deaf to it.

I would have Jackie Uddone killed.

"You okay, Phil?" Pelikan was saying. "You're looking pale around the gills. Hey, you had a bad experience and it's catching up with you. I've been there. Drink some beer. Calm down."

Of course I'd already promised to kill Uddone in reprisal for Catcher. But the promise was made with misgivings and tabled until some indefinite point in the future when I might be able to sidestep it. But this was different. And urgent.

Uddone threatened to kill Sylvia on Monday; he had to die on Sunday.

Tomorrow.

Pelikan said, "Phil, don't it feel nice to be back with good people again?"

It did, but of course the irony was that I had just burned my bridge to the good people community. Drinking in a police bar, I had decided to commit the ultimate felony. There was just one touch of discipline: I decided somewhere during a gulp of beer that I should be stone sober when I gave the order. I did not want to look back on Uddone's death as something I ordered because I was feeling chesty after a few brews.

The chitchat with Pelikan and Milly continued but my mind was racing: Jackie Uddone would be killed because Nicky Vavolizza made a wrong assumption about Sylvia. Even if the Mafia threw open its doors to gender equality and held a news conference endorsing affirmative action, Sylvia would never touch the boss's job. Her idea of liberation was to *not* have this power. Her idea of choice was to *leave* the Mafia.

Perhaps her brothers felt the same way: George had his cleaning company, Tommy seemed to like the moving business, and, odd as it seemed, Jimmy wanted to be a nurse. They had gone into crime because that's what was there for them. They were hardly angels but crime did not have to be their destiny, as it was for Vavolizza and Uddone who aspired to nothing but mob glory and couldn't fathom Sylvia's *not* craving Mafia power or *not* seizing it when it seemed rightfully hers. This blindness led them to their disastrous blunder: they had the real Sforza boss—me—in their clutches but let me get away. Jackie should have killed me when I was naked and defenseless in the locker room. Sylvia would not have taken over as boss. Viv would have refused the job. Jackie would have taken command of the Sforza crew. Vavolizza would have won.

Instead, Jackie Uddone would die, on my order. In the course of my life I never lusted for power and often backed away from it, but now as age eroded my strength and weakened me in virtually every way, I felt the strong appeal of power and embraced it, an exciting suspension of my decline.

"THANK GOD you're safe," she whispered as I slipped into bed.

"In the morning I'm going to have Jackie Uddone killed," I said.

She mumbled something—was it "Congratulations"?—but dozed off.

Then it was eight A.M. and she was shaking me awake. She sat on the edge of the bed holding a newspaper which she thrust into my face.

The story was spread across the front page of the Westchester newspaper:

SUBURB SHOCKED BY DOUBLE MURDER

SLAIN MOBSTERS TIED
TO SCHOOL FLAGPOLE

COPS FEAR MAFIA WAR

WEAVER RIDGE, January 3—The bodies of two reputed mobsters were found tied to the flagpole of the Weaver Ridge Middle School in this Westchester suburb early this morning.

An anonymous caller alerted police to what could be revenge killings related to a Mafia leadership struggle.

Both victims were said to be members of the Vavolizza crime family. The family's boss, Niccolò M. Vavolizza, lives in a $3.2 million estate within walking distance of the school.

The dead men were identified as John Z. Uddone, 46, and Stefano Leccisi, 56, both of the Bronx.

Weaver Ridge Police Chief Jim Farraday said they were killed by small caliber bullets fired into their heads at close range, which he described as "Mob-style executions."

Chief Farraday said the killings occurred late Saturday night. The 9-1-1 call reporting the deaths was received at 11:58 P.M.

Authorities said Uddone was a captain in the Vavolizza family. Leccisi was a "soldier" under Uddone's command.

Leccisi was believed to have been one of four men who took part in the spectacular New Year's Eve attack on the White Plains residence of the late mob boss Jacopo Sforza in which Leccisi's brother Jerome, 53, was fatally shot and three Sforza family members were wounded.

The bodies were found with thick rope holding them upright in sitting positions on opposite sides of the Middle School flagpole.

The grisly scene reminded law enforcement veterans of the murders of Francis and Rocco Sforza, sons of mob boss Tiziano Sforza, in mob warfare some years ago.

The two slain brothers were found tied to a flagpole outside the White Plains residence of their uncle, Jacopo Sforza, who later succeeded Tiziano Sforza as head of the maverick Sforza crew and remained its boss until his death from cancer in December.

Authorities speculated that last night's killings were "payback" for the murders of the two Sforza brothers as well as the attack on the Sforza home and the fatal knifing of John Sforza, 36, in Ricton Correctional Facility on Christmas morning.

Police are concerned that the killings might signal an outbreak of Mob warfare apparently centered on a dispute over Jacopo Sforza's successor. Police promised a crackdown to prevent further violence.

Law enforcement officials describe the Sforza crew as a sophisticated and extremely effective crime unit which operates loosely within the Vavolizza family.

"Didn't you say something to me last night about killing Uddone?"

"Yes, but I didn't order it. I was going to order it this morning. Vavolizza did it and made it look like we did it."

"And it does. But look at this: the article calls us the '*maverick*' Sforza gang and says we '*operate loosely*' within Nicky's family. If mavericks can run around operating loosely, that means there's no discipline left. The commission will come down on us."

I said, "He made it look like we not only killed two of his men but rubbed his nose in it by leaving the bodies near his house. And then he links it to Rocco and Frankie and Catcher. It's like we went out and settled scores for everything, a declaration of war."

"People remember that Rocco and Frankie thing. The tabloids had a horrible photo of it on the front pages."

"Uddone must have left the karate place around ten thirty and rushed up to Weaver Ridge to see Nicky. An hour or so later he was dead."

"What's this about a karate place?"

I got out of bed and headed for the bathroom. "This whole ridiculous 'sit-down' took place at a karate dojo. A hundred parents watching their kids earn cut-rate black belts. Uddone was off the wall, Sylvia. Compared himself to Vladimir Putin."

"*Vladimir Putin?*"

I was in the shower but a moment later she was throwing open the shower door. "Finish the fucking story."

I had to shout over the shower noise. "I tried to convince him the status quo was better than war. I didn't do a very good job of it."

"At least he didn't hurt you."

"He almost did. Then he got the idea I was wearing a wire so he pulled a knife and got me into the locker room. Made me strip. Threatened to slice off my you-know-what."

She was aghast.

"He said it was a waste of time even talking to me because I'm not the real boss of the Sforzas. They think *you* are running the family and I'm the front man. And Uddone said he was going to come over on Monday, take command, and maybe cut you up. That's when I decided to kill him."

"Did you mention this to anybody last night?'

"Nobody. Just you."

"So who'd you go drinking with?"

I pulled on my pants and she handed me a shirt. I fumbled with the buttons, which reminded me of trying to button my shirt with Jackie's knife scraping my ribs.

"You're not going to understand this," I said. "Carl Pelikan and his girlfriend."

That was possibly more shocking and outrageous than the Uddone story. Carl Pelikan: the arrester of Catcher, the would-be arrester of everyone in the family. I cringed like a dog facing punishment for pooping on the rug.

"How the hell did *Pelikan* get into this?"

"I asked him to be there as my security. And when things got dicey in the locker room, he was right there. I could have been on a slab this morning if he wasn't there."

"Why did you even think of involving Carl Pelikan?"

"I figured Uddone's people would spot our people but not him. I didn't think they'd be looking for a cop. But Uddone made him. Also, I wanted Pelikan to see us as pro-peace while the Vavolizzas are pro-war. I want to be on the right side of the cops while Nicky's on the wrong side."

"Great but hasn't Nicky just put *us* on the wrong side of the cops? The whole world thinks we killed Uddone and Leccisi."

"I'll have to convince them Nicky did these killings. I bet I'll get this chance very soon. I bet Pelikan's at the door before I get a cup of coffee. Hint. Hint."

"Okay, we'll get you some coffee. Let's go downstairs, but I have to warn you, they're all waiting to have a big celebration. They're overjoyed because they think you killed Uddone to get revenge for Catcher. You're the man now."

"I won't be the man when they find out we didn't kill him."

"Maybe you don't have to clarify that right away."

Doesn't it always come down to crisis public relations, message management, damage control, and finding the right mix of truth and bullshit? I put on my speechwriter/consultant hat.

"You're right about that, Sylvia. The family won't *want* to believe it because they wanted me to kill Uddone. The cops won't want to believe me because it messes up a neat revenge scenario. The commission won't believe me because it wants to believe Nicky. The public won't believe me because they won't believe anything a mobster says. Roncade knows we didn't kill Uddone, and Bazzanella and the brothers and Pelikan need to know what really happened but why not just let everyone else believe what they're going to believe anyway? *Why lose credibility by telling the truth?*"

"It's so enlightening to hear the kind of thinking that goes on in the big time," Sylvia said. She opened the door and a great cheer arose.

THE ILLUSION of revenge set off jubilation in the house of Sforza. Guests flowed in, some coming from church, some skipping church in their eagerness to start the party.

In my WASPy family, get-togethers are rare but the Sforzas party at the drop of a hat or the death of a goon. In my family, taking pleasure in anyone's death would have been in prohibitive bad taste, but among the Sforzas an enemy's death was an occasion for revelry. And in their view, I had made my bones. I had been "upped" to a level approaching Jake-like stature. When Tiziano arrived with Angela and Beatrice he made a beeline for me and clutched my hand fiercely; I had proven myself.

People came before me in a new way, deferential and slightly awed. There was hesitation about how to address me—"Phil" had become too familiar but it was too soon for a paternal honorific like Poppa or Godfather.

I can't say I was unaffected by this. I could feel my ego swelling. I tried to shrink it back down with a humbling memory of cowering before Jackie Uddone's blade. I knew the truth about Uddone's killing would emerge but in the meantime, I told myself, *use this*. Seize this role; draw size and strength from it. And enjoy it, because it would not last. My unsuitedness for mob leadership would surely catch up with me. My mobster experience would be unforgettable but short, not a retirement solution.

CHAPTER 25

Sylvia gave me two phone messages. One was from Pelikan and DeSens, who were on their way over. Did they intend to make arrests? The other call had come last night from my friend Charlie Benedict. "I'm sorry I forgot to give you his message," she said. "He had a Southern accent and was very nice. Maybe a little drunk."

The doorbell rang before I could get on the phone to Charlie. I grabbed my coat, walked outside, and said, "Shoot some baskets?" Pelikan, DeSens, and I headed to the backyard to what had become our outdoor conference venue, now ankle-deep in snow.

Pelikan said, "Okay, from eight P.M. to almost one A.M. you were never out of my sight, except for a minute or so with Uddone back in the lockers, which would not have been a convenient time to phone in an order to have him killed. So if you ordered it, I don't know how you did it. So, 'splain."

"Vavolizza did it."

DeSens said, "You're saying Nicky Vavolizza executed two of his own men?"

He didn't seem surprised; this was a drill that had to be gotten out of the way.

"Think of it as taking out the trash," I said. "Leccisi was a bum. They call guys like him a *brokester*, a broken-down valise. And Uddone? Well, Carl got a look at him last night. Carl, was that guy stable enough to be of any value to Vavolizza?"

"Stable? No. I would not call him a level guy."

DeSens said: "You're saying Vavolizza killed these guys and tied them to a flagpole a stone's throw from his own house and then called it in to 9-1-1?"

"To make it look like *we* did it," I said. "But getting you to arrest us was only the gravy. The main course was fooling the Mafia Commission. To make the Sforzas look like shit-disturbers so the commission would back a war against us by all five families."

"What's next in this drama?"

"You tell me. You've got two deaths on your hands today—you could have *two hundred* tomorrow. I can't prevent that. But *you* can prevent that."

THEY DIDN'T arrest me so my next move was to summon the war council to the basement where I told the whole story. Roncade knew what happened and Bazzanella had figured it out, but the others were disappointed that Uddone and Leccisi died by someone else's hand.

I went heavy on Uddone's craziness and light on my humiliation because the naked-in-the-locker-room scene would be an indelible blot on my leadership image. Reluctantly I explained why I'd made Pelikan my security instead of Richie's people. Richie didn't like it but he swallowed it. My new stature helped.

I said we had to take the possibility of a big attack very seriously. We got down to planning our moves. We decided that law enforcement couldn't crack down on us if we had nothing to crack down on, so we would temporarily shut down all the family's operations, legal and illegal. We would give our "clients" a brief holiday from payments. We instructed them to report any attempt by Vavolizza or others to poach on our relationships. Ron Taubman said, "I'll tell them loyalty will be remembered. And disloyalty will also be remembered."

The Sforza children would have their Christmas vacations extended; the women would take the kids to a low-profile resort in the Poconos. Bazzanella would heighten his espionage activity. Roncade's security force would be on full alert. Retainers would be called to active duty. The family's two moving vans would be parked in front of the house as protective barriers.

I asked Richie who would win if a war broke out.

"If it's on quality, we win. If it's on numbers, *they* win. They're untrained and undisciplined but they're not cowards. We'd have to end it right away with a devastating offensive attack. Jake had me draw up a plan for what and who to hit. I'd say we'd have, at most, twelve to eighteen hours before the cops could shut us down. We'd kill a lot of scumbags and it would be very noisy."

"Which would mark us as America's foremost enemy of law and order."

He hesitated. "That's above my pay grade, Boss."

"I reject that answer," I said. "I don't want any 'above my pay grade' excuses. Richie, you're now a general. Paul, you're director of our CIA and secretary of state. Ron, you're the secretary of the treasury. George, Tommy, and Jimmy, you're the Cabinet. The old way is over. We share responsibility. I want your assurances as we proceed that you understand our strategy, which is that getting into war is defeat and staying out of it is victory. If this is disappointing because you were looking forward to a big Superbowl street battle, I'm sorry about that. Now, are you with me?"

They all said yes. I think they meant it and it was clear from their energetic camaraderie going up the basement stairs that they were excited to be mobilizing for action, whatever it would be. They were also excited about a boss sharing responsibility with subordinates for the first time in Cosa Nostra history.

None of them seemed to notice that there was no good plan for avoiding war.

CHARLIE BENEDICT had called to tell me he had been given his pink slip, ending his thirty-five-year law career. When I called him back we talked about it for a long time and then he asked, "So what have you been up to?" I didn't look forward to answering so I said, "Let's have dinner."

I think I just needed to talk to somebody. Somebody from outside the crime and police worlds. We met the next night at a small French restaurant in Manhattan.

In recent years Charlie had trimmed his list of life motivations to the single goal of accumulating a substantial estate to be shared by his wife, two daughters and their husbands, and six granddaughters. Because of several serious cardiac episodes, he regarded this effort as a race against time. He understood that aging was discouraged at his firm but mistakenly thought his internal political skills would allow him to squeeze out a few more years of income.

"Is there any chance of getting another job?" I asked.

"Take a look at me," he said with a small smile. He was only a month older than me but surgeries had depleted him: he looked old, talked slower than ever, and his narrow legal expertise did not offer widespread job opportunities.

"As to the value of wisdom, judgment, institutional memory, a sense of history, and other attributes of maturity, I've found that they are regarded as annoying pains in the ass," he said. "Some young lawyer comes to me having totally screwed up and I say, well, here's what we're going to do to fix this and here's what's going to happen and I give him step one through ten and I'm right because I've seen it a million times, and guess what? The kid jumps up smoldering-mad at me. Like I took all the fun out of fucking up. And the word gets around and pretty soon everyone wants me gone. Maybe I felt the same way at their age. The whole thing makes me thirsty."

So I ordered him another bourbon and then it was my turn to talk. It was the first time I'd told the story of my Mafia adventure and I wasn't confident about how to do it. I knew the story challenged plausibility; I barely believed it myself. Would he believe me or think I'd been seized by a delusion requiring medication and therapy? There was also a security aspect; disclosing inside information about the mob was just not smart.

I decided to let instinct be my guide. Instinct advised me to focus on the love story with Sylvia. I revealed that she was a member of a Mafia family—that was bombshell enough—but fuzzed over my role with the Sforzas. Charlie didn't need to know that I was a capo facing decisions about a bloodbath in the city's streets.

He listened thoughtfully, obviously pleased that I had found love and obviously concerned that I was hanging out with the Cosa Nostra. He is a shrewd guy and knew there was more to the story but he asked no questions and voiced no judgments. When I was done he smiled and said, "Your life since our dinner in November has been a tad more eventful than mine. The only thing I've done other than losing my job was to accidentally take a shower with my glasses on."

I walked Charlie to his building as Roncade's hawk-eyed operatives watched from a car rolling along beside us. Charlie said, "I hope the mean-looking bastards in that car are with you and not with the other guys."

Yes, they were mine, I said, but Charlie had read the news stories about impending mob warfare. "Do I have to worry about you?" Charlie asked. "What's going to happen with that?"

"The goal is to avoid it or at least survive it but it looks pretty hairy."

"I lost my job because when the showdown came, I had no big card to play," he said. "That's what you need. Search your assets. Find a secret weapon, preferably nuclear."

We laughed and said good night.

I NEEDED to hear Sylvia's side of the Lou Turco story so as I headed back to Westchester I called and invited her to meet me for a drink at the Auberge. Her answer—"Can we spend the night?"—was perfect. Richie's guys called it in and more guys were sent to provide overnight security.

As we sat at the bar I found myself looking up in search of the bullet hole Lou Turco put in the ceiling instead of Catcher.

Sylvia said, "I know what you're looking for. Who told you?"

"The late Mr. Rat-face."

"Of all people," she said. "Tell me how you feel about it."

We were silent for a few seconds. I said, "Well, I kind of guessed that you weren't a virgin. But your being with a man like Turco sort of—"

"Disgusts you?" she said.

"Not the word I would have used."

"How about 'shocked.' You're shocked because you never thought about some of the seamy realities of my life. But you're right. The whole Turco thing *is* shocking and disgusting too. It's a stain. Not just because I slept with a bad guy. This whole mob life is a stain on all of us. I don't want you to be stained too. Right now it's kind of a novelty for you and the stain isn't on you because you haven't really bought into it yet. You don't understand what a curse this is, how permanent and inescapable it is."

"Maybe it isn't permanent and inescapable."

"*Then get us out.*"

Those black eyes drilled into me.

"Do you really mean that?"

"Yes. But I can't abandon my family. So I don't see how it can be done."

"Tell me the Turco story."

She looked away uncomfortably, then looked back.

"This was a couple years ago. I was going through a lot of confusion. Most of my early boyfriends had been thrill seekers trying to catch a glimpse of real mobsters, trying to see how close they could get to the flame. Then they'd feel the heat and disappear.

"And what did that leave? A small pool of boyfriends that was nothing but my generation of wise guys. I tried to be a Mafia woman. It could be exciting because they had energy and cash and they're good at having fun. And because I was Jake's daughter I was royalty. No man outside the mob would look at me but inside the families I was the princess. And Turco was the prince. It had to happen, we *had* to be a couple.

"Lou's problem was that he was very angry when drunk. When he was very drunk he was *very* frightening. My thing with him only lasted four or five months. He pushed me around a few times and he hurt me in bed but he didn't hit me until that wedding. I guess you heard the story. I'll tell you—try waking up flat on your back on a dance floor with a couple hundred people looking down at you and teeth knocked out and your face swelling up like a beach ball. It was a life changer. Lou was a dead man, I knew that, but I was kind of dead too.

"I went home and tried to deal with it. Getting punched out brought me to my senses. My party girl days were over. I became a spinster aunt. Vera and others tried to get me dates, but I rejected everything. My father wanted to send me to Venice but I wouldn't go. I junked all my old sexy outfits and started wearing the dullest clothes I could find. What did that guy Avon on the train say?—I looked like Mrs. Katz, the school principal? I did. I had no life. I ran the businesses and tried to keep the brothers under control. Then Poppa got sick so I devoted myself to him.

"And then one night I was sitting on a train in Grand Central and this goofy guy came flying in the door. I almost broke out laughing at the sight of him. And then he sat down next to me and passed out. No wedding ring. Nice-looking guy, a little old but so what? He wasn't an Alpha-dog type and I realized I'd had enough Alpha dogs, I needed a guy like this. I knew he was a good man. I *knew* it. I wanted to wake him up with kisses.

"Turco's a bad memory, Phil. Am I glad Catcher killed him? Yes. It happened right about here, in the middle of the bar. Catcher killing Turco and getting sent back to jail and getting killed in jail all goes back to my mistake with Turco. This is something I have to live with, and I hope that you can live with it too. Can we go upstairs now?"

That night as Sylvia slept I stared at the ceiling and slowly realized that my endless, tedious quest for meaning, purpose, direction, etc., was finally over. I'd found all those things. My purpose now was protecting Sylvia. And not just Sylvia but her whole family. And, I realized, Charlie Benedict had given me a hint about how to do it: "*Search your assets,*" he'd said. "*Find a secret weapon, preferably nuclear.*"

CHAPTER 26

"Phil, do you care who's the next president of the United States?"

"I do, Pete."

"Because if I give this speech they wrote for me, it won't be me."

Draybin calling with a speechwriting crisis.

"I got you a room at the Waldorf equipped with a computer, food, bar, everything you need. It's waiting for you now, today. I want you to get into that room and work your butt off. I'm e-mailing Draft #8 as we speak. Try not to vomit."

"Have you got suggestions? Will you send research?"

"No and no. Research will only slow you down and I'm too busy with these campaign donors to think about anything else. I have to give this thing *tomorrow night*, Phil. Take over. Fix it. Make it great. Save my ass."

"Do I have to clear it with the Fromkinator and your other experts?"

"The who?"

"Kitty Fromkin."

"No, she's out. Forget about her. You don't have to clear it with anyone but me. I'll come to your room at three P.M. tomorrow. We'll go over it, bing-bang-boom."

"This is cutting it very close."

"Phil, I'm counting on you. I don't want to bomb before I'm even out of the gate. Ginger sends love. And come to the event. I've got two seats reserved for you at one of the megarich tables—gratis for you, of course. Bring your tux and that beautiful woman. I've got an excellent office picked out for you a few steps from the Oval Office."

A potential president was begging for my assistance and would install me in an office near the heart of power of the Free World. And Kitty was out.

Pete wasn't exaggerating about Draft #8. It was awful. The professional term for it was "a piece of shit," a perfect storm of committee writing, as if consultants, academics, and lawyers fought and bargained over every paragraph in a bitter clash of priorities and value systems, finishing with a product everyone hated but was glad to give up on.

Worse, as nonprofessional speechwriters its authors were ignorant of the cardinal reality of dinner speeches: *the audience is drinking*. A drinking audience will not abide a piece of shit speech. They have no attention span. They stop listening and stop behaving. They talk loudly and check messages and visit other tables. At worst they walk out, right under the speaker's nose. The speaker beholding this audience mutiny suffers the full gut-wrenching impact of bombing; it is a desperate, mortifying, even paralyzing nightmare. Pete was correct to see this coming with Draft #8. I had to help him.

I told Sylvia about it and she said, "You're working for him again? Have you lost all grasp of reality? I'm going to call you Mister Roundheels."

Fifty-nine-year-old writers do not do all-nighters so what I needed was to jump into a brand new draft with an idea that would be smooth sailing, causing no trouble. I would crank out a few good pages to break the ice, sleep, wake up fresh and early, and hammer my way to the end.

My plan was drastic: I would abandon the purpose of the speech. Tindall wanted to demonstrate Draybin's gravitas on a wide range of issues. Screw gravitas. Instead, with thanks to Ronald Reagan, I would introduce Pete as an attractive crowd-pleasing personality rather than a deep thinker. I'd brought along a disc containing all of what we called Pete's Greatest Hits: well-honed anecdotes, jokes, riffs, and reflections that he had delivered so well and so often that he'd developed an actor's polish. I would use this material to describe his life and the lessons that shaped his outlook and character. Hints of substance would be slipped in but never allowed to get in the way. Critics might clamor for meatier stuff but the foremost goal was to keep the audience entertained and friendly. I sat there and tapped away. Busy fingers are happy fingers.

Before bed I summoned Bazzanella to a breakfast meeting at the Waldorf. I also reached Sylvia, who'd arrived in the Poconos with the Sforza women and children and the three brothers. I asked if she could come back tomorrow, picking up a formal gown on the way, and join me among the fat cats attending the Draybin event.

"I don't have a gown. Those gowns are incredibly expensive and I'll probably never wear it again."

I said, "Go down to the basement of the Auberge, find the suitcase with my quarter-million dollars in it, and take whatever you need."

That changed her mind.

I didn't tell Bazzanella what I was doing in the Waldorf and he was too smart to ask. He consumed a gargantuan power breakfast as he told me what he'd learned.

The Mafia Commission would meet Sunday night at a so far undesignated location on Staten Island. Vavolizza would speak and then Bazzanella—not me, I wasn't a made man and was thus not qualified to appear—would be given a few minutes to explain the Sforza position.

We focused on outlining his remarks. He was impressed by my skill at this—there was *something* I was good at—but we knew the odds were against us and that Vavolizza, as a family boss, was one of the five commissioners and would swing strong political weight against us even though, as a party to the dispute, he would be excluded from the deliberations and the vote.

"I got the story of what happened to Jackie Rat-face and the other guy," Bazzanella said. "Wanna hear it or are you better off not knowing?" I was better off not knowing but told him to proceed.

Uddone had been ordered to Weaver Ridge to report on his conversation with me. Finding himself short on content, he tried to extract the message of my muddled analogy about Putin but it made no sense and exasperated Vavolizza. Then—this was a bombshell—it turned out that Uddone (not Vavolizza) had ordered the New Year's attack on the Sforza house, apparently to impress Nicky with his Putinesque executive initiative. Vavolizza had concealed his fury over Jackie launching an attack without permission and considered the attack stupid.

Meanwhile there was the matter of Stevie Leccisi. Nicky saw no point taking a chance that Leccisi would become a government witness. Uddone, who'd been Leccisi's boss for three years, didn't say a word in his defense. Instead, with extreme bad timing, he brought up his karate network scheme. Vavolizza had heard enough of this idea, which he considered idiotic.

Bazzanella said, "So they take Leccisi for a walk down by the school. Leccisi knows what's gonna happen and doesn't try to fight or run. One of Nicky's guys gives him a couple quick ones. Then Nicky turns to Jackie and says, 'You're next,' and the shooter caps Jackie too.

"Then Nicky looks up and sees the school flagpole and gets the idea of the two bodies tied to the flagpole like Rocco and Frankie, which makes me think Nicky had something to do with that years ago. Nicky loves this idea."

It was very strange to be listening to this over a nice breakfast in the Waldorf. I asked Bazzanella who Nicky would put in charge of the Sforza crew.

"Unknown so far. But I wouldn't be shocked if he tried to run the Sforza crew himself rather than sharing it with anyone else. I never heard of a boss running a crew but I don't know of anything against it. And I think he'd like the fame and fortune of replacing Jake."

"How's the breakfast? Want another dozen eggs?"

"Maybe I'll look at the desserts. But I got one more thing. This'll get a laugh out of you. Up at his Weaver Ridge place Nicky's got one of those women—what do they call them?—*au pair*. And this au pair has a hell of a pair. She's a big blonde Danish babe named Mina. She pushes the baby stroller around Weaver Ridge village and it just about causes a riot because she looks like an inflatable sex doll."

"You assume Nicky's banging her and he did, for a while. In the home he shares with his wife and family. This is not acceptable in our culture, Boss. You don't do the nasty with your girlfriend under your wife's roof. In Times Square at high noon, no problem, but not in your wife's house."

"And he got caught?"

"Of course. By guess who? The mother-in-law."

"What a thrill for the mother-in-law."

"She's a buzzard, this woman. Not your sweet little grandma. She knows how the game is played, believe me. I've known her all my life. I called her Aunt Nerezza. My mother has a Tuesday card game with her for forty years. That's how I get this story, from my mom, because Nerezza blabs the au pair story to her girlfriends."

"Does the mother-in-law tell Nicky's wife?"

"No, because the wife's a screamer and will throw it in Nicky's face. She's caught Nicky before and this will rip it. The old lady's got a pretty lush life going and doesn't want to risk getting kicked off the train. She just wants Nicky to behave. So she puts in a call to the son of another old girlfriend, the mother of none other than Ray Rosolini."

"And Ray Rosolini is who?"

"Skipper, Ray is the chairman of the commission. The 'first of the firsts,' as they say. Boss of bosses. So he's above Nicky."

"So the mother-in-law tells the head of the Mafia that Nicky's screwing the au pair behind her daughter's back?"

"Right. Nerezza cries on the phone—these women are actresses, you know. 'Ray, for the sake of the family you gotta talk to Nicky. Ray, I don't wanna make no trouble but this is a nice family and here's this Danish whore and Nicky can't keep his hands off her. Ray, Ray, Ray.'"

"So Ray is amused?"

"Ray is never amused. This thing shows very weak judgment by Nicky and at his level you're not supposed to be acting like this. So the commission talks it over and Ray sends for Nicky. Tells him to zip up his fly. Which Nicky has sense enough to obey."

"How long ago was this?"

"Six months, nine months, something like that."

"Did you pass this story along to Jake?"

"Of course."

"And what did he make of it?"

"He loved it but couldn't figure out what to do with it. A sex scandal might destroy a senator but not a mob boss. And Jake had to walk on eggshells with Nicky because of the autonomy thing. So he decided to put it in his pocket and wait."

"It's a great story."

"Yeah, but now there's a new twist. Everything was settled down in the house but Mina is a lusty young lady. She's got the itch. She starts looking around town and a couple months ago she starts up with a new boyfriend."

At this point Bazzanella started to giggle.

"Wanna know who it is?"

"Sure. Who is it?"

"*The police chief.*"

With that he explodes into mammoth laughter, covering his face with his napkin and pounding the table. "Who happens to be married so he can't take her home and also happens to be the former high school football star recognized by everybody for miles around, so he can't be seen checking into a motel with her. So what's the only place where they can get it on? *Nicky's house.*"

Paul started to choke on his toast. A waiter hurried over with a glass of water.

"Can you believe this?" said Bazzanella. "It's this cop who was quoted in the paper about Uddone. Jim Farraday. Young, good-looking guy. I wonder if they use his handcuffs."

He exploded in laughter again. People from other tables were looking at us.

"Nicky can't whack the cop and it'd be tricky to whack Mina. So does he say, how's it going, Chief, come right in and bang my au pair when I'm not around and enjoy the free run of the house, plant a few bugs, find the hidden guns and the cash and maybe the coke and play with my computer, hey, my casa is your casa? Who knows what he's got lying around, he's so sloppy. The commission would have a stroke over this."

"Has this come out yet?"

"No, but Nerezza knows, which means the old girls in the card game know and they're chirpers, so this will come out. Soon, I bet."

"Amazing. How can we use this?"

"I'm thinking I could put the story out and get Nicky in trouble before the Sunday meeting."

Was this the nuclear weapon I was looking for? Instinct said no. Domestic hanky-panky was not enough to upend Vavolizza or sidetrack a war.

"No, hold onto it," I told Bazzanella. "It's a good card but we have to figure out how to play it."

I went back upstairs and finished what I figured would be the last speech I'd ever write. I e-mailed it to Draybin just before noon. He knocked on my door at three. His security guys stayed in the hallway. Mine watched from afar.

"I had to get out of there," he said, meaning the Waldorf suite where his campaign staff was dug in. "Those people drive me crazy." He eyed the bottle of wine I was saving for drinks with Sylvia. "I wish I could have a drink but I know I can't."

"Have one glass of wine about twenty minutes before you speak. Gives you a little lift-off. But just one glass."

"Tindall and his people hate your draft."

"Just because I rejected every word they wrote?"

"Yeah, plus you changed the objective. But I love it. Should I be worried about looking like a lightweight for telling stories instead of bloviating about issues?"

"Let them call you a lightweight. Just don't let them call you boring."

"Ginger and Leon are here. I'll read the speech to them, in the room. That should be enough rehearsal. This stuff is tried and true. I could give it in my sleep."

"You're always great at this, Pete. If you look like you're having fun, the audience will have fun too. They'll be relieved they don't have to listen to heavy stuff."

"Good. We're done." He kicked off his shoes and flopped down on the bed. We watched some cable sports highlights and he fell asleep. He was a peaceful sleeper. A few snores but generally still and serene.

A little later Ginger called. "The candidate was last seen heading toward your room," she said.

"We talked for two minutes and he fell asleep," I said.

But the ringing phone woke him. "Tell her I'm coming up," he said.

Sylvia arrived as Draybin was leaving. She was carrying a garment bag and an overnight case. Two hours later I watched her wiggle into a sleek black gown. Then she added earrings and a necklace far too dazzling to have been acquired with honest money.

SHE WAS sensational and I was her barely noticed escort as we were led to one of the big-givers' tables. Sylvia was the new face and everyone wanted to know who she was. She used my line about being in "interstate commerce," laughingly deflecting further inquiry.

The ballroom was beautiful and packed with enthusiasts. The after-dinner program began with a comedian, then a woman singer, then a former governor introduced Pete and then he was on, making a presidential entrance with rousing music and a standing o. Ginger was on his arm, beaming. Leon looked dapper.

Draybin gave the speech perfectly. He was at the top of his game—charming, smart, sexy, funny.

Sylvia leaned over and whispered, "This is great. Did you really write this?"

The ovation was thunderous. The room seemed to rumble and shake. He came down from the dais and shook hands tirelessly. People fought to touch him.

Ginger penetrated the throng and hugged me. "He wants to take you to dinner Monday night to say thanks and discuss things," she said. "If you're available."

AVAILABLE?

Eight weeks earlier my heart would have flooded with joy at the prospect of this moment in the winner's circle of life. My career, instead of fading out pathetically, would have been majestically revived as Captain Pete served me his famous seduction platter: a bountiful mix of gratitude, admiration, humor, nostalgia, shared confidences, and anything else he could think of, topped off with White House fantasies galore.

But no, this mobster/speechwriter double identity nonsense had gone on far too long. I decided to go to the Monday dinner but use it to make my break with Draybin, explaining that I was heading for the exit no matter what he offered, telling him I was too old for campaigning and wanted to give all my attention to my marriage.

Jane Dooley called to confirm the dinner. Draybin had chosen an East Side restaurant called Fiori, a place so fabulous and expensive I never considered dining there.

"You're getting a big-time thank you," Jane said. "Meanwhile here's some news you'll enjoy: Dick Tindall insisted on staying with Draft #8 instead of your draft. There was a big fight over this and Pete told him #8 sucked and gave yours instead. So Tindall looks like a schmuck and now he's hanging by a thread. Phil, Fiori at eight o'clock."

Sylvia shook her head over my decision to go. I told her it bothered me that I hadn't been straight with Draybin after all our years together and I'd undoubtedly exposed him to tremendous embarrassment. Parting face-to-face was the honorable way to end it.

"You keep thinking Draybin is your friend," Sylvia said. "He's not your friend. He likes you. He appreciates you. But mainly he uses you. Don't count on any loyalty from him. He would have screwed me in a broom closet at Cape Cod if I'd let him know it was an option. And he wouldn't have felt guilty about it."

I wanted to protest but held my tongue. The notion of Draybin *using* me caught my attention. Maybe I was being too honor-minded about someone who'd betrayed me. If he could use me, maybe I could use him back.

CHAPTER 27

"**I** was so hinked up I almost pissed myself," said Bazzanella, back from the Sunday night meeting of the Mafia Commission on Staten Island. "A guy on my level never gets to see anything like this, all the top guys in one room with their underbosses and consiglieres standing behind them. Stony faces, believe me."

"Where did this happen?" asked Tommy.

"At somebody's apartment over a restaurant called Midnight Rose II on Hylan Boulevard. The bosses sat around the kitchen table. There was no more chairs so the rest of us had to stand."

"So let's hear it," I said.

"Well, I did pretty good. Kept it short like you said, Boss. You should have told that to Nicky. He did the Fidel Castro thing. Long. Yelling. Pounding the table. Finally Ray Rosolini cut him off and said okay, enough, all of you go have a drink while we talk.

"So Nicky and I and the other guys go downstairs to the restaurant and line up at this little bar. I thought the bartender was going to stroke out, you know, having all these wise guys at the bar, all with their ridiculous drink orders. Nobody just says gimme a vodka. They have to top each other by specifying the brand, the age, the shape of the lemon slice. And the shit they order? Mike Partanno orders a Grey Goose with pineapple juice. I almost laughed. Hey, Mike, why don't you have a Courvoisier and paint remover?

"Nicky's at the bar too, still carrying on. Sucking down the scotch. Saying all kinds of shit he shouldn't say. I mean, they had a dining room full of nice restaurant customers. Lots of cops live on Staten Island—there could have been major police brass sitting there for Sunday dinner."

"Paul," I said, "maybe we could fast forward to the commission's decision?"

"Sure, Boss. Basically they're for Nicky on everything. Rosolini does the talking. He says the Sforzas did well with the 'long leash' given to Jake and Tiz and they want those earnings to continue but they won't put up with a crew having autonomy or naming its own boss or trying to break off and become a sixth family. Five families is where it stays, he says. Of course the five would be against having a sixth because it would dilute everything.

"Then Ray surprises me. He turns a little against Nicky and says the commission won't allow a war and demands that Nicky negotiate with us. He says the killing of Catcher, the attack on the house, the two dead mutts tied to the flagpole—this has to stop. He's talking at Nicky, not a glance at me. He keeps telling him, 'I hope you're listening to me.' He says the commission will meet next Sunday, same time and place, and both sides will have to present their negotiated solution. If there's no solution, the commission will impose one and no one will like it. Or the conflict resolution fee."

"How did Nicky take it?" I asked Bazzanella.

"He said okay but he was bitching all the way out the door. Mothafuck this, cocksuck that. Ray noticed, believe me."

I said, "But the commission backed Nicky. What's he so pissed about?"

Bazzanella said, "I guess he don't like being told what to do. He don't think he should have to negotiate with subordinates. And he wants to look like the man because down the road he wants Ray's job."

"Ray knows that?"

"Ray's no fool."

Roncade said, "I can see the four other bosses walking out and asking each other, 'You think we got a problem with Nicky?'"

Bazzanella said, "What I don't understand is what he'd be willing to negotiate. He's won everything already."

I said, "Does the commission think we want to become a sixth family? I never thought of that. Did anyone else?"

"Jake thought of it years ago," said Bazzanella. "He decided we were safer with a lower profile. But I bet he mentioned the idea to some of the big boys, just to give them agita. Maybe it's been churning in their stomachs all this time. Just another reason to come down on the Sforzas."

I said, "What if Vavolizza says screw the commission's orders, I'm going to whack the Sforzas and then present *that* to the commission as my negotiated solution? What would the commission say to that?"

Roncade smiled and said, "Now we're getting down to reality."

Bazzanella said, "Maybe. If Nicky shows them a done deal they might accept it, if the price is right."

"So there are three ways this can go," I said. "One is Nicky kills us. Two is we give up everything and call it a negotiated solution and he kills us anyway. Three is we kill him and most of his outfit but then get arrested and locked up forever. Have I captured the essence of the situation?"

Dead silence.

I said, "Am I wrong? Does anyone see this in a rosier light? If so, speak up."

More dead silence.

"Look, we need leverage," I said. "We have nothing to bargain with. We need more time and we need a carrot to go with our sticks." I was wondering how Draybin would handle this. I wished I could sit down with him and talk it through. That's when I had an idea I couldn't resist.

"Paul," I said. "Call Nicky's people. I want to sit down with him."

"He wouldn't meet you before, why should he meet you now?"

"Because we've been ordered to negotiate. But tell him I've got an idea that will give him an orgasm."

Dead silence again.

"When do you want to do this?"

"Now. Tonight."

"He might not have sobered up from Staten Island yet."

"Good. Let's go to a place where he can drink some more. I'd like him a little off balance."

I felt good. Empowered by a great idea. Forget about my embarrassment with Uddone. I was bouncing back from that. I was finally getting the hang of gangster rock 'n' roll.

AT MIDNIGHT on a Sunday night in the small town of Weaver Ridge there was nothing open except the bowling alley, Weaver Ridge Bowl, which turned out to be the headquarters for the town's riffraff, many of whom filled the bar as I arrived with a security contingent—the Sforza brothers, Roncade and three of his toughest-looking ex-commandos (four more were stationed outside), and Bazzanella, who is not a fighter but has Mafia written all over him.

Roncade said, "You want to sit at the bar, Skip?"

"The stools are all taken," I said.

"Give me ten seconds and they'll be untaken," he said.

"Forget it. Why hurt their business?"

"Sure, Boss," Richie said, but he gave the lowlifes a look before turning away. What a look. The bar was empty in seconds.

"Let's bowl," I said.

Only two or three bowling lanes were active. The crash of flying pins echoed in the cavernous low-slung chamber.

Roncade led our group to the lane farthest from the door. Two thirtyish couples were bowling there but Richie said to them, "You're using our lane." They apologized and departed immediately.

The brothers did the bowling and seemed to enjoy it. Richie positioned the security guys, who were under instructions to be obvious about their presence and readiness to exchange fire. Vavolizza might have realized by now that he should have killed me. I didn't want him to see this as a lucky second chance.

Only twenty-five minutes later Nicky Vavolizza pushed through the door. He stopped for a dramatic pause, scanning the scene with a pugnacious glower as his one bodyguard helped him out of his overcoat. Nicky was good at arrivals and entrances.

I took some money out of my wallet—I'd learned to carry more cash since the humiliation when Uddone stole my forty dollars—and told Jimmy to buy beers for everyone in Weaver Ridge Bowl.

Vavolizza thudded toward us without a smile or wave. His body language signaled the vexation of an important man being called out on a Sunday night to meet with a pissant nobody. He wore dress slacks and an expensive sports shirt with a geometric design that made me dizzy. The shirt was untucked and hung over his belt, possibly to conceal a gun. Roncade stepped forward to frisk him but Vavolizza avoided this indignity by lifting the shirt and dancing in a little circle. No gun. Big hairy belly. I'd bet he'd never done a sit-up but I sensed there was still enough muscle on him to deliver a body punch that would leave you bent over for many minutes.

I rose to greet him but remembered that wise guys don't do polite handshakes and we were obviously not fellow goombahs who would do cheek-kissing. As we came face to face I felt the intimidating push-back of his presence. There was also some push-back from the whiskey odor on his breath.

"You're Phil?" Nicky asked, looking me over and smirking. "You got instructions from Sylvia?"

"Sylvia doesn't give me instructions. I'm the boss."

"I'll take a fucking drink."

"I ordered beers."

"Fuck beers. Chivas."

"In a bowling alley?"

"The best they got." Tommy took off for the bar.

I sat down on the red vinyl banquette where bowlers waited between balls. I noticed that the voice coming out of me wasn't my normal voice: I sounded *strong*. I was surprised by this until I realized I'd given myself permission to play a role, to lie, to be someone much different from the usual me.

"I'll listen but I don't expect to buy nothing you're selling," he said, sitting down. "I don't even know who you are."

"You should have watched my biography on the History Channel."

"Sorry I missed it, I was taking a shit."

"I'll fill you in. I started out in investment banking but that career turned out to be confining, if you know what I mean? So about fifteen years ago I got involved behind-the-scenes with Jake. I worked with him on many deals. I helped him set up his global network. You didn't know he had a global network, did you? I brought in specialists of all kinds, including financial, legal, military, technological. Of course all my good work never came to your attention. Jake wanted it that way. He wanted you to be happy with your 1950s business model while we were getting into the new century."

"We done pretty good," he said. "I ain't complaining."

"You ain't complaining? So why all that screaming with the commission tonight? Sounds like complaining to me, like a man who isn't getting what he wants."

"I'm getting what I want. I won. The game is over."

"You wouldn't be talking to me if it was over. But it'll be over soon. We're heading at each other like two big railroad trains and nobody's going to walk away from the collision. You and I are going to be dead or behind bars forever and our families will be in ruins. I say this happens within a week."

"Maybe I don't see it that way."

Tommy returned with the scotch. "They didn't have Chivas," he said. Nicky tasted it and made a face.

"You're a bluffer, Nick. You tried to bluff the commission with all that noise you made. Don't tell me you don't know better than that. You're not an idiot."

I could see he enjoyed this tiny touch of flattery so I steered in that direction. Nicky was probably not an idiot but he was vain and ambitious, and vain ambitious people will swallow outrageous bullshit if it fits their dreams.

"I've done my due diligence on you, Nick," I said. "I've checked you out from every direction. I know the thinking on you at the highest level. And it's not bad. You get qualified respect. But there are things that haven't come out that reflect poorly on your ability to rise to the top spot that could be ahead for you."

"Such as what?"

"I don't want to get off on a tangent about specific ill-advised things you've done but it's a fairly long list."

The transparent evasion sucked him in.

"Look who's bluffing now," he said. "I think you don't got shit."

"I've got plenty."

"Give me an example. One example."

Bingo.

"If you insist. Just a little one. How about fucking the au pair, Mina."

He blanched. He actually looked around to see who'd overheard.

"I got better than that. Want another one?"

He looked away.

"Okay, Nick, do you know a guy named Jim Farraday?"

"The cop? What about him?"

"Do you know he's been making booty calls at your house? Getting it on with the lovely Mina?"

"Fuck you," he said. All-purpose response.

"First you fuck her under your wife's roof, then a police chief comes into your house and fucks her under *your* roof. How do you think the commission and those above the commission would like that?"

"Whaddaya mean, *above* the commission? What's *above* the commission?"

"Nicky, I thought you were sophisticated."

"Continue," he said, as if he understood what I meant, which I didn't know myself.

Uddone was too crazy to follow anything like this but I sensed that Vavolizza might be vulnerable if I could spin this out-of-the-blue idea about a high crime authority—higher than the commission—that had its eye on him. Mobsters are paranoid and paranoids are eager to believe in sinister secret organizations. This was a promising direction: stimulating Nicky's ambition with the idea that secret powers-that-be were appraising him for future promotion into the stratosphere of crime.

"The way they see it, you're well-positioned as the youngest of the five family bosses. You've still got respect and you have some excellent assets, although it's an egregious deficiency that you haven't *developed* anything."

I had his attention.

"You haven't shown any innovative or visionary dimension, Nick, and that's how you're judged at the top levels these days. You haven't moved beyond traditional core rackets. You can send e-mails but you're a tube steak when it comes to the global potential of technology. Trillions of dollars are flying around the world every minute and you're hardly beyond identity scams and credit cards and some online gambling. Widen your tech-crime horizons, my man. Think Russia. Better yet, think Ukraine or Romania."

That exhausted my knowledge of computer crime so I made a turn toward my intended destination.

"What's even more embarrassing, Nick, is your performance on the basics."

"What basics?"

"Like simple influence. Connections. Juice. It's not enough anymore to own a few judges and politicians. You have to have influence at the highest level. And you need infrastructure. Interlocking layers. Cross-functionality. Vertical integration. Six Sigma. That's what it takes if you want to build a family that'll separate the Vavolizza era from the old days. That's what it takes if you want to get beyond chump change and go exponential. That's what it takes if you want to make *history*."

"Am I supposed to know what you're fucking talking about?" he asked, but he was interested.

I took my eyes off Nicky and glanced at Bazzanella, who was standing behind him, listening. Bazzanella gave me a discreet nod of approval.

"What I'm saying, Nick, is that the Sforza family can provide the platform, innovation, and expertise you need to step up in class. You've got what we both need to build an empire. We have to form a synergistic partnership to optimize our functionalities in the greatest outfit that's ever existed, with a proven superstar as boss. Meaning you."

"Me? You just called me a tube steak."

"No, it has to be you. I'm a behind-the-scenes guy, but you're a natural lead-from-the-front commander, much like Alexander the Great on his big white horse, Bucephalus."

"And you got the, uh, thing for this?"

"Infrastructure? Expertise? Bet your fat ass I do."

Now he made a pathetic attempt to turn the tables.

"So all you're telling me is what I'll have when I own you. But I *already* own you. I don't have to make a deal to get what I'm going to get anyway."

"Nicky, this is an example of how, sometimes, you leave your judgment in your other pants. First, it presumes we're not going to fight you. Do you know my associate, Major General Richard Roncade, US Marine Corps Retired, who's standing behind you to your left? General Roncade now commands our armed security division, which is equipped to wipe out your band of bagels in any given twenty-four-hour period.

"But second, let's say we capitulated in the name of avoiding bloodshed and you took over. You wouldn't understand the op system. You wouldn't know what we're hiding from you. You couldn't hurdle the partitions. If I forget to tell you that a certain important person is on our payroll, how would you know that? We don't write it on the wall in crayon. And if I don't explain how our sophisticated processes work, how would you find out? What I'm saying is that you can't strong-arm your way into our operation. You have to be welcomed in. Partnership is the only way."

"And what do you want for this?"

"Just the status quo, hands-off on our operations, and our rightful piece of the pie as we help you lead the Vavolizza family into the future. You go before the commission next Sunday and renounce all demands for change. You say you've made an executive decision that the Sforzas function best under the current arrangement and that's how it should stay and you're committed to it, permanently. I require that you say that. We keep the same autonomy they gave to Jake years ago. And that's how we'll work it, and you will be strengthened beyond your wildest dreams. And your achievement will be noticed by those who count."

"How about if everything you're saying is total bullshit?"

"Ah, finally the right question," I said, pleased that he'd taken the bait again. "You want proof that I can offer you something special, something you never dreamed of. You want a demonstration. Is that right?"

"Yeah, that's right."

"Okay, I'll give it to you right now. Are you ready?"

He sat back smiling. "Bring it on."

"A minute ago I mentioned influence at the highest level. How do you interpret that?"

"How should I know? Could be anything."

"No, not anything. Do you capeesh the word *highest*?"

Jimmy returned with a heavy tray of beers. I let Nicky's suspense build as I handed out bottles.

"Nick, when I say *highest* I mean *highest*. I mean putting a hook into the president of the United States."

I let that sink in.

"And Nick, that would be *your* hook. Your *personal* hook."

It was not hard to read his mind: I, Niccolò Vavolizza, could have my hook into the biggest whale in the ocean, Moby Fucking Dick, the unattainable jackpot di tutti jackpots.

No mobster had ever hooked a president. Sam Giancana helped get JFK elected (and shared a woman with him) but got nothing out of it. This would top everything.

"Not the current president," I said. "The next one."

His face darkened. "How do you even know who the next one's going to be?"

I laughed derisively. Bazzanella and Roncade took the cue and laughed along with me. The fix was in—people who counted knew who the next president would be, naive wannabes like Nicky did not. But given his view of a corrupt universe, Nicky was quick to buy in.

"Who's it going to be?"

Before leaving the Sforza house I'd rummaged through the old newspapers waiting for the garbage pick-up and plucked out the *New York Times* edition with the front-page story about Pete Draybin's declaring his candidacy. The article included a nice photo of Draybin making the announcement.

"Him," I said.

"You're shitting me? Who's he?"

"Read it."

He slowly read a few paragraphs and looked up. "I gotta get money down on this. What odds are they making on this guy?"

"Nick, I thought you knew about gambling. What do you think the betting world would make of big early money coming in on a long shot like Peter Draybin? Do you think they'd get a little suspicious? What would that do to the odds? If you want to blow the whole thing, go around telling everybody you know who the next president is."

He grumped and harrumphed. But I knew he'd place a big bet on Draybin. Like all hoods, he couldn't pass up the easy score.

"So just how do you plan to do this, putting the hook in?"

"It's *already* in. Jake made the original connection with Draybin and passed it over to me. Over the years we've found ways to be good to each other. We've got a few huge things set up already and there'll be a lot more when he's in the White House. Maybe you and I will go there for dinner sometime. Bring the wives and kids."

He sat back grinning. Sensuous delight seemed to spread over him, head to foot. He turned around and waved his empty scotch glass at Tommy, who understood we were in suck-up mode and took off obediently for a refill.

"Nick, there could be a day when you sit in the living room of your house—let's call it the Weaver Ridge White House—and place a POTUS call on your secure private line and discuss things you can do for each other."

"What the fuck is a POTUS call?"

"POTUS is the acronym for President of the United States. You call him up, you talk deals, regulations, Supreme Court nominations, contracts—and those government contracts are megasized, you know, quintessentially skimworthy. You hang up the phone and you just made, what, millions or billions and you haven't even finished breakfast."

I glanced up at Bazzanella and Roncade. They were smirking about the Weaver Ridge White House.

Nicky enjoyed one long unguarded moment before suspicion returned. "Just one thing I don't get," he said. "What's the hook? You're buddy-buddy and all that but when he's the POTUS, what keeps him from doing business with somebody else? He'll be the boss and won't need you anymore, unless you somehow got him by the onions."

That was a shrewd question which I should have anticipated. I stalled, babbling about Draybin's love for big money and about the value of working with a trusted and longtime partner like me instead of new people.

"Yeah, but that's not having him by the *balls*."

Tommy returned with Nicky's scotch. Nicky took a big gulp as he stared at me, waiting for my response.

By this point I knew where I had to go.

"We *do* have him by the balls," I said.

I was moving into contemptibility. I was having love/hate feelings about myself for coming up with something so brilliant and so despicable.

He was waiting.

"Sylvia," I said.

"Whaddaya mean?"

"Whaddaya think I mean?"

"Something about Sylvia? He's *fucking* Sylvia?"

"And we got it on video. The next president getting it on with the daughter of the mob boss."

I cringed to say this but it was a great lie. And it worked.

He was close to open-mouthed amazement. "No kidding? Sylvia's banging this guy?"

"It was one of the benefits of his relationship with us."

"That is beautiful. Fucking-A beautiful."

And the best part was that as long as Nicky believed he'd have pull with the White House, Sylvia and I were indispensable and therefore unkillable. It was now in Nicky's interest for the status quo between the mob and the Sforzas to resume, undisturbed. There would be no warfare and I would have until the presidential election season to think of a next move. I knew that events would shape new strategies. Time was on my side. Nicky had a high-risk job with many enemies; he had a bad temper and volatile judgment; he was overweight, drank too much, probably had health problems, and would certainly have stressful domestic problems when the Mina story came out. Any of these could be a game-changer in our favor.

"Okay, it's a deal," Vavolizza said. "If you can prove this isn't just bullshit."

"Tell you what," I said. "I just happen to be having dinner with Draybin tomorrow night. We'll be at Fiori in the city."

"I know the joint," he said.

"Here's the plan. I'm sitting down with him at eight. You walk in at eight fifteen and join Bazzanella for a drink at the bar. You've got to play this very low-key. If you come in doing one of your big Al Capone entrances it could blow the deal, okay? He'll get up and run.

"You take a sip or two at the bar and only then do you casually look around the room. You'll see Draybin and me at a table, talking like old friends. Take a good long look until you're satisfied that I've got a close relationship with the next president. Then get outta there. Drive home thinking of the great future ahead of us."

"Maybe I'll stop by the table and say hello."

"*No.* Absolutely not. Nicky, everybody knows who you are. How's it going to look if America's foremost mob boss comes by to shake the hand of a presidential candidate? If Adolf Hitler came by for a hello it wouldn't be any worse. Do you understand that?"

He was disappointed but tried again. "Hey, Italian guys in a restaurant, we go from table to table. 'How ya doing? Hey, what's happening?' It's no big deal."

"It *is* a big deal, Nick. What do you think a photo of you and Peter Draybin smiling and shaking hands would do to his campaign? Destroy it. No more hook, no more big fish. Understand?"

"I'll just shake hands. Wish him well on his campaign. If we're gonna be partners he should look me in the eye, man to man."

"No. Listen to me. If you blow this it could cost us millions that've been invested in electing him and billions in future profits. *Billions.* And so help me, I would walk right into the commission and tell them how you fucked it up. And then I'd go to my other friends too, and tell them, which would end your career and your existence. So keep away from that table. *Do you understand?*"

"Don't worry about it. You're so touchy."

"*Capeesh?*"

"Hey, you're a paisan! *Capisco!*" In a millisecond he'd turned giddy. He had an urge to celebrate and with perfect timing Tommy arrived at just this moment, carrying a bottle of grappa and two whiskey glasses on a plastic tray with a beer company logo.

Nicky gulped the last of his scotch and seized the grappa bottle, filling two glasses to the brim—no, to overflowing. He was so pumped his hand was quivering. His suspicious demeanor was gone and he was now the life-of-the-party don.

"Nicky, one last time. What time are you gonna get there?"

"About ten." He exploded with laughter.

"No coming by the table, right?"

"Unless I want to stick my dick in his ear."

"Tell me you understand or it's off."

"No problem, Phillie. *Salute.*"

I had him.

CHAPTER 28

W alking into Fiori you feel a rich warmth of well-being, as if you had exited an elevator at the top floor of life. A tuxedoed captain led me across the expansive main room where every table was full and every conversation was bubbling. Flowers were everywhere: in lush arrangements in tall hand-painted vases situated around the room and in a magnificent mural on the far wall. The perfume of the flowers blended with the perfumes of the women and the succulent aromas rising from every dish.

I saw Paul Bazzanella at the bar, alone, looking tense as he awaited Vavolizza. The brothers, dressed like young financiers, were seated at a table far in the back. Jimmy rose to get my attention and gave me a supportive punching-the-air gesture.

Then a surprise: instead of seating me in the main room the captain led me to an elegant banistered staircase in the far left corner leading to private dining rooms upstairs. The private room was a fine touch, adding to the grandness of Draybin's gesture. However, as I reached the top stair I realized that it was a serious wrinkle in my game plan. Draybin and I would be dining out of sight. Vavolizza would not be able to look around from the bar and see us together, confirming that I was buddy-buddy with the president-to-be.

Could Bazzanella keep Nicky under control until Draybin and I emerged at the end of the meal? It was hard to be optimistic about that. Nicky was volatile even when sober. He had a celebrity mentality and could not sit quietly or anonymously at a bar. He was hyper about Draybin. How would he behave after two hours of drinking and impatient waiting?

From the balcony I paused to look down at the bar: Nicky had not arrived and I prayed for him to be late, very late. Stuck-in-traffic, even car-accident late.

The captain led me into a dim corridor where he opened the first door on the left and guided me into a predictably beautiful small dining room with a single table. Draybin was already there, seated with a man I didn't know. Both men stood.

Instead of the effusive greeting and crushing embrace I expected from Draybin, I received only a frosty handshake. The other man gave his name as Rob Portis. His handshake was so powerful I almost squealed. He was as strapping and athletic-looking as Draybin but twenty years younger with white hair in a military cut.

We ordered drinks and chatted stiffly about the beauty of the restaurant. There were two flower arrangements in the room and their fragrance was dizzying. Our drinks arrived immediately. Draybin asked the waiter to close the door.

"Phil, are you acquainted with a man named Maxwell Waxman?"

At my age a few bells must ring while the memory struggles with an unexpected retrieval challenge (during which Pete and Portis exchanged glances) but it came back to me: Max from the hospital, the little schmuck whose nose I pinched.

"Mr. Waxman is the cofounder and CEO of Waxman & Girard, which makes him a significant player on Wall Street. He's active in every conceivable civic activity including philanthropy and politics. He and his wife attended my Waldorf fund-raiser. They sat at the table next to yours."

The scotch was delicious, a ridiculously expensive brand I'd never tried. Sensing that I would need it, I drank in healthy sips.

"Maxwell phoned me this morning, extremely upset, and when Maxwell is upset, the earth trembles. I know you've met him, Phil. He's someone you don't forget."

"I've got him now. When I met him he was in a bathrobe and pajamas in a hospital. I didn't recognize him at the Waldorf."

"But he recognized you. And he was outraged to see you there. He said that if people like you were associated with my campaign, he would be forced to reassess his role as a major contributor. You can imagine my surprise, since I don't think of you as someone whose presence has that kind of impact on people."

Was that praise or a put-down?

"Maxwell claimed that you were the personal attorney for a Mafia crime lord. I laughed out loud at that. It got even crazier when he said you were providing legal advice to this guy, who was on his deathbed."

I said, "This was a fairly hilarious misunderstanding that took place when I made a hospital visit to a friend."

"The friend was Jacopo Sforza?"

The noose was tightening. We criminals know the feeling.

"Phil, don't I recall that Sylvia's last name is Sforza? At least that was the name on the sweatshirt she gave Ginger."

"Jake Sforza was her father."

Portis interrupted. "Mr. Vail, I've advised Mr. Draybin that the late Jacopo Sforza was a high-ranking member of the Vavolizza crime family of the New York Mafia and an organized crime figure of legendary stature. Were you aware of that?"

"Yes."

"Can you explain this to me, Phil?" Draybin asked earnestly. "Maxwell also says you physically assaulted him when he was in the hospital being treated for cancer."

"He had a tantrum. You've seen what he's like, a little stinkpot. I hardly assaulted him. I pinched his nose to make him shut up." I hoped for a laugh but none came.

"And he says Jacopo Sforza behaved in a menacing manner."

"Consisting of a few dirty looks."

I'd never seen Draybin so uncomfortable. "Maxwell has promised to make sure everyone in New York politics, philanthropy, *and* the news media knows about my relationship with you *and the Mafia* unless I take action immediately."

"Max is an asshole," I said, taking a big sip of scotch.

"Of course he is, Phil. But he's a *vindictive* asshole and he wants to get even because you embarrassed him. Now he's going to cause trouble and it could be fatal to my candidacy. The whole story is beyond belief. I can't tell you how much this has upset Ginger and Leon."

"I'm sorry about that, Pete."

"Phil, Rob is the head of the FBI office in New York. We've met on numerous civic and social occasions and he was the first person I consulted today after Max called. I've asked him to join us because in the spirit of the great relationship you and I have had over the years I wanted to see if anything can be done for you."

"To rescue me from a life of crime?" His concern about me was difficult to buy ten seconds after he'd spelled out his concern about *himself.*

"I can't believe you're being flippant about this. It's not like you."

Maybe not but I wasn't the same me anymore. When I donned my don suit it became instinctive to stonewall and fend off attacks with wiseass humor. I didn't enjoy acting like this with Pete but this ramrod from the FBI made me even more defensive.

"Mr. Vail," said Portis, "after my conversation with Mr. Draybin I reached out to Special Agent Kenneth DeSens in White Plains. I believe you are acquainted with him?"

"Yes. Is this interrogation being recorded?"

"No and this is not an interrogation. Tonight I'm on your side. It might be different in the future."

I disliked this guy but didn't want him working against me.

"DeSens has briefed me on the evolution of your involvement with the Sforza crew leading up to the violent deaths of a captain and two soldiers in the Vavolizza family. This is a world a person like you should have resisted with all your strength. Instead you seemed to have thrived in it and actually become Jake Sforza's successor. It seems to me you have wandered astray in a way that is without precedent. But Mr. Draybin attests to your good character and DeSens says you've been cooperative in averting further violence. So for now I'm treating you as a good citizen who's made a tragic misjudgment rather than a criminal who should be taken off the street."

"I thought we were going to have a nice dinner tonight, Pete. Pardon me if I feel that you've led me into a trap."

"You trapped yourself, Phil. I mean, I've heard the story but I don't get it. I figure you got pulled in through Sylvia. I can understand how such an attractive woman could manipulate a lonely man of your age."

"She didn't manipulate me."

"On the contrary, I think she bewitched you. You are hardly the kind of person who would join the Mafia, for Christ's sake. Or bring a Mafia woman into my home."

A woman you flirted with like a high school boy. A woman you wanted to hire for your campaign. A woman you probably hoped to maneuver into the sack on some cold winter night during the Iowa primary campaign.

"Is that it, Phil? You didn't know about Sylvia until you were in too deep to get out?"

"If you're saying Sylvia seduced or fooled me into this, you're dead wrong. I saw an opportunity to make my life better and I took it."

"To make your life *better*?" Pete asked, color rising in his face.

"By far. Believe me, it's not the way I would have chosen. But it's what happened."

While Draybin digested that idea, I finished my scotch. I was ready for another.

"And you've been writing for me while getting involved with the Mafia?"

"Yes."

"That cannot continue. You understand I have to fire you effective this moment."

"Understood."

"I'm deeply saddened by this."

He put on his deeply saddened face.

Portis said, "Mr. Vail, Mr. Draybin has requested that I offer you some advice, which I hope is not too late. What I strongly suggest is that you dissociate yourself from the Cosa Nostra as of this moment. I further suggest that you engage an attorney, *tomorrow*, to guide you through the cleanest possible extrication and deal with whatever trouble you've gotten yourself into already. You're welcome to visit my office downtown and discuss possible courses of action."

He reached across the table and inserted his business card into the breast pocket of my suit jacket. "Naturally any reciprocity you can offer would impact beneficially on your prospects going forward."

With that he stood and shook hands with Draybin. He did not offer his hand to me. He turned to go, and that's when the shit hit the fan.

Portis opened the door and there was Nicky Vavolizza, standing in the corridor with his hand raised, trying to decide whether to knock or just stroll in.

He wore a gray double-breasted bespoke suit with an oversized red flower in the lapel (drops of water on the flower hinted that he'd just snitched it from a Fiori vase). Spread across his round face was something I recognized as what we used to call a shit-eating grin, meaning drunk and too stupid to comprehend his own idiocy.

I had a horrible feeling of impending and unstoppable disaster. I realized at once that I'd created a monster with the White House connection fantasy. The prospect of putting a hook into the president had so intoxicated Nicky that he'd carried the intoxication theme to a physical extreme. My strategy had been to have my two worlds touch in a subtle but inspired sting and then bounce apart; instead it would be a deafening crash with unimaginable repercussions.

Nicky bent slightly and peeked around Portis to make direct eye contact with Draybin and greet him in a slurred voice, saying, "Yo, Mr. Future President, how're they hanging?"

I'd never seen Pete Draybin lose his cool or even come close to it but he turned to me in alarm and whispered, "Who the hell is this?"

"Nicky Vavolizza. Boss of the Vavolizza Mafia family."

"Oh shit. What's he doing here? Get him out of here."

But Nicky wanted to strut in and spread goodfella charm. The catch was that Portis loomed in the doorway, blocking him. Nicky raised a heavy arm to brush Portis aside—as he would brush aside any inconsequential obstacle—but Portis roughly seized his wrist and held it tightly. That's when they took their first good looks at each other and realized that fate had contrived a confrontation of opposite numbers, Mafia boss face-to-face with FBI boss.

I would have traded my kingdom for a camera with a wide-angle lens. My photo would begin on the far left with Draybin, still seated but popping out of his skin with anxiety. Moving to the right, past a vase of flowers, was the intense Rob Portis clutching the wrist of the baffled Vavolizza. More to the right, seen through the doorway, was a corridor crammed with large jostling men who, I realized, were professional "muscle": Mafia apes for Vavolizza, Secret Service or private agency guys for Draybin, a tall blond buttoned-down FBI aide for Portis, and the three Sforza brothers for me.

Then, pushing into the doorway behind Nicky, was the immensity of Paul Bazzanella, who sent me two pantomimed messages: first a begging-forgiveness gesture for failing to restrain Vavolizza, then a fast sequence of glass-to-mouth gestures warning me that Vavolizza had downed many drinks. As if I didn't know.

Portis glowered at Nicky. Nicky should have glowered back but he was confounded by booze. Instead of embracing the trophy of a lifetime (Draybin) he was frustrated by the iron grip of his primary nemesis (Portis).

Of all the inflamed motivations in the room the most explosive was Draybin's panicked impulse to escape any kiss-of-death linkage to Vavolizza. A rocket went off somewhere inside him. He reverted to the football player he'd once been, charging the crowded doorway like a fullback determined to blast through the defensive line. Vavolizza, desperately wrenching his wrist free from Portis's fist, made a clumsy attempt to intercept the onrushing Draybin, perhaps to wrap him in a bear hug, anything to keep this greatest of prizes from slipping away forever.

Draybin lashed out with a forearm blow that caught Nicky squarely in his Adam's apple. Nicky's eyes widened in surprise as he stumbled backward, wheezing and clutching his throat. The back of his head hit the doorframe with a sickening crack and he slid to the floor, coming down hard on his broad mobster rump.

Somehow a vase from a wall niche became entangled in his fall and went down after him, landing directly on his kneecap. It looked painful but he didn't flinch; I wasn't sure he was fully conscious. The vase did not break but its water and some of its long-stemmed exotic flowers spilled onto Nicky's lap.

The two mob goons in the corridor pushed forward urgently trying to get to their boss but they were forced backward by the outbound rush of a bodyguard contingent that folded Draybin and Portis into a security bubble befitting a president caught in an assassination attempt. They knew this drill well, moved rapidly, and were gone in a flash. It must have been an astonishing spectacle for diners in Fiori's main room to see them thundering down the stairs and out of the restaurant.

In all this tumult I was the only one who was still. Vavolizza sat on the floor rubbing his head and neck, looking like a disoriented accident victim as his goons and the three Sforza brothers stood over him, pumping adrenaline but not knowing what to do with it. I suspected they were about to slug it out on general principles but Bazzanella asserted himself as the peacemaker simply by moving his bulk between them.

I noticed a waiter rushing by our room with a tray of drinks.

"Grab that waiter," I barked. Tommy Sforza grabbed him and pulled him in.

"Got any scotch on that tray?" I said.

The waiter was tongue-tied but I identified two scotches-on-the-rocks. I took both and waved him away. Then I told the others to calm down, get lost, and stay out of trouble while I talked with Mr. Vavolizza.

Jimmy turned and mouthed, "You okay?" as he went out. I nodded and he left, closing the door.

Nicky was a sorry sight, sitting with spread legs, the crotch of his gray trousers darkly stained with flower water, flowers strewn on his lap. He must have known that colorful descriptions of this mortification would spread like urban wildfire. He would be a laughingstock, a joke, and a mob boss who becomes a joke is no longer feared and a boss who isn't feared is a lion tamer without a whip. They taught this lesson on the first day of Mafia 101.

With a great effort Nicky got to his feet, got a hand on a chair, and sat down heavily. I slid the second scotch in front of him. He took a sloppy slurp, dribbling liquid on his chin. He was in a trance, perhaps bidding farewell to his dream of gloating about his presidential conquest to Ray Rosolini and the gnarly old goats of the commission.

But before I took too much joy in his misery, I thought, I should consider my own predicament. Both of my parallel lives were in ruins. Jake Sforza's baiting of Max Waxman had come back to sabotage my standing with Draybin. My clever-seeming trick to buy time by duping Vavolizza with White House fantasies had turned into a debacle, trashing the last of my bright ideas for delaying a mob war.

I knew what I had to do: I had to *get out*. I had to get Sylvia out. To get Sylvia out I had to get the whole Sforza family out. There was no hope of returning to Jake's status quo. There was no chance of holding off the Mafia's predatory ambitions without a devastating war. I'd failed at everything. Getting out was now the strategy and it started with getting out of this room.

BUT I wasn't going to dash for the door. I refused to give Nicky the satisfaction of seeing me in flight. Just the opposite: I wanted to be as nasty as the baddest gangster, rubbing salt in his wounds and grinning about it.

"You fucked up, Nick," I said. "I've never seen such a fuck-up in my life."

"Fuck yourself," he said, without passion.

"I may have done that already."

"I don't even know who you are," he said groggily. "Who the fuck *are* you?"

"The answer to that is evolving. I'm slowly getting clarity."

"You're a double-talking wiseass, you know that?"

He gave me a black look, maybe the blackest look in his arsenal, and then he said the words that never failed him.

"I'm gonna kill your ass, motherfucker."

A death threat from a mob boss was a peak moment in my crime career, but like many peak moments it was disappointing and trite. Even pathetic coming from this washed-up blob. Murder would be a tall order in his condition. He'd taken serious blows to the head and neck; he was still dazed and under the influence; he was terminally disgraced; he was fifty-plus years old and exhausted. I guessed that the most attractive activity he could imagine was not killing me but falling peacefully asleep in the car and snoring all the way home to Weaver Ridge.

I suppose I saw myself as a cocky matador taunting a wounded bull. But matadors know their business. I was an amateur with no concept of the darkness at the core of Nicky Vavolizza. It was a rare moment of arrogance in my life, but one moment is all it takes to get yourself killed.

"Let me tell you something," he said in a growl. "I am not done. I am going to bury the fucking Sforzas. But first I'm gonna knock your fucking spleen up your ass."

I laughed at that, and the laugh may have been one insult too many. He heaved forward out of his chair and lunged at me. His move was not nimble but it was still 230 or so pounds of gangster beef flying at me.

I'd read about such moments: you watch the danger approaching in slow motion as you try to rouse yourself to action. But I had also read, years ago—I think in a John le Carré novel—a scene in which a protagonist under attack recalls being taught that *any* object could be a weapon and *any* weapon was better than no weapon at all. You don't need a gun or knife. An umbrella or rolled-up magazine could do decisive damage.

All I had was the empty whiskey glass in my hand. Fiori's glassware was substantial. The glass had excellent weight and a squared solid base. It nestled comfortably in the palm like a baseball.

Quickly and with all my strength I slammed it into Nicky's oncoming forehead.

It was a dead-on perfect shot. The base of the glass met the bone over his left eyebrow with a harrowing sound. His head snapped back, eyes closing and jaw dropping. He crumpled and stood on his bent knees, in a prayer position.

At that moment he was lined up for a kill, defenseless and wide open. I had a feeling I've never known in my life, a steep descent toward some primal inner place where violence would be ecstatic. I could have pounded him mercilessly with the glass or kneed him repeatedly in the chin or kicked him in the balls until he fainted dead away. And then I could have killed him with a foot on his neck, crushing his windpipe with a thrust of my heel.

But I didn't. That one great hit with the glass was the bull's-eye of a lifetime. It purged my need for violence and I had just enough clarity to realize it was not smart to be seen running out of a room leaving a corpse on the floor. It was better to leave behind a beaten-up hoodlum who'd been defeated and humiliated by an almost-senior citizen.

I dropped the glass and jumped up. He grabbed at me but I slapped his hand away and went for the door. I'd expected a crowd in the corridor but no one was there.

As I got to the balcony the restaurant scene below struck me as surreal. I paused to look down at it and felt the spinning sensation of vertigo. The whole experience was catching up to me: I was shaking like the proverbial leaf as I started down the stairs, steadying myself with my left hand on the banister and my right hand reaching for contact with the wooden dividers of the enormous wine rack built into the wall parallel to the staircase.

I was a third of the way down the stairs when Vavolizza emerged from the corridor and stood on the balcony. Perhaps it looked surreal to him too. He stood there like King Kong, shouting profanity which stunned the restaurant into silence. He pointed at me, bellowing threats. He would break me in half, kill me, clip me, whack me, chainsaw my fucking ass. It seemed like a theatrical performance with Nicky as the virtuoso thespian, transfixing the audience below as he stormed across the stage in his famous madman scene.

I stumbled down a few more stairs as he came after me. But then he was on me, landing from behind in a fall or leap, a back-breaking load. I had feared his punching power but it was his sheer dumb tonnage that left me staggering, almost buckling. We crashed into the wine rack. My forehead hit something so hard I almost blacked out. Then something else, perhaps the head of a small nail, ripped my cheek.

A heavy punch from behind drove into my ribs with breathtaking impact. More punches followed including several to the side of my head, my ears, and neck. He seemed to have an insatiable desire to damage me. Then he locked his arms around my waist, tugging and grunting, and I realized he wanted to hurl me over the banister. I was aware of panic below—I heard the scraping of chairs and shouted alarms as people stood and jumped back from the area where my body would land.

I knew the brothers would get to me as fast as they could but they had to fight through riot conditions in the restaurant's main room and by the time they arrived I might be airborne. I had to save myself. I struggled with everything I could muster, scared shitless but in a crazy way thrilled by the no-holds-barred desperation of the fight. I reached around frantically for something to cling to. I felt for a grip on the wine rack and found nothing. Then my fingers circled the neck of a bottle.

Vavolizza was yanking hard as I tried to deaden my weight, to make myself unliftable and unthrowable. He was spitting and cursing a blue streak right into my ear. I had to use my left hand to pull the bottle out of a bin. I swung it over my right shoulder.

It hit him across the teeth and nose. I felt warm liquid spurting onto the back of my neck. His blood. He gasped and his grip weakened for a moment but then retightened. The bottle was my hope; I managed to transfer it to my right hand and put the last of my strength into a twisting, over-the-shoulder swing at him, screaming as I did it.

He cried out as the bottle crashed against his temple with a sound like the crack of a baseball bat hitting a ball. The bottle shattered, dousing us with red wine. I felt it running down my back. I could smell the blood, the grapy fragrance of the wine, his gangster cologne and pouring sweat.

He clung to me fiercely, fighting for breath. I had the neck of the broken bottle still in my hand and tried to slash his arm with its jagged edge but it was too wet to grip and slipped away from me. Our feet became tangled; I stamped one of his feet repeatedly, my heel crushing his toes, and I knew it hurt him. He tried to pull the foot out of my range, stepping past the edge of the narrow step. The foot sought a level surface but didn't find one and his fall began with a violent lurch, his grip on me releasing as he flailed for balance, reached out but found nothing, and then toppled backward.

He landed on his head and back, sliding down the stairs face-up. His mighty rump came close to flipping him over in a somersault but he managed to stop in midflip, legs in the air, gray socks and pale shins showing where his trouser legs dropped down. For a moment he was frozen in that position, gasping for breath.

Our battle had seemed endless but it must have been very short. George, Tommy, and Jimmy arrived, charging up the stairs as they'd done at the White Plains train station. Other men including waiters and captains, Vavolizza's thugs, and God knows who else were there in a tangle, trying to join the fight or break it up.

I was jostled and hit and knocked down, finding myself on the floor unable to stand. George got me under the armpits and hoisted me up and then we were out on the street, running. After several staggering steps I sucked in the cold air and felt a surge of exhilaration. I had pain from head to toe but ran—I thought—like a deer. Fleet, agile, floating on air. I found myself in the backseat of the SUV. I was in and out of consciousness, gazing at the cars and yellow taxis whizzing by as we joined the flow of traffic. I saw a Chinese deliveryman riding a bike. A woman crossed a street walking a dachshund. A fruit stand was open, with customers examining the fruit.

I heard Jimmy's voice on the cell to Sylvia, telling her I was a little banged up. They were taking me to White Plains Hospital. It was nothing to worry about. Meet us there.

"You won't believe what happened," Jimmy said. "*The boss kicked the shit out of Nicky Vavolizza.*"

CHAPTER 29

Getting Vavolizza to his feet was a struggle but once upright his rage moved to an even higher level. He fought off everyone trying to help or restrain him and, assisted by his goons, staggered out of Fiori, undoubtedly with hopes that I would be standing there waiting to be murdered. Two police cars with roof lights blazing pulled up. Nicky attempted to give them the finger but instead had a massive heart attack.

That was it for Nicky V. He went down in a heap and was never the same again. He didn't die but his days as a strutting mob boss were over.

I was a patient at White Plains Hospital when Carl Pelikan arrived with this news. The NYPD was perturbed that I'd left the scene of a high-profile crime incident and asked the White Plains police to find me. I wasn't concerned; my self-defense argument was strong since everyone at Fiori heard Vavolizza express intent to kill me and witnessed his attempt to do so.

Sylvia met me at the hospital and assumed oversight in a brisk professional manner. She was well-known at the hospital because of volunteer work and because the Sforzas are well-known everywhere in White Plains. She listened somberly to the brothers' gleeful telling of the restaurant story as she steered me through tests for a head injury, stitches for my cut cheek, and an X-ray for my back, where Nicky's punches had cracked several ribs. I was sticky and foul-smelling and my clothes were stained purple from blood and wine. The grapes of wrath.

Pelikan said the word on the street was that I had won the Mafia's heavyweight championship, having vanquished Vavolizza in a hand-to-hand throw-down. Pelikan found the whole thing hilarious. "You've gone from being a mild-mannered older gentleman to a giant among wise guys. Hang in there and you might have a shot at boss of bosses." I had come around to enjoying Pelikan but Sylvia and the other Sforzas were behind the curve on this so I did not invite him over for a beer.

The world loves a Mafia story and the Fiori incident galvanized the news media. What could be better than a frenzied brawl between two mob bosses at a posh restaurant with a presidential candidate and top FBI official seen running out minutes earlier and one of the mob bosses having a heart attack while making an obscene gesture to police? Eyewitness accounts and excited reporters exaggerated every detail. The restaurant had been full of VIPs including a federal judge and a celebrity real estate mogul who pushed to the front eager for camera time.

A news photographer snapped a memorable shot of Nicky's dopey-looking goons puffing on cigarettes as they stood over him waiting for the ambulance. The story made the front page of the tabloids and was prominently covered in the *New York Times*. And of course it circled the planet on the Internet. Viv called from Venice. He was flabbergasted but his warmth and calmness helped me regain my composure.

All this attention outed me from the Mafia closet. Everyone I'd known from grade school onward would now believe I was a mobster and had probably been one all along. No corporate client would ever hire me. No doubt about it: my old life was over.

I sat with my legs dangling from a hospital gurney as a doctor checked me out under Sylvia's gaze. The brothers and Roncade surrounded me in a protective cocoon. Bazzanella arrived with a big smile on his face and a box of pastries.

I'D REALIZED from the start that Bazzanella's archives were an extraordinary asset. What did he say?—*1,563* pages of details about Mafia activities over the last thirteen years. Jake never explained why he ordered Bazzanella to compile this record. Bazzanella assumed the purpose was tactical: keeping Jake up to speed on Mafia activities, particularly the earnings of rival crews. But it was more than that. Bazzanella's database was the family exit strategy, the card it would play with its back against the wall. It was my challenge to figure out how to play that card. I had to get a look at Bazzanella's pages.

In the morning, hobbling from my rib injuries, I located Bazzanella in the Sforza kitchen and said, "Paul, let's go see your boat."

I ordered up an armed escort and we were off on a nice drive upstate along the Hudson River. We drove for more than an hour, exited the highway, made some turns, and pulled into the boatyard, which looked windswept and deserted on a frigid January morning. A heavy man in overalls stepped out of the repair shack looking nervously at the three-car caravan until he recognized Bazzanella.

They did the "How ya doin'?" thing and then Bazzanella did the nameless introduction thing: "Friend of mine meet a friend of mine." Then he said to the friend, "We're gonna spend some time in the rust bucket. I'll take the ladder."

We carried the ladder across a yard crowded with boats that were out of the water for winter maintenance. Bazzanella's boat, nestled in a tall wooden cradle, was an eyesore, small and rotting with peeling paint and a hull pocked with moldy soft spots.

"You don't actually sail this thing, do you?" I asked.

"Fuck no. It'd go right to the bottom. I used to go out on it as a kid when my uncle owned it. I remember throwing a shotgun overboard once but I forget the story."

We leaned the ladder against the boat and climbed aboard. Bazzanella opened the big lock on the cabin door and stepped down into the cabin, which was so small there was no room for me. He got on his hands and knees and turned a combination lock in a deck panel, which he opened to reveal a green safe.

"This safe's rated top of the line," said Bazzanella. "Humidity-controlled, waterproof, fireproof, burglarproof. It's bolted and welded down so you'd have to destroy the whole boat to get it out. Jake told me to spare no expense."

He punched a keypad, turned the dial, opened the safe, and lifted out three three-inch blue loose-leaf notebooks as if they were crown jewels. He was clearly proud of these volumes but surrendered them to me without sentimentality.

I wanted to sit and browse through them but the cabin was too cold and small and my ribs hurt so we returned to the car and turned on the heat. As I started reading Bazzanella got out and walked back to the shack to gab with his friend and make some calls.

The notebooks were immaculately neat, written in small precise handwriting that seemed surprising coming from an elephant like Bazzanella. There was no connective narrative, just one succinct dated entry after another, a tapestry of Mafia daily life. Bazzanella seemed to have covered everyone (excluding the Sforzas, of course) and everything.

He was a talented chronicler. In addition to details about earnings, deals, scores, beatings, and hits there was information about rivalries, activities of bosses and incarcerated colleagues, the progress of trials, contacts with non-Italian mobs, and connections with nongangsters including some who were clearly important—politicians, judges, bankers, lawyers, cops, municipal and union officials, business owners, and celebrities. Significant items were mixed in with items that were only entertaining, involving sex and girlfriends, health problems, fights, feuds, blunders, rumors, and gossip about who was in or out of favor.

It was riveting reading. The cumulative picture of mob life was as compelling as a great novel. It occurred to me that a publisher could slap a book jacket on these pages and have an instant best seller. Of course it would take a publisher who wouldn't mind being sued for libel by every nonmobster implicated in the book, including some powerful bigwigs. I doubted that such a publisher existed.

But even if it didn't work as a book it would undoubtedly work for prosecutors. Bazzanella had a journalist's eye for facts and figures and included a lot of them. He was meticulous about names, dates, places, and details of bribes, payoffs, kickbacks, and "gifts." He named accomplices and cooperative insiders. Some anecdotes were difficult to follow because I lacked background, and it was impossible to know which information would be valuable in prosecutions, but it was unquestionably a bonanza of raw material and behind-the-scenes intelligence.

What would Rob Portis trade to get his hands on these notebooks?

Bazzanella returned, climbing into the car. "I picked up some good stuff," he said with a big smile.

"First, nobody gave a stack of pancakes about Nicky. He's history. The underboss, Carlo Noto, got upped to acting boss. He's an old-timer. You can find his name all over those notebooks. He's a good earner but not a heavyweight. Nicky would never let anyone but a second-rater stand behind him. The commission's had enough of Nicky's troublemaking so they're probably overjoyed to put in a sheepdog like Carlo, though he won't last long.

"Second, the commission is freaked about the Fiori thing and all the headlines since Jake died. The attention is bad but you know there's also this rule about not laying hands on a made guy, especially a boss. Being bosses themselves they're very serious about it, so they're very pissed at you. In fact, they blame you for everything. I talked to Nicky's old consigliere, Joe Stoffo, and he wants me to tell you to forget about negotiation, forget about autonomy, and go fuck yourself because you're a dead man. So I'd say the chance of war is even greater with Nicky gone. Look for the go-ahead to come at the Sunday night commission meeting. And this doesn't come from Stoffo but I'm hearing there's already a contract on you. I'm hearing $300,000 and rising. They also put a $50,000 contract on Sylvia, just in case she's wearing the pants in the family, which some still think."

"Sylvia will be insulted."

"Sylvia didn't crack a boss's head open with a wine bottle."

"Paul, are you carrying?"

"Carrying? A gun? Yeah. I don't usually carry but these are tense times." He took it out of his coat and handed it to me, a snub-nosed .38. "It was a retired cop's off-duty piece. I bought it off him back in the eighties. Got it for forty-five bucks."

"I think we could spring for something a little better for you," I said.

"Nah, it's good enough. I never use it. Why do you ask?"

"Because this moment would be your opportunity to shoot me for $300,000."

He laughed. "And have George and Tommy and Feeks chasing my ass and maybe Vico giving me a haircut? I don't think so."

I handed the gun back to him. "Paul, can I count on you?"

"Are you serious? Of course you can count on me. I owe a lot to the Sforzas. When I lost my wife they were there for me. When my kid was fucked up, Sylvia got him into a program. The Sforzas are my family. Jake was a father to me. If it wasn't for the Sforzas I'd just be some fat fuck. Skipper, you got no worries with Paul Bazzanella."

"If I came up with a solution that really asked a lot of you, how would you be with that?"

"Hunky fucking dory. Whatever you say."

"Another topic: how much should I be sweating about hit men coming after me and Sylvia?"

"Guys will look into it for a few days and go back and say it can't be done. What they mean is that they can't get away alive. Look at these Roncade guys. The average mob soldier would be in the car sleeping with his mouth hanging open but these guys are set up all over the boatyard. They got a crossfire set up at the entrance. They're serious fuckers. It'd be hard to get you. Richie's good."

"Thanks, Paul. Go talk to your buddy while I read your masterpiece some more."

I NEVER expected a price on my head. Suddenly I imagined assassins everywhere, in every car and window and tree. I worried that any step could center me in the bull's-eye of the sniper's sights; I would hear the crack of the gun, feel the punch of the bullet, and then I'd crumple and lie with arms and legs splayed as life flowed out of me. Or maybe Sylvia would be hit, an unbearable image. Or both of us.

Fear of this moment would come and go, subsiding but rushing back, pushing everything else out of our minds. We tried to laugh it off. I joked about finally being able to put a dollar figure on my self-worth. Sylvia teased me, saying, "I bet it'll be up to $500,000 by the time you've unleashed your master plan."

We felt trapped in the house. Everyone was on edge. I decided Sylvia and I needed a night out despite the risk, so we drove in a minicaravan to dinner at the Auberge, where I told her the full story of what happened at Fiori, including the failure of my scheme to make Vavolizza think he could hook President Draybin.

"I give you huge points for creativity," she said. "I bet you did it just because it was cool to run your two separate lives into each other. Artistic satisfaction. Shakespeare would be proud of you."

I told her how uneasy and even ashamed I'd been lying to Vavolizza that she was screwing Draybin, but she shrugged appreciatively.

"It was a good lie," she said. "If you'd thought of it but *not* used it because you thought it was in bad taste, *that* would have been stupid."

Then there was something she had to say. "People have told me if I was a man I would have been the best choice to run the family—"

"They're right."

"No, they're not. I'd have no idea how to get us out of this mess with the commission. I don't think strategically. You do. You're like Poppa. We all know you're going to find a way to save us."

The admiration in her eyes made me feel ten feet tall. What swiftly brought me back to feeling slightly under six feet tall was the realization that my great strategic mind had produced little more than a hazy notion about starting with the notebooks.

A few hours later, while Sylvia slept in my arms and I lay in her bed listening to soft music, I gave up waiting for a leap of inspiration and tried to think out a step-by-step plan.

I would get up early in the morning.

I would start with Rob Portis. He was the agent-in-charge of the FBI's biggest office, New York, with multiple jurisdictions and a thousand agents under his command. He had major clout.

But Portis was not in the nice guy business. Just handing over the notebooks and hoping for a good deal would not get me the grand-slam home run I needed. This was high-stakes poker and stupendous enticement was required.

Since I was making demands, why not think really big, bigger even than Jake. Leading the Sforzas to safety was the first goal but why not add a second goal, a personal one: wiping my slate clean, cleansing my conscience, reversing the farce that had made me a boss in the Mafia.

This was good. Getting to safety was step one but I wanted step two: *redemption.* I wanted to erase the stain, leaving a better reality behind. I wanted my son, Willy, and Charlie

Benedict and everyone else to know that I'd done not only the right thing but a great thing. And to do this I needed to accomplish a third goal, even bigger, historic.

Gazing at Sylvia's ceiling my pulse quickened and my ambition soared. The notebooks would be more than an exit strategy, more than a defensive treasure to be used in a bargain for leniency or witness protection.

They were my nuclear weapon.

I would have to wreak some serious havoc and the odds were way against me but the plan was to offer the notebooks as the center of an irresistible and convincing reality, a package of carrots and sticks of such magnitude that my demands would be met, allowing me to achieve step three: not just escaping the Cosa Nostra but leaving it in flames.

CHAPTER 30

At seven A.M. I got an FBI agent on the phone and told him I was coming in at ten A.M. for a "sit-down" with Portis. This was apparently equivalent to demanding an appointment with God. The agent gave me a hard time so I told him that if Portis wouldn't see me at ten I would go to the NYPD or the US attorney or the statewide Organized Crime Task Force or the Manhattan district attorney or whoever the fuck else was ready to handle the biggest Mafia story of the century. In the meantime, I said, Portis could kiss off his dream of becoming director of the FBI and the junior agent I was talking to, having wrecked Portis's career, could plan on spending many stimulating years in the FBI field office in Bozeman, Montana.

At ten Portis was waiting behind his impeccably neat desk. His black suit jacket was on, his back was straight, his expression was stern. He did not stand or offer to shake hands. He gestured to a chair.

"Heard anything from Draybin?" I asked.

"About what?"

"You ran out of a restaurant with a presidential candidate after an encounter with a Mafia boss. That should provide material for a conversation."

"Not today. You certainly found a nice way to repay Mr. Draybin for many years of loyalty."

"Maybe you don't know much about Mr. Draybin's loyalty."

"Be that as it may."

"I bet you're getting some intense shit from Washington about what's going on here with the Mafia?"

"Washington is monitoring the situation."

"How do they feel about the Mafia war threat?"

"There's always concern about threats to public safety."

"How do you feel about it?"

"Concern."

I asked, "Do you want to bring this mess to a close?"

"Do you have a solution?"

"Yes," I said.

However, it felt like I was having a conversation with a marble statue. "I'd like a cup of coffee," I said. "If I can't get one here, I bet they'd give me one at 1 Police Plaza."

We sat for a tense few moments until Portis pressed a button and asked his assistant, Peggy, to bring coffee. A few more tense moments went by before Peggy, who was very tall and nervous-looking, hurried in with coffee in an FBI mug. There was no offer of cream or sugar.

"Rob, what's your opinion of the Mafia?"

"It's a cancer on society."

"I agree with that," I said.

"That surprises me, given your current position."

"But it's true. The Mafia is a cancer. And I wonder why the FBI has failed to put it out of business. You were doing well until you got sidetracked by terrorism and cybercrime. Thanks to your divided attention the Mafia's made a comeback."

"That view has been mentioned in the media. I don't subscribe to it."

"I've read about a Justice Department report saying organized crime is the FBI's *sixth* priority."

"Will we be getting to your point anytime soon?"

"I think it's time to destroy the New York Mafia."

"Lovely. And how would you do that?"

"I'm not going to do it. *You* are going to do it. I'm here to rat out the entire New York Mafia so you can burn it to the ground like Sherman burning Dixie. The whole thing, not just the Vavolizza family but all five families. I want to help you put every last Cosa Nostra scumbag behind bars, with the Sforzas explicitly excluded."

"So the Sforzas will have New York crime to themselves?"

"Nope. We're leaving."

"Leaving?"

"You'll enable that too."

"Your fantasy seems to be elaborate, Mr. Vail. Tell me how you see all this happening."

"I'm going to give you a nuclear weapon." I let that sink in before continuing. "I know you won't be able to kill the Mafia permanently because it's like the cockroach that always comes back. But you can decimate it for a very long period of time."

"And what is this nuclear weapon?"

"Information."

"Ah, you want to become an informant," he said, relaxing his posture in an exaggerated show of disappointment. "You're following my advice about extricating yourself. You'll recall that I suggested retaining an attorney. When you do that I'll connect him or her with my organized crime supervisor. We'll assess your offer and if it's significant we'll draft a cooperation agreement."

He stood up as if the meeting was over.

"You're getting it wrong, Rob," I said. "I have very little value as an informant. Hey, I've only been a mobster for three weeks."

He took a long, you're-boring-me look at his wristwatch.

"You've forgotten about the nuclear weapon."

"Oh, sure, your nuclear weapon. Tell me about it briefly."

I'd practiced this: "What I'm offering is detailed inside information implicating every boss of the five families, every underboss, every consigliere, every capo and street boss, many of the soldiers and so-called associates, connected people, judges, cops, politicians, out-of-town bosses and other bad actors, and gangs who deal with the Mafia. You name the badass, press the Search button, and I can give you useful and actionable information on him. I can provide details on probably every significant Mafia crime in the last thirteen years as well as ongoing crimes."

He sat back down.

"I possess a document that I can put in your hands at anytime. The minute this document is in possession of the FBI, the New York Mafia is effectively sodomized."

"Mr. Vail, do you think you're the first person who's come in here with big talk about giving me information on the Cosa Nostra? We've had top mobsters spilling their guts for years, intelligence windfalls better than anything you've got. We had John Gotti's underboss, Sal Gravano, telling us about unsolved crimes, admitting to murders we didn't even know about. Another underboss, Sal Vitale, flipped and gave us three decades worth of information. He had an encyclopedic memory. When these people come to us we require extensive interrogations over weeks or months. They don't choose what to tell us. We get everything. We hold them upside down and shake them until all the coins fall out. If they hold anything back, the deal is off. Plus we have many other sources of intelligence. So if you think your stuff is so much better than what we have without you, you're probably wrong."

"But my stuff *is* better," I said. "You've never had such comprehensive information. And Rob Portis will get the credit. Rob Portis will get books written about the day the mobster walked in and gave him the keys to the kingdom. Rob Portis will move to Washington and have an office the size of Texas."

Rob Portis scoffed. He'd probably heard a ton of bullshit in his career but he wasn't throwing me out, he was only playing hardball. I thought I could sense a physical response from him, maybe even a tingle telling him that a milestone in crime fighting just might be unfolding before his eyes.

"Describe the nature of your document."

"Three loose-leaf notebooks totaling 1,563 pages, compiled on the orders of Jake Sforza. You think of Mr. Sforza as a member of the Mafia but in fact Mr. Sforza was a maverick who felt he had broken away from the Mafia and always believed the Mafia would be his ultimate enemy. He knew there would be a day when he needed an ace in the hole to survive. He assigned a very competent subordinate to take charge of this project. The subordinate made it his life's work. It's a masterpiece of long-term intelligence gathering. It doesn't include the volume of government wiretapping that's been done over the years, most of which is probably worthless goombah chitchat, but I'm confident the accretion of insider information gleaned in face-to-face conversations with unsuspecting Mafiosi in all five families makes it vastly superior to the totality of anything that you or any other agency has ever collected."

I'd rehearsed that speech and thought it went well.

"When can I see it?"

"Not without a deal but you're entitled to a taste. How about right now?"

"Now works for me."

"Give me ten random numbers between one and 1,563."

I took out a pen and index card while he thought about this.

He said, "Okay: 82, 107, 312, 574, 716, 802, 940, 1,005, 1,340."

"That's nine. One more."

"Okay, 1,563."

I'd copied them down. "The fax number on your business card is still operative?"

He nodded.

"Sorry to have to fax but these pages have not been scanned, for obvious reasons."

I took out a "burner" (an untraceable cell phone taken from a drawerful of cheap disposable phones in the Sforza kitchen), punched in a speed-dial number, repeated the numbers Portis had given me, and hung up.

Bazzanella was waiting with the three notebooks on his lap in the lobby of a busy hotel in downtown Manhattan. He removed pages 82, 107, 312, 574, 716, 802, 940, 1,005, 1,340 and 1,563 and fed them into a fax machine in the hotel's business center.

"Tell Peggy to stand at the fax machine," I said.

Instead of telling Peggy he stood up and strode out of the office. I sat and looked at his wall-of-fame gallery, photos of himself with famous people. I stood up and looked out the window at a twenty-third-floor view of Lower Manhattan. Immediately below was a small plaza. Across the street were fast-food joints. The sidewalks were crowded with briskly moving pedestrians.

He returned clutching ten sheets of paper. He closed the office door, sat down behind his desk, put on reading glasses, and read the pages carefully as I waited.

At one point his face reddened and he mumbled, "Son of a bitch."

"Good one, eh?" I said. He ignored me.

At last he looked up and said, "You've got 1,563 pages like this?"

"Want to see more?"

I would have given him a hundred more. The more pages he saw, the more he'd accept the pages as genuine and the better the odds he would find something mouthwatering.

I said, "Of course I'm not familiar with the particular pages you've just read but how many prosecutions could you initiate or at least stimulate based on that kind of information? How much unconfirmed information could you corroborate or supplement? I'm no expert but I bet you could make racketeering cases against every single mobster mentioned in that book. I don't know if this gives you enough for convictions but it gets you started and meanwhile this information probably fills in most of the gaps in the Bureau's knowledge of the mob, including some of what happened in Vavolizza's basement. Are you aware of the activity in the basement?"

"The basement was his clubhouse. Had his capo meetings there."

"Did you ever get a bug in there?"

"I wouldn't tell you either way."

"Did you ever read his notes on his computer or get into his e-mails? They're on his wife's account but I'm sure you knew that."

Portis said nothing but I could see he was surprised. Maybe Nicky's use of the computer was so stupid the FBI never thought of looking into it.

"Many of the people who took part in those meetings talked to the person who compiled my document. I'm confident you could piece it all together from what I can give you."

"It's impossible to verify and assess the value of a particular document after only a cursory glance at a few sample pages."

"Yeah, yeah, yeah," I said. "How about this? I'll get up and go to the men's room and while I'm gone you can call the honchos in Washington and tell them what you got. I'll be glad to send them another twenty pages just to make it interesting."

I'd gotten through the simple part. Now it got trickier.

"But I have one requirement when you talk to them. And it's something you will have to do very skillfully."

"I'm listening."

"You have to stress that this is not about getting a lot of incremental information that'll help in individual prosecutions. It's not about nailing Joey Gobbagooch for hijacking a truck five years ago. It's about a comprehensive attack on the whole Mafia enterprise. I'm offering the document on that basis and that basis alone. If you do anything less with it, I will embarrass you publicly. I'm giving you this document to destroy the New York Mafia. I want that broad purpose acknowledged and I want the government's explicit commitment to it as part of any deal."

He stared at me. "I'll tell them how you see it."

I left his office, found the men's room, and spent a few minutes washing my hands and standing around. Agents came in and out, eyeing me suspiciously. When I returned to his office he gave me twenty more page numbers and we did the faxing exercise again. I took another walk, this time to the lobby and back. When I returned to his office he was hanging up the phone.

"I've been asked to inquire whether the man who compiled these notebooks would be available for additional background and testimony?"

"That would expose him to considerable danger and the process might drag on for years. He'd probably require protective custody for the rest of his life."

"There's no deal without it."

"Have we said there's a deal *with* it?"

"Before agreeing to anything the Bureau will require concrete assurance that this evidence is authentic and reliable and will provide—"

"Rob, shut the fuck up—and I say that with the utmost respect. We're talking about bringing down the entire New York Mafia. At the very least doing tremendous damage to it. So don't be a dick. Let's now move on to what I want in exchange for this."

"Okay," he said. "What do you want?"

"I HAVE a dream," I said, attempting a Martin Luther King cadence. "I have a dream of glistening Adriatic waters and green canals. I have a dream of a family moving on to a new life far away, disappearing lock, stock, and barrel from the New York scene. A family that has—what's the cliché?— *tentacles* into many activities but withdraws those tentacles and moves on to happy crime-free lives across the sea."

"You want to go into witness protection?"

"No, I want to go to Venice. From what I hear the protection program entails being under your thumb for the rest of eternity."

"The WITSEC program is run by the US Marshals Service so you wouldn't be under my thumb."

"I'd be under *somebody's* thumb," I said. "We don't want to be in the program. We'll handle our own security and our own costs. But we need your cooperation and facilitation."

"Who's 'we'?"

"Me and everyone in the Sforza crew. Some will need passports. You'll facilitate that along with whatever other diplomatic papers are necessary. Visas, work permits, I don't have any idea what's needed but you'll provide it. All of these people will require across-the-board immunity from prosecution for anything they've ever done. I'll expect you to guarantee our safety on the way out, and most important I want you to fix it with Italy."

"You want the FBI to relocate you to Italy?"

"No, Rob. I want Venice and Italy to be hospitable to us. I don't want them thinking New York is dumping a mob family on them. I want them to feel that they're taking part in an unprecedented anti-Mafia process. We'll do this quietly and peaceably but we need you backing up the deal. I want a high-ranking Italian official designated as a permanent liaison with us and I want a guarantee that we won't be hassled by Italian cops or any agencies including their tax police. We intend to be model citizens, productive and law-abiding and employed, and we want to feel welcome."

"You want jobs?"

"We'll provide our own jobs. Legitimate jobs."

"You're out of your mind if you think the FBI will approve this and you're even crazier if you think Venetian authorities will go along with this. And what happens when the Italian Mafia finds out where you are."

"Not your problem. Let me worry about that."

"Is that all?"

"No. One other thing: speed. Very bad shit is going to break loose if this moves slowly. It has to be record-breakingly fast."

He gave me a little smile. "Speed is hard. Government wheels turn slowly, you know that. Lots of agencies would be involved in this—Justice, State, Homeland Security, the TSA, Interpol, New York State, New York City. Lots of turf and big egos, meetings, buy-ins and sign-offs, and so on. I can't just make a call and get this done."

"The challenge requires a mover and shaker. That's why I brought it to you," I said. "Find a way. I want this ultra fast-tracked. I don't know what that entails and I don't give a shit. I'll give you a week, Rob. I'll hand you the notebooks next Wednesday afternoon at Newark Airport. Then or never."

"It'll take a week just to—"

"Rob, let me put it this way: the Sforzas are now public enemy number one and the global media is all over this story. If you could make us disappear overnight and do this at no risk and no cost with no bloodshed and no embarrassment of any kind, would that be a good deal?"

"I can't see my superiors accepting it."

"Okay, let's have a bloody mob war instead. Lots of collateral damage to innocent citizens."

"I'll get back to you," he said.

HIRAM TACK, the Sforza IT guy, set up a secure line for a conference call to Italy: Viv and Paola on one end, Sylvia and I on the other.

Viv and Paola were spellbound as I filled them in on the fight with Vavolizza at Fiori, Bazzanella's notebooks, and my session with Portis. I told the stories with a minimum of color. I did not want them distracted by all the juicy details. I wanted them following my thinking as I built a picture of what had to happen next.

"The reality," I said, "is that the Sforza business in New York is on the verge of extinction. A war to preserve it will end disastrously. We've reached an unavoidable turning point. We have to move on to something else, and we have to act fast. So what I told Portis is that the only solution is for the Sforzas to leave."

"*To leave?*" said one of them, or all three of them.

"To pack up and go," I said.

"*Where?*"

There was a moment of dead silence until Viv figured it out and roared, "*Venice!*"

"Yes. Venice."

"That's a brilliant stroke. Allow me to repay my debt to you with permanent hospitality in my city."

Sylvia said nothing. I felt I could see her processing the idea. Then the smile.

"Jesus," she said. "Really?"

Paola laughed.

"Jake's exit strategy had two parts," I said. "The first was secret: the notebooks. The second part was in plain sight: building up a fall-back existence in Venice for everyone in the family. That's what Viv and Paola have been doing all these years."

"Did you say *everybody* in the family's going to Italy?" said Sylvia. "When? When is this going to happen?"

"Wednesday."

"*Wednesday?* We're moving to Italy on Wednesday? Are you nuts?"

But she loved it.

Later we gathered the family and explained the Venice plan. Everyone was shocked but when the shock subsided there was no real resistance. The impending danger was too great and the opportunity to throw off a lifetime as a pariah community was too appealing. Vera, to my surprise, stood up and in a clear and steady voice endorsed the plan. She had become a different person, her bimbo persona forgotten, and her words carried weight. "We're at the end of it here," she said. "We can't go on with this nightmare."

I made it clear that no one would be forced to go to Italy but almost everyone signed up. Sylvia would organize the move. Ron Taubman would close down the family's New York businesses, conducting a "scorched earth" program to erase all traces of the family's connections and to free most of its "clients" (i.e. victims) from depredations by the Vavolizzas. Their new boss, Carlo Noto, would arrive to take over but find nothing to take over.

CHAPTER 31

DeSens called early Friday morning. "I'm shooting hoops."

I went out and met him on the basketball court.

"Bad news, Phil. Robert Portis has asked me to advise you that your proposition has met with impassioned resistance. It will not be approved, especially within your time frame. Portis wants you to know he supported you aggressively but to no avail."

If DeSens had hurled the basketball at me and hit me square in the chest, the impact would not have been as deflating as this blow. Somehow I had counted my chickens; I felt I'd made my case so persuasively that it had to be accepted, wild as it was. I was so confident that I'd brought the whole family into the Venice plan. Now that rug was ripped out from under me.

"I don't know details, Phil, but here's one small fact that'll interest you. In that first batch of pages you showed Portis there was an entry about the mob rigging a jury in a trial eight or nine years ago. That just happened to be a big case that Portis was closely involved with and a hung jury was a severe disappointment. It was obviously jury tampering but we had no proof. The notebook entry said the mob had intimidated and bribed two jurors. It gives their names, tells the whole story."

"Can the case be retried?"

"It's being looked into. But it's what gave Portis a special appreciation of the notebooks. Unfortunately it didn't convince everybody."

"Do these assholes in Washington understand what the consequences will be?"

"They've been warned but it didn't sink in. Portis thinks your proposal was too much to swallow in one gulp. He says they could understand a bunch of new prosecutions but they couldn't visualize the totality of bringing down the entire New York Mafia. What they *could* visualize was the headlines blasting them for allowing a notorious crime family to leave the country with immunity, an escort to the airport, expedited passports, and a hands-off agreement from the Italian police."

"I offer the destruction of the New York Mafia and they reject it because they can't *visualize* it?"

"They just didn't get it. They realize the notebooks are a gold mine and they want to work out a deal with you but that means a lot of negotiation. They're more secure with a slow, careful process than a splashy overnight deal."

"But there's no time for that. The commission's meeting *Sunday night.* That'll be the green light for the war."

"I didn't know about Sunday night."

"You thought they were going to wait six months while we work it out with Washington?"

We looked at each other helplessly. Then we shook hands and he hurried off.

There was a painted white line on the driveway showing the foul line, fifteen feet from the basket. I started shooting foul shots, mindlessly, feeling a roiling, burning sensation I recognized as comeuppance. I'd thought I could play hardball with the big boys. Instead I'd revealed myself as a foolish lightweight on a flight of fancy and ego.

I felt like a bad general realizing on the eve of battle that he'd made an unfathomably amateurish mistake: assuming his adversaries would behave as he hoped. I'd assumed that Portis would succeed in prodding Washington into fast and effective action to do something for which there was no precedent or process. And I'd assumed the Mafia commissioners would live up to their reputation as nervous-nellie politicians, indecisive about going to war. But they would not be indecisive on Sunday night. Their survival was at stake. The Sforzas threatened their authority and the stability of their world. Carnage was coming.

And what of the Sforzas? I had turned these tough people toward a soft and seductive vision of a Venetian future. My fiercest warriors—George, Tommy, and Jimmy—were giving pointers about packing cartons and shipping procedures. Now I had to tell them to forget Venice and rouse themselves for a battle which, no matter how bravely fought, could only end in the destruction of their world.

Thanks a lot, Phil—just as we were thinking you were God's gift to the family, you turned out to be a clown and a curse.

"NOBODY OUTSHOOTS me from the foul line," said Sylvia. I hadn't seen her coming. "You're talking to the sister of four boys and the five-foot-seven-inch former starting forward of the White Plains High girls varsity b-ball team."

This cheered me, but only a little.

"I was watching from the kitchen window," she said. "If ever I've seen body language, wow, like he shot you in the heart. Did the feds say no? Is Venice off?"

I apologized. I could hardly look at her. I explained that it had been a ridiculous stunt. I was crazy to think I could pull it off. Now we had to face the worst.

"I've got a quote for you," she said. "Yield not thy neck to fortune's yoke, but let thy dauntless mind still ride in triumph over all mischance."

"What? Say that again."

She repeated it, smiling as she added, "*Henry the Sixth.*"

My mind worked hard to put despondency aside and comprehend this quotation.

"Gimme the ball, I'm going to crush you in a foul-shooting contest," she said. "Best out of ten. If you win, you can yield thy neck to fortune's yoke and eat the shit of defeat. If I win, you put your dauntless mind to work. Come up with another sensational Phil Vail idea and force those dickheads to give us what we want. I want to move to Venice on Wednesday. Make it happen.

"And that's not all. If I win, we're getting married Wednesday morning."

BY THE time she won, 8-6, we were laughing and goosing each other.

I headed up to Jake's den to sit quietly and try to have an idea. I looked up at the volumes of Shakespeare and wondered if Jake ever sat here needing guidance, wishing Shakespearean wisdom would float down and show the way.

I opened up a paperback *Henry V*, in which Jake had underlined the "once more into the breach" speech. There was some inspiring stuff about imitating the action of the tiger, stiffening the sinews, and summoning up the blood for combat. Exciting stuff, but not what I needed. I read for another few minutes but The Bard had shut down for the day.

It is impossible to force a great idea and what I needed was beyond great: I needed an outrageous move that would make the government act faster and the mob think slower. I had to show the government I was a loose cannon who would keep raising the ante, making enormous trouble until I got what I wanted. Meanwhile I had to distract the Mafia commissioners with a razzle-dazzle stunt, breaking their rhythm as they summoned up the blood for combat.

I got up to stretch my legs and pace around but Jake's den was too small for pacing so I left the room and walked across the landing, opening the door to Carmine's balcony, which had been rebuilt since the attack on the house. And there was Carmine himself, ever-vigilant, perched on his stool, looking down on Sycamore Court.

"Skipper, you shouldn't be out here. A sniper could take you out."

"I'll just stand here for a minute, Carmine. I need some fresh air."

My presence made him nervous. I asked if he planned to join us in Venice. He said he was going to discuss it tonight with his mother and father. It surprised me that mobsters consulted their parents.

The scene was very quiet. A few Roncade men stood around the front lawn. The barricade of the two red Sforza Moving & Storage vans blocked the view of the closer part of Sycamore Court.

Something about the moving vans caught my imagination. When you have to make a big move, you need moving vans. Right?

WE HAD to work fast. The plan was to take the vans and six men in addition to the brothers so the loading and unloading could be done rapidly. Roncade would be there and Bazzanella and I would go along to watch, which was imprudent but irresistible. The Sforza logos on the vans were covered by large panels bearing the logo of a national moving company. This disguise had been useful in smuggling ventures until Jake decided it was foolish to endanger the family's legitimate business.

At ten A.M. we pulled up outside Nicky Vavolizza's mansion in Weaver Ridge. The front door was unlocked, the alarms were turned off, and no one was home. We had confirmed that the mother-in-law and wife were with Nicky at the hospital.

The Danish au pair, Mina, and the children were out of the house and would not return until after two P.M. Mina would parade conspicuously through Weaver Ridge village, pushing the children in their stroller, establishing a presence away from the house. The one thing she was forbidden to do was have sex with Chief Farraday.

The intimidation of Mina had been masterful. It was Bazzanella's inspiration to put Vico the barber on the phone with her. Vico, speaking with a raspy voice that evoked Gothic horrors, told Mina he knew about her "whoring" with Nicky and her current "fornicating in the presence of children" with Farraday. The price for avoiding grotesque punishment was simply to leave the house empty and open for a few hours. Terrified, she took the deal.

Tommy had a gift for the house-moving arts and sciences. He organized his crew efficiently. There would be no time wasted wrapping crockery and knickknacks.

There were two priorities.

The higher priority was to get items with potential intelligence or incrimination value, starting with Nicky's computer and everything in the basement, his desk, a file cabinet, cartons of old papers in the attic. Two handguns turned up—it was assumed he had more artillery hidden away on the property but there was no time for searching.

The second priority was to take personal things whose public display would be embarrassing or infuriating, such as bathroom items, underwear, clothing, jewelry, the enormous televisions and sound systems, the cheesy paintings and sculptures, the garish furniture and the contents of his garage, which included a shelf load of paint cans which, when unsealed, turned out to contain rolls of cash totaling $190,000. The children's room was searched but otherwise left alone. The contents of Mina's room, including her lingerie and vibrators, was carried out to the trucks.

The doorbell never rang. No cop drove past. No neighbor dropped by. Tommy pronounced the house adequately stripped by one P.M. We drove away laughing. Jimmy offered an image of Nicky being brought home by private ambulance and wheeled inside, only to find his house almost as bare as the day he moved in. If all went well, this would cause another heart attack.

The vans were parked in a big garage at the Sforza storage facility, a hangar-sized building. Hiram Tack had no trouble hacking into Nicky's computer and transferring everything to a disc. I had a messenger service deliver the disc to the FBI with an attached note saying, "Rob, here's something to sweeten our deal: the contents of Vavolizza's home computer including his basement notes and e-mails. Enjoy."

Back at the Sforza house I wrote notes to be sent by overnight express to the home addresses of Ray Rosolini and the bosses of the other Mafia families, telling them that we—an undefined "we"—looked forward to moving their household possessions and business records to new locations, promising "discretion and professional care" and giving Nicky Vavolizza as a reference.

Later in the day I called Rob Portis's secretary, Peggy, and asked if he'd received the disc.

"Yes, sir. I can confirm that."

"Tell him I look forward to his reaction."

"I will do that."

"By the way, Peggy," I said. "Cancel your Saturday plans. Portis will need you in the office, very early."

Driving in Manhattan in the wee hours, especially on a Saturday morning, is an unexpected pleasure. There is no traffic and you can fly downtown, though we were careful to heed all red lights and speed limits. We pulled up outside the federal building at four thirty A.M.

I pointed out the little entrance plaza I'd noticed when I looked down from Portis's window. The boys opened the vans and went to work as quietly as possible unloading Nicky Vavolizza's worldly possessions, taking care to arrange them for greatest impact. Nicky's famous basement was laid out in the center, circled by items from other rooms. Artwork and statuary were spread around nicely, with bras and silk jockey shorts hanging from them. The cash-filled paint cans were left on the dining room table, with the tops off to reveal the cash.

A few homeless people approached. We gave each one a hundred dollars out of the paint cans, figuring word of free money would spread and bring a rush of people to the scene.

Using a safe phone we placed calls to the FBI, the NYPD, the US attorney, the Associated Press, the *Times, Post, News,* and *National Enquirer* and all the TV stations as well as social media. One of the movers, who had a rich authoritative voice, volunteered to do the phone work, telling each of them: "The entire contents of Nicky Vavolizza's home are on the sidewalk outside the FBI office at 26 Federal Plaza. You don't want to miss this."

When we heard police sirens we drove away, feeling like fraternity brothers who'd executed the prank of the century. I hoped the audience watching TV reports later would be amused. I wanted lots of laughs, lots of news coverage, and worldwide word of mouth. The circus atmosphere would tighten bureaucratic sphincters in Washington. I called Portis later in the day and asked Peggy if I could leave him a voice message. I wanted my thoughts recorded so he could play them back for everyone in DC who'd blocked my plan.

"Rob, sorry I've had to resort to cheap showmanship but evidently your colleagues in Washington had a problem visualizing my offer. So visualize this! I've provided what are now called optics, which are now providing entertaining viewing on TV. My goal is to make it unmistakably clear to everyone in the world that I'm offering enough evidence for you to blow up the Mafia. I've now sent you Nicky Vavolizza's hard drive plus the contents of his house and on Wednesday, if all goes as I suggested, you'll get the best piece of all, the notebooks. And in a few months, when the notebooks are published unless we make a deal to not publish, you'll get an autographed hardcover copy.

"I'm just getting started, Rob. I plan to keep helping you with more and more evidence. I'm a criminal so the normal constraints on evidence-gathering don't mean jack shit to me. My understanding is that this evidence is admissible because you didn't seize it yourself, you just found it where I'll leave it—on the attorney general's front lawn, the FBI director's favorite golf course, or maybe in Central Park or Times Square or the steps of the Supreme Court. If I'm wrong about admissibility you can cart it all back to the owners. Plant some bugs while you're at it.

"If there's anything else you need, just give me a list and I'll get it for you. If you want to shut off the flow, all you have to do is allow the Sforzas to fly away Wednesday under the conditions I described. Have a nice day."

CHAPTER 32

At midnight someone knocked on our bedroom door and opened it. For a moment I feared an attack but it was a Roncade guy peeking in. "Don't worry, no danger. The agent's downstairs."

DeSens was outside, shivering. It was too cold for basketball so I led him into the kitchen.

I said, "You look like it's been a stressful day."

"Yes, stressful and long. You really kicked the hornet's nest. The powers-that-be were in an uproar and the roar went on until just a little while ago. Finally decisions got made. By whom I do not know, but very high up."

"And?"

"The first thing is that there is no way law enforcement will make an immunity deal with a Mafia crew. Especially on a day when you commit a home burglary and leave the contents outside the FBI office and half the world sees it on TV. However, the consensus is that preventing a mob war on the streets of New York is a supreme priority and the best and only way to do that is to get the Sforzas on the other side of the Atlantic Ocean. So the offer is paperless immunity, meaning nothing in writing but the government doesn't pursue you for anything as long as you get your butts out of here quickly and quietly."

"How about the other stuff?"

"It's done. You'll get the passports and visas and whatever. The Venetian authorities will leave you alone if you keep your noses clean. If they wobble on that, we can jump in for you. You've won, Phil. But don't do any more evidence-gathering for us. That would be a deal-breaker. Do you accept this offer?"

Part of me wanted to jump for joy but there were other serious matters to talk about, starting with the family's safety between now and wheels-up on Wednesday.

"Believe me, we want this to go without incident," he said. "We'll provide security. We'll escort you to the airport. And we'll lay down the law directly to the Cosa Nostra. But I need your help on that. You mentioned a Sunday night commission meeting. We haven't been able to turn up the time and place of this meeting."

"Staten Island. In an apartment over a restaurant called Midnight Rose II on Hylan Boulevard. If you can tie them in knots until Thursday there'll be no more trouble. There's one other thing."

"Which is?"

"I was serious about demanding a commitment to wipe out the New York Mafia rather than just a piecemeal approach. Where do we stand on that?"

"I think you can count on it. I don't know what it took to ram this through but Washington must have finally seen the potential of this thing, not to mention a lot of self-interest in a public campaign to eradicate the Mafia. Amazing as it may be, you get the credit for that. Not *public* credit, but credit."

"Ken, I accept the deal. Can I offer you a drink?"

"No thanks, I have to get home. My kids have games in the morning. Look, Phil, I hope it works out for you. Take my advice when you're in Venice and stay away from the Italian Mafia. Don't push your luck."

"Good advice, Ken. You've been a gentleman."

"This is off the record, Phil: my kids think you're cool. They loved the stunt with Nicky's underwear hanging off the Venus de Milo statue. They're telling their friends I know you."

ON SUNDAY my ex-wife, Joan, called.

"I'm in Paris with Richard. We picked up the *Trib* and read this incredible story about you getting in a brawl with a Mafia boss? At Fiori, no less? The French can't stop talking about this. What is *going on* with you?"

"It's been busy," I said, "and getting busier. Tomorrow I'm getting married and moving to Italy. Amazing how things turn out, isn't it? But I'm very happy, Joan. I think we both got what we needed."

RONCADE WORRIED that snipers would take shots at me and/ or Sylvia outside or even inside the church. An even greater nightmare was a bomb exploding during the wedding, taking out the whole family.

"Isn't a Catholic church off-limits for that kind of thing?" I asked.

"Maybe not," Richie said. "Ray Rosolini will want to set an example people talk about forever."

But nothing happened, possibly because Richie laid on heavy security and we also had FBI security. Ken DeSens headed a detail that escorted us from the house to the church and then to the terminal at Newark airport. Wedding guests who were flying with us brought their luggage to the church where it was loaded into a moving van that took us to the airport.

Carl Pelikan and Milly sat in the back of the church. The Sforzas put up with this.

Sylvia wore a simple silvery dress and looked beautiful. I didn't hear a word the priest said because my thoughts were split between enjoying the greatest day of my life and wondering if I was about to take one between the ears.

DeSens told me a contingent of law enforcement officers had gone to Staten Island Sunday night and barged into the commission's meeting. With the bosses and their bodyguards forced to line up with their palms against a kitchen wall, Portis read them the riot act, telling them they would be under close scrutiny in the next week and any war-like acts would result in mass arrests and a shutting down of their businesses. In the meantime there'd be a police presence at every mob venue and major harassment would be taking place.

Portis was waiting for us at Newark airport and got on the bus before anyone got off. I handed him a backpack containing copies of the notebooks, introduced him to Paul Bazzanella, and gave him our contact information in Venice. He left without a handshake or a smile.

LAW ENFORCEMENT was clearly worried about a bloody attack on us at the airport. Nervous-looking airport police surrounded us immediately, supplementing the FBI detail and herding us at a speedy clip through unmarked doors and stairways to a large brightly lit room euphemistically described as a VIP waiting lounge. But it was obviously a high security area where mob gunmen couldn't reach us. We had our own check-in counter and security screening. Airline reps and TSA agents were exceptionally polite. Our tension faded and we turned into excited travelers. It was a big day for all of us.

I was standing with Syliva on the check-in line when Roncade and Bazzanella pulled me aside. Bazzanella said, "Just got this," and handed me a scrap of notepaper with a name scrawled on it: Ruslan Nayasev.

"Who's this?" I said.

Bazzanella whispered, "The guy who killed Catcher."

I thought I had stepped down as a crime boss but here was one last item in my in-box.

"He's out of prison?" I asked.

"Still in prison, but not Ricton. They transferred him to another prison upstate, Chillicoe Island. Moving him could mean they figured out he did the job."

"Or it could be just routine," said Roncade. "They move the real badasses around so they can't dig in at any one place."

"What do we know about him?"

"He belongs to a Chechen gang. That's probably how Nicky's guys found him. It's also how we found him. He's in for armed robbery but he's probably committed every crime under the sun. These Chechens are real hardcore villains."

In my imagination I saw him: a sullen Slav with a dark stubble, cold eyes, hard and ignorant. God gave him nothing that wasn't brutal and ugly, a thought which did not inspire compassion because he was, after all, a throat-slashing killer. He killed Catcher for money and jailhouse prestige and he probably did it without a moment's regret, and he would consider me a punk if I hesitated about killing him. Which I did.

Roncade said, "It's your call, Skipper."

"Does anyone else in the family know about this?"

"No," said Roncade.

"If I gave his name to the FBI or Pelikan, could they do anything?"

"They'd put it in the system but I doubt if there's any usable evidence on the guy," said Roncade. "So we do it or he gets away with it."

"We can get to him and kill him even though he's in prison?"

"It's no problem," said Roncade.

"Are we certain this is the guy who did it?"

Bazzanella said, "Certain enough. If we kill the wrong scumbag it's no great loss."

Now there was a thought: it didn't matter whether Ruslan Nayasev was the right or wrong scumbag as long as *some* scumbag paid the bill for Catcher. Two months earlier I would have been righteously appalled by that logic. Now, after my experience with another side of life, my moral convictions were not as certain as they used to be. I'd become a gray area guy, and perhaps grayness inclined me to handle the Nayasev decision by avoiding the deep waters of right versus wrong and swimming instead at the shallower level of smart versus stupid.

Here's what would be *smart* about killing Ruslan Nayasev:

1. It would cement my standing as a strong leader and manly godfather.
2. It would fulfill my promise of revenge and prove that my word was good.
3. Everyone would understand why I'd killed him whereas showing mercy would be hard to explain and many would never understand or forgive.
4. Killing him would create closure regarding Catcher, though closure was a dubious concept.
5. If we didn't kill him now, we might never get another chance because someone else might beat us to it. Life was short in the jungle where Ruslan Nayasev dwelled.
6. Killing him would probably have no legal repercussions because he was low-life garbage and no major resources would be wasted investigating his death.

"We could make it happen in a couple weeks, when we're long gone," suggested Bazzanella.

"We're not killing him," I said.

They didn't look surprised. Maybe they expected this, a return of my precriminal soft-civilian mind-set.

"It's not that I respect his life, because I don't," I said. "This is a business decision. Killing this guy would be stupid because it's a crime and we're out of the crime business. We're lucky to be out and we're not going back in."

"The family doesn't ever have to know about this," said Bazzanella, trying to help me manage it.

"Yes, it does," I said. "They're entitled to know. And you can't keep a secret like this. It would pop out sometime. Richie, ask Sylvia and Vera to come over."

While Bazzanella and I waited I said to him, "I want your contacts to get to Ruslan Nayasev and give him a message: '*The Sforzas know what you did.*' That's all, not another word, not a threat that can come back at us, nothing else. But that should be enough to disturb his beauty sleep for a long time."

"I like it," said Bazzanella.

Vera and Sylvia approached, obviously sensing something serious. I'd broken one cardinal principle of Mafia leadership: the one about letting someone live when it was advantageous to have him die. Now I was going to break another: the one about not consulting women.

I told them about Nayasev. I told them I had decided against having him killed, simply because I wanted to put crime behind us. If they strongly felt I was wrong, I would reconsider. So did they agree with me or not?

"Disagree," said Sylvia.

"Agree," said Vera.

The opposite of what I would have bet on.

Sylvia, shocked, stared at Vera, who withheld eye contact.

Vera spoke: "My husband's dead and those other maggots are dead—Uddone, the two Leccisis. And Nicky Vavolizza is as good as dead. That's enough people dead. Fuck this shit."

Sylvia thought for a moment and said, "She's right. That was the old me speaking. Now I'm the new me, changing my vote. I agree."

"How about you guys?" I said to Bazzanella and Roncade. They said they were okay with it. "You're sure?" I asked. They nodded. It was possible they actually respected the decision.

"We'll tell the rest of the family when we're settled," I said. "Let's go to Italy."

We turned back to the check-in line. Sylvia took my hand and said, "Good, Phil."